DARK OCEAN

DARK OCEAN

PATRICK CARPENTER

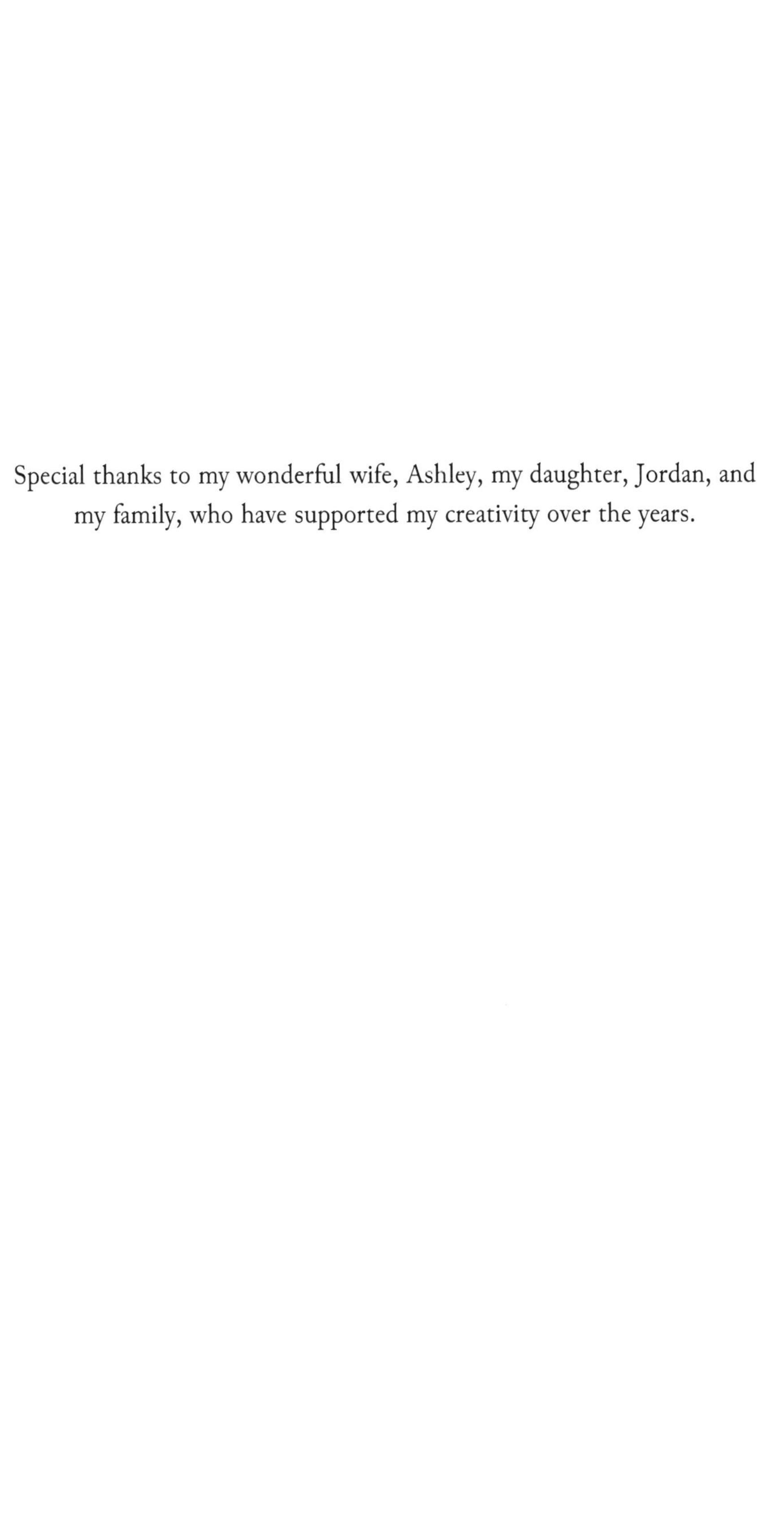

Special thanks to my wonderful wife, Ashley, my daughter, Jordan, and my family, who have supported my creativity over the years.

Foreword

Dark Ocean is a story for all of you who have ever wondered what was out there or, perhaps, what was inside of you. It is for anyone who has ever questioned the infinite, pondered the concepts of higher purpose, or just wanted to know what lies beyond what we perceive.

This story has been in my head for years, though the characters and the particulars have changed or evolved many times over the years. It is with great pleasure that I have finally put together my many inspirations and crafted this tale. I hope you enjoy the story even half as much as I enjoyed writing it!

ADVENT

1

There had always been something about Addy that seemed off. It wasn't a feeling for which any particular word seemed to fit, yet she had felt this nascent, festering anxiousness many times in her life, right before her mind became riddled with the sort of virulent thoughts flooding into her mind on this particular morning.

That smell, a familiar, swanky cologne ... that swagger ... a man, no, two men, had just bumped past her. Where were they? Scanning the bustling marketplace, it took her no time to find them. Both men wore light gray suits, expensive looking and tailored perfectly to their tall and slender bodies. One had loose, shoulder-length hair, and the other was shaved high and tight with a small fade on top and strands of hair spiked in the front. A gold watch shimmered just beneath the cufflinks of the one with long hair. Both wore expensive sunglasses and their shiny wing-tipped shoes glimmered in the sun.

"Addy?" Her brother's voice was a faraway sound.

Who were those guys?

Again, she heard her brother, closer now. "Addy!" The two men turned and disappeared into an alley beside a food truck. When her brother's hand touched her shoulder, Addy jumped and snapped out of her trance.

"What are you doing?" her brother, Alex, asked.

She spun around. "Nothing ... I thought I heard someone calling my name." Not sure why she lied, she deflected. "Where is Rami?"

"Up ahead, getting our place in line. If we don't hurry up, we are going to get crappy seats."

"Okay, right, sorry."

"Who did you think was calling you?"

"No idea, maybe someone from school. It was a weird moment."

As they hip and shoulder checked their way through the crowd to the stadium, Alex did not prod further. Alex was either dense or indifferent with these things. He had always been more of a surface-level guy, which Addy appreciated because it allowed her to confront her tribulations only when she was ready. Whatever this was, this undefined yet passionate hate, she was not ready to describe.

They made it through the crowd and found their way inside. Rami was nowhere to be seen and must have already entered the stadium. A pair of employees stopped them and asked for their tickets, and Alex pulled out his cell phone and flashed a barcode at them. Scanning the code, the men allowed them to pass.

"I feel like I can breathe again," Addy said as she and Alex went into the lobby area and got away from the mobs outside. There were scalpers everywhere. The stadium always sold out, but people found ways to get in anyway. Often, the management would sell your seat if you arrived late and refuse to refund your money, profiting double. As one might imagine, the gates were always flooded with people hoping to steal the scraps. Addy had even seen flash mobs pop up and block legitimate ticket owners from getting in so the scalpers could buy their seats.

Luckily for Addy, Alex was not to be trifled with. Standing at six foot one and weighing about two hundred-thirty pounds, Alex's broad-shouldered, buff, and intimidating frame kept most at bay. That, and his dark, piercing blue eyes could penetrate stone. No one was trying to block him.

"Stupid clowns," Alex said, rolling his eyes.

When they got inside, Rami and another of their mutual friends, Jocelyn, were already there, holding a group of seats for them.

"Yo, Alex! Addy!" Rami yelled, standing on his seat. "Hurry up!"

"Sorry!" Addy apologized. "We got caught in the mob."

"That's why we were not going to split up," Jocelyn said.

"It's fine, girl, don't worry," Rami said as Alex and Addy took their seats.

Alex motioned at Rami. "Give me that." A silver flask passed quickly between them and Alex took a big swig of burning whiskey. Barely flinching, he exclaimed, "Whooo!"

Helping herself to the flask, Addy kicked it back and grimaced. "What is that? Tastes like burning gasoline." The others just laughed and offered no rebuttal.

A couple swigs later, Alex turned around to pass the flask to Jocelyn and inadvertently elbowed a guy in the side of the face. Addy laughed at Alex's clumsy faux pas. She laughed even harder when the fine gentleman gave a reflexive "What the—?!" and miraculously calmed himself once he turned and saw Alex's huge body.

Suddenly the music quieted, and the announcer addressed the crowd. "Ladies and gentlemen; native Calivians and those from afar, welcome to Oric Stadium!" Cheers and applause blew up the stadium.

"Today's event is quite special; our very own Calivian Nighthawks are facing their greatest rivals, all the way from the Sarian Republic Capital City, the Sonics!" The announcer paused, allowing the fans to welcome the away team.

"Without further ado, please welcome our very own Calivian Nighthawks!"

The fans erupted as the arena gates opened on one side and the home team came flying out, skating through the sky at thirty miles per hour on their hover-skates and completing a glorious arc around the arena before stopping in perfect formation on the ground. Soon, the away team followed suit and the players arranged themselves in formation to begin the game.

Addy had always loved the game of airblading. Ever since she was a child and she had first seen it on television, Addy had been enchanted by the game. She loved the grace, the speed, the dexterity of the players—the pure precision required to shoot a ball into a triangular, holographic goal at speeds of up to forty miles per hour was incredible to her. Even more though, the sport of airblading was a great equalizer. No man or woman, no one short or tall, big or small, or whatever else, had any inherent advantage if they couldn't operate the wave suit. Addy respected airbladers so much because of that.

The players lined up for the blitz, the lightning-fast tee-off that would signal the start of the match. Three players from each side lined up on their respective sides of the arena with one hand touching the wall and prepared for a mad dash toward the center of the arena, where the ball would rocket into play from below.

"Here they go!" Rami exclaimed.

With one sound of the buzzer, six players blasted off the walls. Fans went wild as the six converged on the center, boost jumping into the air after the errant ball. They wove an intricate pattern as they crisscrossed in midair, and the fans ate it up. The Nighthawks drew first blood as their midfielder arched his body and drove a thirty-five mile-per-hour shoulder into the chest of the opposing Sonic player, driving her off course from the ball. This allowed Adrian Sky, the Nighthawks' star forward, to secure the ball and land safely in the center of the arena. *Damn, it's a good thing that those suits are made to resist impact*, Addy thought.

Addy and many others screamed as Adrian Sky began dipping and dodging, skating through the Sonic's defense. Meanwhile, the mid-laners from the blitz careened through the air; the Sonic player tried to shake the Nighthawk, but he thrust his skates again, driving his body into hers, until both slammed unceremoniously into the transparent energy-dome between the play area and the audience. The collision happened right in front of Addy and her group, illuminating the dome at the point of contact and making a very loud, hollow smashing sound.

"Oh yeah! Kill her!" Alex yelled. He stood up to cheer and Addy realized she had instinctively grabbed his arm after the clash had startled her. *How embarrassing*, she thought. She'd been at so many of these and had never been so jumpy. Why did she feel so anxious today? She thought for a moment about the men she had seen outside.

Adrian Sky dove between two Sonics and hit his boost jump to vault over a third, then he arched his back, wound up his right arm, and launched a high-speed shot straight into the corner of the Sonic's goal.

An uproar began as the buzzer sounded and the announcer shouted, "GOOOAL! Adrian Sky does it again! That's one for the home team!"

Addy found herself shoved and elbowed repeatedly by the rowdy fans. She turned to one especially annoying bro and scowled. "What's your problem, man?" He may not have heard her over the commotion, but more likely, his scrawny ass was ignoring her. She reiterated, "Hey! Jack-off!" She smacked his arm, which got him looking her way. "Hands to yourself."

"Oh, sorry."

The idiot went back about his business and seconds later "accidently" shoulder checked her as he moved side to side. It was enough for her to stumble into Alex. He looked at her with concern, but she said nothing and they both went back to watching the game. After all, this kind of thing happened all the time and was sort of part of it. Still, inside she was seething.

The players lined up again for the blitz. As the buzzer sounded and the announcer yelled "BLITZ!" the guy rammed her again and started screaming incessantly, way too close to her. *Too bad for metal detectors*, she thought. *If I had a knife, this jack-off would be bleeding out of his kidney*. Actually, a throat spray would be more satisfying. As she pictured it, Addy's rage multiplied.

A moment later, Rami tapped Addy's shoulder and that was it. Her personal space had been violated enough, and she couldn't stand people touching her shoulder! Addy clenched her fist and, without a thought, clocked the guy next to her. Right in the jaw! That jerk-off never saw it coming and stumbled right onto his ass, taking two friends down with him. Addy considered going for blood, just getting on top of him and smashing his face until it was inside out, and if his buddies wanted some, she'd be happy to share. However, security was already on their way.

By now Alex had noticed his sister's altercation and tried to intervene. Grabbing Addy's shoulder, he asked, "What happened?"

"Bitch!" the jerk grumbled, hustling to his feet and stepping up to Addy, staring at her face-to-face and puffing out his chest. Behind him, his two friends were torn between laughing at him and backing away from Addy.

"Hey!" Alex interjected, inserting himself into the fray. "You got a problem?" Alex's usual deterrent effect began to take place as the guy became visibly conflicted about his current situation.

Instead of hitting her back, which Addy could tell he wanted to do, the guy settled on an insult. "Right ... stir up crap and then let your boyfriend come to the rescue."

Now her rage was fuzzy and unquenchable. Her knee connected with his groin and her fist followed, furiously beating on the back of his head until the cocky fool fell again. His two buddies were smart enough to stay back as two big security guards collapsed on the scene, pushing Alex aside and grabbing onto Addy's arms.

"He started it!" Rami tried to defend her.

"Screw you! Get off me!" Addy screamed, squirming to get free.

"You are out of here!" the guard said.

"I know! I'll freaking go! Let go of me, now!"

The security guards complied with her request, but only after jerking her around and shoving her into the aisle, where they followed her to the exit.

Rami argued, "Come on, that's garbage, he started it, I saw!"

"Just enjoy the game," Addy told her friends, submitting to her dismissal.

As she exited the stands, the home team scored again, and the crowd went wild. What a waste of a perfectly exciting game.

2

Oh, sweet cancer. Addy sighed as she exhaled a long drag of her cigarette. The muffled sounds of the game were still drumming in the background as she stood against the outside wall of the stadium and tried to calm down. Most people had moved away from the entrance by now, since admittance after the start of a game was strictly prohibited—unless you paid a hefty price to the guards, of course. Anything could be purchased in Calivia. Addy scoffed just thinking about it. It was probably a fact in most places, she realized, but it seemed like Calivia made it glorious, flaunted it like a fancy hat or an opulent necklace. It had been like this ever since the Grothian invasion: corrupt, chaotic, and incorrigible. Even though the occupation had ended twenty-two years ago, you wouldn't know it if you looked around.

Alex emerged about a minute behind her. "Addy, what happened in there?"

She glanced at him incredulously for a moment. Wasn't it obvious?

"I know that guy. He works at the facility next to mine. Want me to mess him up?"

"No. I will do it myself if he ever shows up again."

There was a silence for a few moments. Alex shifted back and forth and pulled out his own cigarettes.

After a long exhale of smoke, he said, "I've seen better games."

"Yeah."

"Too one-sided this year. The Nighthawks killed it in the draft, and they were already the best team, so now they are unstoppable. There is no balance."

Addy took another long drag and exhaled. "Sorry to make you miss it."

"Nah. We'll catch the next one, eh?"

She instantly felt better. Alex had always been able to center her, ever since they were children. No matter how dismal the situation, no matter how hot she got, Alex was always able to bring her back. It was strange because Alex was not known for his emotional intelligence, normally. With anyone else, Alex was often curt, seemingly disconnected. Sometimes people mistook him as arrogant or uncaring. When it came to Addy, though, Alex was a warm soul, a solemn protector, as an older brother ought to be. They were not related by blood, but their bond was just as strong. Perhaps stronger, even, because they had grown up together in an orphanage here in the city of Calivia. Those postwar days were not easy for any of the children made homeless after the Grothian bastards laid siege to outer Sari, but at least Addy had been blessed with the company of a kindred spirit.

"You know," Addy said after starting a second cigarette, "I felt really anxious today, angry even."

"About what?"

"Nothing specific. Just anxious as ever. It is making me feel ready to snap. Like, I still feel it, even now." That was about half of the truth. There was at least one specific reason for it: the man in the gray suit, the one who had bumped her. His cologne had triggered her. Why? It was the "why" of it that she couldn't pin down. Was it even real, or even the cologne that was the trigger, or mere coincidence? It felt a bit like trying to follow a chirping bird through a dense forest; when you found the bird, was it definitely the one you heard initially?

"I thought that was getting better?"

"It isn't something that just goes away." Addy couldn't hide her frustration. He was doing his best, Addy knew, but Alex did not understand. For as long as she could remember, she had felt this ebb and flow of dark foreboding, as if there were constantly something just on the periphery of her mind. She wished it would just go away.

"Well sure, but ... I don't know."

Alex trailed off and they smoked in silence. Then, something happened. It was as unlikely as it was terrifying, some freak turn of fate, or perhaps a karmic hyperbole responding to her festering misanthropy.

"Addy!" Alex screamed, his eyes staring at the sky. No time to react. An ear-shattering explosion directly above them sent Addy tumbling to the pavement and she just barely managed brace herself from falling face first. After she collided with the pavement, she rolled sideways and tried to look up, but she was concussed, and everything was fuzzy. What was that? A bomb ... a missile? If it were a missile, she'd be dead, Addy decided, but a bomb was possible. Could it be a terrorist attack, from some extremist group making a statement? Calivia had been no stranger to such things in the past, given the tensions between Grothian loyalists and the freedom fighters, but Addy had always been fortunate to not be privy to those events.

When she came to, seconds later, she saw Alex on his knees, with his head down and his hands on the pavement. "Alex! Are you okay?"

Rushing to her feet, she tried to help Alex up. As he sat upright on his knees, Alex held his hands in front of his face and stared at them, horrified. They were bloody and split and two of his fingers were broken. His forearms had gashes in them and blood was trickling down both his arms.

"Oh my God!" Addy exclaimed. "Help! We need help here!" She looked around wildly, now realizing the stadium had been bombed and a huge chunk of the exterior wall had fallen around them. People were screaming, running, and trampling each other to get out and away from the stadium as fast as possible.

She turned to Alex. "We have to go! There was a bomb, can you move?"

Alex just stared at his hands and the pile of debris behind them. Back, forth, back, forth. He asked, "What the hell just happened?"

3

If Zach Brine could have used only two words in the English language to sum up the past year of his life, those words would be *total* and *garbage*, in that order. Yes, there could be no denying that this had been a black-letter year. Even as a diehard optimist, Zach could not find it in him to reconcile his misfortunes of late; at least, not without searching the bottom of a bottle.

First, there had been his job. Zach had always been ruthlessly ambitious, to a fault, some might say, but it all came to a point this last year as Zach began vying for a promotion. If he had succeeded, he would have finally had his own starship and been free to explore his ambitions on a greater level than ever before. Alas, it was not to be.

Zach's wife, Emelia, had always disliked him being in the military, and she especially disliked the idea of him becoming a starship captain, an endeavor which would surely exacerbate the issue. As it was, she was always worrying about his safety and she felt frustrated that their daughter, Jaymi, had to grow up barely seeing her father. Yes, Emelia had been patient throughout his tour in outer Sari quelling the postwar civil unrest. After all, that had been for the greater good, allegedly. Then she had been patient amidst his more recent assignments training cadets for elite positions on Grantitan. But this new job was a step too far.

Second, the castle began to crumble. Zach and Emelia barely spoke when he was home. They never had sex. He wasn't even sure he liked her. She was always so content with mediocrity and forcing him to lower himself, and he couldn't handle it. So, he told her about his affair.

It didn't go as well as he had hoped, and he hadn't expected it to go well at all. Not only did he lose Emelia and Jaymi, but his mistress also broke it off when she found out he was married, which he didn't expect. On top of that, his reputation was ruined. Just like that, the great Zach Brine was nothing but a cheater, a liar, and a stupid joke.

So, Zach did what he always did, which was bury himself in his work. Since he had lost the promotion, it wasn't even satisfying, but it kept him busy. Now here he was, sitting in a coffee shop on Grantitan, sipping some caffeine and scrolling through his work emails on his phone.

"May I top you off, Mr. Brine?" the waitress asked, hovering a steaming pot of coffee over the table.

"What?" Brine looked up from his phone, dazed. "Oh, yes, yes. Thank you."

"Anytime."

As she walked away, Zach reached into the inner pocket of his faded, fur-lined, faux-leather bomber jacket and retrieved his favorite flask. On it was an engraving of a lion and a wolf fused together at the torso and wrapped around one another until their heads came furiously face-to-face. In it was his favorite bourbon. A notification lit up Zach's phone as he poured the bourbon into his coffee: a text from his colleague, Rachel Mccginneas. "You watching the news?"

In fact, the news was on the television over the counter to his left, but he hadn't been watching it. Too caught up in his thoughts. For argument's sake, Zach glanced at the screen as he took a brave sip of steam-garnished bourbon coffee. The anchors were going on about some explosion in space, a ship hit by a meteor storm or something. "Yeah, so what?" Zach texted back.

He lit a cigarette, even though there was no smoking in the diner. What could they do anyway? Zach didn't care. Life had become so monotonous and pointless. Nine hours ago, he had been sitting in an old easy chair with a glass of bourbon on the table in front of him and a gun in his mouth. *I have only one bullet in the chamber*, he had reasoned, white knuckling his ancient sixer. *If I pull this trigger once every day, I can live up to a maximum of six days before my brains become part of the hotel décor. However, if I don't die, I have to give it the old college try, go out in the world and try to find a reason not to pull the trigger again.* As he rationalized through this madness, he also decided the reason couldn't be

Emelia because she would never forgive him. So far, he had the luck of two days and was working on three. Anyway, what could these people possibly do to make Zach feel any worse?

Another text from Rachel read, "How many meteors do you see stray that close to Grantitan?"

Zach thought about that. The nearest asteroid belt was pretty far, and yeah, rogue storms happened, but that's why they invented safe lanes. Those barriers were capable of protecting traveling ships from small objects like meteorites.

"Was the ship off course? Outside barrier?" Zach replied.

"It vanished, Zach. Communication blackout." If it was a storm, the crew would have signaled for help well ahead of the blackout.

"Were they shot down?"

"Looks like it. At Raynor they are being very hush."

"Grothians?"

The waitress came back over and interrupted him, "Excuse me. Sir, you can't smoke in here."

"Hold on," Zach insisted, typing the rest of his text to Rachel, which read, "You probably can't say, eh?"

"Excuse me—"

"Jesus! I said hold on! For heaven's sake, I'll put it out. This damn planet—"

Before Zach could conclude his belligerent rant, he and everyone else in the diner were startled by a huge explosion directly across the street. Horrified screams followed as the subsequent shockwaves shattered the glass windows and doors of the diner and blew the metal door frames right off the hinges and into the specials board. Just as this was happening, Zach dove to the floor, tackling the waitress and covering her beneath him as glass rained down around them.

Zach got to his feet immediately and looked around.

"Stay under the tables!" he directed the people in the diner. Everyone complied, crawling under tables, some huddling together, praying, crying even. Zach had no fear. He was probably going to die today anyway. He glanced over at the shattered window by the front door, and then everything was different. It all changed in one single moment. What happened took all of two or three seconds, but instantly he knew its significance. Tonight, Zach Brine would not pull the trigger. Not tonight, nor tomorrow, nor for a long time, for Zach Brine had seen something amazing, and he had to pursue it.

4

People fled the stadium like stampeding wildebeests. Even the police and the security officers fled, folded into the chaos and assimilated into the panic. No one got paid enough for this.

"Someone help us, please!" Addy pleaded, waving her arms wildly at the errant crowd. As she tried to stop someone, she was rammed by a fleeing couple. Two more people pushed past her with such force that she was thrust into the wall of the stadium and she nearly fell over. Somewhere a child was screaming for his mother.

Addy whipped her phone out of her pocket, frantic and wondering why she hadn't done that already. The screen was cracked from her fall, but it still worked fine.

As she dialed for an ambulance, Addy felt Alex behind her.

"Come on, Addy, we have to get away from the building!" he shouted.

"Hello, what is your emergency?" Someone had picked up on the other line.

"H-Hello?" Addy cried, "There's been a bombing! Someone bombed the stadium! My brother—"

"Slow down. We are aware of the bombing. Who is hurt?"

"My brother! His hands ... he needs an ambulance!"

"Okay, ma'am, paramedics are already on the way. Stay calm and get away from the stadium." Of course, Addy thought, the same thing Alex had said. Alex always knew what to do. Why couldn't she have thought of that and gotten him to safety? Instead she panicked like an idiot. They could have been to safety by now.

She hung up the phone and assessed the crowd, which had mostly moved away from the stadium entrance by now and was stampeding up the street.

"This way," Alex insisted, moving toward the clearing near the entrance Addy had just seen. Smart; everyone else is going the other way.

All they had to do was cross over and they could go toward a different street, free and clear.

"Are you okay? How bad is it?"

"I'm fine," he answered, stubborn as ever.

They wove through the crowd, constantly checking their surroundings for danger, careful not to get separated. As Addy's gaze darted around, she tried to make sense of it all. Who did this? For what purpose? All of these innocent people are screaming and running for their lives, and to what end? That, and her brother had nearly ... well, she couldn't think about it. Actually, it occurred to her that many of these people probably weren't innocent. Perhaps that was why all of this was happening. This city was due for a cleansing, after all.

Then, Addy noticed something amiss. Not chaotic so much as incorrect, out of place, irrational. A man in a black bomber jacket was going the wrong way. While everyone else was fleeing from the stadium, this man was coming toward it, and fast. He was shoving people, bouncing off them, keeping a brisk pace ... if she wasn't mistaken, he was fixated right on her and Alex. As they moved through the crowd, the man's gaze followed them and his tenacity increased. Whoever he was, he was definitely coming for them!

"Alex!"

Turning to ensure that Addy wasn't lost to the fray, Alex saw her pointing to the man.

"Keep going!" Alex urged her, pushing through the crowd. Addy followed Alex out of the chaos and into an alleyway between two large buildings. The man was closing in fast.

"What does he want? Is he the bomber?" Addy asked as they stopped and turned to face the stalker.

As the man came out of the crowd, Alex tensed up and confronted him. "Who the hell are you?" Alex stood at an angle, hiding his worst hand and trying to downplay the extent of his injuries.

"My name is Zach Brine," he said, flashing a very official looking badge. "I'm a Prism soldier. I saw what just happened and I'm here to escort you to safety."

Suspicious, Addy and Alex glanced at each other, then back at Zach. Addy pressed, "What about all of those people?" Something was very off here. As much as Addy wanted to get her brother to the hospital, she wasn't sure she was ready to trust this man, badge or no badge.

"Let me explain after you are safe," Zach insisted, extending his hand toward Alex.

"Piss off," Alex resisted. "We are already safe. Come on, Addy."

Zach offered no argument. Instead, he reached into his bomber jacket and produced a micro-sized pistol. It all happened so fast that by the time Addy had called Alex's name, Zach had already released a tiny metal device from the pistol, an extremely effective taser, and shocked Alex into incapacitation. With well-trained reflexes, Zach thwarted Addy's attempt to grab the gun and tasered her as well, leaving both Addy and Alex unconscious in the alleyway.

5

Addy awoke in a wild, lucid dream. In the phantasmal side of it, she was lying on her back between two great skyscrapers, captivated by their glistening chrome amidst a blustery rainstorm. They seemed to sway above her, like massive trees in a concrete forest. She took a deep breath of the crisp, purifying mist of rain, ignoring for a moment the polluted essence that was Calivia. If only the real world felt like this, but reality knew better. The other side of her lucid state kept waking and promising her that she was indeed still here, tethered to this hopeless land.

Wait a second ... she heard a faint clanking sound. As she opened her eyes, Addy tried to lift her hand to her face and realized abruptly that she was handcuffed to the bed. Panicking, her eyes widened and darted around the room ... a hospital? It must be, she decided upon examining the monitors, beds dressed in white linens, and various medical accoutrements organized near a bay sink. On the wall to her left were two large windows that took up the majority of the wall.

"Alex?" Eventually her gaze fell on the bed next to hers, where Alex lay sleeping, his arms bandaged and wrapped profusely. She noted that his hands were also cuffed to the metal railings on either side of his bed. Though she tried to resist thoughts of the diabolical, her mind was flooded with them anyway. How could she be sure that Zach Brine was a good guy? Prism ... come on. She had heard of them before; supposedly they were a super elite organization within the Sarian military, highly trained and deadly proficient. Prism was also quite secretive, according to rumors, so she didn't know much more about them or what they did. What could they want with Alex? This guy was probably just some serial killer. Hell, maybe he was even the terrorist who planted the bomb at the stadium.

Addy was about to call to Alex again when she heard voices just outside the open door of the room. She closed her eyes and lay still, pretending to be asleep as two men entered the room.

"... No worries," one man said. "You never answered me before, how can you be so sure that he is—"

"Shhh! Shut the hell up," the other, whose voice Addy recognized as Zach's, scolded.

"You owe me."

"Proportionately, it will be you who owes me if I am right."

The other one sighed. "God, it's always some caper you are caught up in. One of these days you are going to get buried so deep you'll never dig out. I hope I'm not here by then."

Addy heard them rustling around Alex's bed and she opened one eye just long enough to see Zach standing over Alex's torso, and the other man at the foot of the bed. The second guy was shorter than Zach and kind of stumpy, with a long, chiseled face and a neat strip of facial hair garnished with a straight goatee. He wore a navy-blue turtleneck and black slacks, and the way the shirt rested higher on the left suggested maybe a handgun was protruding out of his pants, plastered to his lower back. Zach had lost the bomber jacket and now wore just his blue jeans and a tight white t-shirt, which was meticulously tucked in and secured by a basic black leather belt with a silvery buckle. Addy saw that Zach's muscular arms bore several tattoos and perhaps a brand, but she couldn't make out what they were.

"Hey," Zach said, gently slapping Alex on the cheek several times. "Rise and shine."

Alex grumbled and woke. When he saw Zach hovering over him, he reflexively went to punch him, but discovered the handcuffs as they violently halted his lunge. "—The hell?"

"Relax. I'll get those off in a minute; I just needed them so I could explain some things to you."

"You mean why you tasered me and dragged my sister and I here? What do you want?"

"I brought you to the hospital, which is where you need to be with those arms of yours."

"We were already coming here, asshole. I didn't need your help, and I especially didn't need to be tasered and kidnapped!" Alex tried to rip his arm free and winced in pain as he was rudely reminded of his fresh injuries.

"Wow," the man at the foot of the bed commented. "People are so ungrateful these days. This is why I am retired from public service."

A nurse entered the room and started to bustle around behind Zach, preparing a syringe of some bluish liquid. Zach said to her, "About time. I asked for you ten minutes ago."

"You didn't have to wake him," she replied, unfazed.

"What is that?" Alex demanded. "I don't want anything from you."

Addy opened her eyes again to see what Alex was talking about. When she saw the nurse approaching his bedside with the blue syringe, she shouted, "Leave him alone!"

Zach looked at her, irritated, and said, "Settle down. This is a tissue repairing serum. In a few hours your brother's arm will be good as new."

"Yeah right!" said Alex, eyes wide as canyons. "I'm not taking any serums!"

The nurse tried to lean over Alex to administer the medicine and he tried to lunge at her. He winced again and Zach rolled his eyes in annoyance.

"Leave him alone! Let us go!" Addy screamed.

"Goddamn, will you just shut it already?" said the man at the foot of the bed. "Zach, let's just sedate them again."

"Lucas," Zach scolded, putting a finger up to silence him. He turned back to Addy and looked her right in the eye. "Listen, you can't trust the people in this city. I did what I did for your safety."

The calm in Zach's voice seemed to deescalate the situation momentarily, and Alex responded, "Okay, so then, what do you want? We asked you that in the alleyway and you said you would explain once we were safe."

"I will answer you, but first, let the nurse do her job. Hailey is very busy and other patients need her help. It's just a standard tissue repair serum; military grade. It'll have you fixed by the time you go to bed tonight."

"Don't trust these people," Addy urged her brother.

Seeing that they were still nervous, Zach added, "Think about what you are saying; if I wanted to kill you, wouldn't I have done it while you were unconscious? What sense would all this make?"

"Okay," Alex conceded. Addy watched in horror as the nurse, Hailey, leaned in and injected the whole syringe into Alex's forearm. There were things other than death, she wanted to scream.

"Thanks Hailey," Zach said, dismissing her.

"Next time leave them sedated," Hailey said as she took the tray and left the room.

"Alex?" Addy looked worried. What had her brother just allowed himself to be injected with?

Alex reassured her, if you could call it that. "Like he said, they could have done whatever they wanted."

"Smart guy," Lucas said.

"The cuffs?" Alex questioned, locking his gaze with Zach's.

Zach motioned to Lucas. "Get the girl." As Lucas followed instructions and released Addy, Zach reached into his pocket, produced his own key, and released Alex. Immediately, Zach's cohort moved toward the exit, where he leaned firmly on the doorframe, his arms crossed at his chest. Zach backed up and began to pace the room in front of the windows.

Addy got to her feet first and went over to her brother. "Alex, are you okay?"

"I feel fine." Alex sat up and turned toward Zach, his feet hanging off the bed. "Well? Why did you save us, specifically, out of everyone in the crowd? And now, you are here with us. Why?"

"At the time, I thought we were under attack. It turns out it was a freak accident, some space debris too large to have fully burned up in the atmosphere and it just happened to crash into our stadium."

"Under attack by who?"

Zach closed his eyes and rubbed his forehead with one hand as he paced back and forth, as if trying to find his words. Addy just waited anxiously.

"You are aware of what happened, right? Of what you did?"

Alex lowered his brow, looking confused. "What I did? I almost died; I know that. Addy and I both almost died. You are saying that was space debris?" It was obvious that Alex was skeptical. Addy was as well; these things *did* happen, but with all the civil uprising on Grantitan of late, it seemed a fantastic coincidence that some random space debris made it past the barriers that protected the shipping lanes and into the atmosphere without being burned or destroyed, and then hit the airblading stadium, Calivia's famed landmark, of all places?

"Before you got to your feet, what was the last thing you remember?"

"What do you mean? Am I on trial here? We were nearly crushed! It's hard to say what happened. How did you get there so fast, anyway?"

"What about you?" Zach addressed Addy. "You are his sister, but I didn't catch your name. What did you see right before you started to help him up?"

Snapping to, Addy answered him. "My name is Addy, and I didn't see much. I was smoking a cigarette, Alex saw something, called to me, and before I could react, I was lying face down on the ground. Hell, I don't even remember if Alex tackled me or if I was knocked over or what ... it happened too fast."

"Nothing, then?"

"No ... honestly, though, are we being interrogated? Should we be read rights or something? You brought us in here in handcuffs and—"

"Relax, you are not under arrest," Zach assured her.

"Great, then let us go."

"You are free to go any time." Although, the guard at the door seemed to suggest otherwise.

"Fine. Addy, let's go then." Alex slid off the bed and started toward the door. Cautiously, Addy followed him, her eyes locked on Zach, who had stopped pacing and stood with his back to the large window. There was something he wasn't saying, and Addy knew it, but her desire to be free of this room superseded her curiosity.

"You should feel good as new in about four hours," Zach said as they reached the door.

Alex looked over his shoulder and said, "Thanks." He encountered Lucas at the door. For a couple seconds, Alex met his gaze and neither man said anything. Finally, Lucas rolled his eyes and stepped aside, allowing them to pass.

Before they could walk out, Zach made one last attempt. "If you want to find out what really happened, I'll be around." He turned to his cohort and said, "See them out, would you?"

"Wait a second." Addy stopped, curious, and decided to ask after all. "Why bother bringing us here just to let us go?"

"You have not committed a crime," Zach reminded her. "So again, I am not holding you against your will. The handcuffs were merely to prevent you from attacking me. If you want to talk to me willingly, there is much more to discuss, I venture."

"I'm not sure we want to discuss anything with you."

Lucas agreed, "Ha! Yeah, Zach, I think you might have missed the mark on these ones."

"We aren't interested," Alex informed Zach. He looked at Lucas and added, "And we can see ourselves out, thanks."

"Take a right at the end of the hall and you will find the elevator," Zach said.

Lucas shot them a cocky glance as they brushed past him and went into the hall.

Once they were a safe distance from the room, Addy asked, "What just happened?" She was about to follow up by asking where the hell they even were, but she recognized the building after looking around the halls; it was the Hedron Medical Center, the largest hospital in Calivia. Had he taken them here in an ambulance? If they were under attack, wouldn't this place be as unsafe as the stadium? Nothing made sense.

"No clue. You should stay at my apartment tonight, in case that creep gets any ideas about trying to follow you."

"Yeah ... for all we know, he is part of some kidnapping syndicate. I mean, would a Prism soldier really be wasting time on this crappy planet? No one can save this place."

"Prism ... pfft. What a crazy story."

He did have a badge though, and he had let them go. Addy had no idea what to do with this information.

6

She had taken Alex's advice and stayed the night at his place, but she found that even so, she had been crippled with anxiety. It was so bad that she barely slept at all and she found herself waking up the next morning sore, fatigued, and mentally anguished. Alex was gone to work at the Corithiam mines by the time she woke, and she found herself cold and alone, wrapped up tightly in the comforter on Alex's bed. Man, she thought, the heat must be busted again. What was Alex paying rent for? He was too passive, she thought. If it were her landlord, she'd be taking him to task.

Bravely, she released herself from the comforter and went for the bathroom, feeling the deep chill of the uninsulated apartment as late autumn air infiltrated her skin and strangled her bones. The floorboards were like ice. When she got into the bathroom, she turned on the small space heater next to the porcelain sink and stuck her face right in front of it for a few seconds. She could feel the goosebumps all over her body.

When the heater kicked in and she felt a little warmer, she turned on the water and leaned on the sink while she waited for it to warm up. She examined herself in the mirror, running her slender fingers through her long black hair until it was a thorough mess. Her skinny, usually fit body was looking paler and more ragged than usual. Lately, she hadn't been working out much, if at all, and her sleep was sporadic. She couldn't stop moving, tapping her fingers, playing with her hair, whatever. Finally, the water was warm, and she wet a cloth and pressed it to her face.

Perhaps she was just stressed; she had been through a lot. In a way, she wished Alex were home, but at the same time, she could only confide so much in him. There would come a time when Addy would become a burden on his simple life and that was the very last thing she wanted. She had thought of her foster parents, but she couldn't go to them, either. The Palmer ranch was about two hours outside of Calivia, and even if she wanted to make that journey, they were almost never home. Plus, there was nothing there for her. She had never gotten along with Dean Palmer, and Beatrice was just an extension of him. They didn't care about her. If they did, they would have never separated her from Alex in the first place.

Memories flooded her brain of herself, seven and a half, crying on the floor, begging not to be taken from the orphanage. She had only known Alex for a little over a year, but they had bonded so much. She didn't trust the adults. At the time, they said she would be better off, but it didn't feel that way. God, how pathetic she was, crying like that. It was so embarrassing to think about.

Addy pushed it out of her mind and took a shower. Once she was ready for the day, she decided she had to talk to someone. Anxiety was still lurking behind her every thought and she could tell it was something more than stress. Something significant had happened at the stadium. So she called the only person she felt comfortable unloading on, her therapist, Jill, and headed into the city.

"Thanks for meeting me," Addy said when she arrived at a small coffee shop in Eastern Calivia just before noon.

As Addy moved to take her seat, Jill greeted her warmly, insisting on a hug. "Addy, don't be silly! Are you sure you don't mind doing this here?"

"Yeah, we don't have time to get back to the office anyway. I appreciate you meeting me like this at the last minute. So sorry to impose on you during your lunch break."

"Oh, my pleasure. Don't worry about that, it's my job. Further, I care about you, Addy."

Jill was always there on the fly, which was one of the reasons Addy called her.

"Thank you."

"Do you want a coffee? A panini, maybe? They make great sandwiches here."

"Yeah, I think a coffee would be fantastic, I didn't sleep well. I have to insist it is on me, though."

Handing Addy a menu, Jill said, "Addy, it's fine, you don't have to."

"You moved your day around for me; at least let me buy lunch for you."

Their pleasantries were interrupted when the waiter came by and greeted them. "Good afternoon ladies, may I offer you a beverage?"

"Oh, hi," Jill said, "We'll take coffee, please, and a panini for me. Whatever the special is. Addy, are you sure you don't want lunch?"

"Yeah, thank you," Addy insisted.

"Okay, afternoon pick-me-up coming right up," the waiter said cheerily.

"Lovely, thanks so much," Jill replied.

"You're welcome! I'll be right back."

Addy grinned as the waiter strutted away. She could never do that. People annoyed her far too much.

"So," Jill began, "I know we are a bit limited on time today. Do you want to tell me what's bothering you?"

"It's a little hard to describe. It's kind of intangible, even to me." Addy looked at her feet, one crossed over the other, swaying beneath the table.

"Are you feeling hopeless again? Like before, or is it different?"

"It is like that, only, I think I know how it started this time."

"And how was that?" Jill relaxed her chin on her palm inquisitively as she let her elbow rest on the table.

"Well, there were these two men wearing gray suits ... I didn't realize the extent of this event until this morning, you know, when I had a chance to look back on it."

The waiter slid back over with the coffees and a little side plate filled with cream and sugar. "Here you are, ladies. I'll be back with the panini shortly. Enjoy!"

"Thank you," they both answered.

"So, anyway," Addy continued, "I almost died yesterday, and ..."

Jill interrupted, incredulous. "Wait, what?"

"At the stadium. A slab of concrete barely missed me as it fell."

"You were part of that horrible accident at the stadium? Oh, honey ... I'm so glad you are okay. That must have been traumatic."

As she spoke, Jill reached across the table and rubbed Addy's forearm. Normally Addy was not one to appreciate the affections of others, particularly when people touched her, but Jill was okay. Jill could comfort her, which was why Addy had stuck with her. Before Jill, she had seen many therapists, most of whom were full of crap or underqualified for her kind of need. Perhaps the problem was that too many people tried to put a finite quality on Addy, as if this enigmatic shadow that she felt could be defined intrinsically. There was no definition, Addy had learned, only an unknown inhibition, some eternal cloak and dagger manipulating her into primal rage. Jill never thumped any textbooks or assigned any labels. She acknowledged Addy as a deeply complex woman with this darkness about her, this propensity to submit to her cynical and yet culturally reinforced ruminations. In simpler terms, Jill listened to her.

"Thank you. Really, though, it's okay." Addy thought about what she wanted to say as she added cream and sugar and stirred up her coffee. They now knew the airblading stadium had been a freak accident; something went wrong with a freighter and it went outside the shipping lanes around Grantitan, a passing comet collided with it and knocked a big chuck of the ship off, sending it hurtling into the atmosphere. Apparently the chunk was big enough to enter the atmosphere and it just happened to land right here in Calivia, just in time to ruin Addy's smoke break. It had been on the news all morning.

"You were right there when it happened? Were you frightened? Are you hurt?"

"Of course, yeah, I was scared. Anyway, something even stranger happened. After the explosion, I saw Alex on his knees, his hands and forearms were bloody and he was staring at them with these huge eyes, like he had seen a six-headed ostrich." Pausing for a moment, Addy tried the coffee, grimacing slightly as an acrid aftertaste lingered in her throat and crept up into her nose. It smelled vaguely nutty, but with something else, like a sour curd or something. Lifting the little creamer up so she could read it, Addy saw it was one of the fake, processed substitutes that the government tried to subversively replace their food with. Typical, she scoffed, just another example of the fascist government seizing control over the largely choiceless proletariat population of Grantitan. They had to make sure all the good resources were saved for Grothia. Damn, twenty some-odd years had passed since the Grothian war and they couldn't let it go. No, what really happened was the planet was never truly liberated. Even after the war was over, the Grothian influence maintained a vice grip over Grantitan and the other planets of the outer rim of the Sarian Empire. A whole new generation of citizens born in this strip of the galaxy had to be punished because of events they had nothing to do with and because the pandering outer-Sari politicians were too afraid to stand up to those assholes. Perhaps this was why people rose against them in the first place. They were no better than the conquerors and assimilators themselves.

"Oh God, is your brother okay?" Jill touched her arm again.

"Yeah, we were taken by a man who called himself Zach Brine. He claimed to be part of 'Prism,' if that is real. He specifically sought us from the crowd, Jill. As in, I looked up and there he was, coming the opposite way through the crowd like a madman! Long story short, we refused to go with him and he tasered us. We woke up in the Hedron Medical Center to him interrogating us about the incident."

"What did he want to know?"

Before Addy could answer, Jill's panini arrived. "Here you are, ma'am. Anything else I can get you?"

"Not at the moment, thank you," Jill answered.

The waiter made a swift exit to tend to another table across from them, and Addy continued, "He just kept asking what we remembered about the attack ... the accident, I mean, as if he didn't believe us."

"Do you think he was being truthful, about Prism, I mean?" Jill began to eat her sandwich as she listened. "Did you call the cops?"

Like they would do anything, Addy silently scoffed.

"I don't know, but ... but what I do know is that I feel fine today ... about all of that."

"But something else is on your mind?"

"The two guys in the gray suits. I saw them right before the game."

"Right. Who are they?"

"I have no idea, but one of them bumped into me and I smelled his cologne. I don't know if it was that smell or the suits or just the general staleness of the air for the moment that they passed me, but I felt the most intense anxiety I have felt in a long time. Just like last time, when I first came to you. I still feel it today. Even though I almost died, and I basically got kidnapped, tasered, and interrogated, I am focused on those guys."

"Something about them must have triggered you. If I remember, the first time we spoke, you were angry about the way you were treated at the admissions office of the university. You commented on his 'stupid suit' as well."

"That's right ..."

Addy tried to remember the incident to no avail. It wasn't much to fret over, apparently, but whatever interaction she had that day was enough to trigger her at the time. This had happened many other times too, Addy was sure, but she always locked it away when she got that angry. As she pondered this, just to test herself, she tried to remember the guy that got her kicked out of the airblading game yesterday. Some of the circumstances of the altercation were there, but she could not remember his face nor even what he said. All she could remember was the anxiousness, the evolution of it into blistering anger, and then getting kicked out.

"We talked a lot before about your foster father. Do you think your anxiety around these men has anything to do with him?"

"Well, sure, but I don't think that's it."

Jill was hitting all the right notes. Given what Addy had told her about the volatile relationship between her and her foster father, she was right to suspect this link. Dean Palmer's expectations were absurdly high and carried conditional love; of course Addy was anxious around him. He would say he was hard on her because he wanted the best for her, but really, that was him saying he, the prominent and respected politician, didn't want to be embarrassed by her. Once, Addy had even told Jill about how a banker had reminded her of Dean with his smug, elitist attitude. Nothing was good enough for Dean unless it was perfect. However, there was something more. Dean may have sown some of this inside her, but Addy suspected it went deeper than that.

"What else do you think it could be?"

"I have no idea, isn't that what I pay you for?" Addy snapped, then immediately apologized. "I'm sorry."

"That's fine. You are feeling frustrated and you want to know why, I understand that."

"I just don't know, Jill. This place sucks. Everyone here sucks, except you and Alex and a select few others. How can I keep on going like this?"

Jill finished up her sandwich, then answered empathically, "Do you think it may be time to make some changes?"

"You mean go back home? Why, so I can listen to that tyrant tell me I'm not worthy of the Palmer name?" She knew she was deflecting, but Addy didn't care.

"I mean maybe get away for a week, stop thinking about all this. Try making a new friend at school?"

"I don't know, maybe, but I feel like I have tried these things."

"I know. We talked about this once and you said you only came here to Calivia because you missed Alex. You did say that reconnecting with him helped, remember? You also said that you resented Dean and you wanted to get away from your hometown. Honestly, there is probably a lot of residual anxiety from when your foster parents adopted you, and you and Alex were separated. You must realize that those things are not your fault and you can't keep beating yourself up for being sad. We all get sad sometimes. What you can do is try to do things that make you happy."

Addy thought about that for a minute. She did have a propensity to self-sabotage, and this wasn't the first time Jill had called it to her attention.

"You're right, thanks Jill."

"Don't thank me; I'm always here for you, Addy."

"Thank you. Well, anyway, I've taken up your whole lunch break. Let me pay at least?"

"No, no, no. You are not a burden, and lunch is on me. You only had coffee! Which you didn't drink!"

"I insist," Addy said, placing twenty credits on the table. "Thank you again, I'm going to get going."

"You are so welcome!" Jill said, standing up and giving Addy a hug. "So, again, I think you need to make a change. Do something that makes you happy or makes you feel a sense of accomplishment, even if it goes against what others expect of you. You let me know if you want to talk again, you hear? Anytime."

"Thank you."

Addy walked away and started down the street toward Alex's place. Jill's advice seemed spot on, albeit rather utopian. Addy knew she wouldn't follow that advice, at least not today. Honestly, she'd probably just get drunk. *All hail self-sabotage!*

7

Only five minutes until quitting time, Alex thought, wiping the sweat from his brow. Today had been a particularly taxing day at the Calivian Corithiam Mine, both because he was sore from his injuries and because his foreman was rolling the crap downhill after a stern conversation with the higher bosses. Alex must have heard the word *productivity* seventeen times today. It was okay, though; he was working overtime and making tons of money.

He started to gather up his materials and head to his locker when his coworker, Grant, came up beside him and said, "Geez, busy day, huh?"

"Yeah ... it's not too bad, though."

"Screw this mandatory overtime nonsense. I have things to do on my Saturdays."

"At least we have good paying jobs."

Those were hard to come by these days, especially with as little education as many people here had. Most mining operations had been overtaken by automation, but Calivia hadn't quite caught up yet.

"Pfftt ... whatever. I don't see the big bosses workin' on Saturday."

They got into the locker room and went to their individual lockers to gather their things. From across the room, Grant yelled, "What are you doing later?"

"Probably gonna grab some beers with some friends," Alex shouted back. Other miners started to enter the room and the noise became overwhelming. Alex quickly put away his work items, locked his locker, and pushed his way out of the blue-collar frenzy.

Grant was behind him. As they approached the exit to the mine, Grant said, "Well, enjoy your weekend man. What's left of it."

Alex chuckled. "Yeah, you too."

Many of Alex's coworkers were like Grant: hardworking, rough, and a bit simple. Cynical too. They often complained about the work and the boss and the hours, but they still showed up every day and did their best. Alex wasn't quite the same, rather, he was genuinely grateful for his life. He never complained, except to join in the banter, and he regarded his work, his pay, his truck, and his apartment as decent steps above the crowded orphanage where he and Addy had grown up. When he was younger, he hadn't really noticed how poor the conditions of the orphanage were; he had Addy then, and between their friendship and the naivety of youth, he had been happy. Then Addy was adopted, and his loneliness began to open him to the pessimism of it all. When he was older and on his own finally, Alex had told himself he would not view the world that way. He couldn't, it was too hard.

"See you later, bud," Alex said as he and Grant parted ways outside of the mine's exit. He stopped for a moment and lit up a smoke, looking out over the rolling plains outside of Calivia and admiring their early evening beauty. It wasn't quite sunset, not for another hour or so, but the light was beginning to turn to a soft orange, amplifying the golden canvas of rolling countryside outside of Calivia. If you focused on it right, you wouldn't even notice the layers of smog produced by the mines and the nearby factories.

Alex was about to walk to his truck when he noticed something out of place: a man leaning with his back against the wall of the small office building outside the mine, with one foot on the ground and another on the wall. The man wore a familiar jacket and puffed on a big cigar.

"Are you following me now?" Alex asked, turning to the man he recognized as Zach Brine.

"I didn't want to separate you two in the hospital, but it occurred to me that you might not say anything in front of her." Zach puffed on his cigar again.

"What are you talking about? You know, you had best get lost before I mess you up."

"Are you really not curious how you survived? You know, after you caught that big slab of concrete with your bare hands? It should have crushed you and your sister both."

Zach had seen it. There was no way Alex could whisk it away, he knew. Hell, how was he to explain this? Even Alex himself was incredulous of the whole thing. Up until this very second, with the revelation that someone else had witnessed the event, Alex had been uncertain if it had even happened. He had convinced himself, for lack of other evidence, that the rational explanation must be that he had blacked out, imagined the whole thing in a rush of adrenaline. That was certainly more believable than the alternative, in which Alex had done something physically impossible.

Alex tried to deny it anyway. "I must have grazed it, got my arms chewed up by the smaller bits."

"Nope," Zach refuted him confidently. "You caught that big hunk of death dead center. Barely, I'll concede, because you folded almost immediately and let it slide down behind you. Frankly, I'm surprised that you didn't end up dropping it on your sister anyway after all that."

"Look ... obviously that's impossible. I'm not certain what happened; I blacked out. It happened fast and I was full of adrenaline."

"What happened was that you defied physics. Don't you want to know why? I know I do. Come with me and let's find out."

Defensive, Alex refused. "What, are you nuts? Go with you where?"

"Ever heard of Prism? They would crap their pants if they knew someone like you existed."

"No," Alex answered, tensing up. "No Prism, no following me, and not Addy either. If I see you near Addy, I'll rip your head off."

"I venture that you could, with the proper direction. Let me show you how to rip my head off. Come on, Prism is made for you."

"Forget it. You stay away from us," Alex demanded, pointing at Zach.

Alex turned to leave, and Zach called after him, "Your real parents didn't die in a car crash, by the way."

Looking over his shoulder, Alex shouted, "I said leave me alone!"

"I'm at the Haxenburg; you know, the fancy motel downtown!"

Not taking the bait, Alex hurried along to his truck. Man, a drink was going to be magical. It began to hit Alex, as he got into his old pickup and started driving down the dank, industrial parkway leading away from the mines, how intense the past twenty-four hours had been. He had been largely apathetic over the years when things went wrong because frankly, Calivia was not a good place. But he chose not to dwell on it and to try to see the bright side of life. Why Addy had wanted to come here, Alex couldn't understand. It's not as if Alex couldn't have visited her somewhere else, and she could go to university anywhere ... why here? Anyway, since she *was* here, Alex felt like he had to care now. He had to care about this city, about the unrest, about all the things that he would rather just tune out. She could have died yesterday. Also, what was that Zach Brine psycho going on about? How did he know about Alex's parents? It was a bluff, Alex was certain, but even so, Zach must have researched him a bit to learn that he was an orphan. What else did he know, and had he snooped on Addy as well? He realized at that moment that he may have to deal with this guy.

Right now, however, he had to put this to bed and get the edge off; it was time for a drink.

8

Swirling cancer and the sound of whiskey over rocks dominated her senses as Addy entered the tavern. As she surrendered to the familiar blue-collar bliss around her, she felt her stress begin to melt away. Jill was right about one thing; Addy had been through a lot in a short time, even for a normal person. Add to that the fact that Addy was not a normal person, and she could reasonably conclude that she was treading water here. Whatever, though. Alcohol might not stop her from drowning, but it could delay the inevitable for a little while.

Addy marched up to the bar, asserting her way between a couple of guys and signaling her usual bartender. "Hey, Red! I'll take one, on the rocks!" Red knew that meant Jameson and ginger, Addy's favorite variety of triple distilled whiskey. What a perfect way to stave it off.

"Addy!" a familiar female voice called from her left. Whipping her head toward the voice, she saw Jocelyn sitting at the end of the bar next to Alex, Rami, and another of their mutual friends, Trey. Addy waved and signaled that she would join them shortly.

"Evening, Addilynn," Red greeted as he returned with her Jameson.

"How many times? It's Addy." Red was messing with her; she always made fun of his balding head and he reciprocated by forgetting her disdain for her birth name. Addilynn sounded like she was seventy, or at least, like she was some stuck-up princess. Unsurprisingly, Dean Palmer preferred to call her by her proper label, which only served to amplify her disgust for it.

"Sorry Addy," Red cracked. "You know, this bald head of mine feels emptier every day."

"Yeah, whatever. Thanks, baldy." Addy threw a twenty on the table and shifted over to the end of the bar, drink in hand.

"Addy!" Rami and Trey exclaimed in tandem as she slid up next to them.

"Yo," she greeted. "You're in my seat, bud."

Trey took a moment to a moment to catch on as Addy sipped her drink and stared at him. "Oh," he finally said, sliding off the barstool and standing behind Rami. "How rude of me."

"You are the worst."

"Hey sis," Alex greeted her as she took Trey's seat.

"How was work?"

"Same as always. How are you holdin' up, better?"

"I will be in about twenty minutes."

"Cheers to that." She and Alex smacked their glasses together clumsily and tipped them back. Properly finishing hers, Addy beckoned Red for another.

Addy turned to Rami and Jocelyn and asked, "Did you guys just get here?"

"About an hour ago," Jocelyn answered.

"We were just hanging out at Trey's before this. How was class?" Rami asked.

"It's Saturday," Addy pointed out. "Are you drunk already?"

"Right." He laughed. "Where were you all day then?"

"Not hanging out with us," Trey joked.

"What are you guys, ten? We don't have to hang out all the time," Addy said.

"If you'd give me some of that ass, I'd go away," Trey said. He never missed a beat, that one. Trey was in that perfect niche where he was just persistent enough to be annoying, but not quite annoying enough to be banished. Also, Addy knew he was ultimately harmless, so perhaps that was why she let it go.

"Sure, I would, but I'd have to kill myself after."

"Ouch."

Jocelyn interjected and started up a conversation with Rami and Trey. Addy wasn't really listening. Instead, she pounded the rest of her drink and ordered another along with a shot of straight whiskey.

Red brought Alex another drink as well. As Alex watched Addy gulp the shot and slam the glass back onto the bar top, Addy sensed he was considering telling her to slow down and preemptively said, "I'm fine. I feel nothing." Of course, that wasn't true; she felt a lot of things, but drunk was not one of them.

"Something weird happened today," Alex chose to say instead.

"At work?"

"Yeah. That guy Zach was waiting for me outside the mine."

Wide eyed, Addy responded, "What? What did he want?"

Alex took a sip of his drink, contemplating it. "He wants me to join Prism, to go with him wherever and join his cult, or whatever it is."

"Alex, we shouldn't trust him, should we? Why would he want you? No offense, it's just ... Prism? Aren't they some kind of secret special forces? You've never even been in the military."

"I know. I told him to screw off and not to bother either of us again. Then he told me he was staying at the Haxenburg, as if I had said nothing."

"The Haxenburg is a dump."

They had a good laugh about that. Big, fancy Prism whatever and he was sleeping on a rickety box spring in crappy downtown Calivia. One would think he would have at least been put up in a place with a continental breakfast, but the Haxenburg? It was practically a ghetto.

About fifteen minutes and two more drinks later, Addy was feeling the buzz. The guys had started conversing about women and she was dreadfully uninterested, so she excused herself to go outside for a smoke. "I'll be outside," she informed no one in particular. The guys kept laughing but gave a fleeting head tilt to acknowledge that she had spoken.

The cool and moist sensation of an impending rainstorm coated her skin as Addy swung open the door and stepped out of the bar. Moving to the adjacent alley, she lit a smoke and took a long drag. As she exhaled, she looked up at the sky from between two brick walls and felt the smallest sprinkles touch her face. For a moment, she recalled her dream from the hospital. She pictured the brick buildings, like the one she was leaning on, these aging relics of a simple past now indicative of a plebian future, transforming into the magnificent chrome skyscrapers of her dream. They were domineering, sleek, and powerful, touching the sky with their fearless ambition. Beneath these towering structures stretched bold shadows that dared those beneath them to look up. For just a moment, she felt a sadness, a lapse of clarity; what was the point of anything in this world? Are we all doomed to a simple, suffering existence?

At the other end of the alley, a woman screamed. Two people who had been standing near a dumpster fled upon hearing the sound, probably a drug deal. A couple years ago, Addy might have investigated this woman's plight, ran to the other end of the alley, and dashed out into the street, trying to scare a would-be mugger into fleeing. At least she would have called the police. Now, though, she just closed her eyes and took another drag. Nothing mattered; ten minutes from now another mugger would appear anyhow, even if she stopped this one. *I can't save them*, Addy concluded. No one would help her either. Good thing she could take care of herself. If she ever found herself the one getting mugged, she would bleed the person dry.

Finishing off her cigarette, Addy went back inside and found that her group had moved over to the pool table in the corner of the bar. After grabbing another drink from Red, Addy weaved across the crowded room and joined them. Alex was playing nine-ball with Jocelyn as others looked on.

"Hey Addy," Rami acknowledged her. "I've got winner, then these guys are up." Rami pointed to two college-age guys across the table from them and the guys waved.

"Who are they?" Addy asked.

Obviously, she had been louder than she thought because one of the guys answered her. "Elek, and this is Kristof."

As they walked over to her and offered a handshake, the other one said, "Just Kris. Charmed."

"Actually, we know each other from university," Elek mentioned pretentiously.

"Great," Addy mocked. "Good for you two. You look cute together."

Elek laughed that off and replied, "Well, I meant that you and I know each other, but apparently you have forgotten me? Calculus Two, remember?" Addy had no clue who this clown was; it didn't matter anyway, both of them were just generic guys. Both were tall, thin guys, they clearly made it to the gym once in a while, and they had preppy haircuts. One guy was blond, the other had dark hair. Both wore jeans and generic label sports t-shirts. Just a couple of typical college guys, nothing memorable about them.

"I'm sorry ... I meet a lot of people," Addy said.

"Oh, no worries," Elek answered, though judging by the inadvertent frown that briefly crossed his face, there was actually quite a worry about it. Was she supposed to remember every person who breathed the same oxygen as her for two hours during the week?

While they had been talking, Jocelyn sank three balls after a thunderous break and was aiming for four. One precise snap and she sent the four-ball careening decisively into the corner pocket in front of Addy, where it spun for a second before coming to a rest inside.

"Settle down!" Alex pleaded. "Let me play at least!"

"Maybe next time," Jocelyn teased before sinking the five in a side pocket.

"Damn." Kris was impressed.

"She'll clean the table," Addy bet.

"Hey, you guys hear about the stadium?" Rami asked, looking up from his phone at the college guys.

"Yeah, that was nuts!" Kris replied.

"We were there."

"What? No way! Did you get a video?"

"Yeah. Check out my stream. I put a link on my network."

The guys opened their social media apps and found the video on Rami's page. Addy slid behind them and began to curiously watch the video.

"Rami, I didn't know you had a video. Why didn't you tell me?" Addy wondered. Until now, she had barely thought about what it must have been like inside. She had been so caught up in her own experience outside of the stadium.

"I haven't seen you since then."

"Here it is," Kris said, loading up the video. People were screaming right off the bat, and so loudly too. The images were shaky and dizzying to watch, almost impossible to follow. Plus, the sound quality was making the screams pierce Addy's ears. Like anyone could really criticize the video, though ... Rami was fleeing for his life when he shot it. One part that was discernible was when Rami stopped for about five seconds and held the phone up to film the flaming crater in the side of the stadium, then someone bumped into him and the phone went all over the place again. Jocelyn was urgently crying in the background for him to come. Seeing this, then looking around at everyone drinking and joking just twenty-four hours later, made Addy uncomfortable. She realized just how jaded Calivia was. Everyone is so calloused, she thought; they know that this is just part of life now. People fight, people flee, and people die. That was just the way of life in Calivia, and if you could, you just had to try and stay happy despite that. This life couldn't be her reality; this anger she felt, anger masked by this superficial, liquor-soaked brevity, it haunted her ... wow, as she ruminated, she realized how drunk she felt now. She always got a little weepy when she had one too many, and now she could feel the nihilism creeping in, constricting her thoughts like a snake.

"That was when I got caught in the crowd," Rami explained as the video became blurry and incomprehensible.

Kris turned it off and put his phone back into his pocket. "Damn," he said. "You were pretty close to that crater."

"Yeah, it was intense."

"Honestly," Elek said, "This city is going to hell."

"It has always been this way," Rami corrected.

Elek added his two cents. "Yeah, but it's been much worse since those rebels started messing with the loyalists. It runs deep here."

"You think it was the rebels?" Kris asked.

This activated Addy; these guys had no idea what they were talking about. To call them "rebels" was a definition beneath their cause. They were freedom fighters, modern day unsung heroes fighting to protect the fundamental aspects of human liberty. They called themselves Helba and their purpose was to protest the increasingly corrupt and dictatorial policies of the governments of Grantitan, especially those here in Calivia.

"Helba would never attack civilians," Addy educated the young chaps. "That is the prerogative of the fascist government that would rather side with the Grothian imperialists than their own people. Just read a history book; this has been going on for years."

"What?" Elek asked. "What fascists?"

"The ones who force feed us garbage food, ration our utilities, and threaten to jail us for our justified thoughts of distrust in our 'leadership,' Grothian sympathizing bastards. For Christ's sake, how can you not see it?"

"The planet is dying, Addy," Elek pointed out. "It's not fascism, it's survival. We don't have enough resources to go around. We all have to do our part, or else we will succumb to the same fate as planets of our past."

"That's what they want you to think. The Sarian Empire is vast and exuberant, nothing like Earth, Mars, or the others. You are telling me there is no way we can trade or allocate for what we need? We, unlike our ancestors, have infinite ability to network across galaxies. It's not a lack of resources, it's a way to keep us dependent on them so they can maintain power. Inner Sari doesn't care about us. Plus, all of that has nothing to do with it anyway." Thousands of years had passed by since the days of the Milky Way, and yet, humans were still making the same stupid mistakes and offering the same ridiculous justifications. Maybe they *should* have went extinct.

As she was speaking, or yelling, really, it was like she was hanging from the ceiling watching herself. Everything seemed far away, third person, like a recording of herself. She had probably had too much to drink, and it was really starting to kick in.

"That doesn't make sense ..."

"And also, your tax credits are being used to fund the loyalist military and all their boots that will soon be on your throat."

"Whatever." Trying to mask his irritation, Elek turned to watch the pool game.

Addy was so riled up, she hadn't noticed that Rami had switched off with Alex, who was now beside her. "You all right?" he asked.

"I'm fine," Addy insisted. "This clown, though—"

"Hey, hey." Kris started to interfere as he could see irritation in his friend's expression.

"You're probably a loyalist too."

Confused, Alex interjected. "What did you guys say to my sister?"

"Nothing," Elek said. "Just forget it."

"Forget what?"

Kris tried to mediate, "Look, he didn't mean to offend you. Can we just forget about it?"

Though she imagined most people would say she should acknowledge the white flag of surrender and get on with her life, Addy's drunken stupor had more to say. "People like you always want to 'forget about it' when it comes to calling your own stupidity into question."

"Stupid ... you know what?" Elek began, turning away from the pool table and facing Addy.

Before Elek could rise to the next level, Kris put his hand on Elek's chest and said, "Let's just get outta here, screw this."

As they brushed past, Alex warned them, "Don't come back in here."

When they reached the door, Elek looked over his shoulder and yelled, "Your sister is a psycho!" All eyes in the bar gawked at the door as Alex offered the guys a retaliatory middle finger and they slammed the door behind them. A moment later, everyone resumed their merriment as if nothing had happened. Not Addy though.

"Forget about those guys," Alex said, turning his attention back to Rami and Jocelyn.

"I've gotta get some air," Addy grumbled, reaching for her cigarettes and heading for the door.

The misty air outside had evolved into a light rain, which trickled down on her as she lit her cigarette and began walking down the sidewalk in the direction the two guys had gone. Reaching for her left hip, Addy caressed the smooth leather sheath of her switchblade, which was attached firmly to her jeans at just the right spot so she could draw quickly. She touched the butt of the knife with her index finger and fantasized about the blade entering Elek's kidney. She had every right to be furious, she thought as she stumbled down the sidewalk, it was guys like that who perpetuated the rampant spread of poverty and degeneration of liberty on Grantitan with their ignorance and complacency. Someone had to do something about it and quit looking the other way.

She must have gone a block or so from the bar before she lost track of where the guys had gone. *It's for the best anyway*, she decided. Someday, when the time was right, she'd run into them. In the meantime, here she was, standing in the rain at the corner of Jergin and Holland, watching the cars scurry along, and wondering once again what the point of anything was. This was a feeling she had often, the kind that Jill was talking about. "Hopelessness."

She looked at the street sign again and realized ... Holland Street, that's where the Haxenburg was. That was what she was going to do right now. Addy was going to see Zach Brine.

9

The rain was picking up as Addy passed the tacky neon sign that declared the place as the Haxenburg Motel. Which one was his room? She'd march right up to the front desk and demand to know, she decided in a drunken strand of thought. One way or another, Zach Brine was going to give her answers.

Addy had to make little effort, as she found Zach standing outside of room 174, leaning on the wall beside his door and puffing on a cigar. Waltzing right up to him under the cover of the motel awning, she demanded, "Tell me why you want my brother?"

With a cavalier demeanor, Zach puffed his cigar and stared at her, building suspense.

"Are you deaf, or just stupid?" Addy pressed.

Waiting another second, Zach lowered his cigar and inquired, "Had a few?"

Most definitely. It was a little like Addy was watching herself shift on her feet while she was interrogating Zach. It hadn't seemed like she was this drunk when she left the tavern, but now it had certainly caught up to her.

"Don't condescend ... I have a right to know."

"I can smell you even with the rain. Trust me, I know a thing or two about booze."

"Just answer me!" Addy commanded, all too obviously repositioning her hand on her switchblade, too wasted to be subtle. "What do you want with my brother?"

"Settle down," he answered, his eyes on hers but clearly aware of her blade. "Why don't you come inside?"

Addy laughed. "What, so you can taser me and rape me?"

"Your brother can come too." Zach puffed his cigar one more time, then put it out on the cement slab below the motel awning before swinging around and going into the room. He left the door cracked open behind him.

Taken aback, Addy spun around and scanned the parking lot in front of the motel, where she saw Alex's pickup truck on the edge of the lot, partially hidden behind another truck. When he saw her looking, Alex got out of the truck and started walking through the rain toward her. It was really coming down now, drenching Alex as he approached.

"What are you doing here?" Alex demanded as he hurried under the awning.

"You followed me?"

"Of course I did! This city isn't safe, you know that. Why would you meet this guy alone in this sketchy place?"

Addy rolled her eyes and stammered a bit, to which Alex said, "How drunk are you? I'm gonna kill him ..." Without waiting for her response, Alex brushed past her and opened the door to Zach's room.

Following him inside, Addy said, "I can handle this, Alex, don't let him win."

Disregarding her, Alex looked across the shoddy room at Zach, who was sitting in an armchair in the far corner, and said, "I thought I told you to stay away from us?"

"Something about what I said made you wonder, didn't it?" Zach prodded, looking at Addy.

"Hey," Alex redirected. "You are talking to me."

Taking a few more steps into the room, Addy closed the door behind her and looked around the room. Between her and Zach was a perfectly made bed, the sheets and blankets tucked tightly on all sides, neatly stacked piles of documents and folders atop it. Zach's bomber jacket was laid out across the bed in front of where he was sitting, and on the end table beside him were two tidy stacks of books bookmarked with long, fluorescent-colored tabs. Adjacent to the far wall, a sofa table was decorated with liquor and tumblers and a lone ashtray filled halfway with the remnants of cigars. That explained the smell in here.

"Wow." Addy chuckled. "You really are a cliché."

"Not the worst I've been called," Zach replied.

"What's all this?" Alex asked, motioning to all the paperwork on the bed. "You hanging out in this dump, all this stuff? You expect us to believe you are from Prism?"

"Yeah," Addy agreed. "And why are you interested in Alex? Or are you going to dodge that again?"

"Well, I admit the accommodations are not ideal. Have you ever had to pay alimony?" Zach asked, laughing cynically to make a point. "Anyway, Alex, do you want to tell your sister what really happened at the stadium, or should I?" Addy knew her brother well, and she could tell by his body language that he was caught off guard and didn't know how to reply.

Surprised, Addy looked at Alex and asked, "What is he talking about?"

"Nothing. This creep has some crazy theory that I did something impossible, but it never happened."

"What do you mean?" Addy was getting frustrated from being out of the loop, so she turned to Zach and continued, "What theory is he talking about?"

"Well, it's not my theory," Zach replied, standing up from the chair and stepping over to the booze counter to make drinks. "But something about it pertains to your brother."

He poured two drinks and handed one to Alex, who refused, "No thank you."

Anticipating Addy's complaint, Zach glanced at her and said, "I think you are well ahead of us anyway." She resented that but didn't want to get sidetracked.

"Just tell me the theory!" Addy insisted.

"You may have heard of this before, if you dabble at all in mythology. There are stories about an ancient people on the planet Alder, a very spiritual, tribal sort of people. They lived in the most unforgiving of environments, places that required great effort to sustain everyday life. However, this was intentional, because the ancient Alderians believed that by mastering the planet, they could become one with the planet. It all sounds like hippie nonsense, I know."

Addy started to shift in place and Alex had meanwhile leaned against the wall with one shoulder and crossed his arms. Zach noticed their impatience as he took a swig of his scotch and sped up his delivery. "Anyway, it's all related in a bigger way, is the point. What happened at the stadium was that Alex defied physics by catching a slab of concrete with his bare hands, saving your life, Addy."

Certain she had misheard, Addy said, "What? He caught ... what are you saying?"

"That can't be what happened," Alex insisted. "I told you before, you must have seen it wrong."

"Is this what he was saying to you at work?" Addy asked.

"No two ways about it," Zach said. "After the explosion, a chunk the size of a tour bus fell off the stadium and right onto you and your sister. You caught that bus-sized slab of concrete and it nearly crushed you anyhow, so you buckled, and it slid off your hands and fell down behind the two of you. You didn't see it, Addy, because you fell face down after the explosion."

Replaying the incident in her mind, Addy realized Zach was right; she had fallen face first and caught herself with her forearms, then she was there for a few seconds, concussed, and when she had risen, she had seen Alex on his knees, staring at his bloodied hands. Was this true? It couldn't be! That was impossible!

"So, let's say it really happened," Alex said. "Do you have some sort of explanation for it and is that why you have all this stuff?" Again, Alex motioned toward the paperwork on the bed.

"Yes, the answer I suspected, but I had to be certain. You see, there is a myth about an Alderian man who lifted a mountain to save his people after they fled from hundreds of enemies. The raiders were left clueless as the man set the mountain down behind them and it seemed as though the Alderians had vanished."

"So, you think I'm one of the Alderians?"

"A descendent, maybe. I'd say most people would assume—"

"Seriously? You believe that a man picked up a mountain?" Addy interrupted.

"Well, I doubt it was really a mountain. Perhaps a large boulder, similar in scale to the slab that Alex caught, but I have heard once that most myths are based on something. Even if the story itself is hyperbole, we can agree that something significant happened yesterday, right?" Zach argued, "This is what Prism does. We seek the wonders of the universe and try to discern them. Wonders which may someday be our perils, mind you."

"Okay, fine. Why did you have to taser us, though?"

"At that time, I wasn't sure who else had seen Alex catching the slab and I also couldn't be certain if we were under attack. For those reasons, I felt it necessary to remove you from there as fast as possible using any means."

"So, you brought us to a hospital in broad daylight? Are you an idiot? What if we *were* under attack?"

"If I had taken you to one of the hidden bunkers here in Calivia, I would have to explain why to the personnel there. Had we been under attack, I would have made it work, but in the time it took me to get to the Hedron Center, it was clear that we were not under siege. Plus, I have known Hailey for a long time so I knew I could trust her."

"And you don't want to explain it to the people at the bunkers because you don't trust them, yet you want me to trust them and join Prism?" Alex cut in.

"That's fair," Zach admitted. "However, it isn't that they can't be trusted, it's that I'd want you to be ready before the cynics have a chance to dismiss your potential. It was hard enough for me to believe all of this and I saw it firsthand."

"Ready for what?"

"To be a Prism soldier."

"Just stop," Addy said. "Why should we believe any of this? It's total nonsense! A man moving a mountain? Come on!"

"Addy," Alex said in a calm voice, "I don't know if I am sold on this, but I do believe something happened at the stadium. What if he is telling the truth?"

"What if he is? What then? We go prancing off to some foreign planet with this clown and join his stupid club?" Irritated, Addy began pacing beside the bed and chewing her fingernails. She wanted to cry; her head was spinning, and she was all at once hyper-focused and unable to synthesize. How much of this was she just misinterpreting? Was the alcohol blurring her thoughts this much? Her anxiety was as bad as ever.

"Sleep on it," Zach suggested. "Meet me back here tomorrow, preferably earlier, and we will talk more about what this endeavor will involve."

"You say that like we are already going to agree," Alex said.

"You seem reasonable, and I think most reasonable people would recognize that what happened at the stadium was an extraordinary occurrence and, since we have all been woven together by the fate of our mutual involvement, we have an obligation to explore the implications of it."

"And you were just going to stalk us until we agreed with you? Sounds reasonable," Addy scoffed.

"I know what it seems like, but I did what I did for a reason and I know you know it," Zach said, taking one finger off his glass to point toward Alex.

"Pffft ... screw you and screw destiny. It's not real anyway, if that's what you are implying. Come on, Alex, we never should have come here." Addy thrust open the door and stepped out under the awning.

"You stay away from us," Alex said with a tone of finality, and followed Addy out of the room. As he hustled out into the rain, he called out, "Addy, wait!"

Stubborn, she kept walking without acknowledging him, until she felt his hand grab her arm and she spun around violently. "Come on," Alex said. "Get in the truck, you are not walking."

Addy wanted to protest, but it was really raining and she was starting to feel sick, so instead she followed him to the truck and rode in silence all the way back to Alex's apartment. It was obvious that Alex was upset with her for being reckless but holding back saying anything at that moment. She had been reckless, but she had thought about Zach and about Alex and all she wanted was for Zach to say something that eased her mind about her brother. Instead all she got was more confusion and frustration.

10

For Alex, the night was filled with ambiguity. After they had gotten back to his apartment, and Addy had passed out sprawled across his bed, Alex lay on his couch and stared at the ceiling for a long time. Too wired to sleep, he considered all the things that had happened in the past forty-eight hours; everything had been so normal, and in an instant it all changed. In that one moment outside the stadium, he could have died, but instead, he became something else ... something foreign, something supernatural ... what was he to do with this information? He had never been one to believe in fairy tales, yet a part of him knew Zach was right; Alex couldn't just walk away from this.

In fact, as the slow and restless night progressed, Alex found himself recounting the past, wondering how so many crazy coincidences had strung together to guide him here to Calivia. Images of the group homes flashed through his mind: the dirty, musty floors, the crowded rooms, and the old furniture. Alex's parents were refugees that had traveled to escape the war, so when they died not even a year later, there was no one else to take him, and he ended up in the first home. He remembered feeling like he was always in stasis, just sitting there and watching vicariously as the world turned around him and he sat still and alone, waiting for his turn. Of course, that turn never came. Each year that passed added to his resentment, a sort of jealousy, as he watched the others come and go and he remained an orphan. This was not unlike how many of the children he grew up with felt. In postwar Grantitan, there were dozens of these orphanages, many of them overcrowded and understaffed. Some of the kids ended up shuffled between homes for reasons Alex didn't know. There was so much chaos and unfairness in those times. Calivia was still caught in the throes of it today, though it seemed to be waning. Or, perhaps, Alex was blind to it now.

When he was seven, Alex was sent to a different home. It was a place called Mauve Garden, a name that Alex could never quite understand because the place was neither a shade of purple nor a garden. In fact, not only was there no garden, but there were no trees other than a lone dead cypress in the front yard, and no grass except for small bushels of yellowish strands that gasped for life on a vast plain of gray and brown desolation. Inside the home, the thick, dark red curtains were almost always drawn, making the old and dimly lit house resemble a mortuary. Meals were scheduled, schoolwork was oppressive, and the children were strictly monitored at all times. At Mauve Garden, everyone was guilty until proven otherwise.

Alex hated it there. He tried to run away and was locked in a closet as punishment. No one was going to adopt him before, he came to realize, and *no* one was going to adopt him now. Not from this place. Mauve Garden was where they sent the unwanted ones, the kids who were too broken to be fixed. For all his effort, he had been an angry child. Perhaps that was why they sent him there, or maybe he was just unlucky. Alex supposed he would never know.

Then he met the girl who played with knives. The first day she was there, she said virtually nothing to the other kids. Everyone started talking, saying she was a freak and that she had been sent to Mauve Garden because of it. When the kids were laughing about it, she went into the kitchen and came back with a knife, making it seem as if she was going to threaten them. Everyone went silent and watched carefully as she walked over to the table with the knife. She grabbed an orange out of the fruit bowl on the table and started peeling it with the knife, a blank, yet vicious, stare on her face. Addy was only six at the time.

Meeting her was like seeing a specter of himself. Though he was only eight, Alex was mature for his age, and he had been through the full spectrum of emotions that Addy was undoubtedly feeling. She had been abandoned by her parents, found by some woman in a back alley and brought to a church, Alex had heard, and she was allegedly socially awkward and had no friends. "Alone" was a disposition that Alex was quite familiar with. Her anger, too, he understood. Like her, Alex had never known what it was like to be raised by real parents, to have a chance to just be a kid and live free. Instead, their lives had been determined long before their brains could comprehend what it meant to be orphaned.

At first, Addy deflected Alex's attempts to protect her. She ignored him, made fun of him, even yelled at him at times for no good reason. Once she asked him if he had heard the story about her cutting people. Alex figured she was kidding and would jest away her anger and she would eventually laugh and calm down. Somehow, the appearance of a kindred spirit, though grim as their mutual experience was, had invigorated Alex, brought him back to life. It was the beginning of what would become his decision to seek the brighter side of life, no matter how bleak reality might be.

After a few months, Addy became like a sister to him. Some days, she would push him away, but he could tell she was grateful for his effort, for his cheerful spirit in what was such a dark time for both of them. In two short years, their bond was forged forever. Then the Palmers came along, and everything changed again. He just couldn't let her ruin it. As much as it pained Alex to lose his newfound sister, she deserved a better life than Mauve Garden and God knew the Palmers were her best shot at it. Addy was so angry with him.

Years later, he got out of that dungeon and moved to the city. He had never been so happy to be independent, free, and surrounded by so many new people and experiences. Everything fell into place and he finally felt like he had a purposeful life.

Now, here he was.

Alex's mind returned to the stadium and the slab and the assertion that he was somehow supernatural. Unreasonably, he conflated everything in a chaotic heap in his brain. He had never really believed in fate, but still Alex couldn't stave off the notion that somehow everything was connected. Mauve Garden, meeting Addy, coming to Calivia ... all of it led to this moment. Was Zach trying to tell him that everything happened for a reason? What did that mean for the future? It was all so overwhelming.

For the entire night, Alex toiled with his thoughts between broken patches of sleep.

The next morning, he greeted the sun eagerly, an excuse to recuse himself from his struggling slumber in favor of something more productive. Bustling around the apartment, he brewed a pot of coffee, dressed, and cleaned up his kitchen to keep himself busy. Should he go meet Zach? He strained to summarize the previous night's thoughts into a coherent decision. His brain felt like static on a holo-TV. He did know one thing: though he didn't know Zach, Alex felt like he could trust him. Alex, Zach, and Addy had experienced this phenomenal event together and whether that was fate or coincidence, it had bound them together in a way that Alex could not refute. It couldn't hurt to go see him, Alex finally decided while he poured himself a cup of hot coffee.

Addy fumbled into the kitchen, still wearing her clothes from the night before. Leaning in the doorframe between the bedroom and the kitchen, Addy complained, "You are so loud ... what are you even doing up so early?"

"Oh, hey," Alex said, taking a sip of coffee. "How are you feeling?"

"Don't talk to me about it. Any for me?" Alex motioned for her to help herself and moved aside.

"I think I am going to see Zach," he said casually as Addy poured herself a cup of black coffee.

"What? Why? After all the effort we put into telling him to screw off?"

"But think about all the effort it took for Zach to try to convince me. Why would he do that, for no reason?"

"Because he's a washed-up, desperate has-been."

"Plus, something did happen at the stadium, Addy. Were you too drunk, or do you remember that part of the conversation? I caught a giant slab of concrete somehow, and what if that is because I have some special powers, like Zach said?"

Addy considered this, rubbing her forehead, and replied, "That can't be true, Alex."

"Why would he make that up? For kicks? I want to know for myself."

Seeing that he wouldn't be convinced, Addy conceded. "Fine, for Christ's sake. Let me shower and I'll go with you. If this guy turns out to be crazy, I want to be there so I can say I told you so."

"All right," Alex agreed. "I'll wait for you outside."

11

"I knew you'd be back. Please, come in," Zach greeted them as they arrived at the Haxenburg at about ten that morning.

They followed him inside the room and Alex asked, "So, can you explain a little more what you were talking about last night? About Alder?"

"And maybe you want to elaborate on how my brother is supposedly a superhero?" Addy chimed in, taking a seat haphazardly on the edge of Zach's bed while she finished eating a greasy breakfast sandwich. Her head pounded a little as she landed on the bed, just one of the lingering effects of her prior night's indulgence. Hopefully it would fade soon, because the thought of listening to Zach prattle on all morning while she felt like this was making her stomach turn.

Seemingly unfazed, Zach walked over to the closet on the opposite end of the room and answered, "I'll tell you about Alder, Alex, but first, I want you to see something. Come."

"Over there?" Alex wondered.

"Yes, yes," Zach insisted, waving Alex over to the closet. "Addy, you as well. Come here."

Zach turned on a light inside what seemed to be an empty closet, stepped inside, and beckoned for them to join him. Alex got inside, but Addy stood outside the closet with a skeptical look on her face.

"Are you kidding?" Addy scoffed. "All this just so you can cuddle with us in there? You gonna kill us after? Is this your thing?"

"Addy," Alex pushed. "Come on. We came this far, let's keep an open mind."

"It's safe, I assure you," Zach said. Reluctantly, Addy chucked her sandwich into a nearby trash can and packed herself into the closet next to her brother. Closing the door, Zach added, "You may want to hold onto the railings at first." They looked down and noticed the railings around the perimeter of the closet, but before they could process this oddity, Zach did something with his cellphone and the closet began to shift.

"What the—" Alex got two words out and then the floor felt like it was dropping.

Addy let out a surprised scream and grabbed the handles for dear life. Her stomach felt like it had moved up into her chest!

"An elevator?" Alex guessed as they plummeted. Of course, Addy realized. Phew, she was going to live after all.

For no good reason, the elevator suddenly slowed and then came to an abrupt halt, bouncing Addy's brain in her head and causing her to immediately puke up her breakfast. Zach laughed straight from the belly as Addy hunched over and hurled.

"You all right?" Alex asked.

"Why design an elevator like that?" Addy demanded. This thing was not an elevator, more like a roller coaster.

"I didn't design it." Zach chuckled. Then, the most bewildering thing happened: the once-inconspicuous closet door slid back, revealing a huge sub-level room filled with monitors, wires, and complex equipment. Monotonous buzzing sounds filled the background as they entered the room. Addy felt like an owl, twisting her head every which way, observing the various holograms playing above the terminals in this strange, sci-fi wonderland.

"Where is this place?" Alex wondered.

"Wow," Addy said. "This must be why you chose the crappy hotel, huh?"

Zach laughed. "I admit, my alimony is not the only reason I like the Haxenburg. It has housed this secret Prism facility for years. Only certain people know about this place."

"This is amazing."

Zach stopped in the middle of the room so the three of them were surrounded by holographic monitors. Folding his arms behind his back, he scanned the back of the room and called out, "Lucas! Look who made it!"

"When you are right, you are right," a man said, coming out from the back of the monitors and removing a pair of safety goggles. It was the man who had been at the hospital with Zach.

"This is Lucas," Zach introduced his cohort. "He is a friend of mine and we can trust him to help us today."

"A pleasure," Lucas said, shaking first Addy's hand, then Alex's.

"Help us with what?" Addy questioned, feeling a bit nervous again.

"We are going to go in there," Zach answered, pointing at the holograms in front of them. He pointed to the other ones and added, "And there, and maybe there."

Appearing perplexed, Alex looked at the hologram that depicted a glorious valley between two stoic mountain ranges and asked, "Where is that?"

Zach began to pace as he answered, "That is Alder. I told you I'd explain more, but it would be easier to show you."

"A simulation," Addy presumed.

"A-plus," Lucas teased.

"Exactly," Zach said. "We are going to step into these pods and Lucas will help us navigate our consciousness into the simulation. It will seem to us like we are definitely in Alder."

Alex seemed impressed. "This looks way more convincing than any virtual reality I have seen. What should we expect when we get inside?"

"Alex," Addy nudged his shoulder and said quietly, "Should we do this?" She didn't like this at all, giving up control of her body. It was one thing to come talk to Zach when it was her and Alex against Zach and they were in the hotel room, but now they were in some mad basement with Zach and they were supposed to give up their free will to this Lucas guy they had never met?

"If you want, you can stay outside," Zach suggested. "Alex and I can go in, and you can stay out here. I'll even let you hold Lucas' gun."

Lucas objected. "I don't agree to that. If she stays, she has to go upstairs."

Addy ignored him. "No way I'm staying out. If Alex goes, I'm going."

"Well, I guess you are coming then," Zach said.

Everyone seemed to look at Alex to give the final word. He thought about it for a second, and said, "I trust you. Sorry, Addy, but I have to know what happened to me."

After a moment of silent understanding, Addy gave in. "Okay. Let's go in, then."

"Very good! I'll take you over here," Zach instructed, motioning at Alex. "Lucas, you set up Addy over there. After I get in, you can immerse us."

"You got it boss," Lucas said, waving Addy over to a pod two down from the one Zach had reserved for Alex.

Addy approached the pod anxiously. This was like nothing she had ever seen in real life. Slender and cylindrical, it was a cocoon of wires nested around a steeply slanted bed that was just long and wide enough for a standard human adult to lay on.

"This is some serious mad scientist stuff," she said.

Lucas laughed. "Zach is mad, but definitely not a scientist."

"I feel confident."

"It's fine, I've been in the simulator a hundred times. Don't worry." Easy for him to say, he was the one working the controls.

Putting one foot inside, Addy asked, "Do I just lie down?"

"Yeah. Just get in, lie back, and the machine will do the rest."

As he had been talking, Addy was already lying back, because the question had actually been rhetorical. It was rather obvious what she was being asked to do. That said, by the time Lucas had said "the machine will do the rest," the pod had already activated, lights above Addy turned on and a wild buzzing sound revved up behind her. Suddenly, Addy felt her legs and arms touched by something cold and slithery. Instantly she cried out, "What is happening?" The slithery feeling touched her forehead, creeping up both sides of her face and planting something onto her forehead.

"Those are just wires. The machine is integrating you using electrodes. In a moment, you will feel sleepy, that's normal. It means you are phasing into the simulation." Addy didn't like this at all. Her limbs were so stiff she might as well have been made of wood, and the cold sweat was so intense it was inside of her. She wanted to fight this, but instead, she started getting sleepy. In seconds, her body went limp and her eyes closed.

12

A liberating breeze blessed the perfect valley. There she stood, eyes closed, arms wide, her blouse blowing with the wind, smiling at the touch of the north. She breathed the breath of life and smelled the cool, peaceful calm of the moment. She opened her eyes and they took in the beauty, the swaying grass, the humble village below the bluff upon which she stood, the smoky gray and amethyst peaks surrounding them.

"Addy?" Alex called to her from a distance. For a moment, she had been intensely happy, maybe too happy, and then ... well, Alex was here, and if she could hear his voice, then this wasn't real, was it? This was a dream, or perhaps a vivid memory. Although, she was sure she had never been here.

"Where are we?" Addy asked as Alex came to stand beside her.

"No idea. I don't remember what we were doing. Isn't this place beautiful?"

"Yeah. Have we been here?"

"No. I'd remember a place like this."

Thinking for a moment, Addy said, "We went to see Zach ..."

"Right, I remember that too, but that seems like forever ago, doesn't it?"

"Is this ... this is the simulation, isn't it?"

"Correct," Zach affirmed, suddenly joining them from apparently nowhere.

"Where did you come from?" Addy asked.

"I phased in right over there, but you can't see that. It probably seemed to you like one second I wasn't here and the next I was."

"So, this is Alder?" Alex guessed.

"Yes. This is the great planet of Alder, as I imagine it looked hundreds, maybe thousands of years ago," Zach explained, pacing out in front of them and gesturing to the village. "And this is the place where your ancestors lived."

"Wow," Alex said. "It looks so different from Grantitan."

"Who knows if it really looked like this? We can only imagine, after all. Hell, no one even knew *you* existed until I saw you catch that slab of concrete. Alder will probably never look the same again, now that the Grothians control it. Anyway, something tells me that more parts of the mythology are true. The books say that the mountain people would learn the 'power of the golem,' which would give them strength and connection to the planet."

"Wait," Addy interrupted. "Sorry ... why can't I remember entering this simulation?" It was so strange, almost like a dream that she could remember the broad scope of, but the details were like blank faces in the background of a movie.

"Yeah, I don't remember either," Alex agreed.

"That can happen at first," Zach explained. "The neurosensors we use to phase in are designed to trick your mind. It probably feels a bit like a lucid dream, right? It helps to boost to credibility of the experience."

"So you are brainwashing us?" Addy asked.

"You'll remember everything when you exit the simulation. It is only designed to increase immersion."

"That's incredible, that we can do something like this," Alex said, his eyes wildly scanning the valley around them.

"Wait until I show you rykai." Zach smirked.

"What is that?"

A powerful gust of wind passed through the valley and the ground beneath them began to shake. Unsure if she was imagining the shaking, Addy scanned the earth around her. The shaking increased at a rapid pace and soon a small fissure opened up to her left, traveling rapidly to the north and scarring the grassy knolls as it went.

"What is happening?" Addy demanded. Zach said nothing as the earth continued to destroy itself. The environment around them started reshaping itself, terraforming into new land. Grassy hills transformed into a boulder-laden cliffside, trees vanished or shrunk into stubby bushes, and the ground underneath Addy melted peacefully into a barren plateau. Seconds later they stood inside a whole new environment, which looked like the side of a mountain.

"Wow! Addy, do you see this?" Alex asked, astonished.

Addy looked toward her brother, whose face was turned up to see the towering peak behind them, a gargantuan slab of earth topped with an elegant cap of snow. To Alex's left was a man, someone wearing dark clothes, a purple cloak over one shoulder, and a hood covering his face. Who was this man?

Startled, Addy called out, "Alex! Beside you!"

As Alex laid eyes on him, the enigmatic man raised his hand toward Alex and a strange orange glow began growing at the center of his palm.

"What the—?" Addy had no idea what was happening. This was part of the simulation, wasn't it? What was this man doing?

"Don't move," Zach said calmly while he began a strange conjuring motion himself. On his left arm, Zach wore a silver and black metal-plated gauntlet, and as he moved this gauntlet methodically to-and-fro it began to resonate with the ground in front of Alex. Seemingly all at once, the hooded man conjured a ball of fire and hurled it toward Alex; at the same time this happened, the earth in front of Alex shot straight up, forming a wide pillar that absorbed the fire blast and protected Alex.

"What the hell!" Addy exclaimed, running over to Alex to make sure he was okay. "Alex, are you all right?"

Looking shell-shocked, Alex just stared at the pillar in front of him.

"Now, watch this!" Zach said. First, the pillar in front of them crumbled into fragments and scattered all over the ground, leaving them exposed once more to the hooded fire conjurer. Next, Zach pointed one finger toward the man and did some conjuring motion. A second later the gauntlet resonated and the earth in front of the man shook and a long, jagged spike of granite rocketed diagonally upward and stabbed the man through the neck and shoulder. The impact was brutal, lifting the man's thoroughly impaled body into the air as it hung, bloodied and limp, from the killing end of the spike. After sputtering for a moment with blood flooding from his neck, the man gave up and died on the spike.

"Holy hell!" Addy shouted in disbelief.

Laughing with satisfaction, Zach agreed. "Holy hell is right! That's sure one way to get the job done, am I right?"

"You really *are* a maniac."

Collecting himself, Alex asked, "That's the golem, right? The power of the golem."

"Yes, yes! According to the myth, anyway. There is also the phoenix, the gryphon, and the hydra. The four basic Alderian disciplines, each one representing a different synergy with the elements of the planet," Zach explained.

"But how can this be?" Alex pressed. "I still don't understand how I was able to catch the slab. Isn't it still physically impossible?"

"I think so too, but it happened, didn't it? This is just so fantastic! In all my years, I've never been so utterly intrigued."

Zach laughed wildly and once again the earth transformed around them, reshaping itself from a rocky mountainside to a fantastic stone courtyard. Around the courtyard, uniformed men and women sparred with wooden bo staffs, breathing heavily and making grunting sounds as they struck each other's staffs vigorously. One woman outfought her male opponent, striking the back of his knee with the staff and knocking him onto his back. Immediately, she stood over him and pointed her staff at his face as he put his hands up in surrender. A patrolling overseer nodded to her in approval and continued his domineering walk with hands folded behind his back.

Zach changed the subject. "This is Raynor Academy. This is where we will go when you are ready."

"You are still assuming that we believe all this?" Addy was still outwardly skeptical, but honestly, on the inside, she was starting to believe it. Some of it, anyway. Maybe she just wanted to. After all, if it were true, that would mean there was something out there that might constitute some form of destiny, instead of just the dead, monotonous misery of Grantitan. This thought reminded Addy of that feeling of abandonment, of hopelessness that she felt, the one that Jill always alluded to. If Addy wanted it to stop, she had to make a change to get back her sense of purpose. Was this some higher calling? An invisible hand guiding her tortured soul to its proper path?

"The academy is located somewhere in Sari, but exactly where is a secret, for obvious reasons. The Prism candidates that we train here either wash out and are returned home with no memory of the academy or they become the greatest forces to be reckoned with in this galaxy. If I have my way, I will make you the latter."

Alex looked up at the impressive silvery dome of metal and glass beyond the courtyard. He took it all in, speechless for a moment, then he asked, "Why me? Why do you think I can do this, or even want to?"

"It isn't a question of whether you want to. The fact that the power of the golem lay dormant in you so long is marvelous, and now that you know about it, you have a duty to utilize that power. Similarly, I have a duty to cultivate your power, since you don't know how, and I do. Believe me, I do. You see, these things are fated."

Alex paused for a moment, and Addy answered instead. "Oh yeah? Let's say they are. Where do we go from here? How exactly do you make us Prism soldiers?"

Zach grinned and replied, "The same way as these people are learning." He pointed at the students to his left and right.

Alex and Addy wore confused expressions but said nothing.

"When you're ready, I will take you there. Anyway, that's enough for now. Lucas!"

As soon as Zach beckoned, Addy began to feel lightheaded, and her vision began to blur. The simulation was fading. A moment later, she opened her eyes to find herself and Alex back in the pods staring at Lucas, who was sitting in the center of the room manning a series of hologram screens.

"Whatd'ya think?" Lucas grinned, thrusting the holograms aside with a defining swipe so that they collapsed into one spot and minimized into the terminal in front of him.

Addy tore off the neurosensors and climbed out of the pod. Alex was already stumbling into the center of the room.

Zach emerged behind Alex. "The first few times you do it, you might feel dizzy after. It's your brain adjusting to multiple realities. You have all this energy in your mind from what you were doing inside, but your real body has just been lying there. You feel lightheaded, right?"

"Yeah," Alex agreed. "But man, that was amazing." Alex leaned on his knees, catching his breath, and looked toward Addy for validation.

"Actually, it was amazing," she agreed. "How did you build all this?"

"Not me," Zach laughed. "There are Prism facilities all over the galaxy, like this one."

"You guys looked stupid, like lost children," Lucas teased. "Not sure how you are going to sell these two, Zach."

"We'll have to work with them a lot," Zach said to Lucas.

"So, what, do you want us to come here every weekend and sit in a circle with you until we reach enlightenment?" Addy asked.

"You'll need to come every day if we are going to get you into Raynor Academy," Zach corrected.

"What?" Alex seemed shocked. "We can't do that! Addy has school, and I have to work."

"I can pay you more than the mines ever will. Addy, you can get your degree and so much more from Prism. Raynor Academy has a science curriculum that would put Calivian Universities to shame."

"You are going to pay us?" Addy doubted.

"You'd really do that?" Alex asked. "Pay us to train with you?"

"Yeah," Lucas chipped in. "Zach is crazy. Once he is in, he is all in. Take it as a compliment."

"Sounds pathetic, actually. Is this why you were in dumpy-ass Calivia? Too unhinged to train people on the good planets?" Addy asked.

Letting out a deep gut laugh, Zach said, "I've been called that enough, indeed. My passion can be pervasive. I have trained the best of the best, though, and on *all* the 'good' planets. Stick with me, and perhaps someone will lovingly refer to you as 'unhinged' someday."

"Whatever. How much are you going to pay us? I thought you had alimony to worry about?"

"Plenty, and once you become Prism soldiers, you'll never worry about money."

"Okay," Alex said. "We'll do it."

Surprised, Addy replied, "We will think about it, he means."

"I think we should do it, Addy. This happened for a reason, I just know it."

"All right, you know what? We are out of here. Nice seeing you two." Addy motioned for Alex to follow her as she went over to the closet elevator and got inside.

Zach grinned and said to Alex, "Come back in the morning, six a.m., and we'll start the training."

Alex gave Zach a nod of confirmation and followed his sister to the elevator.

"Where the hell is the button?" Addy demanded as Alex settled inside and grabbed the rails tightly.

Zach pulled out his phone, laughing softly, and called out "bon voyage" before pressing a button on his phone and sending them rocketing back up to the crummy room at the Haxenburg.

Addy almost threw up again as she stumbled out of the rude elevator. Someone should seriously fix that. As she leaned on her knees, breathing through the nausea, she questioned her brother. "You aren't serious, right? We can't just jump into bed with this guy."

"I don't know, but my gut is telling me that we should. It's like Zach said; I feel like I have a responsibility to learn about what I am."

"You mean what he is telling us you are? Which, by the way, is a being of myth?"

With an air of frustration about him, Alex replied, "Come on, Addy, it's too elaborate to be fake. Plus, what would he gain from making all of it up? He just showed us a top-secret facility."

"I don't know. Can we just take a minute to think about it, at least?"

"We have taken time to think about it," he argued, "We decided to come here today, didn't we? Addy, you don't understand. Something is inside of me; I felt it at the stadium, and I don't think I could live my whole life without knowing what it is."

"Fine, whatever. Let's just get out of here."

Stubbornly, Addy went ahead of Alex and flung the door open before stepping out into the parking lot. Alex appeared at the door as Addy was already halfway to his truck and she turned back to him and said, "We talked about coming here to hear what he had to say, not diving headfirst into some crazy commitment."

Alex rolled his eyes and followed her silently to his truck.

As they got into the truck, Alex started the engine and reversed out of the parking space. He rolled down the windows and turned on his favorite radio station. A soft, gleeful bluegrass melody filled the silence between them. Scoffing with distaste, Addy leaned out the window and watched the city pass by. She had never cared for this kind of music, especially not in this context. A gray, run-down, hope-drained city was no place for a happy song about sunshine and rolling hills. Or maybe it was just her. Some might argue this was the perfect context for such a song.

"Everything will work out," Alex assured her, placing a hand on her shoulder briefly as he held the wheel with the other. Sure, she thought, but for whom? Honestly, she did understand Alex's yearning for answers. There were plenty of questions she would like answered too, like why her parents decided to leave her on the street or why she ended up here in this city and where she was supposed to go next. Or why she was so angry all the time. That was a good one. Who were the guys in the gray suits? So many questions swirled around her brain. She supposed if she could get the answers, she would. Maybe this quest could lead her to them.

"I know," she assured him with an apologetic glance. Alex smiled and turned up the music as they cruised the rest of the way home.

SHATTERED

1

If there was one aspect of Alex that Addy could be completely sure of, it was that once he had his mind set to something, he was unwavering in his conviction. Add to that the fact that he had always been highly idealistic and carried a strong sense of justice, and it was not surprising to her now that an indomitable destiny had implanted itself inside Alex's head. They discussed it for two hours after leaving the Haxenburg, and Alex seemed convinced of this quest. He was fully indoctrinated now, and the only question left unanswered was whether Addy was going to take the plunge as well.

Alex had left hours ago to meet Zach, disappointed when Addy stayed at the apartment, but she couldn't go, not yet. The whole thing had fueled the furious anxiety that she was already feeling from the events of previous days, and Addy decided she needed to see Jill before she made any decisions about all of this. There were just too many variables, like (just to name the big ones) giving up her school and her life to spend all of her time with Zach and having to leave her home planet and go galloping off to some unknown land to a secret academy. Her nerves were fried from thinking about it.

So here she was, sitting on a train on a Monday morning, heading across town. Briefly, she felt guilty for not going to school, but the significance of her university education was quickly being dwarfed by the impending quest laid before her and Alex. She wondered, was any of this for real? She was still questioning the validity of all this. Was it nihilism, or simply that these were things normal people were not supposed to see?

Addy snapped to attention as the train stopped and people shuffled on and off. She intentionally shifted to the outside seat so no one would try to sit beside her. This wasn't her stop and she didn't want some asshole invading her space. One middle-aged pervert tried anyway and she shot him a death glare, making him think twice. He passed, and she continued to examine the line of degenerates, searching for nothing specific. Somehow, she was still surprised by the human trash produced by this city.

Then it happened.

Two men got on the train, dressed in well-pressed gray suits.

Their hair was dark and slicked, and their eyes were hidden by sunglasses.

One wore a gold wristwatch.

These were the guys that had started it all.

Who were they? Why did Addy think she knew them? Or did she? Something irrational had happened at the stadium and it was happening again now. Her anxiety was through the roof and she couldn't stop her wild and panicked thoughts from bouncing around inside her skull.

As they walked down the aisle, she fixated on them with erratic precision, their frames always in her peripherals as her eyes darted around and her heart beat fast. They came closer and her body tightened. Were they looking at her? One of them was looking toward her, at least. Now both! Should she run?

Addy held her breath and felt her body lifting several inches off the seat. Just as she reached for her switchblade the men stopped two seats in front of her and looked down at the gentleman sitting there.

"Is this seat taken?" one of the men asked cordially.

Without a word, the seated man pushed down to the window and allowed the two men in suits to sit next to him.

"How have you been, Marcus?"

Again, the seated man said nothing. The train doors closed and again the vehicle began moving toward Eastern Calivia.

Addy's eyes were tunnels; the cloudy montage of the city was nothing but a blur in her periphery and all she could see was the back of their necks. One turned and she saw an articulate grin, the grin of a man who had cornered his prey and had only to decide with which knife to carve it. As he ruminated, he chewed gum arrogantly on one side of his mouth.

In what seemed like seconds later, the train was stopping again, and the men rose to get off the train. One of them went into the aisle and the other gestured for Marcus to go ahead, wedging him between the two. "After you, sir," the man said.

Asserting her way into the fray, Addy followed the men off the train, far enough behind to blend in, but close enough to see where they were going. It was an impulse over which she had little control. These men were predators, Addy knew this, and yet her urgent longing for answers was presently more pervasive than her sense of peril. She had to know who these men were and why they had caused her such torment.

"Hey, watch it!" some lady exclaimed as Addy pushed past her on the platform.

"Watch where you are going!" a man added. Addy ignored them and followed the suits down a set of rusting stairs and into the slums below. It was a ghetto of a special breed, a symbol of the dire brittleness of Grantitan. When the planet started to die was when Dean Palmer and those of his kind surrendered to the Grothians, exchanging Grantitan's vitality for subjugated peace. The Grothians demanded everything and the government had to decide how to prioritize what was left. Supposedly, they were making people safe. No longer would they fear for their lives or beg for a chance at happiness and a normal life. It was such a passionate and optimistic message. Needless to say, the people here didn't get a lick of what was promised to them after the Grothians took hold. There were buildings that had holes in the walls, some covered in blankets or tarps, there were busted vehicles, garbage, and junk piled up everywhere ... God, some people were sitting under lean-tos made of scrap metal. The only thing these people got from their heroes in charge was a giant speed rail cutting through their entire neighborhood. It was as if they were being punished for the crime of being poor and Sarian. If only those yuppies from the bar could see this, they'd know why Grantitan needed groups like Helba.

As the crowd dwindled, Addy slipped her hood over her head and found herself a comfortable distance from the suits, who were now walking on either side of Marcus. *They are gonna kill him.* Why was she following them? She already knew the outcome, and yet she kept delving further into the dungeon. People around her stared at her, some curious, others threatening. Addy didn't belong here, but she couldn't stop. She had to know. If she had learned anything from all that was happening with Alex and Zach, it was that uncertainty could be as bad as danger.

A block or so later, the men arrived at the stoop in front of what was probably Marcus's house. The suits flanked Marcus, stood back a bit, and urged him forward. Marcus reluctantly went inside, the men behind him.

Once the men were safely inside the building, Addy hurried up to the stoop and searched for a way to see inside. Next to the door, a ledge containing several potted plants jutted out of the building about five feet below the window. Rustling up there, Addy peeked up over the windowsill and saw Marcus entering what seemed like a living room and dining area.

The window was closed, but she could still make out Marcus begging the suits as they entered the room. "Please, don't do this! I promise I am going to make things right!"

"Marcus?" A woman's voice cried from another room. Oh God, Addy thought to herself, don't let there be kids as well.

"Honey, stay in the other room!" Too late. She wandered right out there into the bastion of death, and she brought the kid.

"Daddy?" The little girl beckoned.

"Marcus, what is going on, who are these men?" the woman demanded.

"We are repo men," one of the suits answered, "And your husband owes a debt."

"Please, no, I'll do anything!" Marcus pleaded, falling to his knees before them. None of that mattered, Addy thought, not to these people.

His wife understood now, and she ordered the child into the bedroom. A few inaudible exchanges happened between the wife and one of the suits, then the guns came out. Great, glistening silver things. Arbiters of death. Addy's anxiety dominated her; she wanted to call out, distract the men, and give Marcus a chance to run. A fleeting thought that she ought to call the police entered her mind and she thought of the mugger and the drug dealers from the alley behind the bar and how nothing mattered. If she called the police, it would be too late, even if they came. Oh God! What was she supposed to do?

Marcus' wife screamed and turned to run as the silver barrels pointed in her direction, but it was too late and she was blown away, her blood and brains exploding from her cortex onto the dining room wall. Marcus had rushed to his feet and charged the one who shot her, but the other suit smashed his head in with the pistol and left him reeling on the floor.

"The Mushida Clan always collects its debts," the suit said. Just then, the little girl ventured out to find her mother dead as could be on the floor and cried out in agony. The same suit regarded the little girl. "This is what happens when you don't pay. Do you understand, girl? Always pay your debts."

The bastard popped Marcus right in front of his daughter. The look on the girl's face ... she was broken forever. Addy couldn't be here anymore; why was she here in the first place? All of this was blossoming something in her, something deep and violent. It was how she'd felt outside the stadium, but exacerbated, as if it were formulating a life of its own, a life of anarchy that threatened to usurp every corridor of her mind.

Her heart racing, Addy fumbled back from the window, knocking over a plant as she tried to descend. The pot shattered on the ground two or three feet below. Oh God ... right before Addy jumped down, she looked back and saw the men turn their heads to the window to investigate the sound.

Seconds later, the men blasted open the door and saw her running into a nearby alley.

"Catch her!" one of them yelled. What had she gotten herself into?

Even though she had gotten a decent head start, by the time Addy reached the next street, the men were almost upon her. They were maybe twenty or so feet behind her.

Careening across the street, Addy narrowly avoided being hit by a car, smashed through a street vendor selling sausages, and scrambled into another alley. The men were in hot pursuit. Once they entered the alley, Addy heard a gunshot followed by a ricochet sound off a nearby dumpster. Another gunshot hit the pavement near her foot. She'd never outrun them; she was already almost out of breath.

As she rounded a corner, the men closing in, she knew she had to make a decision. Should she run into a store and ask for help? Should she run into the street and wave her arms around and hope the men wouldn't kidnap her in broad daylight? Who was she kidding, this was Calivia. People minded their business. She couldn't ask for help and she couldn't outrun them. She saw a group of recycling bins outside of a shop; that was it, she had to hide.

So she found an empty one, dove inside, closed the lid, and prayed.

2

Cold and vile uncertainty constricted her as she huddled inside the bin. Soon, she heard them outside calling and searching and she was drunk with fear. These were not men to trifle with. No, it wouldn't be like the frat boys at school or the dim-witted muggers outside the bar or on the railway. These men were gangsters—blood-soaked, merciless, and unforgiving. They'd kill her, just like they killed Marcus and his wife. Even if she managed to kill them first, more would come for her. The best she could do was never be seen.

"She must have gone that way," one of them said. God ... they were close enough that she could hear them clearly. Why did she follow these men? Even when she had known the forgone conclusion, she had chosen to press on. There was a lesson here, she was certain, and when her heart stopped beating all the way into her temple, she would probably know what it was.

"I'm telling you, she's around here. We would've seen her," the other argued.

"So, what? Shake down the shopkeepers?"

"Who the hell was she anyway?"

An idiot who ought to have minded her own business. That was the lesson.

The voice was even closer now. "It doesn't matter. It's not like this is Western Calivia. No one cares about these people."

"Boss'll have our heads for leaving a witness."

"Well, bro, what about the little girl?"

"What the hell ... dumbo, she is like six or something. What's she gonna do? You know what I meant."

"I don't know."

Sirens began to chirp in the distance, getting louder by the second. Wow, the police were actually coming; someone must have reported the gunshots. Addy thought about the little girl and hoped someone would help her.

In response to the impending law enforcement, one of the men said, "Whatever. She was probably just a bum. We have to get out of here."

"Just don't tell the boss?"

"Yeah. No one is gonna do anything about it anyway. If they do, we'll kill them too."

The voices were fading now.

"You hungry?"

"I could eat."

When the voices were barely audible, Addy summoned her reserve courage and lifted the lid off the bin just enough to peek out and see where the men were. Sure enough, they were walking away from her now.

In this moment, something overcame her, an out-of-body dread, like a fleeting thought wound up in a tornado of fear blowing down her walls. It was here, at last, that her mind revealed itself to her. Succumbing to it, she slipped back into the bin, forgetting the moment and becoming lost in a thread of nightmare.

So clear in her mind's eye were the circumstances, only instead of peering through a crack in the recycling bin, Addy was peeking through a keyhole. In front of her was a bedroom and she could see three men in gray suits, each wearing masks depicting demons in the forms of animals. One man stood by the door of the bedroom and one man stood in the corner opposite the door, both holding machine guns poised and ready. The third man, who wore a mask depicting a white-faced fox, stood with his back to the foot of the bed holding onto a brunette woman from behind. He held one arm around her torso and one hand firmly on her neck. Somewhere to the left of Addy's view a man pleaded with them, begging for the woman's life. Details of the scene were firing off in all directions in her brain ... panic began to cripple her as she huddled inside the bin.

The fox tore the woman's blouse and helped himself to her, letting her ruined clothes fall and hang haphazardly at her elbows. He unbuttoned her pants; she resisted this, and the fox responded by producing a large knife and placing it against her throat.

"Leave her alone! I'll kill you!" the man out of sight screamed.

"Shut up!" one of the goons shot back, pointing his gun at the bed.

"Is her purity important to you?" the fox inquired, running his fingers along the length of her while he waited for a response. His voice was calm and calculating, the voice of man who has decided.

"Please ... I'll do anything you want!"

"Liam ..." the woman cried. "I love you ..." Addy couldn't see the woman's eyes, but her limp limbs and the way her body slumped apathetically into the fox told a tale of surrender. She knew she was going to die.

"That's sweet," the fox sneered, turning her so that her naked torso faced the man on the bed.

Trying desperately, the man begged, "I love you, baby! Come on, please! There must be something you want!"

"Shhhh!" the fox sounded, placing the knife over the woman's lips mockingly. "Now, now, I respected you once, and I think she is, at worst, corrupted. That matters to me, Liam."

"No, stop, I'll kill you!"

"Liam ..." she cried, her face moist with tears.

"Since I do think highly of you, or at least of her, I'll allow her to die a pure woman." Without hesitation, the fox bunched up her hair in his left hand and with his right hand he lowered the knife to her neck and opened her up from ear to ear.

Screaming and crying, Liam cursed the fox as he held onto her hair and balanced her body against the bed frame, allowing the blood to spray frantically. Laughing wildly, the fox pulled on her hair, opening the chasm in her neck and covering the bed in blood. He finished his work by completing the decapitation with his knife, letting the woman's body fall to the floor with a thump.

As the fox dangled the head by the hair, he stood up on the bed, threw the head at Liam, and shouted maniacally, "I am God!" Taking a machine gun from one of his cronies, the fox towered over Liam, who was just out of view from the keyhole, and pointed the gun at him. "You see, Liam, you screwed up. You upset the balance of things," the fox continued, Liam bawling his eyes out and begging for his life. "You have upset the balance of things because you can't see the truth. Why did you have to put me in this position?"

"I—I don't know, please, I don't know! Oh God, please help me!"

"Didn't you hear me? If your God exists, *where is he*? To hell with your God! There is only one, and that is me. I am God. I decide who lives and who dies. You had to upset the balance, Liam, and now you have forced my hand!"

"Nooo!"

The fox emptied an entire clip on him, then laughed like a total maniac again and tossed the empty gun back to his goon.

"Leave the mess," the fox instructed. "Let Calivia see for themselves what their alleged 'God' believes in."

After this, the men in the masks left the room and Addy could finally cry. And boy did she cry. She must have stayed locked in that chest for hours, huddled into a ball in the corner, full of fear and sorrow, before the police arrived. At first, she was too scared to call out to them. She just wanted to stay huddled in there forever, much like she was presently in this recycling bin, and just vanish, crawl into herself and disappear like a listless Sunday afternoon.

In at least one way, she *had* vanished. She couldn't remember what happened next ... after the cops found her ... the orphanage ... oh God! They had always told her that her parents had left her at the church when she was an infant; it all made sense! Addy must have forgotten it all, her survival instinct preserving her brain with a fog of repression. This darkness of hers, the passenger Addy had sensed for years, the one Jill had acknowledged but falsely attributed to Alex and Dean and feeling abandoned, this was its true form. She *was* abandoned, but that wasn't why she felt anxious; no, it was much darker. Addy's parents had been brutally murdered in front of her! There was no way this could be fake ... the memory was too vivid, too specific, too grotesque. Oh, her poor mother! There had been so much blood on that bed!

Over and over, Addy played the scene in her mind and collapsed into tears. That crimson scar, once her mother's trachea, just wouldn't cease; the whole damn room was covered in her blood and the fox was giddy about it. Addy realized she had underestimated the depth of the evil inside of her. It wasn't purely darkness or anxiety; it was total and complete evil.

Addy was absolutely crippled, crumpled up with her arms around her knees, floating in tears. She'd never come out. She was going to stay in this recycling bin forever. No way she could ever tell Alex; this was too dark, too putrid. It would corrupt him, and his soul was too good for that.

Suddenly, the lid of the recycling bin ripped off and a startled business owner cried out, "What the—!"

Surprised, Addy tried to uncoil herself and inadvertently leaned to one side, toppling the bin onto its side and ejecting her awkwardly onto the pavement.

"Are you all right?" The businessman asked as he stood over Addy, who lay on her back, her body limp and her eyes glazed. "Ma'am, do you need help?"

"I'm fine," she muttered, staring blankly toward nothing in particular.

"Okay ..." The man lingered for a moment, confused, then went on with his life. So would everyone else. He didn't care, they didn't care, nobody cared. But they would, someday. Now they walk to-and-fro, checking their phones, giving much ado about nothings of every kind, never knowing that someday their worlds would be shattered too ... like hers. Then what? What were they to do then?

In her peripheral view, Addy could see two large dumpsters wedged into the alleyway. Geez, she should have gotten into those. Too late for hindsight. She dragged her body into the alleyway and lodged herself between the dumpsters, where she allowed herself to collapse.

3

Time had passed in a vacuum. Addy had no idea how long it had been before she crawled out of there. She felt dead, and yet fully alive, in tune with the most intimate recesses of her soul. From the depths of these recesses came a sort of clarity that engulfed her in an errant firestorm. It was all so simple to her now; the world she knew was full of rot, and those who were making it rot had to be stopped. Anyone who had the power to stop the rot had a responsibility to do so—not just for themselves, but for the unknowing who would someday be shattered as she had been today. When Zach Brine spoke of destiny, this was the closest thing Addy could determine that was meant for her. There was no real "destiny," after all, that was just a construct humans built to rationalize the rampant chaos and coincidence that would otherwise overwhelm their ability to cope. No, she refused to refer to all this as "fated." It was nothing but rampaging chaos. One thing was for sure, though: as long as she was breathing, Addy wouldn't let this be.

When she finally did stammer out into the street and start walking back to the train platform, the first thing that occurred to her was to call Beatrice. She thought of Dean too, of course, but screw him. Why hadn't they told her?

After four rings, Beatrice answered. "Hello, Addy?"

Silence penetrated her ears until Beatrice spoke again. "Addy? Are you all right?"

"How could you?"

"What? Addy, how could I what?"

"You said my parents gave me up. They were ashamed ... never wanted to meet me." There was no outward emotion in her voice, but inside, Addy was ready to explode.

"Oh Addy," Beatrice began, clearly off guard. "Your parents wanted you to have a better life."

"I bet they did. A better life than the one they had, right?"

"We never met them; that's what the orphanage told us. Addy, did something happen?"

Tears formed and Addy started to get angry. "Yeah, something did happen! My parents were murdered! My mother was hacked to pieces and you knew it, didn't you?"

"What? Where did you hear that?"

"You knew, just admit it! You and that asshole Dean adopted me because you felt sorry for me and because you knew it would make you look heroic in front of all your constituents, right? You must have known!"

"Why would you think that? Honey, what happened? I'm coming to Calivia."

Now Addy was screaming into the phone. "No! Don't you come here! I don't want to see or hear from you two again! Liars!"

"Addy—"

"The police came! I was locked inside a chest and they had to break me out; there is no way you didn't know! I bet it was all over the news! How did everyone hide this from me? Why? I deserved to know!"

"You were just a kid. We didn't—"

"It wasn't your decision!"

"I'm coming there, Addy. Please try to understand."

"Screw you both! Don't come here!"

Decisively, she hung up the phone and screamed into the sky. Collapsing to her hands and knees, she bowed her head and let the tears fall onto the gray, weathered pavement. Her hair brushed back and forth across her face as her stomach and her chest heaved and her head bobbed up and down. Her arms were shaking and her hands were turning white as she tried futilely to rip up the ground. All these years ... it made so much sense now. The anxiety she felt, the dark passenger she sensed but couldn't discern, it was no defect of genetics, no preconceived locus of control, no. In fact, she had been born from blood. Inside of her was a rage with a purpose. A purpose of vengeance.

Beside her, she felt a small vibration and she saw a light flash in her periphery, a notification coming to her phone, which she had discarded beside her. That's right, she recalled, she had been on her way to see Jill. Having absolutely no concept of how much time had passed, she realized people were probably looking for her. She grabbed the phone and unlocked it to find that she had several missed calls and texts. Two calls and a text from Jill that read, "Addy? Are you all right?" Soon after, Alex had tried to reach her and had texted her asking her to call him. Guilt for having worried them flooded Addy. At the same time, she wasn't certain she could muster the energy to talk to them. She'd have to explain this, and she couldn't say what the real problem was. She stood by what she had thought initially, back in the alley: this was too dark, and she couldn't stand the thought of it corrupting Alex as it had her. Or, who knows, perhaps she was just afraid of looking vulnerable. Either way, she wasn't ready for this.

Addy inhaled fully, closing her eyes and lifting her upper body so she sat on her knees. With lungs full of air, she tilted her head toward the sky and held her breath for a long time. *Time to collect yourself,* she decided, finally exhaling.

Getting to her feet, she texted Alex back. "Be at the apartment soon, sorry."

She headed back to the train.

4

"You'll have to do better than you did today," said Zach as he sat on a log across from Alex in their makeshift camp. Lucas sat between them, chuckling like a hyena on a ledge as he poked at the fire.

"Are you kidding me?" Alex replied. "How many hours was that?"

About seven, if Zach figured correctly, and that was nothing. Normally, Alex would be right to expect some sort of learning curve, but Zach was not a normal trainer and Alex was not a normal pupil. This was a special paradigm and had to be treated as such.

"I told you he was crazy, didn't I?" Lucas reminded Alex.

As they spoke, Zach began to methodically break apart the charred meat of a small animal Lucas had caught in the late afternoon, and carefully sort the pieces into equal portions. Next, he combined them with some gathered berries and edible plants and served them on wooden planks.

"Thank you," Alex said. "This looks excellent!"

"You're welcome," Lucas answered.

"Seems like you've done this before. Have you two spent a lot of time in the wilderness?"

"Prism demands an array of skills," Zach answered. "You can't always rely on technology and convenience, advanced as it may be."

"You are right. Technology couldn't present a meal like this." Alex admired the spread and took a long-awaited bite of the flame-cooked meat. "Wow. Amazing."

"You must respect the resources presented to you. This is why we invest our time to achieve perfection. Those who squander lack the compassion for Prism."

Alex paused before replying, "So, wastefulness is immoral?"

"Rykai is an intimate mastery. It is not a question of morality; it is whether you can make yourself vulnerable. Can you respect and love the process and the resources involved enough to become one with them?"

"That's why we meditate," Lucas added. "We reflect on our actions, our blessings, and our failures; you know, what we could have done differently."

"No, not what we do *differently*," Zach corrected. "We reflect on cause and effect. We can never do things differently. What happens is just an event. The only significance to such events is how we synthesize them. Such is fate; it is our ability to seize the moments in front of us and recognize the cosmic significance of our interactions with them."

Alex wasn't sure he understood. "I thought you said our meeting was 'fated'?"

"It was, in the sense that we both recognized our mutual destiny. I could have ignored your catching the slab and you could have lived in denial, but we both recognized that something was amiss and chose to be here, in this moment, preparing for Prism." What was truly "immoral," Zach thought, was ignoring such signs. Unfortunately, most people did. Or they just weren't capable of critically understanding what was in front of them.

"Okay." Alex accepted what Zach said and changed the subject. "So you are going to teach me rykai, right?"

"You are a way yet from rykai, but yes, I am going to teach you."

"How long does it take to get good at it?"

"Pfft!" Zach dismissed him and started eating his meal. What a ridiculous notion!

A moment later, Zach added, "You don't 'get good at' rykai. It's not tennis or gardening or video games. Rykai is a precise and intimate pursuit of perfection." It was always rather frustrating to try to explain rykai to a new recruit, especially one so green as Alex. Rykai wasn't really a thing, but more of a concept, and it wasn't to be defined. Some of the best rykai fighters were completely surreptitious until the moment they struck, and they never struck the same way twice. How could he encompass that thought into something meaningful? Zach tried his best. "You will understand once you begin to practice rykai. If you lose focus for even a second, it could be the difference between who lives and who dies."

Alex continued to engage, seeming quite interested, "Are there many varieties of rykai? You showed us the 'golem' in the simulator, right? And there are three other types, or are there more?"

"There are four Alderian Pantheons, yes, but rykai is as vast as space itself. No two people will use it exactly the same way. This is one reason why you have to be so prepared for Raynor Academy."

"Okay, I get it now. Rykai is a practice, not a skill, right?"

"Exactly." He did get it. Every moment that passed, Zach grew more confident about his chosen prodigy.

Zach was about to continue, but Alex stood up suddenly and said, "I'm going to step away for a minute."

Alex wandered over to the top of the bluff and started toying with his phone. As he waited, Zach leaned back on the log and fell into introspection. Finally, he had Alex on the hook; now, all he had to do was deliver. How fantastically whimsical and grandiose would it be for Zach to show up at Raynor Academy with a real, live Alderian myth come alive? If he could figure out how to bring out Alex's power again and teach him to harness it properly, Zach would be a legend. What's more, the galaxy would be forever changed, as this knowledge could be the key to finally defeating the Grothians. Not to mention, he would finally get his starship. So many considerations!

Lucas interrupted his fantasy. "You know that Addy is not Prism material, right?"

Of course he knew that.

"Yeah. It will take a hell of a lot of work to get her ready for the test," Zach replied.

"Why bother? I say we invest our energy in Alex. I mean, he is going to be a monster when he is complete."

"He won't be complete without Addy. Alex's loyalty to her is too deep. We can figure out how to deal with her if the test filters her out, but until then, we need to train her too so we can keep Alex on board. As it is, I am going to have to get her if she doesn't come tomorrow."

"Okay boss, I'll do my best."

"You can't fail, Lucas. We have to succeed. Do you understand fully what Alex means?"

"Obviously I do. I've been doing this as long as you. I just think Addy is too undisciplined and erratic."

"Well then, Lucas, do your job and she won't be."

"All right, you got it. She is going to dislike us," Lucas said smugly.

She certainly would, Zach thought. That was part of it. Everyone hated them, until they loved them. It wasn't as though people went to sleep one night and woke up with the clarity required to be Prism soldiers. Those who made it to the level Zach and Lucas had achieved saw the world differently. It was up to them to awaken and cultivate that perspective in others. Sometimes Zach felt Lucas had become too jaded. Even so, Lucas was worth his weight in great whiskey.

"I need to get home," Alex explained as he returned to the camp. "Addy didn't show up at an appointment and she isn't answering the phone."

Zach ignored him for a moment, contemptuously fiddling with his knife instead.

"Same time tomorrow?" Alex pressed.

"If you think you can fit it into your schedule," Zach finally answered.

"I'll be here," Alex assured him, gathering up his knapsack and slinging it over his shoulder.

"Don't let her distract you," Lucas warned. "What you are doing here is too important."

"Better yet," Zach added, "Bring her with you. She is already behind."

"You got it. I'll see you bright and early."

The two men nodded at him as he turned to go.

Lucas yawned. "Whatd'ya say we get some sleep?"

After a brief silence, Zach said, "Yes. Meet here in the morning. Five a.m. Good job today."

Lucas nodded and the two parted ways. As Zach wandered back to his hotel room, he suddenly pictured his revolver, sitting there on the sofa table, fired twice and chambering one bullet that had been intended for his skull. How frivolous and stupid he had been. He knew now he could not, and would not, pull that trigger again. No, the significance of his quest was too great. No one else could do this; it had to be Zach. He had to succeed.

And he would.

5

"Addy? Are you here?"

By the time Alex got back to the apartment, Addy was just a few whiskeys from oblivion and sprawled out on the couch, hanging halfway off it and staring at the ceiling.

"Addy?" He said again, catching sight of her. "Are you okay? Jill called me."

"I'm fine." She answered blankly, offering no explanation. All afternoon, she had been pounding liquor and swiping away on her phone, ignoring Beatrice's texts and calls, and scouring the internet for anything related to her parents' murder. Nothing to be found. It was as if they never existed. Granted, she didn't know their last names or even her mother's first name, but something like this had to be recorded somewhere. She tried searching for "Liam hotel shooting," "woman decapitated in Grantitan hotel," and dozens of other queries and not even a whisper of it was anywhere. Was she just crazy? She couldn't be. This memory was too real, and what she was feeling now, it was what she had always felt. This was her dark passenger, she knew it.

When her search for the murder turned up nothing, she fell down a different hole, trying to find anything she could about the Mushida Clan. They were one of several gangs in outer Sari, perhaps the most prolific of them, and they apparently had quite a bit of influence on Grantitan in particular. Most of what Addy found suggested that the clan became prominent following the war, when everything was still in upheaval. She had heard of the clan before, but one thing that turned up in her perusing that she hadn't known was that there was suspicion about the clan being somehow connected to ARMs Corporation, a large, interplanetary energy company. Allegedly, the clan had bullied local governments into approving contracts for mining operations, including the one Alex worked at. One thing led to another, and soon Addy was reading articles about Helba protesting the corporation as they moved more operations to Grantitan. She got a funny feeling as she read all of this, like there was more to the connection between the Mushida Clan and ARMs Corporation. But there wasn't enough evidence to be conclusive.

"What is going on with you? Seriously, first there was the bar, then going to meet Zach alone, and now you are skipping counseling and getting drunk at five p.m.?" Alex tossed his bag on the floor and stood across the room with his arms crossed. A confusing combination of concern and frustration was on his face as he looked at her and waited.

Addy sat up and leaned back into the cushions, refusing to meet Alex's eyes, and she mumbled, "I don't want to talk about it."

"Well, okay, I get not wanting to tell Jill, but come on, Addy, I'm your brother."

Yeah, she thought, but you just don't get it. He never would. Alex always wanted wounds to be patched up and moved on from, for fingers to be splinted and for minds to conquer matter, but that was all too simple. This was not a surface-level problem; it was rooted deep in her being, a critical darkness that could neither be bandaged nor cured.

"Just leave me alone. I'm safe, that is your concern, right?"

Clearly frustrated, Alex stroked his chin and went into the kitchen. When Alex was agitated, he always made himself busy. Addy wanted to feel bad for shutting him out, but it was for his own good. Plus, she didn't have the bandwidth right now.

He called out to her from the kitchen, "Do you want anything?"

"If you are already cooking, yeah."

"You know," he said as he shuffled around, "I know we don't agree on doing this training and I can understand why you would be upset with me for doing it anyway, but have you thought about why I want to? Why we ought to?"

Ridiculous. Addy practically laughed out loud. He really thought she was drowning in liquor over that?

Just to humor herself, Addy asked him, "Why exactly is that?"

Alex filled a pot with water and turned the stovetop on. "Well, like I said before, something amazing happened at the stadium, and it all seems too coincidental to me, everything that came after. It has to be fate, doesn't it?"

"You are asking me? I thought you had this figured out. I mean, we've spent two days talking about it."

Sensing the sarcasm, Alex leaned into the archway between the kitchen and living room so he could see Addy. "Look, I'm sorry. I have told you why I want to do it, but I want you to come with me. I understand if—"

"Yeah, I get it," Addy interrupted. "Believe it or not, I have done some thinking of my own, and I don't care what Zach or that Lucas asshole say about it. I'm going to become a Prism soldier, but not because of them, and when I do, I'm going to whoop some ass all across the galaxy. How's that for 'fate'?" Even she knew she was equivocating, but the liquor was doing most of the talking anyway, so screw it.

"Huh? I thought—"

"Forget it," she interrupted again. "If those clowns can be in Prism, so can I. I've always wanted to see the galaxy. You know, leave this planet." Addy jumped up, grabbed the bottle she had set beside the couch, and took a wild swig, dripping booze all over herself as the liquid hit her lips. While the whiskey dribbled off her chin, she said, "Alex, we *have* to get out of here. I don't want to live here anymore." Laughing at her own drunkenness, Addy set the bottle down clumsily on an end table and danced over to the other end of the room with no specific destination. She continued this pattern of movement as she began to rant. "Tomorrow, I am going to go with you, and I'll tell Zach that he had better train me or I'll drain his throat while he sleeps. Ha! What a weird way to say that, eh? 'drain' his throat ... powerful imagery, right?"

"Addy, maybe you should lay down." Motioning at the bottle on the end table, he asked, "Did you kill that whole bottle?"

"Who cares? I'm fine. I will be, too, just wait. What are you making?"

"Pasta. It's quick. I ate already, anyway. The training is no joke, Addy. I'm exhausted and I gave it my all."

"And you don't think I will?"

"I do, it's just that you're going to be hungover if you keep it up."

"You sound like Ms. Keaten. Addy, you can't do anything because you are a piece of garbage. Yeah, well, who taught me? What does that say about you?" Rage began to boil inside of her as she thought of that wretched woman from the orphanage. She could feel it like steam permeating her brain as she imagined that judgmental look, those condescending eyes, and that scraggly voice. Ms. Keaten, the witch, she could make a songbird commit suicide with that voice. It was like a slap in the face to anything happy in the world, a stark reminder to any child who entered her grim sphere that, in fact, there was no creativity, no hope, and no happiness. No, all that existed was order and responsibility and the penance that accompanied imperfection, a penance which had befallen Addy disproportionately.

"Oh, come on," Alex argued. "Obviously I believe in you, I just don't want you to mess it up."

Addy paced the room and took the liberty of more booze. "Yup. You sound exactly like her, and all the other ones too. Listen, it's not about destiny ...." She paused to take another swig and pointed obnoxiously at Alex, assuming he knew that was meant as a slight. "Nah ... only thing 'fated' is that people don't change. I'm tired of feeling helpless. I won't let the people who are making this world rot get away with it anymore. When I'm a Prism soldier they will tremble at the sight of me."

"What are you talking about? What people?" Appearing confused and flustered, Alex held up a finger and said, "Hold on," and rushed into the kitchen.

When he returned seconds later, Addy was still pacing, her hand on her forehead and her head lowered. Before he could speak, she continued her rant. "All of them. Those multiplying degenerates. All those disgusting parasites and the failed governments that foster them. The Grothian scum that started all this. Haven't you looked around? No one gives a damn. I'm sick of letting them win; sick of doing nothing. That's 'destiny,' brother. We are going to *do* something."

"Yeah," he agreed, trying to walk the line and calm her down. "I've seen it, and yeah, we are going to do something. It's a way off, though. We won't change anything if we fail Zach's test."

"We won't fail though."

"I know. I'm just saying, don't stress about it now. Let's just eat and get some sleep. Tomorrow we can focus on training, and when we pass the test, we can focus on changing those things."

"Sorry I'm not as shortsighted as you. When was the last time you went to tarp city? It's been adding up for so long that it can't be ignored and I'm sick of people telling me to ignore it or that I can't do anything or whatever."

Alex threw his hands up. "Whatever Addy! No matter what I say you're going to be angry, right?"

As he went into the kitchen, Addy followed him to the doorway and argued, "Yeah, 'cause you always try to tell me the bright side, like I don't know already. 'Stressing' about it is called motivation. Quit telling me what to do and do something yourself!"

"I am doing something," Alex snapped back. "What were you doing today?" He didn't mean that, and she knew she had pushed him there, but she blew up nonetheless.

"Screw you! Why do you have to be like that?"

"Why do you have to get drunk all the time? All I try to do is help you, Addy! Of course I see how crappy the world is! Do you see how crappy this apartment is?" Alex waved his arms wildly, showcasing the drab accommodations around them. "You think I don't know?"

"Yet you do nothing to change it. Always 'one step at a time.' If Zach hadn't basically forced you to do this, you'd work at the mines and live in this dump forever."

"You are a piece of work, you know? Why don't you go sleep it off, you drunk!"

"Yeah, whatever, asshole." Having had enough, Addy thrust the contents of a nearby countertop onto the floor and retreated into the bedroom to the sound of the crashing kitchen accoutrements. Screw that, she thought, locking the bedroom door behind her and collapsing onto the bed face first. Grabbing Alex's pillow, she buried her face and screamed the most epic scream until she felt a pounding in her head and her temples threatened to burst out of her forehead.

Her parents had been brutally murdered.

There was nothing for her here.

She hated everyone and most of them hated her.

Screw this planet.

As her scream reached its climax, it transformed into bountiful tears. She had no control over it and didn't want to. Instead, she let her natural emotions exist, her body heave and contract, and her face flush until the pillow felt like a misty shower. Alex calling her a drunk really knocked her back. Rarely did he speak to her like that. In fact, she could barely remember the last time they had fought that vehemently. Maybe it was when she was adopted; she had been looking for every reason to resent going, to avoid the inevitable, and of course, Alex had been stubbornly optimistic then too. "It'll be okay," he had promised her, and said something about how the Palmers seemed nice and how they would still see each other. At the time, she was so mad. How could he advocate for something that sent her away? She saw it as him betraying her, not wanting to look after her anymore, but now she knew that he had wanted her to be happy and have a chance at a real life. That ship had sailed for Alex and he probably knew it. All he wanted was for her to avoid that same sadness. That's what Alex was doing now, too. Deep down, she knew he was protecting her. That's what he was always doing, because he was the best brother she could ever ask for, and boy did she ever need him to be. Addy was such a terrible sister. What a mess.

Tomorrow would be different. It had to be.

6

A bowl of pasta with crusty red sauce lay at the doorway the next morning. Even after Addy had treated her brother like trash, he had still left her food and let her sleep in his bed. Feeling both physically and emotionally ill, Addy droned her way into the bathroom to get water and maybe puke. There, she saw the second thing Alex had left for her: a note scribbled on lined paper and taped to the mirror.

On it were the words "I'm sorry, love you sis" and instructions telling her where to find him, Zach, and Lucas. Well, this was it, today it was ride or die. If she didn't go all in, she might as well give up, and that she could not do. She might have been drunk before, but what she had felt was one hundred percent real. No longer could this world rot before her eyes while she stood around helpless. Besides, Alex deserved better than her worthless meandering. It was time for her to stop complaining and do something about it.

So Addy got herself cleaned up and began her quest.

When she found them, they were on a boulder-strewn plateau six miles north of Calivia. Lucas watched from a high perch as Zach instructed Alex to perform circuits in between attempts to combat him. Addy could see the midday sunlight glistening off the beads of sweat dripping from Alex's face as she approached the training grounds.

"That's it?" Zach Brine demanded as he towered over Alex, who was flying up and down, performing jumping jacks into pushups. Zach interrupted this routine by launching a devastating boot into Alex's ribs, which knocked him onto his back. "You must be able to do better than that!"

"Damn it!" Alex choked out, rolling onto his knees and starting again.

"You enemies will kick harder and more frequently. How do you expect to keep up?"

Addy walked nervously into Zach Brine's arena. Lucas spotted her from above and shouted, "Hey Zach, look who showed up!"

At the sound of Lucas' voice, Zach whipped around to face Addy. He stared, daring her to say the first word. Meanwhile, Alex stopped his regiment and watched curiously as Addy stared Zach down.

"Well." Addy stood her ground. "Are we going to do this, or what?"

Disgusted, Zach replied, "What makes you think you deserve to train with us now? Is it somehow more worth your time today than it was yesterday?"

"I want to be a Prism soldier. I'm ready to do whatever it takes."

"So do thousands of others, most of whom are better than you. I gave you a chance. You have been nothing but argumentative since the beginning."

"She is—" Alex began, only to be silenced by a quick thrust of Zach's arm and the decisive palm of his hand. Zach was testing her; she knew it. Addy had to stand her ground.

"I want to do this, and I *will* do this. If you refuse to train me, I will return every day until you agree," Addy said.

Lucas laughed from his rocky ledge.

Addy spoke louder. "I understand now what you meant about fate. I don't know if I believe in higher powers, but I know that there is nothing for us here and we were meant to do something. So here I am, doing something. Now train me."

As she finished her proposal, Addy clenched her fists and felt her toes curling into her shoes. Zach showed no emotion as he silently considered her. The anxiety she felt, the tension of that moment, was palpable. This was not a man to disappoint, Addy understood as she absorbed the taste of his scorn into the back of her throat and swallowed the lump of it with great effort.

"All right," Zach finally said. "Come over here."

She approached with caution, her heart beating faster and more nervously with every step. He pointed to his left and said, "There."

Complying, Addy filed herself there, between Zach and where Alex was watching with anticipation, and stood as straight as she could. Taking a step toward her, Zach examined her with disdain. Without warning, he buried a boulder-crushing fist deep into her gut. Addy doubled over, practically folding in half, and fell to the ground.

She tried to curse, but only a winded yelp came out as she doubled over, curling up her knees and wrapping her arms around her abdomen in agony.

Lucas laughed.

Zach turned to Alex, who seemed to be trying to resist his temptation to tend to his sister, and demanded, "Why have you stopped? I want you on double time, now!"

Alex obeyed and began Zach's circuit once again.

Addy choked as she rose to her knees and heaved toward the ground. She tried to get up, but as she did, Zach's powerful backhand cracked the side of her face, sending her tumbling to the ground again.

"You are worthless," Zach said as he loomed over her, ready to strike again. "Deserving of no pity. You are as bad as the rest of this garbage planet."

"Damn you." She tried to get up to face him. Zach's boot smashed her chest and forced her onto her back, where he pinned her to the ground and crushed her into the dirt. Desperate, Addy wrapped both hands around his enormous combat boot and kicked her feet as she tried to break free.

"Can't even get off the ground!"

"Let me up! Fight me without the cheap shot!" Addy insisted.

"Your enemies won't fight fair if they can help it," Zach pointed out as he crushed her diaphragm.

She thought her chest was going to collapse. Her breathing became labored and she felt her strength waning as Zach put more weight on his step. When she was on the edge of begging him and it felt as though he were going to pulverize her bones, Zach finally let up, taking his boot off her and walking away from her as she wrapped her arms around her chest.

"Hurry up!" Zach yelled at Alex, who was jumping up and down on a boulder. "You can do that faster!"

Addy got to her feet. "I'm not quitting; you can't ignore me."

His back remained toward her and he said nothing.

"Damn it! Turn around and fight me fair!"

Again, Zach refused to acknowledge her.

Angrily, Addy spit on the ground and made her decision. With all her gusto, she rushed Zach from behind and went for a choke hold, which Zach answered by carelessly tossing her over his shoulder and onto her back.

Fearlessly, ravenously even, Addy got to her feet and tried to strike him again. She paid for it with a hook to the jaw followed by a punishing kick to the knee. As she buckled from the sting of the kick, Zach twisted up a fistful of her hair and yanked her viciously down into the dirt. With her hair still in his fist, he bounced her face off the ground a couple times before pulling her up to her knees and taunting her, "What about now?" As he said this, he pulled her hair and forced her face to stare up at his so she could see his stupid grin.

She responded by grabbing onto his wrist with both hands and digging her fingernails into his skin as forcefully as she could manage.

Zach laughed and pulled her to her feet. She cried out in agony as her legs didn't respond quickly enough and her scalp momentarily bore the weight of her entire body. Just as she caught herself on two feet, Zach caved in her stomach again with a devastating punch. Instinctively, she lurched forward, but Zach's iron grip yanking out her scalp stopped her.

"Stop it! Stop it!" She found herself pleading. "Let go, you bastard!"

She stopped trying at his wrist and started punching and kicking at Zach; anything to get free, God, she was getting desperate. The pain was incredible.

Zach seemed apathetic. He allowed her hits for a moment, deciding carefully how to end her.

"You filthy, cheating asshole!" she yelled, fully furious. "Let me go! Fight me for real! Come on! Come on!"

"Give your enemies an exploit, and they will abuse it."

He tightened his grip on her hair and pulled her head back again to punctuate his point. Her hands returned to his wrist as he ripped and tugged and forced her back down to her knees. She closed her eyes and grit her teeth as Zach twisted one more time, forcing her whole body to turn so that her back was to him. She had never felt such complete agony and humiliation. How could this be happening to her? She was just sitting here, legs curled up under her, arms flailing above her like an idiot, and Zach was towering over her, totally in control. He was a grizzly bear and she was a camper with a marshmallow stick.

"My God, is this it? Are you going to try at all?" Zach asked her.

"Let me up," she dared him. "If you have the guts." No way she was going to lay down. That's what he wanted.

"All right."

Without warning, Zach began dragging her briskly through the dirt. Addy screamed in pain as her legs unfolded and weight was put on her scalp again. She kicked and struggled as he dragged her, but it was no use. Her bottom and her thighs bounced off rocks as she went, tearing a hole in her shorts and leaving a gash on her thigh.

A few long seconds later, Zach stopped, yanked her up again, and finally released her hair as he thrust her body into a slab of rock at the base of the ledge from which Lucas watched in amusement. She stuttered forward after the impact, and Zach finished her with three quick and brutal gut-punches, leaving Addy on her hands and knees gasping for air. A second later she puked and tears welled up in her eyes.

Zach loomed over her. "Totally worthless. Why should I waste my time?"

"Enough!" Alex finally said.

"She won't stay," Lucas said from above as Alex approached. "Might as well forget about her."

"Shut up," Alex dismissed. He bent down beside Addy. "Are you okay? Can you get up?"

She was shaking and crying and a drizzle of snot was swinging from her nose. Her face twisted in embarrassment and she couldn't even look at him.

Out of the corner of her eye, she could see Alex holding out his hand.

"I'm ... fine. I won't give up."

Although Addy was certain he had heard full well, Zach asked, "Did you say something?"

Alex stood up and answered him. "That's enough. You didn't beat me this badly."

"You showed up on time."

"Screw you," Addy stammered, getting to her feet and facing Zach. "I said I won't give up."

"Addy—" Alex started, but he saw the burning vigor in her eyes. Just like that night in the bar and so many others like it, he knew when it was time to step back. Addy was nothing if not passionate and tenacious. No matter what he said, she wasn't going to stop.

After a moment, Zach replied, with a slight nod to Alex. "Also, you weren't an asshole." And he punched Addy right in the face as hard as he could, knocking her down and out cold.

7

When Addy came to it was swift and rude. There was no wellness check and no apology. Instead, she got Zach's version of "walk it off," which included twenty miles of hiking, running, climbing, and jumping. In between laps around the mountain, Zach conditioned her with more punishment until every part of her body felt black and blue. Alex got it too, but Lucas's mean streak had far less bravado than Zach's. For hours, she did her best, but each time Zach pummeled her, she fell further behind. Before she knew it, darkness was upon them and Lucas had gone into the tree line with Alex to get food while Zach started a fire. The tension between them was an obvious, brooding resentment. When the others returned and began to cook, it was a welcome comfort. Everyone settled in around the fire, but although she should have felt comradery, instead she felt awkward and scorned.

The warm, luminous campfire was an hourglass between them. Every crackle of wood and flicker of sparks flipped the sand again, refreshing the doubt in Zach's eyes. Addy stared back, eating in silence while casting a shade of her own. Seeing his pause, Addy felt both saddened and resentful, like a scolded child. The way he had humiliated her she would not soon forget. It was Zach who had stalked her, who had indoctrinated her, and now she was not good enough for him? She wanted to hate him, but somehow, she felt a burning desire, hot as the flames between them, to gain his approval.

It had been like this for several minutes. No one was speaking. Lucas finally decided to break the silence and offered a compliment to Addy. "You did well for your first day."

"Yeah," Alex agreed. "Better than I did. I'm sorry I acted like I doubted you yesterday."

Addy didn't acknowledge them and kept staring at Zach.

"I'll work with you tomorrow. Meditation and mantra; it will help with the anger," Lucas said.

"Mantras?" Alex was curious. "You mean like prayers? Like monks?"

"Yeah. It helps clear the mind, a critical skill for a Prism soldier."

They continued speaking, but Addy tuned them out. She was focused on something else. Beside her, she caught a glimpse of the razor-sharp, straight-edged knife that Lucas had used to skin their meal. The perfect killing edge glimmered with reflections of fire and speckles of blood left over. What a wonderful splatter that would make of someone, she thought, picturing herself stabbing a man over and over with merciless fury. To her surprise, it wasn't Zach on her mind's canvas, but it was instead a person she wished she could just erase, a man with no name, only a gray suit and the face of a fox. Whoever he was, he was part of the Mushida Clan, or ARMs Corporation, or maybe both. It was all connected somehow. Someday, somewhere in the vast, infinite blackness of the galaxy, she would find the right man in the right suit, and when she did, God help him.

The fire spit up a bouquet of sparks and Zach sighed disapprovingly, still looking in her direction. Addy was tired of this! Her eyes stayed on Zach as she considered the blade beside her. In a moment of spontaneous discovery, she knew what she had to do. Grabbing the blade, she stood up slowly, without a word, staring down at Zach. With her free hand, she reached behind her head and corralled all her long and cumbersome hairs into one loose ponytail. She raised the edge of the blade to the back of her neck and, with one swift slice, liberated herself from the exploitable locks she had once loved.

"Addy, your hair!" Alex, taken aback, stated the obvious as he saw the bundles of it on the ground.

Still looking at Zach, who showed no emotion, Addy said firmly, "Addy is gone. I am Lynn now, and I am going to be a Prism soldier."

For the briefest moment, Addy saw the shade of Zach's countenance shift in her favor.

CITY IN SPACE

1

Forty-seven days passed before Zach Brine acknowledged Lynn as a legitimate pupil. Every day, she went with Alex up into the mountains outside of Calivia, and every day Zach beat her into the dirt and ignored her presence as he trained Alex. She swallowed her pride, licked her wounds, and did whatever Alex was doing. Lucas found it hilarious, she could tell. Finally, on the forty-seventh day, she managed to sweep Zach's leg and knock him down.

"Haha! Very good!" He had laughed while Lynn stood over him, covered in bruises and boiling with rage. After that, he included her in the tyranny of his training.

Over the many months that followed, Alex and Lynn endured rigorous physical and mental trials. Zach pushed the limits of their bodies, and Lucas taught them to release the tension in their bodies through introspection and meditation. After some time of this, Lynn understood how to channel her emotions and release them in productive ways. Instead of being crippled by them, she was empowered, untethered by the tribulations of her past. She didn't forget, though; she would never forget. Instead, she would use her darkness, control it, and become unburdened by it. And one day, she would kill the fox.

When their minds and bodies were sculpted and ready, Zach Brine taught them the governing principles of rykai, the fighting style of the Prism soldier. The science was an art, and the art was a science, Zach drilled into them. Every Prism soldier designs a combat suit that conforms to their preferred style. No two suits are the same, thus, a Prism soldier must be adaptable, quick-witted, and able to think critically in the midst of combat.

To prepare them for the tests ahead, Zach asked the two of them to design their own suits, using the simulator. It took weeks of trial and error for them to find the perfect suits. Lynn's chosen armaments were surreptitious, including a full-body cloaking device, exploding ninja stars, and her signature weapon, a hidden chamber on her forearm that, with a firm flick of her wrist, would release deadly poison in the face of her opponent. Her style might best be described as that of a ninja: quick, deceptive, and deadly. She practiced by shedding the blood of the hopeless holograms inside of Zach's simulator until she could kill them all with flawless precision, avoiding even the slightest scratch on her virtual body.

Alex trained with a similar intensity, but toward a different end. Zach warned Alex that his gift, the strength of golems, would be coveted by many and must be kept a secret at all costs. With this in mind, Alex designed a suit that would mask his true power as purely a function of the suit. His gloves synchronized with the magnetism in the earth, creating the illusion that he could manipulate its crust without the mythical capabilities of the ancient Alderians. Zach forbid him from ever using his intrinsic power. Instead, Alex had to rely on the simple structures he could create with the gloves.

In the meantime, things on Grantitan were evolving. The tension between the Sarians and the Grothians was intensifying, and the people who felt it most were the citizens of outer Sari. Power continued to consolidate among those who supposedly sought peace, but the freedom fighters knew better. Groups like Helba grew in size and influence as they protested the government's rationing of supplies, mandated curfews, and media censorship. All of it just served to solidify Lynn's decision to leave and join Prism. She and Alex both agreed; there was nothing they could do now, but someday, when they were powerful Prism soldiers, they would return and liberate this place.

Calivia wasn't the only casualty in these tough times; Lynn's personal life had also fallen to pieces. Shortly after she had remembered her parent's killing, Beatrice had shown up at the university, looking for Lynn. To her surprise, Dean had come as well. Boy, did she have words for them. Somewhere inside the bramble wood of her brain she knew that Beatrice and Dean did the right thing for her, but she wasn't ready to accept that. Maybe she never would be. Regardless, after two days of them trying to reconcile with her and convince her not to throw away her education and her life on Grantitan, she told them to shove it and to let her decide for herself. The next day they left, and she hadn't seen them since.

For a little over a year, she and Alex trained relentlessly with Lucas and Zach, until their prowess met Zach's approval. Then, one cloudy day in April, Alex reached the apex.

He stood, eyes closed, arms out, embracing the cool wind on the mountainside, and before him was a great boulder. This boulder was one he had stood before many times, contemplating its impressive stature. On this day, he did the impossible. As the others looked on from a safe distance, Alex focused all his energy into his hands and his intentions with the slab of granite before him. Rain began to fall in gentle and forewarning drops as Alex touched the stone. Moments passed and the anticipation grew, but Alex just stood there with both palms on the slab. The distant rolling of thunder reminded them of the impending storm. Alex pulled back his hands, forming them into a sort of crescent shape, and thrust his palms forward with both the grace and the brutality of the golem. The next rumbling they heard was not thunder, but was the compromising of the great slab as a decisive fault formed from the center of the boulder and traveled all the way up and down the surface. Moments later, the massive rock fissured and collapsed into two pieces that rolled on their sides and left a jagged scar in the earth.

Lynn was mystified. Impossible things could happen ... now she had seen it with her own eyes, twice. First the stadium, and now this. Zach had known all along. He had known Alex from the moment he had seen him. Even in Lynn, an ordinary human who resisted him at every turn, Zach had recognized a tenacity and a ferocity that would lead her to greatness. And indeed, Zach had shaped her into that greatness. She knew now why Lucas said he was the best. In this moment, this fantastic and inexplicable exaggeration of reality, she suddenly felt closer to Zach, like she had all at once understood something about him. No one could fully understand Zach, not unless they had been here and witnessed something like Alex striking a mountain in half with his palms. Not even his wife or his daughter. That must have been an impossible burden to live with, to never be able to explain the infinite fantasy of the universe. What's more, to be the person who knows what to do, how to identify and cultivate it. How lonely that must be. Lynn imagined someday those feelings might find her too.

After that day, Zach decided they were ready. So, they gathered what little belongings they needed and prepared themselves for the long journey ahead. Lynn did not feel anxious for once in her life; she felt mature, empowered, and determined. It was time to put an end to the aimless suffering of her youth and direct her pain toward higher purpose. This was her destiny.

2

Halfway between the outer band of planets and the more developed inner sphere of the Sarian Empire, a wondrous hub orbited around the planet of Pailon. A gathering place for the diverse travelers of the galaxy, the Pailon Space Station became known as the City of Drifters. "City" was a fitting term; the station was so massive that it was easy for one to forget it was floating in space. Main Street Pailon was populated by dozens of purveyors of everything from spaceship repair to cold craft brew. The Pailon Bazaar, as it was known, was a place of intrigue, but also a place of potential danger, peppered with dubious traders, traffickers, and bounty hunters. It was best to travel in a group in Pailon and stay in the part of the city closest to the docking bays, where it was more likely that you could find law and order.

Zach had made all this abundantly clear to Alex and Lynn on the way, but as they docked the ship and walked through the hangars and onto Pailon's impressive Main Street, Lynn felt like she just had to see everything. She had never left Grantitan and man this was a hell of a first weekend away from home! Everywhere she looked, Lynn saw things she had never seen before. People were selling odd plants and peculiar pets, and groups of people circled merrily around unknown games with oddly sided dice and colored marble stones. A man and a woman with reptilian skin and slits for eyes leaned against the side of a shop and spoke in some slithery language. Lynn could have sworn she had even seen an elf dashing across the bazaar.

"We are going left up there," Zach said, pointing to an intersection up ahead. "About a block that way."

There was so much noise, Lynn hadn't heard him. "What?" she asked, trying to talk over the bustling bazaar.

"That way!" Zach repeated.

"Can you believe this place, Ad ... Lynn?" Alex asked. Even a year later, Lynn could tell Alex still felt awkward calling her that name. At first, he hadn't understood why she wanted to change her name. She thought it was obvious, but then, as she had noted so many times before, Alex tended to overlook things like that. "Addy" was part of the life she had left behind, part of the bitterness and the self-loathing she so detested about herself.

"It sure isn't Calivia, huh?" Lynn replied with a smirk.

"No kidding!"

"It has some similarities," Zach reminded them. "Keep your guard up."

Lynn stroked her hip, where she had her pistol holstered, a beast of a blaster with which she had practiced hundreds of hours in the last year. Somehow, she doubted anyone was going to mess with her while she was flashing this piece around. Even if someone snuck up on her, she was equipped with two very serious combat knives crisscrossed on her lower back beneath her black leather jacket. Between her jeans and her left boot, her good old switchblade lay in wait as backup. Whoever decided to attack her would soon be a gut fish.

As they rounded the corner, a mob of people clogged the street, all gathered around what looked like a grotesque alien cockfight. Whatever animals were ripping and tearing at each other, Lynn had never seen them before. They looked like mini-dinosaurs, with their scaly bodies and bird-like structures, but their heads—if they could be called that—were like Venus flytraps.

"Oh Pailon, we have missed you so," Lucas joked.

"What are those?" Alex wondered.

"They call them cat-traps, because they eat your pets. Probably a scientific name for 'em."

"Don't worry about them," Zach said. "Push through."

Lynn led the way through the rowdy gaggle of spectators, dodging elbows and fists, until she and the others were clear of the chaos. Before them stood a massive structure of steel and neon lights. Sliding glass doors were at the center, opening and closing relentlessly as travelers funneled in and out. A constant ray of yellow light poured from the doors and the dozens of perfectly symmetrical windows that rose high into the space station. Lynn was still in complete awe that this city was so big, and it was built in outer space! What other things was she going to see when they got to inner Sari?

"This is the rally point. We'll stay here tonight along with all the other Raynor Academy cadets. There are probably a few inside already," Zach said.

"What makes you say that?" Lynn was curious.

Lucas answered, "Zach's bestie's ship was in the hangar. She'd only come here if she had business."

"Another trainer?"

"Aye." Lucas chuckled. "She is good too; Zach will tell you."

"It has been awhile since Rachel Mccginneas has picked anyone," Zach said. "Whoever it is, I'm sure she trained them well."

"Do you guys compete or something?" Alex asked. "I mean, are all Prism cadets handpicked?"

"Not exactly."

Lynn snickered. "I bet you do more than compete."

She could tell by the tone of Zach's voice, the subtle creasing of his lips on one side, and the way he shifted from one foot to another when he talked about Rachel that she was more than a rival. Lynn had spent so much time with Zach in the past year that she probably knew him better than she knew anyone at this moment in her life. Though Zach had been careful not to reveal himself to her, Lynn had observed him deeply and she knew his subtleties.

"I'll talk to you more in the morning. Check in at the desk and get some rest. We have another long flight before we reach Raynor Academy." Before Lynn could respond, Zach went ahead into the hotel. Lucas nodded farewell and followed.

Alex, who had been carrying his luggage along with Lynn's since the hangar, was eager to get inside. He lifted the luggage off the ground where he had set it and said, "Well then, should we go in?"

"Yeah," Lynn said. "Here, let me take that, sorry." Grabbing her luggage from Alex, she took one last look around the wild bazaar and turned to go inside.

3

The inside of the hotel looked different than its generic and tired outward appearance. Everything looked modern and high tech, from the eggshell-shaped swivel chairs postured around oval glass tables to the tabletop hologram displays of airblading games and the chrome-encased concierge desk.

As they approached the desk, a concierge addressed them. "Hello travelers, welcome to the Pailon Hub, may I help get you situated?" Something sounded weird about this person.

"Hi," Lynn responded. "We are from Grantitan. We are here for Prism. Our names are Lynn Palmer and Alex Shaw."

"Excellent! I have you checked in now, your room keys will dispense below. The front desk is open twenty-four seven and can fulfill any requests you may have. A list of commands may be found beside your beds." As the man finished, a compartment opened up in the smooth chrome, and a tray bearing two sets of keys slid forward. Each of them grabbed one and the tray slid back in, closing again into the perfect surface of the desk.

Another employee came up beside them and said, "May I help with your bags?"

As this happened, yet another arrived and offered them two champagne flutes garnished with strawberries. "Welcome to the Pailon Hub, Alex Shaw and Lynn Palmer. We hope your stay is pleasant."

Alex raised his eyebrow as the other employee took their bags. "Thank you ... wow, you really don't have to take those."

"Damn, this isn't bad," Lynn complimented the champagne as she sipped it. "Can we get more of this?"

"Complimentary minibars are provided in all VIP rooms, or, if you prefer a social setting, you may venture into the Pailon Oasis, down this hall and to the right. Drinks are served until two a.m."

"Are you kidding me? Alex, we have to go!" She turned and shook him by the shoulders. "I haven't been to a bar in forever!" All the excitement of being in a new place had Lynn giddy and ready for an adventure. And for the first time in as long as she could remember, she wasn't feeling lost or hopeless. She was on a quest and serving a purpose. Why shouldn't she be allowed to let loose?

"Hell yeah, let's do it!"

"Awesome!" she exclaimed. "Brother and sister back at it again." She gave Alex a playful high five before turning back to the concierge and asking, "Where did you say it was?"

"Where is what?"

An awkward silence occurred while Lynn looked at him with incredulity, then she said, "The bar? The one you *just* mentioned?"

The concierge replied, "Complimentary minibars are provided in all VIP rooms, or, if you prefer a social setting, you may venture into the Pailon Oasis, down this hall and to the right. Drinks are served until two a.m."

Squinting her eyes in disgust, Lynn asked, "Are you stupid?"

"They are robots," someone said from behind them.

Lynn turned around and saw the most intimidating, tan-skinned woman standing there, looking like a renegade in a basic black tank top and camo pants with a bag slung over one shoulder and her other hand in her pocket. She had short dark hair that was shaved and faded on the right side and feathered on the other. The shaved side of her head exposed a tattoo of some spiritual symbol that began near the top of her head and had a thin trail of ink that trickled down the right side of her neck and disappeared over her shoulder. Her left arm was also covered in tattoos of various beasts and symbols. All of this, though, was upstaged by her most blatant feature: her right arm was made of metal.

Taking a step forward, the woman addressed the concierge bot. "Sam Nyguyami, checking in."

The bot did its whole cycle again and Lynn cracked up. "That makes sense."

"Wow!" Alex laughed. "No way!"

"I'm Sam," said the woman, offering Lynn a handshake.

"Lynn."

Alex shook her hand next. "Alex. A pleasure."

"Pleasure is mine," Sam insisted as she received her free champagne. Lynn absently wondered where all those drinks were coming from, laughing to herself a bit as she pictured the inside of the concierge bot as a set of tumblers and champagne glasses spinning forever on some infinite turntable.

"So, you are going to Raynor Academy too?" Alex asked.

"At some point." Sam laughed, giving her bag to the second concierge bot. "Right now I'm going to get drunk. Is that something you all do where you are from? Which is ... where, by the way?"

"Grantitan, and yeah, we are pros at that." Lynn assured her. All at once, Lynn was remembering what it was like to live life. For the last year, she had been cooped up in Zach's boot camp from hell, grinding for hours every day in the simulators and depriving herself of everything but rykai, and now that Zach was gone for a night, she could feel herself so ready to release.

"Grantitan, eh? Been there once or twice. I have to say, I've yet to find a corner of the galaxy where a good grog doesn't bring people together."

"True," Alex agreed. "So, what corner are you from, then?"

"Taland, I suppose. I've been all over, though."

"You are from the capital?" Lynn asked.

"Born there, but I can't say I spend a lot of time there. You all hungry? I've gotta get something in me." The mention of food made Lynn's stomach scream. It had been such a long, exhausting trip from Grantitan, and she had been running on adrenaline since they got to Pailon, not realizing just how tired and hungry she was.

"Oh God yeah, I'm starving."

"Yeah, me too," Alex said.

"Well all right." Sam led the way down the hall. "You all been here before?"

"We've never been off Grantitan."

"Really? How'd you like space travel?"

"Sick of it already," Lynn cut in. "It took us two days to get here." It was rough, too. Sometimes it felt okay, but for a few hours the turbulence had felt worse than any boat or plane. A couple times, Alex had gotten sick and Lynn had declared him "space sick." Some of the crew were laughing at them and assured them it was something they would get used to, but Lynn wasn't sure if that would prove to be true.

"You've been here before?" Alex guessed.

"A few times," Sam confirmed. "Pailon is about halfway to everywhere."

"What's the most messed up thing you've seen here?" Lynn asked.

"Ha! Depends on where you compare it to. I saw a guy bite off someone's finger once over a poker game."

"Damn!"

Alex said, "Wow, the most messed up thing I've seen was someone breaking a beer bottle over a guy's head once." Well, Lynn thought, unless you count catching a slab of concrete with your bare hands after a piece of space debris blew up a stadium behind you.

Music that had been distant before became boisterous as they approached the end of the hall and a large screen with the words *Pailon Oasis* etched in digital cursive letters. Beneath the sign was a door barraged by people of all kinds. A large group of patrons loitered in the hall outside the lounge, some of whom were from places Lynn couldn't even guess. She wondered how many of them were Prism hopefuls. This ought to be interesting, she ventured.

4

It was as though they were phasing into another world. All around them, the room was illuminated by soft and colorful lights, and the floor beneath them rippled like the surface of a lake when they stepped onto it, making it appear as though they were walking on water.

"Whoa! Look at this!" Lynn exclaimed, stomping on the ground and activating a series of powerful ripples.

"That's awesome!" Alex said. What a fantastic effect, Lynn marveled as she followed the aquatic simulation all the way up to the massive bar, which was a long glass fish tank filled with exotic fish, coral, and plants. Behind the bar were huge, colorful displays of what must have been every liquor and craft beer in the galaxy.

Sam marched up to the one open seat and called the bartender, a thin blonde woman covered in flashy tattoos.

"What can I get you?" the bartender asked.

"Rum and coke," Sam answered. She spun around and asked, "What do you all drink?"

"I'll take a rum and coke as well," Alex said.

Lynn shouted past Sam to the bartender. "Jameson and ginger please!"

"A whiskey girl, huh?" Sam said.

"Until I die."

The bartender whipped up their drinks and Sam passed them around. She slid off the barstool, thanked the bartender, and motioned for Lynn and Alex to follow her into the booth area, where the floors were dull and normal and the air was filled with the sounds of laughter and the smells of Pailon's delicacies. Sam looked around for a moment, finding that all the booths were full.

"Pretty crowded in here," she said.

"Man, I am starving," Alex complained.

"Hey!" a voice shouted from their left. They turned toward it and saw three men sitting in a circular booth with half-eaten plates of food in front of them and several beer bottles scattered on the table. The one on the left who had called out asked, "Are you here for the academy?"

Lynn shot back, "Who's asking?"

"Us too, come on, come over here and eat with us!"

The man on the right stood up and apologized. "Pardon us, my friend can be very forward. I am Jett Shorin, and these are my mates, Blake Santos and Leon Cravich." Jett came toward them and held out his hand.

"Lynn Palmer," she replied, shaking his hand.

The other two exchanged pleasantries as well and Jett said, "A pleasure to meet you."

"The same to you," Alex returned.

"Here, come eat with us," Jett insisted. Lynn was skeptical at first, but she was hungry as anything and these guys looked normal enough. Except for their clothes. They kind of looked like pretty boys, wearing garments that Lynn could describe only as something she would expect to see in old Victorian-style literature, with their hand-cut tailored vests and slacks, pressed shirts, and pompous accessories. Compared to some of the people she had seen here so far though, this seemed a mild anomaly.

Lynn, Alex, and Sam obliged and slid into one side of the semi-circle booth. Soon, a drone flew over and took their order. While they waited for the food, Lynn crushed the first whiskey in her traditional manner. She soon realized that it had been awhile since she had drunk significantly, as she started to feel a good buzz.

"So," Sam said, "You guys are Prism hopefuls also?"

"Yeah," Jett confirmed. "We just arrived hours ago, and you?"

"More like minutes ago."

The forward one, Blake, jumped in. "Yeah, you look a little fresh off the drop. Where are you from?"

"My sister and I are from Grantitan," Alex answered.

"Ah, Grantitan! Plenty of excitement out that way, eh?"

"I guess so."

Sam asked, "You guys are Corithian, right?"

“Very good,” Leon said. “Have you been there before?”

“Sam has been everywhere,” Lynn said expertly.

Before they knew it, the food arrived, and it was glorious. Lynn ate so fast she nearly choked; it was one of the best burgers she had ever eaten.

Everyone ate and laughed and became twirled up in the levity of the evening. These men weren’t terrible; they were lively, somewhat funny, and objectively pretty handsome. Especially Jett, with his dark, brooding hair, chiseled face, and deep, powerful blue eyes. He was definitely the leader of their outfit, Lynn decided. It was obvious by the way he spoke, the way he carried himself, and even by the precision of his speech. An aura of confidence surrounded him that made him seem to be a natural leader. It was funny, really, because most people that Lynn knew spoke ill of the Corithian people, but Lynn never gave too much credibility to it. Historically, it made some sense, as the Corithians had selfishly remained neutral when the Grothians first attacked outer Sari, while every other planet in the galaxy joined forces to fight. Ever since, the Corithians had remained friendly, but refused to get involved with Sari, either in politics or military. Some people said they were self-interested snobs. At the moment, Lynn could care less.

Something was poking her curiosity though, and Lynn had to ask, “So, how did you guys know we were here for the academy?”

“You seemed to fit the bill,” Blake said.

“We look that out of place?”

“Actually,” Leon interjected, “My mate here was sayin’ you had a fine ass and he was asking us how to get you to come over here.”

“Now hey, hey,” Blake defended. “I did say that you seemed like the Prism type, and yeah, I did say that, but it’s not misogynistic. I’m just saying, objectively, that’s a nice caboose!”

“Not misogynistic at all,” Alex cut in. “I appreciate the compliment.” The table went into an uproar.

“Seriously, though, we all kinda look like badasses, right?” Lynn said.

"Of a certain persuasion, yes," Jett agreed. "I have seen plenty of colorful individuals in here, though."

"You guys met any other Prism cadets?" Alex wondered.

"Just you folks," Leon said.

"Then again, we supposed not all of them would be good company," Blake reminded them. "After all, this shindig is a competition."

"You forget about that," Sam said. "Comin' up is all about teamwork."

Lynn asked, "Are you a soldier?" Stupid question, she scolded herself. Of course Sam was a soldier, everyone here was ... except her and Alex.

"Was a marine. Worked my way up to fighter pilot. Wouldn't trade it for the world. You?" Great, now she had to explain herself. Great going, Lynn. There was an awkward silence for a second while Lynn racked her brain. Why hadn't she come up with an answer for this?

Alex came to her aid. "Lynn and I are horses of a different color. We had the 'pleasure' of learning rykai from Zach Brine. Yup, he saw something in us. At first, it was brutal, but you get used to it." Thank God for his graceful dodge. The last thing either of them wanted was for their competition to know that they had no military experience. Zach had told them parts of this test would be team based, but individual performance would be heavily weighted as well. If the Corithians or Sam or anyone else found out their secrets, Lynn was certain they would be ganged up on and taken out quickly. The best thing they could do was make allies and try to blend in until they understood things better.

"I hear Zach Brine is kinda washed-up," Sam scoffed. "Word on the street is he is hittin' the booze pretty hard."

Feeling defensive, Lynn said, "Whoever said that is an idiot. Zach is not washed-up, trust me."

"Okay, don't get riled up, that's just what I heard."

"Anyway," Lynn digressed, drawing the attention away from her credentials, "What about you guys? What's your story?"

"We are soldiers," Leon explained. "Taught rykai by Captain Solari of the Corithian special infantry."

"Oh yeah? What was your specialty?" Lynn asked, hoping for a peek at her potential opponents.

However, Jett was not to be fooled. "I venture that you will be able to guess it once we all enter the simulators."

Sam changed the subject. "Hey, you guys want more drinks?" When everyone emphatically agreed, she went and got another round from the bar.

"I'll be right back," Lynn said, taking the opportunity to steal away to the side door she had seen on her way in and go outside for a smoke. With one drag she remembered another thing she had been missing in the last year: these precious few moments of peace and pleasure. Lucas had shown her a lot about inner peace, but if she was being honest, there was nothing like the clarity of nicotine and a good buzz. She felt herself loosen and exhale the rigidness of Zach's training.

But then a gaggle of rough-looking types came out of the bar, smoking and joking nearby, ridiculing one of the guys in their group, and being quite annoying. She was tuning out whatever they were saying, but one of them had the most incessant laugh, like a parrot repeating a hyena. She was about to move away from the area when one of them said something that stopped her cold.

"I think the Fox would kill you if he knew you said that."

Some of them laughed and another said, "He can sniff out pussies, you know."

"Shut up!" one of them demanded. "You don't know the situation."

"I don't know," one of his cohorts said. "I think Toshiba is right. If you are going to speak ill of the Fox behind his back, you had best be prepared for the consequences."

"He hears everything, you know," another guy chipped in.

"In fact, we should rough you up for that, or the Fox will kill us, too."

The men closed in around one of their comrades as he pleaded, assuring them that he was only joking. Lynn couldn't listen to this anymore. In an instant, her anxiety was threatening to overtake her, to erase the progress she had made in the last year. There was no way it was a coincidence; these men were talking about the same guy, the same "fox" who had murdered her parents. What else could they mean? There couldn't be another person like that on Pailon; there was just no way. Or were these men from Grantitan? Either way, she couldn't think about it. There was no way of knowing and even she wasn't foolish enough to ask these dangerous men in an unknown land a question like this one.

When she went back inside, the only thing on her mind was drinking herself into oblivion, and the fresh Jameson sitting on the table in front of her seat was a perfect start.

"Got you a drink," Alex said as she returned.

"You rock," she replied, pounding the first half of it. Already she was tipsy, and this was likely not going to be good, but Lynn didn't care.

As she was standing there, tipping her drink back, Sam looked at her waist and commented, "That's a nice tool you have there."

Looking down, she realized Sam was admiring one of her knives.

"Oh, yeah, check it out," Lynn bragged, unsheathing the beastly blade and laying it on the table.

Sam picked up the knife and turned it around in her hands. "You could kill a bitch real good with this." She ran her finger along the blade, then handed it back to Lynn.

"It's impressive, but if you want a proper blade, check this one out," Blake said, placing his on the table. Soon everyone joined in, laughing, drinking, and comparing steel.

Lynn held Blake's knife in her hand, examining it, and asked, "How many people have you shanked with this? It's got no teeth."

"Well, that way is better for sticking in the back," Blake said. "Pull the piece under the—"

As he was halfway through saying it, Lynn found the lever and clicked it, transforming the smooth edges into tissue-shredding shark's teeth.

"Damn!" Lynn admired, kicking back more whiskey, and putting the knife back where she found it. There was such limited technology on

Grantitan; Lynn was realizing it the more she saw here. How was she supposed to know what was coming? Zach could only prepare her so much.

"He acts like he can hit something with it," Leon jabbed at Blake.

"I can hit more than you, can't I?" Blake shot back.

"With this one?" Sam asked, holding up Blake's knife, now reverted to the smooth edges. "I'd like to see that."

"All right," Blake said, standing up from the booth. "You're on, mate." He took his knife and examined the room for a moment. Looking toward the corner of the lounge, just a couple booths away from where they were sitting, he held out the knife and pointed toward an open area with high tables and two big wooden targets standing in front of a long wall with an assortment of posters plastered along it. A group of three burley men were throwing axes at one of the targets. Of course they were, Lynn thought, amused. If they allowed the drunken patrons of the Pailon Oasis to throw deadly weapons inside the lounge, it said a lot about why Zach had advised them not to leave the hotel.

The others watched with excitement as Sam stood up and accepted his challenge. "All right, you better put up or shut up then. Who else is in?"

"Hell yeah!" Lynn accepted, quite eager to do it. Throwing was one of the skills she had practiced the most while she was with Zach, because it played perfectly into her style and she loved the finesse of it. Here was a chance for her to validate herself with this new group.

"Why not?" Jett said, rolling his eyes. "It seems like a smart idea."

They all migrated over to the table closest to the targets and set their drinks down. As they settled, the axe throwers were finishing up. It dawned on Lynn, as she sipped her whiskey, how buzzed she was. Her ears felt warm when she tipped her head back and her mind was starting to get that fuzz, that welcomed feeling of slipping into careless levity.

Sam stepped up to take the first shot.

As she unsheathed her knife, Blake said, "Let's see it then."

With perfect power and form, Sam flung the vicious steel into the wood, less than an inch from the bullseye. Everyone cheered and she took a bow.

"Your turn, slick," she said as she returned to the table and took a drink. Sam had quite the swagger, Lynn noticed. Both the way she moved and the way she spoke was confident and smooth. She was what they would call an initiator, the kind of person that made things happen when she came into the room.

"Not bad," Blake admitted, taking his place in front of the target. "But how about this one!" A flick of the wrist and Blake sent his knife soaring, planting it an inch or so to the left of the bullseye.

"Oh man! That one looks a bit far away, man!" Lynn taunted.

"Yeah, yeah, warm-up shot. Let's see you do better."

"Yeah Palmer," Sam said. "Let's see what you got."

Stepping up to the target, Lynn bent down and snapped up the knife in the front of her boot, a smaller, lighter knife perfect for throwing. For showmanship, she flicked the blade open and closed a couple times before grabbing the tip of the blade with her other hand and throwing it gracefully at the hunk of wood. A perfect bullseye.

"Nice job, sis!" Alex cheered.

"That's how you do it!" Lynn postured, pointing to her bullseye. Dancing her way back to the table, she polished off her whiskey and slid the glass to the center of the table. By now, the liquor was soaking in and she was feeling quite drunk, but it was of no concern to her.

Looking over at Alex, Lynn said, "Hey, bro, go get us some shots, huh?"

"Yeah, shots!" Leon agreed with enthusiasm.

"All right," Alex agreed. "Be back in a shake."

Blake and Sam both took turns at the target, neither hitting the mark. Then it was Jett's turn to throw and Lynn watched him as he went over to the target and pulled the knives out of the wood. He laid them carefully on the table beside them before drawing his own knife and stepping into position.

"Now," Jett said, "Allow me to demonstrate a proper throw."

And what a proper throw it was. Another perfect bullseye. Everyone cheered and Jett returned to the table with a sly grin on his face. That confidence of his, the way he walked and the looks he gave, just the very presence that Jett portrayed was interesting to Lynn. It was odd, really, because nothing he was doing was particularly unordinary, but still, she found herself gravitating toward him.

"Not bad," Lynn said. "I guess my first impression of you was wrong."

"In what way?"

"Kinda thought you looked like a pretty boy."

"Who says he isn't?" Blake joked, having overheard.

"Yeah," Leon jumped in. "Why do you think he needs us?"

Jett scratched his head and laughed. "Pay them no mind."

"Shots for everyone!" Alex announced as he returned to the table. A standing ovation was offered in return as everyone grabbed their shots and stood around the table.

Jett offered a toast. "Tomorrow we must work for the future, but tonight, we celebrate new friends."

"To friendship!" Leon seconded, quickly followed by the rest of the table. They clinked their glasses and tipped the liquor into their mouths.

"Hey, Blakey boy," Sam teased. "Bet you fifty credits you can't get a hit."

As the boys were cracking up over his new nickname, Blake accepted her challenge. "All right, lass, next round is on you."

Blake stepped up to make his throw, but Lynn wasn't paying attention. Instead, she returned her attention to Jett and asked, "So, what's with the clothes?" Wow, she thought, that sounded drunk and stupid.

She saw the confused look on his face and corrected herself, doing as poorly as her first attempt. "I meant, why are you dressed like that?"

"How should I be dressed?"

"I don't know, just ... people on Grantitan don't dress like that. Never mind."

Embarrassed at herself, Lynn returned her attention to the game. Blake had missed and now Sam was taking a turn.

"Double or nothing says I can hit it," Sam was saying.

"You're on," Blake accepted.

Perhaps sensing her discomfort, Jett changed the subject. "So, you are from Grantitan, right? I admit, I have never been there. What is it like?"

"It's okay, I guess," Lynn replied dispassionately. She had no desire to discuss that rotten place right now. Part of her was aware of her rudeness, but she felt only partially in control of it. The Jameson was doing a lot of the talking.

Sam smirked as she stepped up to the line and, without even aiming beyond the general direction of the target, lifted her metal arm and triggered something with her left hand, firing a swordlike projectile at breakneck speed toward the wall. Upon impact, the blade split the target clean in half and sent wood splinters flying everywhere and knives clattering to the floor. Just for drama, when Sam turned to face the Corithians, she slammed her knife into the table so it stuck and swayed side to side momentarily right in front of Blake and Leon.

"How about that?" she boasted, slamming her hands on the table before chugging the rest of her drink. The men laughed and held their glasses up for a toast and everyone was high fiving her. A few people from the nearby tables were staring.

"Can't beat that," Alex laughed.

"Hey, hey!" Leon motioned. "How about one more round, for the road?"

"One more," Sam agreed. "On Blakey boy."

"Yeah, yeah," he grumbled as everyone laughed.

As Blake made his way to the bar, Lynn finished off one of the drinks in front of her and slammed the glass on the table with little concern for whether it was hers. Looking down at the glass, she laughed a little to herself. This definitely wasn't good.

When she looked up, she happened to catch a glance of those assholes from outside. They were sitting at the bar now, laughing it up and enjoying each other's company. Who the hell did they think they were, anyway, prancing around like regular guys?

"Gotta piss," Sam informed no one in particular. "Be right back."

"Me too," Lynn realized.

"We'll keep the booth warm," Alex said.

Sam started across the room and Lynn scurried after her. The whole time, she kept her eyes on the guys at the bar. They didn't seem concerned with Blake, who was ordering drinks near them. Something else she noticed was that the one they had just been kicking around outside was with them, acting as if nothing had happened. Just another day in a culture of violence. Was it like this everywhere? Had it always been, or was this merely, as she suspected, the by-product of the Grothian war?

Lynn turned back around and noticed Sam sliding through the crowd.

"Wait up!" Lynn called, but Sam had already gone into the bathroom. Suddenly it was really crowded. Lynn tried to push through, but it was hard to do anything with all these stupid people hanging out in a narrow space by the bathroom. She absolutely hated that. Apparently, people on Pailon were just as stupid as the people in the dive bars in Calivia. Why would anyone choose to be over here? Specifically, there was one couple dancing together right next to the door, drinks in hand, bodies flailing around. No wonder the floor was wet.

"Hey!" Lynn yelled, aggressively tapping the guy on the shoulder. "Excuse me, you are blocking the hall!"

"Who the hell are you?" The guy asked, whizzing around and holding his arms out in protest, spilling some of his drink in the process and adding another layer of filth to the floor. When he turned, Lynn could see that he was not human. He had some scaly textures to his face and his pupils were vertical ovals, like exaggerated snake eyes.

"Excuse me," Lynn repeated.

The guy brushed her off and went back to dancing.

"She said excuse me!" Sam said rudely to the reptilian man as she emerged from the crowd. One look at Sam's metal arm and huge knife on her hip, and the man was feeling much more flexible.

"Pssh ... whatever," he brushed them off, tugging his girlfriend's wrist and dragging her away from the area.

"I could've taken him," Lynn said.

"Yeah," Sam laughed. "I know."

She thought she sensed some sarcasm in Sam's voice, but chose to ignore it in favor of a more pressing issue.

As Sam came toward her, Lynn grabbed her forearm and said, "Hey, hey, hold on."

"What's wrong with you?" Sam sneered, pulling her arm away.

"You see those guys at the bar? Near Blake, four guys."

"What about them?"

"I saw them outside. They were saying something about a person called the Fox. You've traveled the galaxy, right? Ever heard of someone like that?"

Sam closed her eyes for a second, contemplating Lynn's drunken inquiry, and responded, "Can't say I have."

"How about the Mushida Clan? ARMs Corporation?"

"What the—" Sam said, sounding serious. Tugging on Lynn's arm, Sam leaned in really close and warned, "Don't bring that up in here. That's a good way to get killed." Then she stormed off toward the table.

That got dark pretty fast. Honestly, it should have been obvious what Sam was telling her. After all, people like this had murdered her parents, they killed Marcus and his wife in front of a child, and undoubtedly committed thousands of other atrocities over the years. It was just so hard seeing them and not knowing the connections and yearning so badly for revenge.

Frustrated, she went into the bathroom and tried to brush it off.

When she returned to the table, it seemed as though everyone was finishing up. That was quite all right, she decided. She was beginning to not feel so well.

"Are you okay?" Alex asked.

"I think I am going to go to bed," Lynn answered.

"Yes," Jett agreed. "I venture it is time for us to go as well. Tomorrow will surely be arduous, and we must be rested."

Sam pounded the last of her drink and said, "Yup. It's been real, boys and girls."

"Nice meeting you, lass," Blake said, waving goodbye.

"See you all tomorrow," Alex chimed in.

"Later," Lynn managed to say. She was leaning on the table, feeling very dizzy and lightheaded, and her stomach was beginning to churn.

Alex noticed her discomfort and stood up beside her, placing his hand on her back. As he leaned down to look at her, he asked, "Do you want me to walk up with you?"

Embarrassed, she didn't answer right away. Normally she could hold her own, but apparently she had gotten carried away.

Alex read her expression and suggested, "Yeah, let me go up with you."

"Sorry," Lynn apologized as they left the bar.

"Don't worry about it," Alex reassured her. "We've been training so hard. I guess we don't have as much tolerance as we used to."

A few minutes and one sickly elevator ride later, they arrived at Lynn's room. Alex followed her inside, turning on the lights as they entered the room.

Lynn dodged into the bathroom, where she splashed water on her face and leaned over the sink.

"Are you going to be okay?"

"I'll be fine. Just need sleep."

"Make sure that you drink plenty of water. You don't want to be hungover tomorrow. Anyway, text me if you need anything. I'm going to head back to my room."

"Okay, thanks."

"Good night, sis."

"Night."

Lynn took her brother's advice and pounded a glass of water. Feeling dizzy, she collapsed back over the sink. Man, she had never felt this sick, and what horrible timing. She was so mad at herself, letting her anxiety take hold of her and letting herself lose track of her inhibitions.

Oh well, it's done, she told herself. No use feeling sorry; tomorrow was too important. She had trained for over a year for this and nothing was going to stop her.

Getting herself together, Lynn drank another glass of water and took a cold shower. She was still feeling sick, but it was getting better. She would sleep the rest of this off and everything would be good tomorrow. At least, that's what she hoped.

5

It was approximately six a.m. when Zach heard a knock at his door. He glanced at his watch and waited a second until the knock happened again, more obnoxious this time.

"Zach, what are you doing in there?" Rachel shouted. "You better not be sleeping!"

For kicks, Zach leaned back on the white metal bars of his private terrace and took a long puff of his cigarette, ignoring her for a moment. Rachel was always so intense. If she wasn't early, she was late. If it wasn't perfect, it wasn't good. In many ways, Zach was the same, but according to his watch, there was still plenty of time for solitude.

Again, Rachel knocked and called out, "Come on, Zach! I know you are in there!"

"All right! Christ!" Zach said, hustling over to the door and allowing her in.

"What are you doing?" she said, wasting no time. "The cadets will be down there in thirty minutes. We need to check in with the dropship crew."

"Yeah, yeah, just give me a minute."

The cigarette still dangling from his mouth, Zach meandered back out through the sliding glass doors onto the terrace and gazed out at the beautiful purple and orange hues of the morning sky. The holograms all around him were so clever; if one didn't know that they were on a space station, they would never know the difference.

"I'm pretty sure you can't smoke in here." Rachel patrolled the room, examining Zach's alleged readiness.

Zach grinned, taking a long drag. "Then why have terraces at all?"

"To enjoy all that fresh artificial air."

"Yeah," Zach laughed. "The only thing fresh in this place is the bull crap."

"You are so cynical in your old age."

"Just real. Old age comes with wisdom, you know. Among other ... proficiencies."

Rachel rolled her eyes. "Not according to what I've heard."

Zach watched her from the terrace and took another drag, wondering how she could still be so beautiful at age forty-seven. Here he was, on the brink of decline, and she was still vibrant and youthful, even in her full Prism attire. For a brief moment a deep lust overtook him, redirecting all of his thoughts to the idea of him and Rachel between the sheets. His desire wasn't even that genuine, he knew, but it had been so lonely after Emelia.

A moment later, Rachel followed up. "I still don't get why you told Emelia about Alexis." Yeah, he didn't either. Guilt, Zach supposed.

"She deserved to know."

"Come on. Everyone in our line of work strays. We are away for months at a time. I don't see casual sex as infidelity, I'm sorry. At least, not in this context."

Although Zach really didn't want to go there, he knew Rachel well enough to know she would harp on it until he satiated her curiosity, so he answered. "Emelia thought it was."

"Yeah, because you told her. I'm saying most people have casual sex because otherwise we'd go insane traveling through space and being away from home months or even years at a time. No one blames you, except that you had to blab."

"Sure, whatever," Zach said halfheartedly. "Not too many other ways to relax out here."

Although for Zach, sex was never casual. Like everything else he did, he put his entire soul into it. That was one of the major problems with Emelia; once they fell out of love, he couldn't do it anymore.

"Yeah. Anyway, I don't get it, but it's not my business. Also, how long does it take you to smoke one cigarette? Come on, I don't want to be late."

"We still have twenty minutes," Zach said, putting out his cigarette on the outside of the railing and flicking it down onto the street. As he came inside, Zach changed the subject. "So, who did you sponsor this year, anyone I would know?"

He had wanted to ask that last night, when they had been in the officer's lounge with a group of colleagues, but by the time he got around to it they were already several martinis into the night and business had been long left behind.

"Well, I'd give that a hard maybe. I found an entourage of Corithian boys with spectacular talent. You might recognize one of them, albeit by name only, I suspect."

"Yeah, Corithians tend to be fairly isolationist. Who is it?"

"Jett Raeliegh Shorin, and his friends, who you wouldn't know, Blake Santos and Leon Cravich."

Zach was taken by surprise. "Shorin. Wait, you mean, as in, *Baron* Shorin?"

"As in, prince of the Corithian province of Zalia, son of Baron Clive Shorin."

"Wow. Why is the baron's son interested in joining Prism?"

There could be no doubt this was huge news, whatever the reason for Jett's appearance at Raynor Academy. Corinth was a unique and amazing planet made up of many provinces, each one ruled by a baron and his council. Although the Corithians were drastically different from the Sarians in terms of government and belief systems, they had always been friendly with the Sarians. Still, the Corithians were proud and individualistic people, deeply rooted in tradition and preferring to work parallel to their allies instead of directly with them. If Zach recalled correctly, the Prism elites had spoken to Clive many times, attempting to persuade him to allow Prism to train some of his most promising soldiers and allow his province of Zalia to work with Sari toward mutual goals. Clive was cordial, but always firm: Zalia was quite content to go about it as they always had. Zach would love to know what had changed.

"There is quite a story there, actually. I'll fill you in on the way down though; we really ought to get going."

"Yeah, okay. Wow, Rachel, you always surprise me."

"I hope you brought some decent cadets yourself. I wouldn't want to embarrass you."

"Ha, we will see who is embarrassed, won't we?"

Zach slung his bags over his shoulder and followed Rachel out of the room. What an interesting year this was turning out to be. Zach had found a man who could very possibly be the last living Alderian and taught him how to channel the golem, and Rachel had somehow rustled up the renowned Baron Clive Shorin's son and convinced him to join Prism. What other surprises would Zach encounter this year at Raynor Academy? He simply couldn't wait to find out.

6

Alex slept surprisingly well; all things considered. It must have been the rum. Alex had forgotten how great it was to kick back with good people and strong drinks. Thoughts of the jokes and the fun of the previous night flashed through his mind as Alex showered and dressed for the day. Hopefully more people in Prism were like those guys, Alex thought. If they were, he was going to fit in just fine. It was so important that Alex remembered to make positive connections and keep his spirits up, lest he succumb to the incredible weight of his destiny. What he was to become was too important for him to fail. This fact was not lost on him; the passionate sense of purpose and incredible urgency that came with it had driven his thoughts for most of the previous year.

When he was packed and ready, Alex made his way down to the desk and waited for as long as he felt comfortable for his sister. Soon, he would be risking being late himself, so he sent her a text asking, "Are you almost ready?" Five more minutes passed and she finally answered, "10 minutes." Laughing to himself, he wondered how hungover she was. Not wanting to be late, Alex decided to go on his own and sent Lynn a text that said, "I'm going to the hangar, meet you there."

There was a sort of ruckus going on at the back of the crowd when Alex arrived at the hangar. At least two hundred people, presumably all Prism candidates, were gathered near one of the dropships, and most of them were turning their attention to a small group in the back, where some type of confrontation seemed to be happening. Alex recognized Sam from a distance and joined her.

"What's going on?" Alex asked. He noticed that Jett was one of the people everyone was watching. Blake and Leon were behind him and, facing Jett with his back to the crowd, was a cocky soldier with a brutish build and a spiked blond haircut. The guy was posturing, puffing out his chest and trying to intimidate Jett.

"Oh, hey. No idea. This guy just started harassing Jett, says he is a prince," Sam explained. A prince? As in, royalty? Alex wondered why someone like that would care to join Prism. Certainly he had other priorities to tend to, and besides, he would have other people to fight in his place. Alex must have been missing something.

Jett didn't seem scared of the man. He calmly stood his ground and said, "I believe we got off on the wrong foot. What do you say if we do not assume each other's intentions and have ourselves a proper competition?"

The man snorted, addressing the crowd. "Anyone else smell a set up?"

"Like they are going to turn down the baron's son," a woman agreed.

Leon interjected, "Baron Shorin has nothing to do with us being here."

"Leon, please," Jett corrected him. "We have no qualms here. Just as the rest of you, we are here to compete for a chance to join Prism and represent Corinth."

"Kill him in his sleep," someone mumbled from Jett's left.

"Yeah, Brock, forget it," another person said. "We'll kill him first."

"Hey!" Alex jumped out of the crowd and confronted Brock. "What is your deal, man?"

"Mind your business, boy," Brock threatened.

"Rather rude, don't you think?" Blake commented. "To kill a man while he snoozes? What, are you afraid to fight us man to man?"

"Aye," Sam Nyguyami agreed, coming forward from the crowd. Standing before the Corithians, Sam looked Jett up and down and put her metal hand down roughly on his shoulder and said, "I mean, come on." With her hand still there, she turned her head to the crowd. "When I kill a prince, I want to brag about it." People seemed to enjoy that and started clamoring among themselves again, wondering who this new, half-metal prince slayer was.

"Hey, watch yourself," Leon warned Sam as he went to remove her hand.

Sam backed off on her own. "Relax, man. We are friends, remember?"

Alex weighed in, addressing the group. "Listen, we are all from different places and different backgrounds, right? We all want the same thing, though. So, let's keep it civil."

"I'll be civil just as long as it suits me," Brock answered. "Just like all of you. When it comes time though, I won't go easy. Prince or no prince."

"I look forward to competing with you," Jett said.

Brock narrowed his eyes and began to stare down Jett, but his bravado was interrupted by the arrival of Lynn, who walked awkwardly up to the scene. "Hey guys! Are we boarding yet?"

"Ad—Lynn, geez! I thought you were going to be late," Alex greeted her as she came up beside him. He understood the new name, but at the same time, changing her name didn't change the past, right? All it did was confuse everyone, and it would be a while before he was used to it.

"Are you kidding? No way I'd be late. After everything we did to get here ..." She trailed off as she noticed Jett and Brock and the tension in the hangar.

Jett refused to look away and Brock finally ended the contest. "Pfft! Like I said, we'll see what happens."

"What's his problem?" Lynn whispered to Alex.

"Some people are worked up, I don't know. I think they are threatened by Jett."

Having overheard them, Blake answered, "Because they are bloody scared of us, that's why."

Before Lynn could reply, Zach's booming voice silenced the room. "At-ten-*tion*!" At the sight of Zach marching down the ramp from the Prism dropship, everyone turned to face him and stood straight, forming fluidly into two straight lines in front of the ship. Alex and Lynn were among the last to conform, stumbling into the second row and mimicking the postures of their peers.

Zach was in a full navy-blue Prism uniform, including a long peacoat tailored with gold trim and buttons and fitted shoulder pads. On his left breast, secured to his coat, was the emblem of Prism; connected to this was a thick black leather shoulder pad from which a long, black, cloak-like tassel hung down to Zach's lower back. This cloak, Zach had told Alex, was awarded only to those who had reached the highest achievements in Prism, and bestowed the title of "Black Rose." Beneath and around the emblem of Prism were Zach's many "seeds," the badges of honor awarded by Prism. For Alex, and probably everyone in the hangar, Zach was an inspiration as he stood there before them, symbolizing their hopes and aspirations.

"My name is Zach Brine, but from this point forward, you will call me 'Instructor Brine' or 'sir.' These are my colleagues, Instructor Mccginneas and Instructor Terif. You will show them the same respect that you will undoubtedly show me."

Zach began to pace back and forth as he continued. "Today there are two hundred twenty of your sorry asses. Some of you are here because you have achieved greatness in your fields, others of you for unique and marvelous talents, and some of you, well, just because you are lucky or well connected. You all know which ones you are and the rest of us will soon find out. The trials ahead of you are complex and dangerous. You will not be helped, we will not coddle you, and you will not be comforted. Some of you will get injured, maimed, or even killed. Those of you who survive and pass the tests will become legends. Do you all understand the gravity of getting on this ship?"

"Yes, sir!" everyone yelled in tandem.

"Once you get on this ship, there is no turning back. Anyone who is not up for the task need only walk away, go back to the Pailon Hub, and pick up a one-way ticket to whatever garbage heap you came from, on me. This is the only charity you will get from me; do you understand?"

"Yes, sir!"

"Anyone want to bow out now?"

"No, sir!"

"No one?" Zach halted his patrol in front of a blonde woman with a prison barcode tattooed on her neck. Adopting his most misanthropic expression, he scoffed at her. "You think you are tough? You'll be crying and begging me to put you in a cell in less than a week."

Skipping five cadets, Zach stopped again in front of Brock and said, "Your stature means nothing. I've seen a million meatheads come and a million meatheads die in a fit of frivolous bravado. Don't get used to your seat on that ship." Though he shifted uncomfortably, Brock was wise enough to take his chastening in silence. All of them were. After all, Zach's reputation preceded him.

Continuing to flaunt his disdain for the cadets, Zach stopped in front of another man and commented on his slicked back hair. "What is this, a high school prom? There is no time to waste on glamour in my academy. The sight of you disgusts me. It reminds me why I find your generation grotesque and insufferable."

Deciding that he was through evaluating them, Zach returned to the bottom of the ramp, where he said, "Well, then, let's go! What are you waiting for? From the right, two at a time, onto the ship!" Cadets began filing into the ship quickly and efficiently and all the while Zach berated them. "Come on, hurry up now! Remember, if you get on this ship, there is no turning around! Cowards, dimwits, and buffoons do not waste my time! Quit now and spare us all the embarrassment!"

It went on like that for several minutes. As Alex entered the dimly lit, tightly packed dropship, he felt an ominous twinge in the pit of his stomach. Though he was no stranger to Zach's belligerence, this time was different. This test was real, and everything rode on it.

No one spoke as the last cadets funneled into their seats and the instructors came up the ramp behind them. The air was thick with anticipation; clearly everyone felt the pressure of the performance that awaited them at Raynor Academy.

The dropship ramp slid into the floor and the doors closed behind Zach as he entered the cabin and made his way up to the front of the ship. While he progressed through the crowded seats, Zach provided a brief synopsis of the journey ahead. "We will dock inside Sal Brigande's cruiser,

Leviathan, in approximately twenty minutes. I know, you wish we could ride in this sardine can for the entire journey, but I'm afraid that without lightspeed, this vessel would take a lifetime to get where we are going. Once we are on the *Leviathan*, we will use the lightspeed lanes to travel to the coordinates of Gran Karisu. There, we will pile back into this dropship and descend into the atmosphere. Raynor Academy is located in a remote location on Gran Karisu. You will be given further instructions once we reach the planet. The entire journey will take about eighteen hours, so I recommend that you get some rest while we are at lightspeed and prepare for the trials ahead. Any questions?"

No one dared speak.

"Very well," Zach concluded. "Then let us go." He tapped on the door at the front of the dropship and someone opened it from the other side. "Let's get this thing flying," he ordered, passing through the door and into the cockpit area. The other two instructors followed him, and the door shut behind them. A moment later the engine roared and the cabin began to shake. Alex glanced around as the dropship lifted off, observing the various expressions of his peers. Most seemed apprehensive, some were progressively more nervous, and a few seemed totally at ease, like they had done this before. Even in the midst of everything, a few cadets still continued to give dirty looks to Jett, Blake, and Leon. Hopefully it would pass once they got into the test and everyone could work together.

After several minutes of light shaking, engines revving, and the cabin turning, the dropship suddenly thrust forward, momentarily gluing the cadets to their seats as it burst into flight and rocketed out of the Pailon Space Station. *Well,* Alex thought*, this is it, let the trials begin.*

7

Order was the primary directive of the officers who awaited them in the docking bay of the *Leviathan*. Each cadet was ordered out of the dropship quickly, hurled their gear, and made to form into neat lines. Everyone tried to avoid eye contact with Zach for fear of targeted reprisal. This Zach seemed different than the one Lynn had known up until now. In fairness, he had told them it would be this way, but it still surprised her.

"Listen up!" Zach demanded as the last cadets received their bags. "We will be on this vessel for about fourteen hours. You will find tags attached to your bags; on these tags is a number. That number is your room assignment. You'll forgive the lack of privacy; I'm afraid the dormitories are a tad crowded given the number of you. Don't worry though, most of you won't last. There is a dining hall and other facilities that you may use, however, stay out of any areas marked restricted, as those are for officers and crew members only. Am I making myself clear?"

"Yes, sir!" the group answered.

"Good. We wouldn't want anyone expelled for wandering curiosity, would we?"

Rachel stepped forward and added, "And don't screw each other in the showers. There are only a few of them and we all have to use them and so does the crew. Anyone caught doing anything in the bathrooms other than pissing, brushing their teeth, or washing their grimy ass will be disciplined."

"We say that every year," Zach followed up. "Yet every year someone can't keep it to themselves. Listen well: if that happens, the whole group will be punished."

"So just to summarize: no screwing, no masturbating, no smoking, no drugs, no board games, no sewing circles. Pissing, teeth brushing, and washing. Do you understand?" Rachel asked.

"Yes, sir!"

"Finally, do not talk to the crew. They have jobs to do and they don't need your stupid asses distracting them. Half of you are has-beens to be, and nothing that you say needs to be heard by anyone anyway. Are my expectations clear?" Zach pressed them.

"Yes, sir!"

"You are dismissed."

Everyone broke ranks and began heading out of the docking bay and into the main arterial hallway of the *Leviathan*. This walkway was wide with tall ceilings and had warm white lights every six feet or so along the length of its walls. On either side there were periodic doors that led to different parts of the ship. The hallway itself extended for miles in a sort of oval around the entire perimeter of the great starship.

As soon as they were out of the bay, Lynn felt comfortable to speak to Alex. "Can you believe we are really here?"

"It still seems like a dream, all of it," Alex admitted.

"When we were riding up here, I was trying to picture Gran Karisu. I wonder if it will be like any of the simulated biomes that Zach had us fight in?"

"I can't even imagine it. I mean, before the simulator, I would have never pictured Alder. It's like, you know there are other planets, but most people never actually travel to them, you know? We actually get to do that now."

"I know, it's incredible. A little scary, too."

"Yeah." Alex trailed off for a moment, then said, "So, how are you feeling?"

Embarrassed, Lynn answered, "A little woozy, but I'll live."

"We went hard last night. Even I am feeling it a bit."

"It was fun, though."

Alex laughed. "Yeah, those guys were all right."

They came to a door that most of the cadets were going into labeled "Quad," and followed everyone through it. On the other side was an amazing circular room furnished with dozens of tables and chairs, couches, armchairs, and hologram televisions. A huge blue and green pattern of Leviathan, the great Greek water serpent, was monogrammed into grayish-white floors and complemented by Greek-inspired art and décor garnishing the walls and tables.

"Someone has a fetish," Lynn joked as she admired the room.

Cadets were coming into the massive quad from behind them and to the right of them. It seemed the quad was a central room, around which the main hallway wrapped, and each of the room's six doors led to one of the many junctions in the ship's pathways. Most cadets came in and started examining the maps near the doors, and some just threw their bags down by a couch and crashed.

"Do you want to find the dorms and put our stuff down?" Alex suggested.

"Yeah. I am starving, they have food, right?" Lynn suddenly recalled that she hadn't had time for breakfast.

"I think so."

They were crossing the room toward the crowd in front of the maps when they were flagged down by Blake. "Hey!" As they looked his way, Blake pointed to their left and said, "The dorms are through that door."

"Awesome, thanks," Alex said as he and Lynn approached the table where Blake sat with Leon and Jett.

"Did you guys already drop your bags?" Lynn was surprised.

"Yep, we went straight there. There were signs in the hall," Blake said.

"So, what do you think of this ship?" Leon asked.

Alex answered, "It's pretty incredible."

"Are you all scared yet?" Lynn joked. "No turning back now, huh?"

"Anyone who is not a fool is apprehensive," Jett said. "This trial has a reputation for depravity."

"Yeah, we are nervous too," Alex agreed. "Hey ... I'm just curious, what was all that about you being a prince? Is that true?"

Remembering the morning's odd interaction, Lynn asked, "Wait, a prince? What are you talking about?"

"Before you got to the hangar this morning, some people were saying that Jett was a prince and that he didn't earn his spot here." Quickly, Alex put his hands up and corrected himself. "Not that I think that. It is just what they were saying. I'm just curious if your dad is really a king?"

Jett laughed. "Not a king, a baron, and yes, technically I am a prince."

Lynn asked, "A baron? Well, what is the difference exactly?"

"My father and his advisors carry out the will of the people."

"Why have a baron at all, then? Why not just have elections?"

"It's not that simple," Leon started.

"Weird how you didn't mention being a prince last night. Seems like an important part about you," Lynn sassed. "What, are these two your bodyguards?"

"I'm sorry," Alex interjected. "We don't mean to be rude; I was just curious."

"No, it is quite all right," Jett assured him. "While neither my father nor I constructed the political systems that rule Corinth, we are bound by them due to the current complexities of those systems. We do our best to honor the people within the confines of that." Instantly, Lynn started to hate him. That sounded like an answer Dean Palmer would have given at one of his forums back on Grantitan, always arguing in circles and providing vagaries that, while answering the question in a roundabout way, could never be traced back to a specific position, should his answer turn out to be wrong. All politicians were the same. To think that she had started to fall for Jett's charm last night.

Unable to help herself, Lynn stirred the pot. "Don't you think people have a right to be suspicious of you, then? A lot of people in the galaxy are suffering right now, and many of those people rightfully blame our leaders."

"Lynn, come on, don't be like that," Alex pleaded.

Ignoring him, Lynn kept at it. "On Grantitan, our leaders have bowed to the Grothian's demands while the people of Grantitan live in squalor. It's part of why we are here. People have been stolen from for too long. Someone has to stop it."

"It is why we are here as well," Jett informed her.

Blake agreed. "The Grothians have taken much from Sari. We want to make things better, just like you."

"I'll believe it when I see it," Lynn decided, taking her leave of the group.

"Sorry, she doesn't mean it," she heard Alex say as she walked off.

Lynn walked out of the quad and into the dormitory, which looked more like a prison block than a dorm. The entire room was off-white with lighting to match, there were twin-sized bunk beds lined up in a U-shape across three walls, spaced out only a few feet just to give the cadets enough space to climb in and out of them. Each bunk had hooks on the ends of the top bunks where cadets had hung their bags and clothing. Other than the beds, there was nothing else in the room.

"Hey," Alex huffed, catching up to her. "What is your problem? Those guys are our friends."

"It looks like someone didn't finish this room," Lynn joked, ignoring him.

"Are you listening to me?" Alex pressed.

Annoyed, she snapped back. "We just met them last night, you talk about it like we have known them for years."

"No, I just think they are nice, and it could be good to have allies in this thing. Who cares if he is a prince? He is here like the rest of us, right?"

"Come on, you don't think the test is rigged?"

"No, I don't. I trust Zach and I don't think he would bring us here if it weren't legit."

"Pssh. I guess," Lynn conceded.

They walked around the cramped room and found the two bunks with their numbers on them and hung their bags on the hooks.

"All right," Alex said. "Let's just forget that stuff for now. I guess we are going to be in flight for a while. Do you want to go get something to eat?"

Lynn sat down on the edge of the bed and replied, "Yeah, just give me a few minutes. I'll meet you down there." She rested her palm on her forehead and sifted through her hair with her fingers.

"You all right?"

"I'm fine, I just started feeling overwhelmed. Just give me a few minutes."

"Okay, well, I'll see you over there, okay?"

Alex left her alone and Lynn fell into her thoughts. She could feel her good old nihilism crawling into her brain, and she had to rebuke it. Alex was a superhuman, Sam was a superstar pilot, and Jett was apparently a prince. What was she? Some orphan girl from Grantitan who dropped out of college to play space ninja? She felt sick to her stomach; here she was, overbid and outclassed and unable to turn back. All that could follow was humiliation or death, or perhaps both.

No, she wrestled with herself, *get it together*. What followed this would be victory, glory, and a chance to do something greater than anything she would have ever achieved on that god-forsaken planet of Grantitan. She just had to breathe, to use the techniques Lucas had taught her to curb this anxiety and get her mind straight.

Placing her palms together in front of her chest, Lynn closed her eyes and meditated, blocking out everyone else in the room and letting her mind go numb.

Ten minutes passed and so did the negativity. Lynn felt refreshed enough to socialize and went to the cafeteria, where she found Alex sitting with the Corithians. Though she still felt skeptical of Jett, she sucked it up for Alex's sake. Notably, no one else was bold enough to befriend the prince and his pals. Alex hadn't been kidding about the others, who shot clear looks of disdain toward Jett. Lynn wondered if this alliance would be their undoing once they got to the academy. Nothing else was worthy of note. They ate, they drank, and they made friendly banter. It was a little different than Pailon, Lynn noticed; the men seemed tamer, more conscientious. Clearly, it was game time.

After the meal, Lynn wandered into the gym on the other end of the quad, where she let off some steam by lifting weights and smashing her fists into a sturdy black punching bag.

In the middle of punishing the bag, a voice startled her. "Hey."

Lynn spun around, irritated, and Sam said, "You got a lot of power, girl."

"What, do I look weak or something?"

"No. Relax, I'm just giving you a compliment."

"Thanks."

"Anyway, about last night—"

Interrupting, Lynn apologized. "Yeah, I know, I had way too much whiskey."

"Ha!" Sam dismissed. "I don't care about that. I just wanted to ask you something."

"Okay," Lynn said anxiously. "What?"

"You said you and your brother have never been off Grantitan, right?"

"Yeah, why, is it that obvious?"

"Well, you asked me about the Fox last night, do you remember that?"

Definitely she remembered that, it was one of the contributing factors to her being here in the first place. Now she was fully interested in this conversation.

"Yeah, and you said you had never heard of him."

"One thing you should know out here is that you can't talk about the Fox on a whim. If I were one of his enforcers, you'd be a dead woman."

"So, you do know who he is?"

"I know *what* he is, like everyone else in outer Sari. The Fox is a mythical warlord, a symbol of death. Wherever he appears, people die. No one knows who he really is, only that he can be anywhere, and he controls everything."

"Wait, what do you mean, he controls everything?"

"I mean his followers are everywhere, like those guys at the bar."

"Are you saying he is some kind of god?" Lynn flashed back to her memory of the fox in that hotel room, telling her father that he was God. That couldn't be. Things like that weren't real, were they?

"Not exactly, but I don't really know, I don't mess with it. My point is, just don't talk about the Fox, because trust me, you don't want to find out."

Lynn thought about this for a moment, then replied, "Okay, thanks for telling me that."

"No problem, catch you later, eh?"

"You bet."

Lynn went back to her workout, pummeling the black leather bag even harder and faster than before.

Later, when most cadets had piled into their tiny bunks, Lynn found she was not ready to sleep. She wanted to hang on to this last bit of peace, the final calm before the vicious storm that she was certain awaited her in the morning.

Lynn decided that instead of tossing and turning she would have a walk around. She wandered through a door marked "Observatory" and entered a long room filled with benches and small tables that faced a wall of windows. Outside, the psychedelic winds of hyperspace cruised by incomprehensibly, splashing maddening colors across the usual blackness of space. It would have been impossible for Lynn to describe what it looked like to anyone back on Grantitan. Seeing hyperspace in movies or on holo-TV was not at all the same experience. Staring at this was like standing at the cusp of oblivion, teetering between enlightenment and insanity.

As she stood there hypnotized, Lynn succumbed to a deep rumination. Was the Fox really some all-knowing, all-powerful being? That couldn't be. People like the Fox, those who carved their empires with tragedy and fear, thrived on myths. The more arcane and inexplicable he seemed, the more people would fear him, and thus, the more power he would gain. Whatever he was, Grothian or Sarian, mortal or deity, Lynn would never bow to him. Someday, she would reach behind the curtain and find out the truth.

And so would the Fox.

After a short while, she felt herself fading and let out an epic yawn. It was probably better if she was well rested before tomorrow. All of this could be pondered another day. So, she gave up on the mystery for the time being and cleared her mind before heading back to the dormitory and drifting off to sleep.

THE DREAD WOODS

1

Being on the dropship felt different this time, almost like a lucid dream. A cocktail of anxiety, excitement, pressure, and anticipation intoxicated Lynn as she strapped herself in and prepared for takeoff. This was it; the Prism warship was now orbiting above Gran Karisu and all the cadets were about to be launched into the atmosphere, where they would land at Raynor Academy.

The morning had been a blur. She barely had time for breakfast before Zach and the other officers were scurrying them into one of the "restricted" hallways in neat lines. They were led into a chamber that looked familiar to Lynn, like the secret room Zach had shown them at the Haxenburg, except in this one, instead of holo-screens and simulation pods, the circular walls were covered with stalls separated by thin walls. Inside each compartment was a raised, circular platform upon which the cadets would stand. Next to the platforms were small terminals. Upon activation, these terminals brought up a holo-screen before each cadet, allowing them to select the armaments that would come with their rykai suits.

When Lynn selected her armaments, the avatar on the screen updated in real time. Amazingly, when she was done selecting, the wall behind her platform opened and several metal claws on long, flexible arms flew out and expertly attached all of her weaponry to her body.

As soon as she was outfitted, the instructors were yelling and rushing them into the hangar and onto the dropship.

Alex must have sensed her having a mini anxiety attack as they sat there waiting for takeoff, and he leaned over to her and whispered, "We are in this together, okay?"

She nodded her head in agreement and looked up at the ceiling.

Working his way up the center aisle, Zach gave them one last disparaging rant. "Well, I must admit, you all look slightly less pathetic in your full rykai suits, albeit still not worthy of Prism. Indeed, it takes more than looks to pass the tests ahead. Since we have established that it is too late to quit, I will leave you jerk-offs with this piece of advice about the weeks ahead: just because you have made it here does not mean you are worth a damn. Bring your best every day, both in terms of your bodies and your minds. You will have to dig deep, push yourself to your physical limits, and be able to critically think with unprecedented mental agility. Stay focused and do these things and you will be successful. Do not and you will fail. Do you understand?"

"Yes, sir!" The cabin echoed as the cadets shouted emphatically.

"Very well. Then I wish you all the best of luck."

Without another word, Zach vanished into the cockpit of the drop ship and the engines began to roar.

"Here we go, boys," Brock sneered as they felt the ship turning and revving up. They were sucked into their seats as the ship blasted out of the hangar of the *Leviathan* and into space.

A few minutes later, the ship stabilized, and some cadets were talking amongst themselves. Some were laughing and jeering, but Lynn was just feeling sick. Well, lightheaded, really, and it was making her feel nauseous. That had been a particularly rough takeoff, she privately resented, not like when they had left Grantitan or Pailon. Maybe it was something about departing from another ship that made it different. Whatever it was, it had left her feeling nasty.

"What do you think it will be like down there?" Alex asked.

Lynn sighed, rubbing her palms on her cheeks. "I don't know ... I can't think about it now."

"You all right?"

"I feel woozy."

"Yeah, me too a little bit. Not as bad as you, apparently."

Brock inserted himself again. "Gran Karisu is dangerous, you know. They have to keep forcefields up around the cities to protect them from the wildlife."

"What?" Alex asked, raising his brow. "What kind of freaking wildlife has to be kept out by force fields?"

A large clunking sound on the outside of the ship was followed by an erratic jerk to the side, refreshing Lynn's motion sickness.

"What was that?" Lynn said, annoyed. An even worse movement came next as the ship suddenly seemed to slam the breaks and drop downwards what seemed like a few meters. She was certain she was going to throw up.

Watching her, Brock laughed. "Re-entry is fun, eh?"

Was this normal for ships entering planets? If so, she hoped it was something she would get used to, because if it was like this every time, she was going to be seriously in for it.

"It's pretty rough," another female cadet said. "This isn't normal."

The ship rattled and jerked again, followed by a rapid dip. Lynn held her stomach and closed her eyes.

"Oh, shut up," Brock said. "It's always a party up here."

"I don't know, something feels wrong."

Something definitely felt wrong; there were more rattling and clunking noises and the whole cabin began to shake violently as it pressed forward into the atmosphere of Gran Karisu.

"It's gonna be okay," Alex said to her, putting his hand on her back and rubbing in circles.

"I know," she replied, "I just—"

No time to finish that thought.

An awful collision tumbled the vessel onto its side. The breath was abruptly torn from Lynn's lungs as she was thrust violently forward into her straps, where she dangled momentarily as the ship tossed and tumbled and tried to correct its course.

Soon, Zach's urgent voice came onto the intercom. "Attention, cadets! Do not panic. We have been struck by an unknown object, compromising our entry into Gran Karisu. We will be making an emergency landing at the first available site. Be advised we may be in for a rough landing."

"Oh, man ..." Alex trailed off.

Another impact battered the dropship, this time hitting the underside and sending the ship into a nosedive.

"We are going to crash," Alex came to realize, grabbing onto Lynn's hand and holding it in his.

"The hell we are. Don't say that!" She might have been a cynic, but she wasn't ready to accept that she was going to die.

"I love you, sis."

She couldn't say anything else before a massive explosion blew open the side of the cabin and fire proliferated around the edges of the rift as air was rapidly sucked toward the opening. She saw sunlight, briefly, and realized they had made it through the atmosphere. Now they just had to survive the fall. Please, she prayed to whatever cosmic power could be, let us survive this fall. Her head smashed against her seat and she blacked out as thc ship was broken in half.

2

First, there was sound, a faint monotony of voices behind the crackling doom of fire and wreckage. Then, blindness as the oppressive sun penetrated a thick cloud of smoke. Lifting her arms to shield her still adjusting eyes, she next felt the pain of her bruised abdomen from being thrust against her straps. Blood slowly trickled from slashed flesh at Lynn's ribcage and two small pieces of shrapnel protruded from just above her hip. When her eyes could finally assess, Lynn saw the precariousness of her position. About fifteen feet to her right and at a steep angle was the long, dark, and defeated cabin of the Prism dropship, a single light flickering and sparking above the mostly empty seats and the occasional bloodied body. Flames consumed the bottom of the cabin and smoke crept up and engulfed Lynn while she sat there, trapped in the nearby treetops.

Lynn felt around frantically, touching everything, trying to figure out the best course of action. So many thoughts raced through her head. Those flames had to be near the fuel tank. Wait, which half of the ship was she near? Where was Alex and the others?

"Hey!" she screamed down into the cabin. "Hey! Anyone alive?" No one answered.

She tried calling out, "HEY! UP HERE! HELP ME, I'M UP HERE!" After trying this a couple more times, she realized she was too high up and no one was responding. What was she supposed to do? She couldn't go back into that ship, no one could hear her up here, and she couldn't stay. As she considered this, she tried her seatbelts again, finding them frustratingly jammed. For a moment, she wanted to cry, but instead she stopped writhing, took deep breaths, and cleared her mind.

Okay, she reasoned, once she could get these belts off, gravity was going to suggest that she go down, so she would need a firm grip when she released herself. She'd have to climb up out of this seat and get onto a solid branch. Hopefully from there she could find a way to climb down the trees.

Examining the area beside her, Lynn found a long, firm branch that would do just fine.

When she tried to wrestle out of the seatbelts, she accidently brushed her arm against the shrapnel in her hip and cried out in pain. Damn, she'd have to remove that first. Closing her eyes, she tightened her fist around the smaller of the two pieces and yanked it out with blind courage.

"Damn it!" she cried out again as she dropped the shard of metal down through the canopy. One more. This one was harder because it was bigger, and because she already knew it was going to hurt.

With one deep breath, she yanked the other one out with furious resolve. "Damn it that hurts!" She held her side as blood escaped the cavities in her abdomen and seeped between her fingers. Thinking quickly, she realized she was still wearing her rykai suit and reached for the small satchel attached to her right leg. In it was a mixture of clay and certain compounds that she scooped out and smeared onto her exposed wounds. The slightly viscous, malleable solution bonded to her skin enough to offer a short-term solution.

With her body intact, Lynn shifted, and tugged and finessed the belts until at last she broke free. She found her way up and onto the sturdy branch, and from up here, she could see through the canopy and into the wild scenery of Gran Karisu. It was neither a bog nor a coniferous forest, but a whimsical exaggeration of both, with long, harrowing brooks cutting through dense and tangled underbrush between massive, willow-like pines and a yellowish-green forest floor peppered with dark and murky ponds. What was more, there were huge brown and black birds the size of small planes sweeping across the sky and being followed by hundreds of smaller birds. It was not unlike a dream, except that it was a nightmare.

Before she began her descent, Lynn took note of a clearing in the distance, apparently to the northwest relative to the sun's position, where a pillar of smoke rose up above the trees: the other half of the ship.

Lynn made her way down the tree, carefully vetting branches before she committed herself to a descent. Eventually, she came to a branch about twenty feet above the ground and found herself with nothing but trunk and bark between her and the dirt below. The bark was like shingles, she observed, peeling off a piece, and it was too frail. There was no way she could just shimmy down the tree. Could she jump? Not from this height.

She heard voices and a group of cadets came into view below her.

"Hey!" she called out. "Up here!"

The group down below stopped and a few of them looked up. One of them she recognized as Jett and he yelled up to her, "Lynn! Is that you?"

"Yeah! My seat landed in the canopy!"

"Hang on! We'll get you down!"

"Can we catch her if she jumps?" one of the cadets asked.

"It's risky without a stretcher," someone else decided.

Emerging from the periphery, Alex interrupted. "I have a better idea. Move away from the tree."

"Alex! You are okay!" Lynn cried with relief.

"Hang onto the tree," Alex instructed as he held his hands out in front of him with his palms facing the ground. The other cadets moved aside hastily as the ground near the tree began to shudder. Alex's gauntlets sparked with power and his hands slowly turned palms up as he commanded the planet's crust to rise into the shape of a tall, cylindrical spire that stopped just a few feet from Lynn's branch.

"Incredible," a cadet marveled at the pole.

Lynn hopped over to the smooth rock and slid down with ease. Her feet on the ground, she said, "Wow, you really did get good at that. Thank you."

Alex gave her a huge hug. "I was so worried about you, sis."

"It's been awhile since I've seen a golem," Jett commented. For a moment, Lynn froze and looked at Alex, who also seemed ambushed. Did Jett know? How could he? Zach had assured them the suit would hide Alex's Alderian heritage and yet, even though he had taught Alex to make this structure hundreds of times, it had blown his cover immediately.

"Yeah," one man agreed. "Tough ARMs to use. Good when they are done right, though." Alex and Lynn both breathed a sigh of relief. ARMs (atomic reconstruction mechanisms) were the technical labels for rykai weapons. Apparently, they meant "golem" to refer to Alex's rykai suit, not his ancestry.

"Yes, well done. Alas, we haven't time to prattle on," Jett reminded the group. "Have we gathered everything we can use?"

"I think so," a woman answered.

"No way anything is left in the base of that ship," Lynn assured them.

"Then let us reconvene with the scouts," Jett said.

"Where are the others?" Alex wondered, a reference to the existence of only a dozen cadets out of what started as two hundred twenty. Some would be at the other crash site, but at least a hundred ought to have been at this one. Lynn thought of the bodies she had seen in the cabin and wondered how many others had been flung into the dense trees.

"Dead," the woman from before said.

"Or missing, perhaps, as you were," Jett reminded her. "The best we can do is rendezvous with the survivors from the other half of the ship. There are bound to be several, as there were here. Also, the other site is the front of the ship and it contains the GPS device, so if Prism is locating the crash, that is where they will go."

"What if there are others that were ejected?" Lynn objected. "We can't just leave them."

"We will come back once Prism sends another dropship," Jett said.

"What if they die before then?"

"We would expend ourselves as well, searching for them on foot. Prism will have recognized that we crashed and have likely dispatched a ship already. We need to be at that other site when it arrives so that we can tell the rescuers where to look."

Lynn knew he was right, but she couldn't help being offended, having been minutes away from being one of those left behind.

"What if I hadn't escaped? If I were still up there?"

Alex interjected. "I was searching for you. I wouldn't leave you behind."

"Who cares?" one of the men said. "We have to go."

Jett agreed. "We do not have time to have this debate. Everyone, grab some of the supplies and we shall go."

Feeling illegitimate, Lynn asked Jett, "So, I guess you are the leader now, *Prince* Shorin?"

"To anyone who follows, I suppose." None of the others seemed to object, which Lynn found strange, seeing as just eighteen hours ago some of them were plotting to "kill him in his sleep." It was funny how quickly people abandoned their convictions when their lives were threatened.

"Sis," Alex said in his best "don't screw up" voice. For now, she heeded his advice and chose a rucksack of supplies to carry.

Jett summoned a communication device from his wristwatch and spoke into it. "Blake, have you ascertained our position?"

"Vegetation is too thick," Blake's voice crackled back. "Sam is in a tree, this crazy bugger. We see smoke, but it is hard to see what is between us and it. Hey, you get in touch with the ship yet?"

"No word from the *Leviathan* as of yet. The com channels are still blank."

"Dang. What do you make of it?"

"I am unsure. We found Lynn in a tree. Say, which way did you scout?"

"West, toward the smoke."

"Come on back, we are done here, and it is better to travel together. We don't know what is out there."

"Roger that, mate."

Lynn cut in, correcting Blake. "The smoke is north, northwest from here."

Jett considered this for a moment, then asked, "Did you see the crash site from up there?"

"Yeah, it is northwest, that way." She pointed.

Jett was about to answer when a commotion started happening on the other side of the crash site where other cadets were gearing up.

"What is happening over there?" Alex asked. It was unclear at first, like approaching the scene of a traffic accident, and then, like the moment the jaws of life come into view and the realization of severity occurs to the unwitting observer, it overcame them.

3

"Rippers!" A male cadet warned too late. The dogs of war were upon them, bursting out of the brush and tearing into the first two cadets with an unquenchable lust for blood. The man let out a stomach-turning scream as the wolf-like creature pounced on him and sliced his chest open with its bladed headbutt. The creature landed on him and immediately opened its mouth and clamped serrated jaws down on the man's neck. Blood sprayed into the air as the creature bit and tore his face apart.

"Oh, God! Alex, please don't die," Lynn's thoughts spilled out. It was a weird thing to say, but the first thing that popped into her mind. She would lose it if anything ever happened to Alex.

"Stay together," Alex said, readying his ARM.

"Their back is armored and sharp," Jett warned them. "Attack the underside."

There was no time to discuss it further, as the rippers were upon them. One cut in from the left, and Jett released a pulse of energy from his left forearm which expanded into a dome-shaped energy shield. He rebuked the charging ripper with a head-rattling shield bash, and following up instantly he drew his blaster, fired off several shots, and hit the beast twice on its exposed underbelly. The ripper screeched in pain and fled into the brush to die.

Two more came at them from the front and Alex tried to catch one by raising rock spikes from the ground, but the rippers jumped over it and advanced too quickly for another attempt. Meanwhile, Lynn had drawn her blaster and emptied a clip to no avail; they were just too fast.

The rippers lunged and Alex and Lynn dodged in opposite directions. Lynn jumped and rolled onto one knee, unsheathing her knife as one of the rippers quickly corrected its path to face her. Seeing the beast up close was the sort of thing people had nightmares about. It was the size of a coyote, but with a leaner body and longer legs, and its long, stiff gray hairs were hard as steel and sharp as the horn of a rhino. No mercy existed in its yellow eyes or its two rows of hungry, flesh tearing teeth.

It went for her and Lynn knew she wasn't getting her knife in its belly without taking serious damage herself. Instead of attacking, she flung dirt in the creature's face and jumped to the side again. In an instant, the creature reset and prepared to lunge.

"Hey!" Sam's voice commanded from somewhere behind Lynn. "Come and get me!" She heard a loud whistle. Instantly, the ripper's slanted ears perked up and he changed targets, rushing toward Sam. Lynn turned just in time to see Sam, fully adorned with her cybernetic rykai suit, thrust forward like a fired cannonball and smash her metal fist into the ripper's head in a collision of dust and sparks. The ripper yelped before its neck snapped and its body went tumbling several yards across the forest floor, snapping twigs and saplings until it crashed into a boulder and folded up into a bloody heap. Sam ran toward three more rippers that were rampaging among the other cadets, yelling, "You want some too?" and thrust herself forward and up ten feet in the air. Seconds later, she came crashing down on one of the rippers, driving its skull into the dirt with her fist.

Blake and Leon came out of the woods behind where Sam had been, weapons in hand, and Blake yelled to Jett, "The cavalry is here, mate!"

Lynn got to her feet and saw Alex was in trouble. He was lying on his back, underneath one of the rippers. He had molded stone bracers around his arms, which he was using to hold the ripper above his face. Drool rained from the ripper's hellish jaw as it snapped its teeth over and over.

Lynn called out to her brother, rushing over to help him. As she approached, Alex got one of his stone-covered arms up into the beast's mouth and pushed himself to the side, thrusting the ripper off of him. Lynn could have killed the beast as it landed on its back, but she hesitated, afraid the beast would flip over and its body would slice her up if she tried to stab it. In the second she failed to act, the beast got back to its feet and faced Alex, who was scrambling to his feet with fear and desperation in his eyes. Damn it! She had to do something!

"Back away from it!" Blake commanded as he prepared his attack with three double-edged, foot-long blades perfectly curved off a circular hilt. With great force, he launched this bladed boomerang toward the creature. The weapon intuitively began to spin the blades around the hilt until it was whizzing like a buzz saw. The noise caught the attention of the ripper, but not in time for it to react. Blood and gore spilled across the forest floor as Blake's vicious weapon sliced the beast in two diagonally from shoulder to ribcage. Following the carnage, the weapon whizzed on, completing a one hundred eighty-degree arc in midair and flying back to Blake. To complete the brutal sweep, the boomerang stopped spinning and retracted its blades before returning deftly to Blake's hand.

"Thank you," Alex said, getting to his feet and breathing a heavy sigh of relief.

"No worries, mate."

"We have to help the others!" Lynn reminded them.

By the time they reached the other side of the crash site, Jett had dispatched one ripper and Sam got another, and the remaining rippers fled into the tree line. Lynn's heart was still pounding. She had fought all manner of things in Zach's simulations, but the real thing was so much more intense. At least three people had been killed by the rippers, as far as she could tell by looking around. It couldn't get more real than that.

Jett retracted his pulse shield and came toward the center of the camp, where everyone left was gathered, and he asked, "Is everyone all right? Are there any injuries?"

Lynn caught Alex feeling his shoulder and noticed a slit in his rykai suit. The area was wet and discolored. Reaching out and touching him, she asked, "Was it a bite?"

"No. When I flipped it over, one of the arm blades caught me."

"I can heal that up," Leon offered, producing two tiny metal spheres from one of the satchels attached to his belt. At first, Lynn thought her eyes were playing tricks on her as she witnessed the spheres levitate out of Leon's palm. Two smooth metallic spheres began floating toward Alex, transforming in midair into micro-drones with tiny instruments. They circled the wound on Alex's shoulder, analyzing the damage while Alex and Lynn watched with wonder.

"Take off your shirt," one of the cadets instructed Alex.

Alex complied, revealing a great gash that crossed his right pectoral all the way to the collarbone.

Lynn gasped. This was all her fault; when she'd had a chance to help Alex, she hadn't done anything. She'd panicked, had no idea what to do, and was so concerned about herself that she had failed to protect her brother. What kind of sister was she?

Within seconds of analyzing the exposed wound, the drones began working. One sprayed a sanitizing mist, and the other deployed a green beam that looked like a micro-laser and began crosshatching a pattern across the wound. It was applying stitches! Except instead of stitches, it was just closing the wound and repairing the tissue. While the one drone did this, the other one began going behind it and applying a skin graft over the top of the repaired muscles. Lynn caught herself marveling at the technology she never imagined possible, realizing that as a Prism candidate, she ought to know about it. Suddenly she was anxious about blowing their cover. Come to think of it, maybe they had bigger problems. What if their enemies used wild ARMs that they could never even dream of? They would die, that's what. Perhaps this was a mistake after all. She hadn't even been able to fend off rippers, so she couldn't reasonably expect to beat Leon, Blake, Jett, Sam, or any of the others who would use critical thought.

"We lost three people," another cadet pointed out.

"Yes. Unfortunately, we have no time for mourning. We must make it to the other crash site before nightfall," Jett said. "Gran Karisu is a dangerous place, especially at night."

"Yeah, and if we stay here, this wreck is likely to bring more wildlife," Sam pointed out.

The drones finished their work on Alex, who appeared good as new. Looking at Lynn's abdomen, Leon said, "It looks like you could use a tune-up as well."

She looked down and noticed her clay solution was all but gone and fresh blood was trickling out of the shrapnel wounds.

Leon redirected his drones to Lynn, and she felt a twinge of pain as they began working. It got worse as they continued and she bit her lip, trying not to cry out. It felt like getting stitches without anesthetic. It burned too, oh man did it burn!

"It hurts," she mumbled to Alex.

"No kidding. Crazy, though, right?" he whispered back.

"So, anyone else hurt?" Jett asked. When no one answered, he said, "All right. Then when she is finished, we go. Sam, what did you three find?"

"There is a ridge about a quarter mile west," Sam said. "We get up on that—"

Blake interrupted. "This broad is crazy. It's a fool's ridge, that one."

"It will keep us off the floor with the rippers, and it cuts northwest into the mountains. We can come down on the other side and it should put us a mile or two from the crash site."

"Yeah, if we don't fall to our bloody deaths before then!"

Jett considered this and argued, "The ridge will take time and energy to traverse. It also takes us around the forest. The fastest way is through it."

Sam objected. "The forest may be fastest, but also rife with more of those rippers and who knows what else."

"How do we know those things can't climb?" Alex asked.

"They can," Jett confirmed. "And if we encounter them on the ridge, we will be more limited in our mobility. So, I believe that while the forest is more likely to yield further encounters with wildlife, it is overall the safer and more efficient way."

Leon's drones finished up on Lynn's wounds and drifted back to Leon's palm, where they collapsed back into perfectly smooth orbs before he deposited them back into the satchel.

"Thank you," Lynn said.

"You're welcome. They are pretty incredible, eh?"

"Yeah. Too bad they don't sew."

Sam interrupted, "We don't have time to mess around. So, is it the woods, then?"

"I agree with Jett," Alex reiterated.

"Me too," Lynn seconded. Blake smiled smugly as the rest of the group voted in favor of the direction he had first suggested, though credit had been assigned to Jett for articulating the particulars. One thing Lynn could admit was that Jett had shown great leadership in this dire situation. It was starting to make more sense why those who had denounced the Corithians back on Pailon would be willing to be led by one now. Fear and uncertainty often made people seek shelter wherever it could be found, and Jett was certainly offering some security with his calmness and his wisdom. Lynn was impressed.

"All right, then," Jett said decisively. "Let's go." All in agreement, they followed Jett away from the crash site and into the dense and dangerous forest.

4

It took a while for Lynn to reconcile her emotions enough to properly apologize to Alex. At first, she had so much adrenaline circulating through her body from the crash and the fight that she couldn't possibly sort her thoughts. Once that began to subside, the reality of the current situation set in. Most of them had died, either in the crash itself or at the hands of the wildlife, and for some reason she had been granted the chance to live even though she had failed when the rippers attacked them. Now, eight of them remained: her, Alex, Sam, Jett, Blake, Leon, and two others who had introduced themselves as Siefer and Kiah. Somehow the eight of them had to escape this place.

"I'm sorry," she finally said as they stepped over rocks and pushed through the brush.

"For what?" he asked. Naturally, he would be humble about it.

"I froze when that thing was about to attack you. If Blake hadn't gotten it—"

He interrupted, "No, don't do that. You did what you could."

"No, I could have done more. I was close enough to it. Anyway, if it ever came down to it, it should be me, not you."

"I'd never let that happen. We will protect each other, how about that?"

"Sounds fair. Again, I am sorry, though."

Overhearing at least part of the conversation, Sam jumped in. "You have a point, you know. You were close enough to make the kill, but you hesitated."

"Hey," Alex scolded her. "You mind your business."

"It *is* my business. If it were me relying on one of you, I need to know you won't hesitate."

"She won't."

Lynn stopped Alex. "No, Alex, it's okay. It won't happen again."

"It better not," Sam reiterated. "Do your job next time."

"Screw you!"

There was an awkward silence as Sam stopped for a second and stared at Lynn with raised eyebrows. She repeated herself with a condescending tone. "Just do your job, that's all. No one else has to die."

Sam walked on ahead and Alex tried to comfort Lynn, "I'm sorry. I know you did what you could."

"No, she's right. I have to do better."

The two of them fell back into silence and focused on the journey. Lynn couldn't help slipping back into the same insecurity she had felt on the *Leviathan*. Everyone else had something going for them; everyone but her. Why couldn't she have been the one that got the superpower? Why Alex? Or, why not both of them? She tried not to resent her fragility, but right now, it was all she could think about.

A while later, after they had been walking through these creepy woods for what seemed like hours, Lynn had to figure they were lost. Exhaustion was setting in. There was still no communication with the ship, though Jett had tried several more times. To add to their tribulations, the sun was starting to go down and the landscape beneath the canopy was becoming dimmer by the minute.

Thick and lumbering trunks covered in dangerous black spines threatened the cadets as they traversed a familiar boggy bank. Beside them was a blackened pond covered with insects and green and white foam. Lynn could only imagine what lurked beneath it. As they dodged around the spines and stepped over fallen logs, Lynn felt a lapse of clarity, as if her mind suddenly escaped her body, flew around the treetops, and swan-dived straight back into her. It was as if she had seen the land from up there and seen herself within it. Then she was certain she had been here before.

"We passed this bog already," Lynn said.

The others stopped and Leon asked, "What makes you say that?"

"These two spiny trees; the way they bend over this log, I remember ducking to the side to avoid them, like this." As she articulated, she also demonstrated, moving carefully between the virulent, urchin-like spines.

"No way," Siefer disagreed. "We've passed a lot of those trees."

"Yeah, they all look the same," Sam seconded.

With visible disinterest in Sam's point, Lynn argued, "No. We have passed these specific trees already. Look at the arrangement; it is unique. Around that bend up there will be a big willow growing out of a hillside."

"So the trees are growing lopsided? That's how you navigate?" Siefer asked.

"She navigates better than you, obviously," Alex defended Lynn.

"And what exactly is it that you do?" Siefer demanded, his tall and bulky frame matching up to Alex as he stepped closer. "Make some fancy rock sculptures? Great job." He had one of those cocky faces; he looked like the kind of guy who threw a great football in high school, and now the only thing he did that well was overcompensate. Lynn could tell by the grin on Alex's face that he wasn't amused by this loser either.

"Keep it up and he'll shove one up your ass," Lynn jumped in.

Meanwhile, Jett had gone up to the bend to have a look and called back to the group, "She is right, the willow is here, on the hillside."

"No kidding." Blake was surprised. Lynn shot Siefer and Sam her cockiest grin.

Jett returned to the group just as Leon asked, "Okay, then where did we get turned around?"

"I've been following a north-northwest bearing the whole time," Jett insisted. "It is impossible for us to have gone in a circle."

"Your compass is busted, bud," Siefer concluded.

"No," Blake said. "My reading is the same. There is nothing wrong with the compasses."

Kiah asked, "Leon, can you send your drones up above the trees?"

"If he could do that, don't you think we would have done it in the first place?" Siefer questioned, rudely.

"My drones are designed to scan lifeforms, not terrain," Leon confirmed.

Sam paced in impatient circles around the swampy grass. "We should have taken the ridge. This is getting us nowhere."

"That's enough," Jett said. "We must not fight amongst ourselves. Let us accept the current situation and discuss how we may overcome it."

"We need to reacquire our bearings," Blake said. "Let's find a high ground and figure out where we got turned around."

"We did that already," Sam reminded him. "I think we need to double back and get on the ridge. This undergrowth is too thick to navigate."

"I agree with Sam," Alex said.

Reluctantly, Lynn agreed.

"It'll be dark in an hour, at best," Blake pointed out. "By the time we get back it will be too late."

"So, what should we do?" Leon asked, looking at Jett for an answer.

"I believe we need to ascertain our current position, but I also believe we are placed dangerously at odds with the sunset and we do not want to be unprotected at night. Two of us should find a high point while the rest of us make camp."

That sounded rational to Lynn as well. As she listened to them debate, she realized her lack of experience was seeping through. Each perspective had benefits, but she did not have firsthand experience with wilderness survival, and it was hard to say for certain which plan was the soundest. All she had to pull from was the barrage of information Zach had fired at her during the earlier parts of their training. Shallow equivocations were bouncing around her brain like a tennis ball as she considered what to do. Perhaps staying quiet was best for now.

Kiah objected. "What about the rescue ship? If we stay here, we will get left behind."

"It doesn't seem like we have a choice," Alex said.

Sam took Kiah's side and said, "I don't think we should stay here. We are sitting ducks."

In response, Jett offered a modified solution. "Then, let us set up camp at the base of the ridge. It is more protected there and we can get our bearings and leave at dawn."

"Okay, that sounds logical," Leon agreed.

"That wreck can't be far," Siefer said. "We must be circling the area. If we just find a high point, I bet we are close enough to reach it by nightfall."

"Perhaps," Jett replied. "However, it stands to reason that if a ship were coming, it would likely have arrived by now, given that we have been hiking for hours. It is also reasonable that if they do not account for every cadet, they will send another ship tomorrow. The risk of not having a protected camp tonight is a higher priority than getting to the crash site within the next hour, and most likely waiting there until tomorrow regardless."

The group seemed convinced and finally Sam conceded. "All right, let's get to it then."

"The ridge juts out that way," Blake explained, moving his flattened hand up and down along a westerly trajectory.

"Damn," Siefer sighed. "How did we get caught up in all this?"

Jett motioned toward the ridge as he began to lead the group. Everyone followed, watching their peripherals carefully as the darkness slowly permeated the forest and strange noises began floating around the trees. For the first time since she was six years old and in a strange, new orphanage, Lynn felt fearful of the dark.

5

A cool, dank wisp of wind fluttered through the dark forest and across the windswept slate behind their improvised camp, carrying with it the chilling sounds of the night. Alex had stretched the rock out of the cliffside and shaped it into two curved outcrops, forming a small, cave-like shelter for them to sleep in. It wasn't perfect, but at least it shielded them from the elements. Doing this had drained Alex's rykai suit, forcing him to load his backup power cells into his gauntlets. Taking inventory of the group's supplies, they realized that between them, they only had a half-dozen power cells, and that was not accounting for the fact that Jett and Sam's cells were half-depleted at the moment. Hopefully they could avoid another encounter with the rippers. Otherwise, they would be dangerously low and perhaps unable to use their ARMs.

In the entrance to the shelter, they had built a fire and began to boil water. There had not been time before sundown to hunt any wildlife, nor did it seem particularly smart anyway, given the dangers known to them on Gran Karisu. Luckily, Jett had ensured that they searched the wreckage and took with them anything that could prove useful. Among these provisions were enough rations for about two days. Granted, it would not be a lavish meal, but it would suffice.

Lynn sat with the other cadets in a semi-circle around the fire, eating a ration of dried meat and nuts. The feeling in the air suggested to Lynn that the others were starting to feel disheartened, just as she was. Sam was keeping to herself off in the corner of the cave and playing with her knife. Jett, Blake, and Leon sat together and were still obsessing over planning the next morning. Alex, Kiah, and Siefer sat near Lynn, speaking occasionally in exhausted voices.

"It shouldn't take long once we climb up there," Leon said.

"Well, climbing down will be the heck of it," Blake reminded him.

"Regardless, it is the best way," Jett said. "At first light, we must traverse it."

"Yeah. We will be fine," Leon concluded.

"You know," Kiah piped up through shivering lips, "They say the forests of Gran Karisu are haunted."

Lynn perked up. "Haunted?"

"They say the spirits taunt weary travelers by tricking their minds, forcing them to walk in circles for days. There are all kinds of stories of people who got lost here and never came back."

"Well, it sure feels creepy out there," Blake commented.

"Haunted, though? You believe in that stuff?" Lynn asked. She had never been one to believe in ghosts. Everything had an explanation, she found. People who believed in ghosts, gods, and miracles often did so because they needed those explanations and they either couldn't get them or refused to accept them.

"There have been people who have made it out," Kiah kept harping on it. "This one guy, an explorer from Sinca, claimed he had seen a demon in the shape of a minotaur. It kept appearing whenever he thought he'd found an exit and it would chase him back into the forest."

"I remember that guy, what a nutjob," Siefer recalled.

"Yeah, it was all over social media. The guy had to be committed."

"The experience of one man hardly breeds cause for concern," Jett said firmly. "The supernatural, if such concepts are real, affect most deeply our minds. If we do not focus on them, we shall not succumb to them."

"I wouldn't be so sure," Alex said.

Amused, Lynn looked at him and asked, "You believe in ghosts? I thought you said that stuff was nonsense."

"I don't know what I believe. I thought I knew what was out there." Oh, right, she realized, Alex had defied physics. The supernatural was the entire pretext upon which this journey was based. She supposed, then, it was possible that a forest could be "haunted." If it were true, it was probably best, as Jett had suggested, not to think about it.

Sam emerged from the shadows and stood between them with an aggravated look on her face. "There are worse things than ghosts. Why is no one talking about the elephant in the room? I know someone else has thought of it."

Everyone was silent, so Sam followed up. "Grothians. Anyone else realize that we may have been shot down? It would explain the coms not working."

"Yes!" Lynn agreed emphatically. She had thought she was being paranoid when they were in the dropship, but hearing Sam say it out loud made her realize it was a real possibility.

Jett dismissed the notion. "There is no evidence of that."

"Plus," Leon added, "Do you think they attacked the *Leviathan*, a Prism warship, this far into Sarian space?"

"Where is the rescue ship, then?" Sam wondered. "It's been twelve hours. A Prism ship the caliber of the *Leviathan* could detect the crash and send a ship in twelve minutes."

"There must be another explanation," Alex reasoned. "We have had peace for over twenty years ... why would they attack now?"

"Maybe," Siefer chimed in. "For all we know, Prism has been fighting them all along. The Grothians haven't exactly lived up to their end of the bargain. We all know how much they have overstepped in outer Sari. We can't trust them."

"At this time, all of that is conjecture," Jett reminded them. "It offers us no utility to speculate."

"Except there may not be a rescue ship and we need a contingency plan if no one answers the distress call," Sam pushed.

Jett tried to reassure them. "If that were to be, we would travel to the nearest city on foot. It may be arduous, but we would survive. Whatever happens, we must remain positive and stay together."

"Fine, but if they do show up, we can't fight them with so few power cells."

"Not to mention we may need those cells if we run into more of the locals," Siefer added.

"Yeah," Leon agreed. "We have to be careful how we use our ARMs."

"That seems prudent. We should conserve our supply until we find rescue," Jett said.

It was silent except for the crackle of the fire and the rustling of the trees as the group considered the information laid before them. Sam looked disenfranchised, as if not buying into Jett's optimistic message. There was a good reason for that, Lynn knew. Tensions between the Grothians and the Sarians had been mounting for years and it was only a matter of time before the cold war broke. Hell, there was never peace in the first place, only a false ceasefire so the Grothians could set up strongholds in outer Sari. This whole organization they were part of, Prism, was founded on that suspicion. Or, at least, that was what Zach told her and Alex.

Siefer stood up, stretching and letting out a huge yawn. He crossed his arms and said, "Well, that's enough ghosts and Grothians for me. Sleep in shifts?"

"Yes. We ought to have two at a time awake," Blake suggested.

"I'll be first," Alex volunteered.

"No," Lynn objected. "Let me. I won't sleep anyway."

"I will as well," Jett said.

"Are you sure?" Alex asked.

"Absolutely," Lynn replied.

"I'll take second shift then," Alex volunteered.

"Aye, me too," Sam said. The rest of them decided their order and began to retire. Jett and Lynn sat near the entrance on opposite sides of the fire, leaning against the walls.

"We need to keep this going strong," Jett advised, stoking the fire and adding a piece of wood from a nearby pile they had gathered. "It will deter smaller predators."

Lynn nodded and relaxed herself against the wall. Like she didn't know what a fire would do, she thought.

After a short while, everyone was asleep except the two of them, and Lynn was watching the wood pop and crackle to keep herself occupied.

"Have you ever been away from home like this?" Jett asked suddenly.

"Huh?" Lynn asked, shaking herself out of a funk.

"I mean, to outer space?"

"No, I never left Grantitan before this. You've probably been on ships like the *Leviathan* before, right?"

"No, never."

"Shut up. You are a prince, right? Doesn't your baron father have a warship?"

"Corinth is a unique planet, you would find. We have warships, but not light speed capabilities. Our ships do not have cafeterias or showers, either," he joked.

Skeptical, Lynn pressed. "What, is your planet, like, third world or something? Do you have electricity?"

"Yes, of course. I am afraid we are just a little behind the curve. As I mentioned earlier, we are an isolated people. This has had some benefits and also some detriments." Lynn knew what that was like. Grantitan didn't even have real food.

She laughed a little. "You are kidding me? So, you've never been in space?"

"No, not until last year when I began my training for Prism." He laughed as well. "Though I had wondered about it many times."

"Yeah. When I lived in the country, I used to love looking at the stars. Never imagined all this stuff was out here, though."

"As an adolescent I was often ensorcelled in fantasy, much to my mother's dismay, I admit. She was always pushing me to focus on my studies and preparations. It was 'very unbecoming of a baron to have his head in the clouds,' she would say."

"I get that. My foster parents are politicians and they always wanted me to look prim and proper. They made me take all kinds of lessons to get scholarships: music, tennis, horseback riding, private tutoring, you name it. I hated all of it. As soon as I was old enough, I abandoned that ship."

A moment passed, and Jett replied, "You just wanted something different for your life. You want to change things, right?"

"Yeah. I'm tired of hearing lies; tired of seeing people suffering and not being able to help them. You know, really help them, not the sort of help where that same thing happens five minutes later."

As she said that, she thought of the screaming woman she had heard in the alleyway outside of Red's bar back on Grantitan. She hadn't bothered to help her because she was too jaded, and she thought it wouldn't have mattered anyway. She thought of the tent city, and the poor family torn apart by the men in the gray suits. She had almost been killed herself ... and her parents. Her nerves stood on end as the thought of their murder crossed her mind and she had to block it out. How many more lives had been changed forever by the evil and corrupt forces that held her planet in their relentless grip?

"I know. That is what I want as well. We must not forget, however, that everything that has befallen us pertains to the path ahead. I count my blessings for being given the station in life to affect such change."

Frustrated, Lynn said, "So, things happen for a reason? There is that fate crap again. Why is everyone obsessed with that? I thought we lived in a time of science, not blind faith."

Jett turned and looked at her. "You do not believe in fate?"

Honestly, she wasn't sure. On the one hand, she kept telling herself she was here for a reason, but on the other, it had all been a result of her own choices and unrelated to any kind of cosmic coincidence, right? Except for Alex catching the slab and Zach being there to witness it, which she supposed led to all this.

"I think people have destinies, in the sense that we have inherent abilities and dispositions that lend themselves to certain paths better than others, but fate, no. Coincidences followed by actions are still coincidences."

At any time, Lynn could have said no to Zach and so could have Alex. The fact that they followed through did not make the incident at the stadium "fated." All it meant was that Alex and Lynn were destined to leave Calivia, one way or another. They were both wayward souls with a broader purpose than the life of the proletariat.

"I disagree. I believe actions lay the foundation for fate. You know, I used to look at the stars a lot as well. When I was growing up, my mother rarely let me leave the palace, and I would get bored sometimes and climb up the towers and sit there. I often dreamed about the world outside the palace. This was especially true about space. I had learned that there were other planets and different species of people and animals out there somewhere, beyond the stars, and I just wanted to see them. To me, the night sky was not unlike a deep, dark ocean, whose vast and mysterious depths may never be known to me."

He paused for a time and Lynn thought about his assertion. She wasn't sure if she was convinced, but there was something compelling about imagining that her actions had meaning, that some invisible loom was somehow weaving together the threads of her intentions into a better future.

"I did know one thing," he continued. "I knew that someday I was going to find out what was up there. What if, through the tribulations we face in Prism, we stumble upon an answer to a question that people have asked for centuries? Would it not be our actions that changed the fate of the galaxy?"

Thinking for a moment, she answered without commitment. "I suppose so."

They stared at the fire for a minute until Jett finally said, "Well, we should get some rest. It's about time to switch shifts. Lynn ... Palmer, was it?"

"Yes, and you are Jett ... uh ..."

"Shorin."

"Shorin, okay, sorry, I'll remember now, okay?"

"All right. It was a pleasure speaking to you, Ms. Palmer."

"Yeah. People should get to know you." Lynn was surprised at herself for letting that slip out. Just a couple days ago, she would have spit on his shoes, and yet, there was something about him that suggested he was different from the others of his kind. She may have felt something for him that night, but if so, she didn't care to admit it.

"I think they will know about both of us soon."

"Definitely. Call me Lynn, by the way."

"Okay, Lynn."

The two of them switched with Alex and Sam and settled into the back of the cave. Lynn made herself as comfortable as she could against the wall next to Alex, which was not very comfortable. She tried to close her eyes and relax, but they kept fluttering, opening slightly every few seconds until she forced them shut. Her brain was going faster than a mustang on the run and she struggled to lay still. Prism, Pailon, Gran Karisu, the Grothians starting a war, Jett the prince, minotaurs ... she couldn't turn it off.

Thirty or so minutes of restlessness passed. Alex and Sam occasionally exchanged muffled words, but mostly she just heard the deafening sounds of her anxious thoughts tumbling around in her head.

Wait ... something critical clicked into place in her brain. All this information synced together in one wild, uncertain, and yet completely sensical proposition. Her eyes went wide at this thought and Lynn jumped up and approached Sam and Alex.

"Lynn?" Alex looked concerned.

Staring intently at him, she asked, "Do you remember what you were doing right before we got on the dropship?"

Confused, he answered, "You mean, on Pailon? I had breakfast and met everyone in the hangar. You were late—"

"No," she interrupted. "On the *Leviathan.* Right before the dropship left the warship, do you remember?"

"We were all doing the same thing ..." Alex clearly didn't understand what she was getting at.

Sam just watched curiously as Lynn went on. "I guess I mean, do you remember the dropship itself, before the turbulence started?"

"Sort of. I was so scared ... my mind kinda mashed it all together, I think."

"Me too, it's like everything happened within minutes and I remember that right before the crash, my head felt foggy, just like the first time we went into the simulator at the Haxenburg."

"I had a headache, but it was a bumpy ride and we had traveled a lot. What are you saying, exactly?" How could he not get it? Her mind was firing everywhere, trying to lock onto an idea with enough precision to blow the lid off it. She just wanted him to see the words she was struggling to construct a sentence with. Her brain shook like a machine gun on full auto.

Finally, she just spit it out.

"Don't you see? This *is* the test."

6

"Whoa, whoa," Siefer stopped her. "You think we are in a simulation? I get what you mean; I felt weird on the ship too, but what if you are wrong? What if this is real?"

She had been ruminating all night, trying to figure out how best to convey this hypothesis. Jett and Alex had accepted it more easily than she had expected, but she could tell by the incredulous looks of the other cadets that they would not be quickly persuaded.

Lynn explained, "Yes, all of this is a simulation. We are being tested *right now* for Raynor Academy. That's why they had us put on the rykai suits on the *Leviathan*: to trick us so that when we had the suits on in this simulation, we wouldn't suspect it."

"You know that sounds crazy, right?" Kiah asked.

Blake stepped to the front of the cave and argued, "And what happens if it isn't a simulation? What then?" Lynn had been through this with Sam the night before and had plenty of practice in overcoming this objection.

"It doesn't matter, does it? Don't we want the same outcome either way? To get out of here and not die, right?" Lynn answered.

"Except that if it *isn't* a simulation, we *actually* die," Sam pointed out.

Leon interjected. "No, no, but she does have a point. We don't want to die in the test, either, or we probably fail. So, we just don't die."

Even in the dim, rising light of the breaking dawn Lynn could see the resentment on Sam's face at the suggestion that she was wrong.

"Look, anyway, when Alex and I were training, we were told that if you use the simulators too much, you don't feel the transition as much," Lynn pushed. "We didn't use the simulator much recently, so we still felt it phasing us in. I'm telling you!"

Siefer joined in again. "So, who cares? If it makes no difference whether it is a simulation or not, then why are we discussing it? Let's just get out of here."

"Yes!" Sam threw her hands up and agreed. "Thank you."

"We are discussing it because while the avoidance of death is a goal of both scenarios, whether it is real or a simulation changes the location of our escape," Jett explained.

Blake was amused. "Fascinating ... what would the goal be then, mate?"

"Zach said 'not all of us would make it to the academy.' The goal is not to get rescued, the goal is to find Raynor Academy," Lynn said. It was the only thing she could think of that made sense. Zach knew all along that they would be phased into this test, they would crash, and they would have to fight the rippers. That explained the rykai suits, the crash, the coincidence, and everything else in between.

"Zach said 'the academy is located on a remote part of Gran Karisu.' That must be the goal of the simulation," Alex followed up.

"Yes! Somewhere that we could reasonably get to out here, we will find it, and then we pass the test."

"You believe all this?" Blake asked, looking at Jett.

"It seems a likely possibility, given the infamously mysterious nature of the Prism test and the unlikely circumstances surrounding what we suspected to be a Grothian engagement."

Raising his eyebrow, Siefer nodded and said, "Yeah, I was thinking about that. The Grothians aren't fools."

"They would not engage a Prism warship so deep in Sarian space. Even if they did, we would likely have seen smaller ships enter the atmosphere by now. The simulation would also explain why there has been no rescue vessel."

"I wouldn't put anything past those sons of bitches," Sam grumbled.

"Anyway," Blake moved on, "What if we go galloping around for the academy and it isn't here? We could miss the rescue ship."

"If there is one. You don't think they can track us anyway, with all the technology they have?" Lynn insisted, "I mean—"

Lynn's point was cut short by a sudden, desperate scream from within the forest. It sounded like a woman, and she was definitely in danger.

Everyone looked toward the forest and Jett pointed east. "It came from over there!" He rushed into the tree line. All the cadets followed behind him and prepared their weapons for a fight.

"Should we be running toward the danger?" Blake wondered as they battled through the undergrowth, being snapped at and torn up by the thorny brush.

"Someone is in trouble!" Alex reminded him.

"What if it's a simulation?" he asked sarcastically. "We want to win, right?"

"What if it isn't?"

They heard the scream again, this time practically on top of them. Then a low roar, too deep and powerful to be a ripper. No, rippers made more of a snarl, this was akin to a bear or a large cat.

Or perhaps an ogre.

Jett and Lynn were the first to break out of the trees and into a flat, overgrown clearing, where they witnessed a huge, four-armed goliath of a creature rampaging around a formation of rocks and a massive, ancient tree that had fallen over it. Between the rock and the sturdy trunk of the tree was a short, skinny woman looking terrified and helpless as the ogre tried to reach for her. A dark-haired man was on top of the biggest rock, reaching down into the gully and calling for her to take his outstretched hand. The tree started to crack as the ogre shoved up against it, reaching wildly in between the rocks as the woman dodged side to side and cried for help.

Fearlessly, Jett rushed toward the ogre and yelled, "Hey! Face me, animal!"

To Lynn's surprise, the ogre seemed to understand Jett, and it turned and grunted something barely comprehensible. It raised its arms and leaped at Jett, who quickly sidestepped before the ogre came crashing down into the ground with a big puff of dust. Faster than Lynn would have thought possible, the ogre thrashed at Jett again, but Jett deployed his pulse shield in time to thwart the beast's crushing fists. It roared in pain and irritation, recoiling away from Jett as the barrier delivered an electric shock. The force of the ogre's attack had been so great that it had sent Jett sliding backward through the dirt.

"Jett!" Lynn called out, rushing in to join the fight. As the ogre turned its attention to her, Lynn drew one of her throwing knives off her left hip and flicked it expertly, burying the blade into the ogre's chest. It roared and Lynn sunk a second knife into it, this time near the ribcage.

"Die, human!" the beast seemed to say as it charged at Lynn. Panic set in as she realized her knives were like splinters to this creature. It hadn't even bothered to remove the blades before it rushed at her.

The other cadets came rushing out of the woods and Alex called out to Lynn, "Hold on, sis!"

He held his hands out and his gloves began to resonate as he channeled the earth in front of Lynn. She felt the ground tremble and knew a spike would surely rise any second and pierce the ogre's heart. She stood her ground, baiting the creature into the spike.

Sam called out, "Yo! Rippers! Watch out!"

It was too late. A pack of frenzied rippers burst out of the trees and engaged the cadets at the edge of the clearing. One ripper pounced on Alex, interrupting his channeling and pinning him to the ground. In the process, the ripper's bladed body gashed open Alex's right arm and hip. While Alex struggled for his life, the others engaged the pack.

"Go right!" Sam ordered the Corithians. "You two, left!"

Meanwhile, Alex's trap had failed, and the ogre was upon Lynn. Desperately, she tried to dodge out of the way, but it was too late, and the ogre's big, powerful hands latched onto her.

"No!" she screamed, struggling as it grabbed her right arm and wrist with its two left arms. Lynn went dead-weight and tried to slide under the ogre's legs, but it rudely yanked on her arm and lifted her up, her feet leaving the ground for a second. Something popped in her shoulder and she cried out. Ignoring the pain, she reacted by drawing her blaster with her left hand, but the ogre quickly batted it out of her hand. Oh God, she feared, what if this wasn't a simulation? Her heart was slamming out of her chest and she was urgently churning ideas around her brain to try and stay alive.

Suddenly, the ogre roared and bucked its hunched over torso into the air, pulling Lynn around like a rag doll and practically shattering her eardrum. Her arm couldn't be in the socket anymore, she decided as she dangled painfully.

After she had been lifted into the air, Lynn could see that Jett was firing his blaster into the ogre's back. The other man, who had been on top of the rock when they emerged, was coming up on the other side of the ogre.

This was her chance. Her left hand was still free.

The ogre spun around to face the two men, and the second that Lynn saw an opportunity, she flicked her left wrist at the ogre's face, activating the poisonous spray hidden beneath her armor.

Reeling in agony, the ogre dropped Lynn and all four of its hands clawed at its face. Lynn tried to scurry away, but a second later, the ogre swung its arms like thick, flying logs in a full, blind arc, battering Lynn and launching her into the air. Lynn bounced off a rock several feet away and fell face first on the ground. Pain surged through her body like someone was beating her bones with a mallet.

"Oh, God! Are you okay?" A woman's voice asked from a distance. Everything sounded like echoes. Someone touched her but Lynn couldn't get up to see who it was. She turned her head, but her vision was blurry. The ogre was still there and the men were flanking it. At least, she assumed so, because they looked like faraway mirages. Was she dying? If she was, would she be so aware of it?

"Hey!" the woman screamed again. "Hey! You stay alive, you hear me?"

Lynn felt herself being rolled over and then she could see the sky. Clouds were rolling in, the kind that would probably bring rain. It smelled wonderful. The woman came into view, and she looked down at Lynn and spoke reassuringly to her. "It's gonna be okay. You are okay, you hear?"

"You have to help them," Lynn choked out.

A familiar clinking sound burrowed into Lynn's ear and she looked down her chin to see Leon's drones unfolding their tools and working on her wounds. The pain from the drone's healing process was stinging and constant as they moved around her body. Squeezing her eyes shut, she gritted her teeth and prayed that it would be quick so she could get back up and help.

"Okay, your wounds are healing, you are okay, hun," the woman said. What was she doing? *Go help Jett!* She wanted to scream. The woman continued, "I have to do this, I'm sorry." What was she—

Lynn screeched as she felt the woman tug on her arm and pop it firmly back into place.

"So sorry!"

"God!" Lynn winced, getting to her knees.

When she looked up Jett was being thrown to the ground with massive force and the ogre was preparing to crush him. The guy from the top of the rock emptied his last clip on the ogre, exacerbating its rage. Lynn wondered to herself how to kill this crazy thing. It must have some type of carapace to take all those bullets.

Instead of stomping Jett, the ogre turned around and caught the other man's wrist just as the gun started to click empty. A primal roar escaped the ogre's larynx as he got hold of the man's other arm and he yanked the man into the air. The ogre's two lower arms wrapped around the man's torso in a bear hug and began crushing his ribs. The poor, helpless man could only scream bloody murder as the ogre held his arms straight out and broke his bones. With one big, bloody roar, the ogre ripped both of the man's arms clean off before discarding the deformed and destroyed body on the ground.

Lynn was completely shocked. She would never forget the sounds that man made before he was ripped apart.

Jett had gotten up but decided better of facing the ogre head on again. He tried to get away, to get closer to the others, but the ogre was upon him too quickly, and soon he was scooped up just like the other man had been. Lynn knew what was next.

Ignoring her fear, she rushed into battle and yelled, "Hey! Attack me, you asshole!"

It seemed the ogre would not be distracted, and it began to crush Jett. She had to do something! There was one thing she hadn't tried.

From about ten feet away, Lynn pulled three four-point ninja stars off her belt and tossed them skillfully at the ogre's legs, sticking two in the left leg and one in the right. The murderous beast bellowed angrily, but it wasn't the end. These were not ordinary throwing stars. At the tip of each point there were sensors, and when these sensors detected significant impact, such as being thrust into the flesh of an ogre, they triggered a mechanism inside the device that caused the star to explode, inflicting massive damage. In this case, the explosions, while minor enough to avoid damaging Jett, were significant enough to blow the ogre's left knee entirely off and to leave a gaping hole in the calf of the right leg.

Finally, the ogre released Jett and went crashing to the ground.

"Jett! Are you okay?" Lynn asked, rushing to his side as he fell to the ground.

"I'm fine," he assured her. "Finish it off!"

Alex called from behind them, "Move aside!"

They quickly obliged as Alex stood before the ogre, his gloves channeling. The ground shook beneath the ogre and his bloody stubs of legs and there was no chance left. Three rock spikes burst forth from the earth, one at a time, impaling the beast through the abdomen twice and through the head once.

At last the ogre went still.

The rippers had been dispatched as well and everyone gathered around the ogre's body, staring in awe at the skewered death.

"Thank you for saving me," Jett said.

"You're welcome," Lynn replied, elated at the idea of having contributed in a meaningful way, unlike the previous day at the crash site.

"That's the last of it," Sam said, as she examined the tree line for signs of any other monsters.

"Any injuries?" Leon asked, his drones floating in his hands while he circled the area where everyone was gathered. Alex tore open his suit where the ripper's body had left a gash, and Leon began to work on it.

"I can help too," the new woman said, producing her own drones. "I am a healer as well."

Lynn perked up. "Was it you that healed me? I thought it was Leon."

"Just little old me. I'm Reanyn. Thank you all so much for saving me."

"Thank you for healing me. My name is Lynn. I am sorry about, well, you know." Her eyes went briefly toward the heap of crushed bones and bodily fluids that used to be a man, and she thought better of saying more.

"Was he your mate?" Blake wondered.

"We found each other after the crash. Both of us were ejected. We didn't know each other before, but he helped me, and I was so grateful. Poor Karson ..."

There was an awkward silence until Jett stepped forward and said, "My condolences. You must be shaken. I am Jett Shorin, and may you rest assured, you have a place in our group."

"Yes, welcome," Leon agreed. "Glad to meet another healer. I am Leon."

"A pleasure. Thank you so much again! We would have both been goners if you hadn't come along."

Siefer chimed in, "Hey, no problem. We have to get moving, though. More of those things could come. All this commotion has probably got half the forest headed this way."

"Yes. Let us return to camp and gather our supplies. Then we shall proceed to the ridge," Jett instructed them.

As Jett led the way, everyone began to follow. Lynn waited behind with Alex, to take up the rear.

"I am so sorry, sis," Alex apologized. "I didn't stop it in time."

"It's okay. We made it, right?"

"Yeah, but you could have died."

A hand came down heavily on Lynn's shoulder, causing her heart to skip.

"Good job," Sam said.

"Thanks," Lynn replied, annoyed and shrugging Sam's hand off her shoulder.

Sam completed the compliment anyway, even though Lynn was walking away. "That's the kind of grit we need. Keep it up."

Lynn kept going, Alex right beside her, and didn't acknowledge Sam. Still, she wasn't able to stop the grin from forming at the creases of her mouth at the thought of Sam being impressed by her. If Lynn could keep going like this, she had a real shot at making it into Prism. Maybe she could do this after all. For now, she returned her focus to their next move and marched back to the cave with her head held high.

7

Debate sparked up again when the cadets returned to the camp. Not everyone agreed that they were in a simulation or, if they were, that the end goal of said simulation was to find Raynor Academy. Few alternative views were offered, and in the end the majority voted to follow Lynn's hypothesis. To compromise, Jett proposed to the nay-sayers that they chart a course that would take them near enough to the second crash site to see if there were survivors there or if they had moved on as well. No one disagreed that a ship hadn't flown over them, so if the second crash site was empty, it meant there was nothing there for them.

They embarked up and across the crumbly shale ridge that enclosed the forest, watching their steps as they traversed the narrow and shifty terrain. On the other side of the ridge, a blustery plateau stretched for miles as far as Lynn could see, its bright green and yellow grasses and occasional tall and shady trees undulating in the uninhibited wind. It reminded Lynn of the outskirts of Calivia, except without the pollution from the mines. Kind of like the countryside estate she had lived in when she was with the Palmers. Unexpectedly she felt a twinge of longing, a grasping pain for a lost life. Things *seemed* so hard and complicated in those days, when she was missing her brother, resenting her foster parents, and being forced to learn to ride horses and play the piano. Now, things *were* complicated. Life back then had been simple and peaceful, if only she had recognized that at the time.

To their surprise, the second crash site was not empty. Brock and three others were there, sitting by a campfire while they fiddled with the communication device from inside the cabin. Apparently there had been a vote in the second camp as well, only there had been less respect for the outcome. Half the group had left the site in search of the academy, having come to the same conclusion as Lynn's group, and Brock and the others had stubbornly stayed, not wanting to miss rescue, should it come. This had happened the day before; Brock and his group had been at the site alone for around eighteen hours before Lynn's group arrived, and they had since changed their tune about rescue.

So the two groups merged and set out over the ridge once again, this time going down the other side. Someone from the new group had an interesting theory: the academy was somewhere on the plateau. He thought this because it was the most open and unassuming slab of Gran Karisu that they could reasonably reach, and that was the trick. Anyone could look over the ridge at this endless stretch of plateau and assume nothing would be found there. Of course, if this was wrong, they'd be in trouble. It would be a lot harder to find food and shelter out there.

As they reached the plateau, they fanned out into a sort of semi-circle, covering their flanks. It had been harder to move on the ridge and it felt much safer here. Unless one believed there were Grothians out there, Lynn supposed.

Glad to no longer have to concentrate on not falling to her death, Lynn asked Alex, "Do you think we will find it out here?"

His face scrunched as he thought.

"I really do," he answered.

"Don't worry about before. I messed up at the crash site, so we are even, right?" Even though he hadn't said anything, Lynn knew her brother and she could tell he was beating himself up over letting the ogre get ahold of her.

He smiled. "Yeah, I guess we are."

Light-hearted as they were about it, Lynn assumed Alex understood, just as she did, the gravity of it all. Even if they were in a simulation, someday they wouldn't be, and some unfortunate guy would have been getting his arms ripped off for real.

Reanyn caught up to them, winded, and said, "Hey, I wanted to say something earlier, but I never got a chance to talk to you."

"Me?" Lynn asked, pointing at herself.

"Yeah. Just ... I already told Jett, but I ... it's just that I am not much of a fighter. I am so sorry for not helping you kill that big monster."

Sympathetically, Lynn said, "You did help me, you healed me."

"Yeah, but anyone can do that. All they have to do is learn how to operate the drones. What you and the others did was way courageous."

"We all had to learn our skills, just like you learned your drones," Alex reminded her. "We are all in this together and everyone is important."

Reanyn blushed and said shyly, "Jett said something similar."

Lynn couldn't help but ask, "If you don't mind me asking, if you are not a fighter, then how did you get endorsed for Prism? You have to get endorsed, right?"

"Sis!" Alex scolded.

"What? I am just curious."

"No, it's okay," Reanyn said. "A lot of people have asked me that. I am so weak; people think I am a joke."

Alex put his hand on her shoulder and looked at her compassionately. She shied away from him, her eyes falling to the ground as he said, "Don't say that about yourself. You are amazing at something, right? That's why you are here."

"I am good at programming," she admitted with an air of shame. Damn, even Lynn felt sorry for this woman. She didn't think it was possible to have such low self-esteem, and Lynn was an authority on the topic, being a person who had cut off her hair and changed her name just to escape her own identity. Honestly, at first glance, Lynn couldn't be sure what exactly there was to be insecure about. Reanyn's body was fit, and her dark skin looked smooth and beautiful, with her lustrous, thick black hair and dark brown eyes providing great complements as well. Certainly, she was pretty, but also, if she knew how to program well enough to be endorsed for Prism, she must be mind-blowingly intelligent as well. Wasn't that the whole package?

"Really? What kind of programming?" Alex removed his hand, but still looked at her with interest as he spoke.

"Any kind. If it has a circuit board or a microchip, I can figure it out." She sounded more at ease already. Alex could do that to people. He had done it to Lynn enough times.

"That sounds awesome!"

She smiled and laughed a little. "Thanks."

Lynn was about to weigh in when something happened up ahead. Jett, Blake, and Leon were the first to encounter it, then Sam and Siefer came up right behind them and saw it too. Everyone could feel it once they were upon it.

"This is it," Jett said proudly, as all of them gathered around him. "Great job, Lynn."

For no apparent reason, there was a massive forcefield in the middle of the plateau. Standing in front of it, they could see heat rising off its transparent surface and they could feel subtle pulses of energy emanating from it. They could even hear a low buzzing noise, like the sound of an electric fence, coming from the barrier.

Jett reached forward with two open palms and placed them on the forcefield, causing it to surge with energy around his hands and pulse outward in a series of ripples. As he stepped forward, the forcefield parted upward and out, like a backward zipper, revealing the most amazing city Lynn had ever seen.

Three massive, small-city sized spires rose at various levels above the plateau, each containing complex grids of high-tech buildings and skyways. Small aircraft zipped back and forth between the spires and in and out of the cities on top of them. It was the stuff of Lynn's wildest dreams.

"Welcome to Epilogue City," Zach Brine said as he appeared before them from seemingly nowhere. Lynn started to feel sleepy, her head became fuzzy, and the wondrous planet of Gran Karisu faded to black.

THE GAUNTLET

1

More than half of the cadets never saw the academy. Once Lynn and the others phased out of the simulation, they found themselves back on the dropship in the exact seats where they had been before the crash, completely unscathed but a little dizzy. Somehow the neurosensors had been placed on them, just like in the pods below the Haxenburg. One other thing was significantly different as well: many of the seats around them were now empty and only one hundred forty of the original two hundred twenty cadets remained on the ship.

Before the ship dropped them safely atop the western spire of Epilogue City, it was explained to them that as soon as the cabin was sealed they had been subjected to a powerful sleeping gas. It was subtle but powerful and none of them had even realized it. Once the cadets were asleep, the officers phased them in by activating the neurosensors in their seats. As for those who were no longer on the ship, their resumes had been seen and duly declined, and so, they got to have the honor of dying in the crash simulation for the sake of the immersion of the survivors. They had been deposited back on the Pailon Space Station while the others were being tested.

Lynn was beside herself but there was no time to think about it. Soon after they phased out, they were on the ground and whisked out of the dropship and onto the landing pad.

Zach was the first to speak. "Well, here we are. Congratulations to those of you who proved yourself and made it this far. Do not get too cocky; some of you died in the simulation but performed well enough prior to that to skate by. That won't work here."

Lynn noticed Karson standing across from her, looking peeved with himself.

Zach continued, "You are the top one hundred forty candidates in the galaxy, and you will be treated as such on this campus. There is no set number of you that will make it to Prism. Rather, we shall only take the worthy. Now, for the second part of your test."

Second part? As if Gran Karisu's wilderness had not been enough ...

"Your existence here at Raynor Academy is not yet proof that you are worthy to be called a Prism soldier. As you train and learn our ways, you will endeavor in this next challenge, one which will test your critical thinking and your rykai skills in never-before-seen ways."

He motioned toward Rachel and said, "I give you the mastermind behind this test, Instructor Rachel Mccginneas."

She cracked her knuckles and addressed the group. "All right, then. Listen up! The first part of your test was a warm-up. Instructor Brine always likes to pitch softballs to the newbies, but understand this, I am not Instructor Brine. My pitches will be fast and hard and if you can't keep up, you will go home. I will have no backtalk, no bitching, and no incompetence. Do you understand me, you screw ups?"

"Yes, sir!" the cadets answered obediently.

"And around here, we say "Yes, Instructor," you got that?"

"Yes, Instructor!"

"Better."

Zach smirked and said, "Regrettably, I must take my leave to attend to an important matter. Try not to cry."

He stole away to the back of the group and disappeared across the campus while Rachel examined her playthings. The first person she went up to was Karson, the unfortunate little man, and she taunted him, grabbing his shoulders and asking, "How are the arms?" She laughed and moved on.

"You big idiot," she said to Brock. "Zach calls 'em like he sees 'em, huh?"

As she marched back and forth, she insulted a few more cadets that Lynn had never met, then she turned her focus to the test. "Some others of you did marginally well in there, but I wonder, how well would you do against other rykai fighters? It's one thing to kill a bunch of mindless beasts and another entirely to have to outsmart a trained, critically thinking soldier. For example ..."

Abruptly, she stopped right in front of Lynn and reached behind her back, grabbing hold of something small and cylindrical and instantly transforming it into an electrified bo staff. As fast as she had produced it, she spun it around with back-breaking speed and struck the back of Lynn's knee, sending awful jolts of electricity through Lynn's body and knocking her flat onto her back. Her mouth tried to let out a yelp, but the wind was gone from her chest and all that came out was empty air.

Rachel was standing over her in a second with her staff pointing at Lynn's face. On the end of the staff was a steel point in the shape of a pyramid and it was inches from Lynn's eye.

"Get up!" Rachel demanded.

As the staff retracted, Lynn got to her feet.

A second later, Rachel drew her staff and knocked her down again. Lynn's head started pounding after it bounced off the landing pad. No one dared to object.

"You got lucky to have stumbled upon the Corithians," Rachel scoffed at Lynn. "You don't deserve to be here."

Hatred was eating Lynn alive as she stared spitefully at Rachel. She wanted so badly to unleash on her, to tell her what she deserved, but she gathered all her mental strength and resisted. After all, she hadn't come this far to be failed for such an infraction.

"Get up."

Lynn prepared herself for a third strike, but one never came.

Instead, Rachel returned to the center of the landing pad. "This test is called the Prism Gauntlet. To receive consideration to graduate this academy, you must complete the test. More will be explained tomorrow. For now, you will remain in your lines and you will follow Instructor Terif into the academy and to the armory, where you will remove your rykai suits. Then you will be escorted to the dormitories. Most of you don't deserve to see these walls, so count yourselves lucky that Instructor Brine has allowed you to be here. Any questions?"

Obviously, there were questions, and obviously no one would ask them.

"No, Instructor!" The cadets answered instead.

"Well, get to it then, go, go!" She rushed them, waving her hands toward the campus with irritation.

"Right this way!" Instructor Terif guided them away from the landing pad and across an intricate stone walkway toward the academy.

"Yes, Instructor!"

Lynn wanted so badly to talk to Alex and the others. Her nerves were just about fried from everything and she just wanted a few minutes to vent and let her brain catch up. Instead, she had Rachel behind them and Instructor Terif in front of them yelling and making them jog down the pathway. Lynn's eyes couldn't decide what to focus on; all around them were big brick buildings, ivory towers, and mystical gardens. Looming over the beautiful campus, there were massive bunkers housing turret cannons and anti-air lasers. Prism soldiers patrolled the grounds and various military vehicles were traveling back and forth to different installations. Everything was so impressive and so prestigious, exactly as she had first seen this place inside the simulator back below the Haxenburg.

Soon they were funneled into the grand hall and led around the outer perimeter of the massive building, eventually leading them to a pair of sliding doors that opened up into a massive dome-shaped room, much like the armory they had gone into on the *Leviathan*. In much the same fashion as before, the cadets were instructed to walk up to individual booths and stand on the circular platforms in the center. On command, robotic arms came from above and behind them and removed their weapons and armor, piece by piece, until the cadets were left wearing simple body suits.

"This room will be your church," Rachel explained. "It is both an armory and a simulator. You will spend much time here."

They were whisked away again, down a couple more hallways and into a huge rectangular room that harbored a beautiful courtyard separated from its exterior walkways by white cylindrical columns. The walkways covered three sides of the courtyard, with the fourth being an open outdoor pathway to the greater campus.

Alex snapped her back to reality. "We made it, sis."

"Yeah, we really did."

"Stop!" Instructor Terif commanded, suddenly halting and turning to face them. The cadets swiftly formed into lines and stood at attention.

Instructor Mccginneas came around to the front of them. "Ahead of you is the dormitory. On each of your bags is a room assignment. Find your room and get settled, then take a few minutes to acclimate yourself to the layout of the academy. I will accept no excuses tomorrow. If anyone is even a minute late to any activities, I will personally boot your ass out of here. Do I make myself clear?"

"Yes, Instructor!"

"Very good. You are dismissed."

"Yes, Instructor!"

Finally, they were at ease. Lynn breathed long and easy. For just a moment, she felt like the hardest part was over, though in the back of her mind she knew that couldn't possibly be true. Whatever this Prism Gauntlet was, surely it would be hellish.

Jett approached Lynn and Alex as the cadets broke away toward their rooms. "Congratulations. Your performance during the first test was impeccable."

"Thanks, but I think you did more than we did," Alex replied.

"Yeah," Lynn agreed. "I could have done a lot better."

"It was because of you that we identified the primary objective," Jett reminded her. "Take the credit that you well earned."

"I guess so."

Blake and Leon appeared, and Jett said, "We should find our rooms, but we will meet again soon. I look forward to our continued success together."

"Right back at ya," Alex reached out and shook Jett's hand.

"Later mates," Blake said, and the three of them walked off, talking amongst themselves.

Sam walked by and startled Lynn with a soft punch to the shoulder.

"Nice work," she commended, winking at Lynn and hustling on to find her room.

"Jett's right, you deserve credit for figuring out Zach's trick," Alex insisted. "You were awesome, sis."

"Thanks, you are right. Come on, let's find our rooms. I want to put my stuff down." Lynn started down the long hall that had all the dormitory rooms along the right and the courtyard to the left and Alex followed right beside her.

"Sounds good. Hey, you think they have food around here? I'm famished!"

She joked, "No, I'm sure they'll just make us starve."

He laughed, stopping abruptly before room eighty-two. "Well, this is mine. Catch up soon?"

"Oh, okay, yeah. Give me a few. I'm gonna smoke, I'll see you in the courtyard."

Alex smirked and said, "Okay, later, sis."

He went inside and left her to find her room alone. Everyone else was chatting and joking, some yelling, hustling, or wrestling in the halls. This assault on Lynn's ears made her realize that she wasn't feeling particularly social. Actually, she was completely drained. When she thought about it, she realized she had no real concept of how long she had been awake. How many days had passed since they arrived on Pailon? Was the passage of time inside the Gran Karisu simulation a true depiction of reality, and did that reflect on her unconscious body? Whatever the answers were, all Lynn wanted to do was pass out.

When she finally found her room, she threw her bags haphazardly onto the floor beside the bed and went over to the vanity in the corner of her room. With great pleasure, she stripped off the body suit and her sports bra and let out a huge breath as she tossed the clothes on the floor. For a moment, she examined herself in the mirror: she looked a mess, exhausted and beaten up. She couldn't help but dwell on what Rachel said. To some degree, Lynn was being carried by the others, and that couldn't go on.

Eventually, she had to shine on her own. Maybe she could learn from the others. No matter what, she couldn't doubt her choices. *Just remember why you came here*, she kept thinking, *and never give up.*

Lynn slid on a pair of shorts and a gray tank top and tried to stop thinking about it. If her mind got going too much, she wouldn't sleep again, and she was going to need all her energy for tomorrow.

She took a few deep breaths, reset herself, and grabbed her cigarettes before heading out into the courtyard. Plenty of cadets were already smoking and joking, so it must be okay. Alex found her after a minute and they smoked for a while, reminiscing about old times and trying not to stress. After about twenty minutes or so Lynn retired back to her room, took a quick shower, and collapsed onto the bed. As she lay there on her belly, half-asleep, she prayed: *Please, let me succeed tomorrow.*

2

At exactly six a.m., just as the sun was peeking out from behind the distant mountain range, Lynn received a hard awakening. Sirens and bells rang loudly as Prism officers raided the dormitory and compelled the cadets to dress themselves and report to the courtyard for roll call. In two minutes, Lynn was primed and ready and rushed outside to line up. This, Instructor Terif assured them as he patrolled the courtyard in front of them, would be standard practice every day, followed by a three-mile run around campus, then breakfast. The rest of their morning would be spent on calisthenics and classroom activities. After lunch, they would spend the entire afternoon in the simulator, perfecting rykai fighting. They would repeat these activities six days a week, stopping to recover only on Sundays, until the worthiest group of cadets presented themselves, at which time they would become Prism soldiers. There was no set time frame for this, Terif informed them, as there was no way of knowing how long it would take for worthy cadets, if any existed, to emerge. If at any time during the trials, cadets proved definitively unworthy, they would be removed from consideration and asked to leave the academy. It was also possible no one would make it.

And so, the cadets ran.

After a hearty breakfast, the cadets were hurried into the classroom, where Instructor Mccginneas stood before them and gave a lecture in front of a three-dimensional holo-terminal that was portraying images of Grothian soldiers and weaponry. As the images cycled on the screen, Instructor Mccginneas explained the history of the Sarian's political affiliations with the Grothians and the importance of preparation against them.

They were a proud, spartan people, Mccginneas explained, valuing strength, honor, and vigilance over all other values. Piety was also important to them. The Grothians believed they were children of the old gods, the deities who allegedly created the universe. All Grothians worshiped the old gods and strived to cultivate themselves in their images. Those who rose to the height of the Grothian caste system were the soldiers, and the best of their soldiers became known as "templars." To qualify as a templar, one had to master at least one form of psychic power; often templars would be telekinetic, or telepathic and able to communicate through unspoken mind frequencies. It was thought the ability to learn these powers meant the old gods accepted templars as their galactic crusaders.

If you ever encountered a templar, you had to assume it could read your mind. The only way one could win against an opponent that could predict your every move was to block all new thoughts from being plastered across your mind. This was where mantras came in—by repeating the same phrase over and over in your mind, it would prevent the templars from knowing your moves. Zach had explained briefly that these would be needed, and Lucas had drilled it into Lynn and Alex. Everything was coming together now.

There had been a lot more to the lecture, but Lynn's mind kept wandering. Her stomach dropped every time she thought about the test coming this afternoon. So much anxiety ... she just wanted to get in there and get it over with.

Finally, after an hour that seemed more like four or five, Instructor Mccginneas dismissed them to the gym, where they would spend the rest of the morning with Instructor Terif doing circuits and calisthenics. Then the cadets had lunch, and at last it was time to enter the simulators.

Everyone reported to the armory, where they were assigned to their pods and given five minutes to select their rykai suits. In the center of the room was a massive holosphere, a three-dimensional display that depicted two Prism soldiers dueling each other with electrified bow staves. Two steel catwalks in the shape of an X overlooked the room from above, converging at the center of the holosphere and connecting at each end to the upper level of the dome, an area accessible only to officers.

Rachel loomed over the cadets and she bellowed, "Hurry up, time's a-wastin'! It is high time for me to eliminate you! The more of my time you waste, the more annoyed I become!"

When the cadets' allotted time expired, Rachel explained the test before them.

"You are about to enter the Prism Gauntlet," she informed them. "Inside this simulation the conditions may vary in an infinite number of ways. No two runs will be the same. The goal is to outwit and outlast your peers. When the algorithm decides you are worthy, the simulation will end on its own. If you die, you fail. The first group of ten cadets that finish the Gauntlet will graduate and become Prism soldiers without contest. All others who finish the test will be considered according to a plethora of factors. This will be your life for however long it takes. Do you understand?"

"Yes, Instructor!" the cadets answered.

Lynn wasn't sure she understood Rachel's vague explanation, but there was no time to ruminate. Rachel commanded them to activate their pods and begin phasing in, and within seconds Lynn was feeling that familiar drowsy feeling and everything went black.

3

Rain fell on Lynn with gentle foreshadowing as the lunacy of lighting forked across the distant sky. Around her, the arid canyons sang in relief as the precious drops turned the dusty orange landscape into slick, smooth burgundy. From a clever shelf carved into the side of the mountain, she could see the lay of the land. For miles in either direction were jagged canyons and pillars of rock. Quite far to the northeast, there appeared to be a waterfall. Wait, what was she doing here?

The sounds of death were creeping up the cliffside from the labyrinth below and suddenly she recalled that she was in the Gauntlet. She wondered if she would ever get used to the transition into the simulator.

Lynn felt her brain hyperfocusing. Zach had dropped them into many scenarios like this in their training, where they were phased into unknown landscapes and made to survive whatever came into it. Knowing that she was in a simulation emboldened her. This was much different than her debut on Gran Karisu, when she had thought it was real. This was what she had trained for.

She decided she would seek the waterfall.

When she scurried down the ridge, the rain started to pick up and the thunder clapped closer and louder. Up ahead, she saw two other cadets entering a ravine, no one she recognized. Lynn snuck up to the edge of a rock pillar and peered around the corner. She activated her suit's cloaking device and carefully stalked them into the ravine. Was she supposed to kill them? It was a competition, right? Rachel had offered no advice in this way.

She waited a few seconds, and her patience was worth it. Suddenly, a barrage of gunfire rained down on the two cadets in front of her from somewhere up above.

With impossible reflex, one of the men turned around and unloaded three rapid fireballs in Lynn's direction, forcing her to react to the incoming salvo.

She managed to get away from the wall before the explosion, but she didn't avoid damage completely. The impact of the blast flung her to the ground and she was covered in rock and dirt and one large piece of the canyon wall had fallen on her ankle, pinning her to the ground. She shrieked in pain and her cloaking device failed, revealing her to the conjurer. God, how embarrassing. She was going to die already.

Luckily, another barrage of suppressing fire rained down upon the conjurer and his crippled comrade, keeping the attention away from her. Lynn couldn't see who was firing, but she capitalized on the distraction, rolling the rock off her ankle and stealing away into the shadows of a nearby overhang. From here she watched the two men get slaughtered by the hail of bullets. Nothing seemed to happen after the killings. That settled it, they were supposed to kill each other.

Seconds later, she heard Brock's voice. "I know you're here, little lady. You're next, you know."

Brock and two other men laughed and joked amongst themselves. They were on the rocks right above her. Looking at her chewed-up ankle, she figured there was no way she could run from them. Her best bet was to cause a diversion and get the hell out of this ravine.

Before she could form a plan, the men jumped down off the rock and started looking around. She cloaked herself quickly, her heart beating out of her chest. Her invisibility used a lot of her power cells and she couldn't do it for long. Something had to happen.

"She's here somewhere," one of Brock's minions said.

"Yeah," Brock agreed. "She was just right there ..."

Lynn watched with terror as Brock examined the rock under which her ankle had been caught and began to trace the ground, following the drops of blood and scuffs of dirt all the way to her outcrop.

Decisively, Lynn bum-rushed the huge men, fighting through the pain of her ankle, and buried her serrated combat knife into one man's collarbone. His blood gurgled up his throat as he struggled for life and fell to the ground. She turned to his friend and flicked her wrist at his face, releasing her venom. The big man screamed and fell to the ground as well, writhing in agony as he clawed at his eyes and cursed at Lynn.

Brock wasn't close enough to pick off, she decided, and quickly dashed away. Her ankle was on fire.

"You bitch!" Brock yelled, firing reckless, fully automatic rounds in her general direction. She almost escaped unscathed, but just as she reached the corner of the ravine, a high-caliber bullet tore into her shoulder with such force that she stumbled and fell, cursing in pain and crawling to safety behind a large boulder.

As her cloaking device failed, she gripped her savaged shoulder and winced in pain. Quickly she applied her clay to the wound to stop the bleeding momentarily, then drew her pistol and laid it on her lap.

She listened for Brock.

Her ears were ringing badly from the explosion and the gunfire, but she could still hear a low clicking sound. Why? What was—

She cried out as she was startled by a sudden, searing pain. She covered her mouth in terror, but then she noticed the little drones going to work on her shoulder.

From a nearby bush, she saw Reanyn with her finger over her mouth, telling her to shush.

"I hear you!" Brock said, apparently quite close. Reanyn's drones retreated to safety and went quiet, so as to disguise their position. Both women readied their weapons and Lynn tried to peek around the boulder.

Brock was right there.

It was too late to hesitate; he had seen her, and she only had a second to react. Spinning around, Lynn fired four rounds over the top of the boulder; two connected and staggered the massive man. His body armor was so thick he didn't even fall over from her puny bullets.

"Damn, that smarts!" He laughed, unloading a barrage of his own and forcing Lynn back into cover. Reanyn stayed hidden, her hands over her head. What the hell was she doing?

Ok, she was going to try something else.

When she heard the gunfire stop, Lynn popped up again and flicked two explosive ninja stars at Brock and ducked back behind her cover.

Seconds later, two micro-explosions echoed through the ravine and she heard Brock yelping in pain. She showed that asshole. That was, what, four kills now? Not bad at all. Lynn pat herself on the back; she really was a student of Zach Brine.

She stood up to bask in her glory, but it wasn't a mangled corpse she saw.

Brock was right on top of her, his torso stripped of armor and burned significantly, and before she could react, he grabbed her by the neck with his bionic arm and lifted her off the ground.

Dashing out of the bush, Reanyn held a pistol up, but Brock was faster than her. Lifting his free arm, Brock fired a lethal shotgun blast from a cannon on his forearm, blowing Reanyn to smithereens before she could even fire a shot.

"You whore!" he cursed as he crushed Lynn's windpipe and she kicked and pried and desperately tried to break free. The malice in his eyes multiplied with every second she remained alive. She felt the life draining from her and, at first, she thought she could hear a faint whizzing sound, like the hum of a computer hard drive. This must be her dying, she thought, and she was hearing the sound of the simulator processing her strangulation and phasing her back into the real world.

As it turned out, she was one step ahead of herself. Seconds later, the buzzing came closer and more apparent, but before she made the correlation, Blake's bladed boomerang sliced through both Lynn and Brock, dicing their bodies into unrecognizable bits and blending their blood and guts together into frenzied macabre on the canyon floor.

Everything went black and Lynn woke up in her pod, gasping for life.

Bursting out of the pod, she examined herself and took several deep, heavy breaths, trying to quell her anxiety. It had been quite a while since she had died inside one of these. By the end of Zach's training, she had gotten quite good at living. Suddenly, she was forced to relive the trauma of all those times she had been torn to pieces by just about anything Zach could think of. Man, she had forgotten how badly one suffered as they phased out through death. It was like waking up from a horrific nightmare, barely able to breathe, dizzy, and terrified.

When she composed herself, Lynn saw all the dead cadets out of their pods and gathered around the holosphere, watching the remaining cadets fight it out. At first glance, it looked like nearly all the pods were empty. Had she made it that close to the end? That was good, wasn't it?

Lynn slid through the crowd and found a spot in front of the holosphere, next to Reanyn. Above them, Instructor Terif and Instructor Mccginneas patrolled the catwalks. Every few seconds, the holosphere shifted to display the avatars of different cadets that were still in the battle. Blake appeared, exiting the ravine where he had brutally ended Lynn and Brock, then Alex came into view, using the golem to camouflage himself as part of the rock wall next to the roaring waterfall. Lynn laughed a little to herself; it was quite impressive how he had used his weapon to hide instead of fight. Lynn was the one who could become invisible, and yet, she hadn't thought to just stay out of the fight.

"He is smart," Reanyn said.

"Yeah, my brother is pretty amazing."

"Wow, there are only seventeen left!"

"What? How do you know?"

"Over there." Reanyn pointed to a terminal on the wall behind the holosphere. On it, displayed in bold, blue lights, was a zero, one, and seven. Beneath it, a multitude of statistics were calculating in real time as the action happened in the holosphere. Static numbers seemed to be assigned to some areas. Lynn guessed it must be how they were assessed, though the meaning behind any of it was anyone's guess.

Her thoughts were bludgeoned by obnoxious voice of a stupid cadet next to her screaming, "Kill him! Kill the Corithian!"

Jett appeared on the holosphere, faced with two cadets chasing him through a dusty cave system. He prepared to deploy his pulse shield as the men flanked him and blocked the only easy exit back into the ravines. Inexplicably, Lynn noticed the ground shaking and the terrain beginning to shift. Mutual panic postponed the fight as Jett and his two attackers quickly fled the cave, escaping just in time to avoid its total collapse.

Outside, the landscape continued to terraform, the canyon walls flattening and becoming devoid of all features. The ground beneath them seemed to die; the grass went limp and yellow, and the few small trees cracked and fell before turning to dust. Other cadets were forced out of hiding as the landscape became bare and desolate. Now, the holosphere shifted to a woman Lynn didn't recognize, who looked bewildered as she peered across the naked canyon, now a brown and gray hallway of death. The exposed cadets stared ominously at one another, aware of the finality of their situation, and finally, the fight broke out.

Around the holosphere, the cadets kept jeering and shouting as the final sequence of the test played out. When Jett came on the screen again, he was capitalizing on the confusion from the terraforming arena, easily dispatching his two attackers with some kind of guided laser blasts. Lynn watched as the big blue ticker behind the holosphere turned to fifteen. Another cadet attempted to ambush Jett but was quickly sawed in half by Blake's blade.

"Jett is going to win," Reanyn guessed.

Lynn didn't answer. Instead, she watched intently as Alex finally revealed himself and prepared to fight the unwitting Corithians. Of course she didn't want to bet against her brother, but she had to admit, the Corithians were incredibly good, and there were two of them.

Alex got the drop on them, and to his credit, he made the first strike count. First, he raised the hillside beneath Jett into an uneven and hazardous surface, achieving two things: throwing Jett off balance and distracting Blake. Second, as Blake was drawn to what was happening to his friend, Alex channeled the ground behind Blake, calling forth a ruthless spike that sliced through Blake's abdomen, just below his ribs. Jett grimaced as he watched his friend's guts spill out the front of the jagged rock. Lynn watched the wall ticker turn to fourteen as Blake's life waned and dissipated.

Within seconds, Alex met Jett in the center of the canyon, both staring each other down with looks of determination and mutual respect. One had to die.

4

Almost two years before this unforgiving test, Alex had been hanging out with Rami and Trey in his little apartment, kicking back beers and playing video games. It had been a long week, and if Alex remembered correctly, Rami was having a pretty bad fight with Jocelyn and just wanted to forget about it. The best way to do that was to just be with friends and do something pointless and fun.

They were playing some shooting game; Alex couldn't even remember the name of it now, but the object of the game was to kill all the other players in the match and be the last one standing. Everyone spawned into the game at random locations and received only one life. Alex spent half the night screaming at the TV as he rounded corners or entered buildings and walked straight into the barrel of another player's gun. Alex started ranting, complaining about how he kept dying at the beginning and having to sit there and spectate for ten minutes while everyone else played.

"You have to find a good vantage point and hide," Rami explained. It all seemed obvious when he said it. If he never engaged, he couldn't die. All you had to do was kill the second to the last guy.

Alex still never won the game, but one thing he did do was learn the perfect strategy for the Prism test before him today. It was funny how such a random experience could so perfectly apply to such a different context.

So Alex hid behind his stone wall, ensuring he had a small opening near his face so he could peer out into the waterfall basin and see where everyone else was. Early in the challenge, he had assumed two things based on the landscape: Lynn would try to come to the waterfall and the battle would inevitably convene here. It was the most discernible landmark on the map and would attract many of the others, he reasoned.

It turned out he was right, and when he saw the arena shrinking and Jett picking off two cadets in the narrow canyon, Alex decided it was time.

Just as he dropped his rock cloak, Alex saw Blake's boomerang fly in from his right and slice through a cadet who had tried to sneak up on Jett.

Alex watched the boomerang return to its source and saw Blake coming down into the basin. It was clear that Blake had not spotted Alex yet.

Thinking quickly, he seized the opportunity for an ambush. First he caused a ruckus by raising the ground beneath Jett, throwing him off balance and grabbing Blake's attention. Then he called forth a rock spike and impaled Blake from behind.

He and Jett came to the center of the shrinking arena, facing each other for the final duel. For a moment, Alex wished he had ambushed Jett instead, as he thought perhaps Blake would have been an easier opponent, but he brushed it aside and focused on winning.

"May the best man win," Alex said.

Jett nodded in agreement and readied himself for combat.

Alex began by lifting the ground under himself, raising him several feet above Jett. Really, this was a distraction so that he could create a spike behind Jett. Perhaps he could pull off the same trick twice.

As the ground trembled, Jett rushed forward and planted something on the raised pillar of rock upon which Alex channeled, then he activated his shield while he escaped to a pair of nearby boulders. Alex gave up on the spike, conserving his power cells. He heard a beeping sound, a bomb! Too late to react though. A huge explosion blew out the base of Alex's roost, sending him hurtling into the ground where he was pummeled by falling pieces of rock.

Immediately Jett's rifle fire was upon Alex, forcing him to erect a small barricade of rock in front of himself. His heart was beating out of his chest while he listened to the bullets bounce off the stone. Alex looked down at his dirt-covered suit and took heavy breaths as he planned his next move. Suddenly the gunfire ceased. He had to act now.

He tossed a grenade over the wall to draw Jett out from the boulders, then drew his pistol and aimed it at where he expected Jett to come out. But Jett never appeared.

Alex took cover as the grenade exploded and decimated the area behind the boulders. Rock shrapnel fell everywhere, making a chorus of chaotic sounds as it rained down around Alex, but then it was silent. Where the hell was Jett?

His heart started beating faster again as Alex desperately scanned the battlefield. To reinforce himself, Alex erected walls on the other side of himself, such that he was crouched in a sort of raised foxhole, and he crafted himself stone bracers, just in case Jett got close to him.

None of that mattered.

Suddenly there was a low, heavy crashing sound, followed by the sound of rushing water. A massive wave appeared on the horizon and Alex barely had time to brace himself and take a huge breath of air before the errant wave overtook him and sent him careening down the canyon at breakneck speed. Alex felt like he had been hit by a car as he struggled against the current and tried desperately to breathe. The last thing he remembered after he surfaced was seeing the rocks in front of him; that jagged, inevitable death right in the path of the current. He felt the impalement in his gut first, followed by a bluntness accompanied by blindness and blinking, starry lights when his head smashed off the jagged rocks. Almost instantly, his body failed, and he was waking up in his pod, choking for air.

Furiously, Alex burst out of his pod and cursed, "Damn it! I was so close!" Feeling dizzy, Alex leaned on the wall next to his pod. His limbs felt weak from lying down and then suddenly jumping up.

A loud clamor ensued in front of him as the cadets surrounding the holosphere reacted to the conclusion of the second Prism test. Only four cadets had survived the white-water death, and within minutes of it, two more cadets were eliminated and only Jett and one other cadet remained.

They were about to begin the final duel when a strange, vertical scar of blue energy emerged before them and morphed into the shape of a humanoid lifeform. The lifeform was tall and brooding, with sleek and minimalist armor covering its entire body and a strange helmet that covered only the top half of its neck and the top of its head, from the eyes up. Its ears were elongated, like an elf in some fantasy story, and its skin was a light purplish hue. Only one lifeform that Alex knew of looked like this. A Grothian templar.

Before either of the men could react, the templar dashed with incredible speed toward Jett, so fast, in fact, that it seemed to vanish. Appearing behind Jett a moment later, the templar drew a long orange blade and slashed at him. Jett wasn't fast enough and the blade sliced right through his torso like butter. The templar's blade seemed to glow, as if it were freshly tempered steel, straight from the forge, and it left similar glowing orange traces around the edges of Jett's torso where it had cut.

The last remaining soldier seemed craven as the templar dashed toward him. All attempts to defend were futile. In a bloody flurry of incomprehensibly fast slashes, the templar divided the cadet's body into a dozen pieces before flicking the blood off his blade and returning it to its sheath at his side. With great Zen, the templar stood amongst his conquests, meditating for a moment. He collapsed back into blue energy and vanished.

When Jett came out of his pod and joined the group, Alex congratulated him. "Nice job, man. You were way better than me." It pained him to say that. Not because it was false, but because Alex had always hated losing. Especially when he knew that if not for the flood, there was a chance he could have won.

"Good fight," Jett commended him. Yeah right, Alex thought. He would get him next time.

By the time the last cadet had approached the center of the room, Rachel was coming down from her roost and yelling at everyone to get into formation.

"Attention!" She demanded as everyone lined up. "I must say, that was one of the most pathetic attempts I have ever seen at the Prism Gauntlet, and I have seen a lot of attempts. So we will conclude this portion of this test having proven none more worthy than when we began. Given that there are so many of you wasting my time, I am thinning the herd yet again. There are one hundred and forty of you now; on the scoreboard behind me,

Instructor Terif will post fifteen names. Those fifteen will take their bags and go back to the launchpad, where you will leave immediately. Understood?"

"Yes, Instructor!" everyone replied.

"You are dismissed."

A mad hustle began as all the cadets rushed over to the scoreboard, where names were quickly appearing. Even though he was confident his would not be there, Alex was still nervous.

"Alex!" Lynn called to him as she came through the crowd. "Alex, I can't believe you made it to the end!"

"I got lucky I guess," Alex joked.

Reanyn was with her and shot back, "Yeah right! You had a great strategy." It was good, wasn't it? Alex felt validated to hear someone else say it.

"I hope I'm not up there," Lynn said morosely as the last few names were appearing.

"If you are, I probably am too," Reanyn said.

"I'm sure neither of you are," Alex reassured them. It seemed like the names had stopped appearing and Alex counted them. Fifteen names, and none of them were Alex, Lynn, or Reanyn. Relief poured over Alex and he let out a big sigh.

"What a relief," Lynn said. "It's not us. That was stressful."

"I bet they will keep eliminating people," Alex guessed. "We have to make sure we are not the first ones killed."

Reanyn said, "I guess I should be more like you next time. Will you teach me good strategies?"

Alex smiled at her. There was something warm about Reanyn, something that reminded him of good times, like country music on a sunny afternoon. Maybe it was her peppy voice or her pretty smile that inspired his confidence. Maybe it was just that she seemed to admire Alex. All he knew was that he liked having her around.

"Stop," Alex teased her. "You do well on your own. You don't need to be like me. I'll teach you things if you want, though." He shot her a look, a subtle flirt, just to test the waters, and she seemed to blush, retreating her eyes to the floor.

Lynn rolled her eyes. "All right, hotshot, we get it. Let's get out of this freakin' place. I don't know about you, but I'm hungry and tired and I'm sick of looking at simulators." Alex couldn't help but laugh. His sister was always trying to block him when he flirted with women. Why, he could only guess. With her sick sense of humor, it was probably a game. Little did she know, Alex didn't care. Usually it just made women want him more.

"Okay," Reanyn agreed. "I'm gonna find my room and I'll catch up with you later, okay?"

"All right," Alex said. "Catch you later."

Instructor Mccginneas came up behind them and startled Alex. "Why are you still here? Get out of my arena already!" Her voice was so intimidating it made Alex's hairs stand up all over his body.

Only a few cadets were lingering in the arena now and they quickly shuffled out as Instructor Mccginneas berated them. Outside, the sun was setting, and the sky was shifting into brilliant shades of orange in the western sky. It almost felt weird having the cool evening breeze touch his skin, having spent so much time wandering between realities recently. There had been Pailon, the massive starship, the simulators ... so many different worlds that Alex had never seen before, and yet, here he was, and he was in the top fifteen. What a strange feeling. Alex only hoped he could keep living up to the expectations of everyone. After all, it was because of him that all of this had started.

"You all right?" Lynn asked suddenly, snapping Alex out of his thoughts. It seemed like she had been talking to him and he had been zoning out.

"Sorry. Man, I need a cigarette."

"God, me too."

The two of them headed across the courtyard and Alex decided to put his brain to bed for the night. As long as he was surrounded by great people like his sister, Reanyn, Jett, and Zach, he would be able to fulfill his destiny. He was certain of it.

5

Days passed and the cadets endured the same rituals. Each time they went into the Prism Gauntlet, it seemed as though Lynn was doing worse. She did everything she could think to do, and yet, whatever contingency she *didn't* prepare for was the one that got her. How was she supposed to prepare for a test that was different every time?

Honestly, though, it all seemed like a joke. One time, Lynn had phased in on top of a skyscraper with Sam and some other guy and they were immediately pursued by an attack helicopter. Sam thrust jumped to another rooftop and the other guy freefell off the edge. Lynn managed to get inside the building through the access door before the chopper shredded her. She got down about two floors before rounding a corner and ending up in a knife fight. The guy had a stupid shotgun attachment on his arm and that was the only reason he beat Lynn.

Another time, she was in some dense jungle, attacked by tribal people with spears and axes. After fending off a half dozen of them, and avoiding a pair of archers, she dodged a series of volcanic geysers that arose from nowhere. All this, and she was killed from behind by one of Brock's assholes.

In her most recent attempt, she had actually found Alex and Reanyn inside the test and they worked together to defeat several other cadets. It seemed like things were going well, but a dozen rippers suddenly attacked them, and it was over.

Hours after the day's trials were over, Lynn found she was still frustrated by all this. Every second she dwelled on it, she could feel her external locus of control sneaking back in, threatening to revive the nihilism that had controlled her for so long.

Alex and Sam were both in the courtyard already when she got there.

"Hey," Alex greeted her.

"What's up, girl?" Sam asked.

"I'm pissed," Lynn answered, lighting up a smoke.

"Me too," Alex agreed. "We'll do better tomorrow."

"That test is rigged."

Sam laughed. "Yeah. People told me this place is off the rails."

Everyone chuckled and took drags from their cigarettes.

Alex looked out at the darkening sky. "The sunset from here reminds me of Calivia."

"This place is nothing like Calivia," Lynn disagreed. There were much worse things in that city.

"Come on, it had its charm."

As they were talking, Reanyn came up beside Alex and sat on a white stone slab, close to the ground, looking rather somber as she slumped over.

"Yeah, it has more types of pollution than any other city, pretty unique."

After she had been there for a minute, Reanyn quietly said, "Sorry I am not much help to you."

Realizing she had rudely failed to acknowledge her, Lynn replied, "Oh, no, it's fine. You did help me a couple times."

"I won't betray you, if you are worried about that." Reanyn's voice was so soft that Lynn could barely hear her. She was certain she must have heard that weird thing Reanyn said incorrectly.

"What?"

"I said I won't kill you, as long as you don't kill me."

Incredulous, Lynn said, "That sounds swell and all, but what is in it for you?"

"What do you mean, isn't it obvious?"

"This is a competition," Alex piped in. "How are you going to win if you never kill us?"

"I probably couldn't even if I wanted to," Reanyn explained. "I am not a fighter. I am here because of my exceptional knowledge of computers and AI systems. All I have to do is finish in the top twenty-five percent in everything and I will make the cut. Just let me team up with you and I'll heal you and cover you. I'll even die in your place if it maintains our arrangement."

Sam belly laughed. "Well, hell, how do I get in on this deal? If all you want is to get to the top twenty-five, I can get you there better than these two. Why don't you heal me?"

Offended, Lynn asked, "Excuse me? The only thing I have seen you do is run."

Ignoring Lynn completely, Sam was still cracking up over Reanyn. "That's classic; I'll heal you if you don't kill me!"

Alex seemed to notice Reanyn was embarrassed and said, "We all have different skills. All she is suggesting is that we combine them. What is so crazy about that?"

Sam just laughed harder.

"Because it is a competition," Lynn reminded her brother. "I don't know about you, but I want to win it."

"Winning isn't everything," Reanyn pointed out.

Alex agreed, "Yeah. Why can the others team up against us, but we can't team up against them?" Everyone stopped and thought about that. Sam stopped grinning and looked at the ground, considering. Lynn supposed Alex was right. Brock and four of his henchmen had aligned against her in their first trial. Another time, Leon had found himself alone against three others, who teamed up to kill him. Why not even the odds?

"That could hurt our evaluation," Sam guessed. "Those others are cowards."

"If the rules prevented us from doing this, why has no one said anything?"

Sam seemed stumped.

"I don't know," Lynn said. "Let's think about it. We don't even know what all those numbers on the board mean. They could well be accounting for this."

"I promise our alliance will be worth it," Reanyn reiterated.

Putting out her cigarette, Lynn replied, “Maybe. Anyway, I’ll see you all in the morning.”

She started heading back to her room, but there was no way she could sleep right now. There was too much going on. Whether they were supposed to work together was an interesting question, but not Lynn’s top priority. What she needed to worry about was how to improve her personal performance and prevent elimination.

After some time of following her feet around the campus with no specific direction, her mind as busy as the Pailon Starport, she decided to forget pride and do what made sense. Ironically, she had been thinking of Mauve Garden and that wretched Ms. Keaten. She couldn’t stand that woman, but there was one expression that she used to scold Lynn, and it kept coming into her head now: “One’s act, one’s profit.” It made sense, in a way. Even if other factors were holding her down, ultimately, the instructors would not care. It was time that Lynn took matters into her own hands, and she knew exactly what she ought to do.

6

Lynn decided to seek advice from the one person she had yet to see falter in these tests, despite how many of his peers would try to derail him. Recalling the first day of the academy, she remembered that Jett had been walking with her and Alex and had split away from them in front of room ninety-four. Now, here she was, knocking on the door and hoping she wasn't about to embarrass herself.

To her relief, Jett answered the door, half-dressed in cotton pants and a tight gray V-neck t-shirt. "Lynn, hello. What brings you here?"

She cut right to the chase. "Tell me how I can do better in the Gauntlet."

"Okay, well ..." His brow furrowed and he stroked his chin as he contemplated, clearly surprised by the question and probably her forwardness. "I presume you have watched the replays?"

Realizing she jumped the gun, she asked, "You want to get dressed first?"

She wished he would, because she was feeling attracted to him, though her mind was trying to deny it as she was looking past his awesome, chiseled body. Who was she kidding? If she was candid with herself, she had thought he was sexy the moment she had met him on Pailon. And she had been attracted to him the night they were together in the cave on Gran Karisu, and even more so after he had rushed valiantly into battle with the ogre. Jett was strong and courageous and handsome, all the typical heroic tropes that she couldn't help but feel affinity for. It was almost pathetic, really, her being so cliché about it.

"Oh, yes. I suppose that would be polite. A moment, please." Jett held up one finger and went inside briefly, and when he reappeared he had on his blue uniform slacks and a basic white button-up shirt with the top two buttons and the wrist cuffs undone. His hair was slightly messy, but in a good way. Lynn couldn't recall ever seeing Jett without perfect attire until this moment, and actually, she was into it.

"Are you sure you don't mind? It's late."

"It would be my pleasure. Shall we go to the armory?"

"You gotta stop that proper talk," Lynn teased as they began the long walk across the campus. "People already hate you enough."

"Yes," Jett conceded. "My lineage is a badge I wish not to wear at times."

"Well, plus, your clothes are terrible," she joked. "And that hair ... well, you could use some modernization."

"What is wrong with my clothes?" he asked, insecurely buttoning one of his cuffs.

Lynn laughed and grabbed his arm, unbuttoning it again. "You dress like a politician. I mean, I know you *are* one, but if you want people to trust you, you gotta act relatable."

"When I was training to come here, Instructor Mccginneas mentioned that as well, citing my speech as a potential opportunity for me as a cadet."

As they entered the grand hall and went toward the armory, Lynn laughed at him and said, "See? That's what I mean. Just say 'Rachel.' She isn't here right now, so who cares?"

"I suppose, though it is strange to think of her in the informal sense."

"It's weird to think of her as anything other than a ruthless bitch."

Jett smirked and replied, "There are many sides to people." Something about that made Lynn remember the day Alex had broken the mountain back on Grantitan, when she had glanced at Zach and seen the cosmic Zen in his eyes, that sort of convergence of understanding and fate and significance. It was a feeling that, even now, Lynn couldn't describe, but she had felt it too. Experiencing something like that with someone gave a person a perspective that could never be discerned by others. Perhaps Jett had felt this way about Rachel.

"Yeah," Lynn said as they entered the armory. "Anyway, let's do this."

"Okay. If I may, I could start by suggesting some alterations to your rykai suit?"

Lynn stopped in front of one of the pods and questioned him, "Wait, what? I thought you were going to look at the replays and tell me what I did wrong?" She liked her suit the way it was. It had taken her weeks to decide on the perfect setup and it had been working fine so far.

"I can do that; however, I know one way you can improve without even seeing them."

Insulted, Lynn challenged him. "Oh, really? Seems like you have thought about this, eh? Enlighten me."

"My suggestions are two-fold: you have no real defensive abilities and you have no true long-range attacks. As a side observation, your poison spray, while a sure kill when it hits, is point-blank range and makes you vulnerable since, again, you have no defense."

Wow, she thought, such immediate and detailed feedback. He had noticed these weaknesses before and didn't tell her. What he was saying made sense, but she was too annoyed to respond. Instead, she stood there, looking at the ground, pretending to be in thought. Why hadn't she realized she had no defense? And why would Zach allow her to enter the academy with an imperfect suit? She wasn't sure who to be more upset with.

Jett continued after a moment of awkward silence. "You are very skilled, Lynn. To have performed so well in spite of my observations is impressive. If you—"

"Don't patronize me," Lynn interrupted. "What, then, would you suggest, since my suit is so awful?"

"You need maneuverability and surprise in your kit."

"Everything I have is a surprise." Lynn knew she was being insufferable. She was acting just like the people she had hated the most back on Grantitan, those ignorant, excuse-mongering ingrates. They never took accountability for anything. Plenty of them had crossed her path before. It was just so hard. She had spent over a year of her life perfecting this fighting style and Jett was so quick to point out the flaws.

As he spoke, Jett started cycling through the weaponry on the screen next to Lynn's pod. "You have a lot of attacks, yes, but enemies expect attacks. You need defensive rebuttals. Trust me, try my pulse shield. Add this attachment; it has a voice command to overclock the shield and deliver an outward burst of electrical energy. If anyone catches you, you can escape in a pinch. I would also add a long-range attack of some kind."

"Okay, fine, I'll try it," she said, swallowing her pride. "Will you watch me and tell me if you notice anything?"

"Of course."

"All right, I'm going in."

Lynn phased herself into the replay of the skyscraper match. At first, she did the exact same thing by escaping through the access door and descending two levels. This time, she would know about the shotgun on the guy's arm and she had Jett's shield to stop it.

With her shield ready to deploy, she rounded the corner where he would be. Sure enough, there he was. He pulled his knife and went for her like before, but this time Lynn used the shield and bashed him back into a file cabinet. Unconsciously, she lowered her shield when she went to draw her pistol and the guy blew her away with the shotgun anyway.

Furious, she phased back into the armory and yelled, "Damn it! Lucky asshole!"

Calmly, Jett critiqued her. "You have to kill him or disable his arm instantly in such a tight space. Even if the shield had blocked the shotgun, the force would have put you on your back and at his mercy."

"I thought you said to be more defensive?"

"It is situational. Sometimes offense is better."

"Screw that."

Lynn tried the same scenario again, but this time had her pistol out before rounding the corner. This time, she did kill him, but he got a shot off after her first round went in his chest, and Lynn was left bloody and clinging to life in the hallway. Irritated, she shot herself and phased back into the armory.

"Don't even say it," she said, preparing to phase herself into a different replay.

Three times, she went into the canyon from the first day, when she and Brock had been killed by Blake's boomerang blade, and all three times, she was defeated easily. She was too annoyed for words.

As she came out the third time, Jett consoled her, "You are doing well. Just remember, you have never used the shield before, and it takes practice."

"I'm not doing well."

"You are also putting too much pressure on yourself. Perhaps we should rest for the night?"

Easy for him to say, she thought, he is in the top ten percent. He did have a valid point, though. Lynn was exhausted and irritated and probably not going to be productive at this point.

"Maybe you're right. Okay, let's call it."

Lynn shut down the pod and she and Jett turned off the lights and left the armory.

"We can practice together next time, if you like."

"Actually, that sounds nice. You know, Alex was saying earlier that he thinks we should all team up in there." Lynn wasn't certain whether she thought that would be against the rules, but she was curious to see what Jett would say.

"It is certainly an interesting proposition, but how would we all find each other without also finding opponents?"

"I hadn't thought of that. Brock found his buddies, right? Do you think it was luck?"

"I am not sure. I am also curious if we would have to kill each other at the end."

"They never said anything about killing, only surviving, right? I wonder if we just refuse to fight each other if the simulation will eventually end?"

Jett thought about it for a moment, then said, "I suppose that is true."

The two of them ended up discussing strategies and bouncing around every possible contingency for quite some time. They had tacitly ignored the dorm rooms and kept going, walking all the way to the edge of the campus, a secluded, grassy ledge near the edge of the western spire. Sitting crossed legged, they could see the northern spire below them and the eastern spire directly across, lighting up the night with the brilliant white lights of the city. What an incredible fantasy, Lynn thought, humbled.

They kept talking, and eventually Lynn was so tired that things started to seem silly. The conversation got kind of comical as they joked about finding unicorns inside the Gauntlet and riding them to victory or being attacked by a windstorm filled with piranhas. It was nice to let the seriousness of it go for a few minutes.

Eventually their laughter faded into yawns and they went silent for a moment, watching the hover-cars dart around the northern spire.

"It's pretty late," Lynn observed.

"It is easy to lose track of time when you are used to being sleep deprived."

"Yeah, no kidding."

They should probably go to bed, Lynn knew. The Prism Gauntlet was not a test to be taken lightly and they needed to be at one hundred percent to stand a chance. It was just so easy to talk to Jett, for some reason. Still, one thing was weighing on her curiosity, and she had to get it off her chest.

"Hey ... you've been helping me since the crash, but you didn't have to. We are technically each other's competition, so ... anyway, thanks."

"You are welcome, and it was my pleasure."

"Why, though? Again, wouldn't it be better if I were helpless? Plus, I treated you scornfully at first, just like Brock and the others."

"If I am to succeed as a Prism soldier, and one day, a captain of my own starship, others will depend on me, and I cannot allow the trivial to interfere with my duty to those people. As well, you were the one who articulated this, but because of the mixed history of Corinth and Sari, it is not without reason that anyone would bear suspicion against me."

Normally Lynn would have been bitter, filed away Jett's response in the cynical part of her brain as just another flowery thing that people say to make themselves seem significant, but not this time. She could tell he meant what he said. Jett was one of the rare few who wouldn't just tout his intentions, he would really do it.

"You are so courageous," she complimented him, both with envy and adoration. "I wish I could believe in people the way you do."

"I think you do. That's why you came here."

"Sometimes I don't know."

As much as Lynn wanted to believe things could change, there was a deeply embedded darkness within her that refused to release her mind. Her faith was bound and gagged by the specter of revenge. The Fox was her true intention. She knew that unless she wielded a sword in hand, those like the Fox would never change, and the fear, misery, and violence they created would be inevitable. Some people were just evil and those who understood this had to be the equalizers. Her coming here was as much obligatory as it was vengeful, she supposed. Someone had to stop the madness.

"I do," he assured her.

She looked up at him and there was a sincerity in his eyes that matched the sound of his voice, a sort of clarity that only kindred spirits understood. He too knew the pain of injustice, the sting of powerlessness. But how? He was a prince, and he couldn't possibly understand what she felt. Yet her heart was telling her that he could see her. They looked at each other for just a moment, but in that short time, he had become fully versed in her, mastering every aspect of Lynn.

"It's so hard," Lynn protested, returning her gaze to the dirt.

"I know, but ... there is always hope."

"I want to believe that, so bad," Lynn said, her nerves on edge and her mouth dry as she subconsciously made the decision to let her soul slip out. "But there is this part of me ... something I have never told anyone, and it is impossibly dark."

Jett just leaned on the grass beside her, looking at her with concern as he waited.

"When I was just a child, barely five years old I think, my parents were murdered in front of me. I was locked in a storage chest ... I saw it through the keyhole. The man who decapitated my mother wore a mask of a white fox. Before he left me there, he laughed like a total maniac ... claimed he was God."

"Oh, Lynn, that is horrendous. I am so sorry that happened to you," Jett replied, reaching out and taking hold of her hand, softly stroking her fingers with his thumb.

"I'm not," she said, her eyes on the ground in front of her. "I mean ... yeah, it wasn't fair, and I wish like hell my parents didn't have to suffer like that, but at the same time, I am on the cusp of something now that I would never have been if it hadn't happened."

"Surely you do not mean that. No one should have to experience what you did."

"That's my point. How many more people have to watch their parents be slaughtered? How many cities must burn, how many empires must fall? Most people see evil but turn a blind eye. Because I have been broken, I have no choice. I have to stop him."

At the height of her impassioned rambling, Lynn couldn't help letting the tears come. This was, she realized, the first time she had said all of this out loud since she had recalled her past. The dam was bursting and emotions were flooding everything.

She felt Jett's finger touch her cheek and brush one of the tears off her face. Looking up at him, she apologized. "I'm sorry. I didn't mean to dump all of this on you."

"No," he said. "Do not be sorry." He slid over to her, so he was sitting beside her, and she felt his hand rubbing her back.

"Why am I so pathetic?" Lynn wondered, doing her best to suppress the tears.

Jett replied, "You are not pathetic. You are strong. You choose to face the bleakness of the universe in spite of the personal consequences. I know you say you have to stop the Fox, but I can tell there is more than that; you want to help people overcome this strife. Lynn, you are a stronger woman than any I have ever met, to have come here like this."

She gazed at him once more and that was it. No more resisting. No more walls. Leaning into him carefully, Lynn closed her eyes and pressed her lips against his. The kiss lasted only about two seconds, but it unlocked something inside of her. As he started to pull away, she reached for his head and kissed him again. There were no words to describe what was between them at that moment, a melting pot of wild emotions that were completely jumbling and indiscernible. All Lynn knew was that she wanted him, and as she leaned in for another kiss, she could feel his desire, as warm and genuine as her own.

She felt his hands beginning to touch her body, grazing her thigh and the small of her back, and eventually finding the nape of her neck and pushing her hair up and through his fingers.

"You are beautiful," Jett said. "I have thought about it since I first met you. Not only beautiful, but strong and passionate. You will give your people hope, even if you don't believe it now."

They kissed again and Lynn nuzzled into him, resting her forehead on his for a moment.

"I'm glad I met you," she said.

"Me too."

Unrestrained passion took hold of them as their lips met again and Lynn slid her tongue into his mouth. Lynn pushed on Jett's chest and he allowed her on top of him as he lay back on the grass. They kissed furiously as Lynn pressed her body against his. With one hand on the grass, she held herself over him while she unbuttoned his shirt with the other. She could feel the touch of his strong, gentle hands sliding under her shirt and stroking her skin. In this perfect moment, everything felt right.

Until a switch flipped in her brain and suddenly, she panicked. She shouldn't be doing this, not here, not now.

She sat upright and lifted herself up off Jett, fixing her hair and looking quite flustered.

"Are you okay?" Jett sat up.

"Nothing," She lied. "It's just ... it's late. We have to be at our best tomorrow."

Lynn was looking away, scolding herself for losing control, and all the while she could feel Jett's bewilderment.

"Did I offend you? I deeply apologize. Perhaps this was not the right moment—"

"No, you did nothing. I just think I need to focus on the test. This ... would only distract us. I don't know what I was thinking."

"I understand," he said with what sounded like sincerity, though Lynn assumed he must be disappointed. "That seems wise."

"Sorry."

"No need to apologize."

Well, she thought there was. It wasn't fair to lead him on like that, but she knew deep down that getting involved with someone was not in her best interest, or anyone else's. This was especially true of someone like Jett, who was so pure of heart and full of hope. All she could do was corrupt him. Plus, how could she be sure this was what she wanted? There were too many emotions firing off in her brain right now and it was best not to jump into anything.

"Anyway, it's late. I'm going to go to bed," Lynn said.

"May I escort you back?"

"I'd rather walk alone. No offense, I just need a few minutes to myself."

"All right. Well, I will see you in the morning. Sleep well, okay? If you need to talk, I am around anytime."

"Yeah, you too, and thanks."

Feeling awkward, she turned to go and halfheartedly waved goodbye, then lit up a smoke and started across the field and back to the campus.

Damn it, why was she so stupid?

Most likely, he wouldn't carry on their friendship, if friendship was ever the right way to describe their relationship anyway. Here she was, baring her messed-up soul to this guy, teasing him, and running away. God, she scolded herself again, why did she have to complicate things? The stress of her quest was already enough, and here she was trying to add the uncertainty of love into the equation. There was no way it could end well. Every time she had put her heart on the line before, it had been for naught. Hell, even with Alex she maintained a level of distance, a portion of her true self hidden from view, and this was exactly why.

When she finally reached the courtyard, Lynn put out her cigarette and went to her room. Realizing at once just how tired she was, she didn't even bother to wash up. Instead, she tore off her uniform and launched herself face first onto the bed, letting herself cry for a while before falling asleep in a jumble of mixed feelings.

7

Weeks went by, and what Lynn had assumed would be rather awkward interactions between her and Jett were instead rather pleasant. The morning after they kissed, Lynn tried to apologize again, but Jett insisted he understood her purpose and would respect it. Since then, he had kept his word, keeping things platonic and practicing with her every evening in the armory, helping Lynn improve her use of her new suit. As time went on, Lynn could feel herself growing stronger, more effective, and more calculating.

In the Gauntlet, Lynn was improving, as were the others, but still no one got the approval of the algorithm. One of the key roadblocks seemed to be that none of the cadets were able to defeat the Grothian templars that would often appear at random. She supposed this was a good indication that they were not ready, but honestly, no one could be sure. At one point, Lynn began to question whether it was all a joke and the instructors were laughing at them. If at some time, they would just choose the worthiest cadets by some arbitrary and unstated metric and they would learn there never had been any algorithm.

Alex, ever the optimist, wasn't convinced. He stuck to his theory that the test was intended to be done as a group, and after a while, Jett, Sam, and the others started to agree. Whenever possible, if the simulation placed them together or they happened upon each other during the test, they would team up. The only hole in Alex's theory, Lynn pointed out, was that they could never get all seven of them together at the same time.

Other than that, everything was going well, and Lynn was feeling optimistic for once.

The long and intense summer days soon waned into crisp, cool autumn, and on one seemingly routine evening on Gran Karisu, the inevitable finally happened. Lynn first heard about it when she was in the gym running on the treadmill. She was only half-listening to the news program that was perpetually playing on the holo-TV in the center of the room, but one particular headline broke through her subconscious and punched her in the brain. Grantitan had been attacked by Grothian templars. What? Instantly, she perked up, slowing the treadmill to a walk so she could pay closer attention.

Apparently, the Grothians were tired of being resisted, for they had rained hell upon Calivia and other hotspots all over the planet. Lynn couldn't understand. This was not how it was supposed to be. Why did they surrender so easily? Did this mean they were at war?

Oh God, she realized, her foster parents! Her friends, her old classmates, were they okay?

Powering down the treadmill, she grabbed her towel, slung it over her shoulder, and rushed out of the gym. When she got outside, she wiped the sweat from her brow and took out her phone, scrolling through internet sites to find out more details. What she found shocked her. The Grothians had sent only six templars. Those six templars had defeated all the Helba freedom fighters alone, without any help from the loyalists. Once they took Calivia, the rest of the planet surrendered and the Grothians locked them down. Now, the Grothian fleet was just sitting in orbit, stopping ships from coming and going. Damn ... *six* templars?

As she finished watching a video someone posted of the siege, she decided she had to call Beatrice, conflicted as she was. What was she supposed to say to them? She hadn't spoken to them in over a year, and now this was happening. Still, if something happened to them, and Lynn left things as they had been, she would never forgive herself. So she decided to call and just say whatever came to mind. Don't worry about the state of things, she coached herself, just make sure they are okay.

Four rings later, no one picked up. Lynn tried twice more, but nothing.

Lynn bit her lip and closed her eyes. She leaned on the wall behind her for a moment and let herself cry freely. It was a confusing cry, for it was specific and full of worry for her loved ones, and also it was transcendent, a grand yet elusive sadness cast over the entirety of her existence. Things always changed—love and hate, life and death, hope and desolation. One second, you were fighting with your parents, telling them to go to hell and die, and the next they were swept away by the dark, pitiless undertow of God's universe, never to be seen again. There was no way to ever predict the bounds of depravity in which she would become entangled, but she was supposed to live with it.

Honestly, Lynn always kind of knew it would come to this. For every event that gave her hope in this galaxy, two more sent her plunging backward. She hated the Grothians. They had taken everything from her. There was an aspect to her bitterness that was drifting away slowly, making its way toward Prism. She could blame the Grothians, sure, but their motivation was marked by domination and they held no empathy for Lynn's people. Prism, on the other hand, was supposed to help them. All her youth, Lynn had never seen one Prism ship until Zach Brine. What the hell had they been doing all these years while the Grothians slowly usurped outer Sari, and what exactly did they expect, that the Grothians would just honor some arbitrary peace treaty with no threat or incentive to do so? Maybe, if she really wanted to save this galaxy, she was in the wrong place.

She had to go see Alex.

When she arrived at his room, Lynn's eyes were still moist and her face flushed from tears. Alex opened the door and gasped. "Sis, what's wrong?"

"They attacked our home. Did you hear?"

"What do you mean? Who attacked?"

Alex moved aside and motioned for her to come in. Accepting his offer, she went into the room and sat on the edge of the bed. Shuffling through her phone, she found the video she had seen at the gym of the streets of Calivia being patrolled by Grothian soldiers.

"Look," Lynn said, showing him the video. The seriousness of it melded into Alex's expression as he saw the place where they used to work, go to school, and drink beer with friends dominated by armed enemy soldiers.

"Oh God," he said in awe. "I hope our friends are okay. Lynn, what about your parents?"

"I don't know, I tried calling and I can't get through."

"I'm so sorry. They are okay, though, I know it."

Irritated, Lynn asked, "How could you know that?"

"I just do. Your parents are smart. Plus, Rami and Jocelyn and the others ... they are all resourceful. I am sure they are smart enough to keep their heads down."

"I guess. God, it looks like martial law there." Lynn clicked on another video that showed Grothian soldiers escorting people down the streets and forcing them into their homes. Some people resisted and were met by the butts of Grothian rifles and hard pavement.

Angrily, Alex asked, "Why are they doing this? We made peace with them!"

"Zach knew this would happen. He said so. That's why we came here, Alex."

"I just can't believe this is happening," he said, collapsing into a chair in the corner of the room and running his hand through his hair nervously.

"Can you imagine if we hadn't come here? We'd be at home now."

After a short silence, Alex stood up and said, "We have to pass the Gauntlet so we can become Prism soldiers and help them." He started pacing the room and stroking his head again, apparently deep in thought.

"I know," Lynn agreed. "But how? We still don't even know the point of the test."

"What *do* we know? We know the computer will tell us when we win, right? We know we have to kill everyone else, and—"

Lynn corrected him. "Actually, the instructors never said anything about killing. We've been doing it right along, but no one is winning."

"Okay," Alex conceded, thinking about that for a moment. "So, we just have to survive?"

"Maybe. We do a lot better when we team up. The problem is, we all phase in separately, so it's impossible to group up."

"Not to mention everyone teams up on us, too."

At that moment, hearing everything out loud, a sudden clarity swooped over Lynn and she could barely contain her excitement. Jumping to her feet, she practically blurted it out.

"Wait a second, Alex, that's exactly right. I know what to do."

8

It must have been at least two years, no, more like two and a half, since Zach had been called to the Prism Assembly. Somewhere along the timeline of his drunken, adultery-ridden bender he had stopped receiving invitations to these secretive, high-profile meetings. Around the time he had gone to Grantitan and met Alex, he had asked his good friend and former captain, Sal Brigande, what the authorities thought of him. Sal was pleasant enough; he told Zach it wasn't that people thought he had fallen from grace, it was just felt that perhaps he needed time to sort himself out after his family disowned him and his life fell apart. Surely he had used all the sugar to coat that reassurance, for Zach knew better. They may be "understanding," as in, they were not going to fire him, but there was a reason he hadn't been offered a starship again.

Anyway, this evening he had been called to the Prism Assembly by none other than General Mezane himself. This could really only mean one of two things at this hour: either he was in trouble, or the galaxy was burning down. Judging by the headlines proliferating across every network on the holo-TVs and the notifications blowing up his phone, Zach assumed the former.

When he walked into his office, Zach wandered over to the big, black leather swivel chair positioned perfectly behind his red oak desk and fell into the perfectly sized imprint. Kicking his feet up on the desk, one over the other, he reached to his left, into his desk drawer, and produced his favorite Sincan cigars and a book of matches. He put one in his mouth and he puffed on it as the lit match began to burn the other end. Soon, the smell of old tobacco and burning wood filled his nostrils. Really old, good tobacco. None of the cheap stuff. He shook the match to put out the flame and closed his eyes for a good rip. Man, the smell of matches was almost as good as bourbon and hot coffee on a chilly morning. Some things were better done the old-fashioned way.

Zach wanted to remove his cape and other outer adornments, lose the tie, and unbutton his shirt so he could get more comfortable, but if he was going to be on a holo-call with the assembly, he had best look sharp. So he remained in full vestments as he anxiously awaited his invitation. Moments later, he received a text from Sal Brigande telling him the call was starting in a moment. His nerves went wild and a cold sweat came over him, which he attempted to remedy by walking over to his small liquor cabinet in the corner of the room and pouring himself a scotch.

The holo-terminal at his desk began beeping and flashing, indicating an incoming transmission. He took a sip of scotch and accepted the transmission. Robert Mezane, a prominent general from Sinca, was the first to appear on the holo-screen, then Sal appeared beside him and several others. The whole Prism Assembly was here.

"Oh, Zach," General Mezane greeted him, "Thank you for joining us. It has been a while, hasn't it? I hope you have been well?"

"I have never been better, and please, it is my pleasure to join this conference."

"Good to hear. Well, I hate to cut the pleasantries short, but we have a pressing issue to discuss and I know we all have limited time, so I'll get right to the meat and potatoes. First of all, what we are about to discuss here is classified and must not be shared outside of the present company." After a brief pause, the general continued. "We have been in a cold war with the Grothians for twenty-two years now, ever since we first encountered their species and repelled their initial attacks in outer Sari. The ceasefire between Sari and Grothia was largely predicated on mutual fear. Neither of us truly knew the powers of the other side and decided to stay in our own camps instead of shedding blood on unknown battlefields. It is possible that we mistook each other for enemies, or I should say, it *was* possible. Anyway, we made certain concessions to the Grothians over the years to maintain the peace—"

"General," Fleet Admiral Anita Perez urged, as she often did when the general began to ramble.

The general put up his hand. "Yes, yes, I am sorry. Anyway, by now, I suspect that all of you are aware of what happened on Grantitan."

There was a low mumbling in the assembly as the general let them speculate.

"The Grothian fleets entered the atmosphere of Grantitan about seven hours ago," Anita informed the group. "The specifics are still unclear, but what we do know is that they are now occupying the planet and its surrounding orbit with several fleets."

Someone else asked, "Why would they do this now?"

"We are not yet certain," General Mezane replied. "But we are activating contingencies for a potential full-scale invasion. We have to assume that the Grothians intend to continue this pattern of aggressive behavior."

"Are we mounting a counter-attack?" Sal asked.

"We are in the process of planning to retake Grantitan," Anita answered.

"However," the general followed up, "Our first priority is fortifying and establishing fleet presence on the other outer planets. Should the Grothians aggress further, we need to be prepared. A counter-attack will also be more effective if we win on the defensive."

"So, we are leaving Grantitan to suffer?" someone asked.

"Are we alerting our allies?" Another talked over him.

Zach added his two cents. "So, are we to assume that the Grothians are voiding the treaty?"

The general said, "We are not leaving anyone, and yes, we will be contacting our allies. All the details will be in your files, which will be sent to you at the conclusion of this call. Zach, for now, we have to assume anything is possible. If you have any questions, Admiral Perez and I will be reachable on this server. For now, we will end this call and you all are to return to your current duties. Read the documents ASAP and be prepared to act accordingly when it is time for action. Does everyone understand the situation?"

"Yes, sir!" the council replied in unison.

"Very good. Oh, and, there is one more thing you all should be aware of."

The general deferred to Anita, who cleared her throat and said, "Also, we received several reports from Grantitan regarding the appearance of the Fox. As you know, the Fox has been a high value target for Prism for years."

"I didn't know the Fox was real," someone commented.

"Of course he is!" another said. "He has appeared in several encounters around outer Sari."

"This is no impersonator," Anita stressed. "Not one of the petty criminals or local enforcers waving the Fox's colors around; this guy was a templar. The reports claim he had nine tails and he moved impossibly fast."

"At least ninety people were confirmed dead after three alleged sightings of the Fox," the general added.

"We believe he will appear again, and when he does, we need to be cautious," Anita said. "Should he appear, you are not to engage the Fox unless it is in a heavily armed, coordinated attack. Understood?"

Everyone confirmed and the general moved on. "Very well, then you are dismissed, but allow me to simply reiterate, this information is highly classified. I do not want to hear about any leaks regarding this call or the contents of the documents you will be receiving."

As the general terminated the call, Zach slumped back down into his chair and stared at the wall as he mulled everything over. It wasn't as if this was particularly surprising; Zach and most others with his intimate knowledge understood it was only a matter of time before the Grothians betrayed their peace agreement. What *was* surprising, however, was the appearance of the Fox. Zach had always heard the rumors about him, a supposedly elite templar with abilities far beyond that of other templars. In the past, he always assumed a degree of folklore to the stories, but now that he had seen Alex, he was inclined to believe the Fox may just be real.

It was ironic that all this would happen now. After all, this conflict was why Prism existed and it was for this explicit purpose that Alex's power was so significant. The wheel of fate never ceased to amaze him. Without warning, a realization hit him like a punch to the gut: he could get called away to fight! That would disrupt everything, leave his work floating in the wind! He had to call Lucas.

9

The next morning at breakfast, Lynn gathered everyone together in the mess hall to discuss her plan. Alex had already bought into it and helped Lynn to talk out the particulars, and she was hoping her success at predicting the first test would help to convince the others.

Everyone ate and listened intently as Lynn spoke. "So, what we know about the test so far is: it is infinite, until someone wins, the algorithm determines when such a win occurs, and the condition of this win is unknown. We also know that killing the others is not the main goal, if it is part of the goal at all, because otherwise, the last one alive in each scenario would have won."

"That all sounds right," Blake said.

"Right, but what Alex and I were thinking is that the point is survival instead of killing."

"We've been surviving," Sam argued.

"Let's hear her out," Jett said.

"Maybe not long enough. The challenges in there are too great for one person. What if all seven of us group up and manage to live longer than any of us have so far?"

"Sounds great, but how can we all group up?" Leon wondered.

"I'll send up a flare and you guys can come to me," Lynn answered.

Sam laughed. "Oh, why didn't I think of that? You'll alert everyone else too and then we will all die."

"Exactly," Lynn shot back. "Except without the dying."

Alex jumped in. "Lynn will shoot the flare, use her cloaking device, and travel due north of the flare approximately a mile."

"And we will meet there," Lynn finished.

"That's bloody brilliant, lass!" Blake said. The rest of the group considered this for a moment. Leon and Sam were nodding their approval.

"Yeah, guys!" Reanyn seconded. "Great thinking!"

"I have just one criticism," Jett said. "When we arrived at the academy, Instructor Mccginneas stated that the 'first group of ten' to finish the Gauntlet would become Prism soldiers without contest. We have only seven, so we ought to utilize the other three positions in our group."

"I forgot about that. Are you sure that's what she meant?" Lynn asked.

"We assumed the 'first group of ten' meant the first ten individuals to finish, not an entire group of ten people working together. That is what they want us to figure out; ten of us have to make it to the end, not one of us," Leon paraphrased.

"Yes, I believe that is correct," Jett said. "We haven't won because it is not sufficient for one person to survive the test."

"Okay," Lynn agreed. "I think you are right. So, who should we pick up?"

"Siefer, Kiah, and Karson," Sam suggested. "They were with us in the first test and I think we can trust them."

Everyone nodded in agreement.

"I'll get Siefer," Sam volunteered. "Reanyn, you have a rapport with Karson, right? Get him on board. Leon, can you get Kiah?" Reanyn and Leon agreed.

"All right," Jett said, "It is decided, then."

"To summarize, I am going to fire a flare once we all phase in and the ten of us are going to meet up a mile due north of the flare's location. Got it?" Lynn reiterated.

Following up, Jett said, "Remember, if this theory is correct, all ten of us have to live, so do not take any chances. Follow the flare and group up, engaging only when necessary."

"We are going to do it this time," Alex assured them excitedly, "I know it."

That's right, Lynn thought as the group expressed their consensus. They were.

Soon after, the instructors were bellowing at them to hurry up and get to their classrooms, and the seven parted ways. The rest of the morning and early afternoon flew by, which was good, because Lynn had butterflies in her stomach the whole time. This was her plan and her part in it was paramount.

Around two p.m., she met up with Jett in the courtyard. There had been no issues with convincing the other three to join them. So, that was it. They had their group of ten and a solid plan. It was time to beat the Prism Gauntlet.

10

It was midday and they were surrounded by the ruins of an ancient city. Great stone pillars stood stoic, peppered between crumbling walls, overtaken by moss and vines. There were chunks missing from the once-marvelous architecture of walls, archways, and columns of the city. Some of it had eroded and fallen away, but other, larger gaps had a man-made quality about them, as if they had been carved out by some long-ago siege.

Lynn was on the second floor of an ivy-covered temple. Its impressive dome-shaped ceiling was two-thirds of the way destroyed, exposing the partially clouded sky above, and the remains of it cluttered the floor in piles of rubble. Beside her was a window etched into a still-intact portion of the wall. A few feet from there, the wall crumbled away and formed a sort of off-center V-shape in the stone.

"Nothing yet," Blake said as he watched the sky intensely from below the outcrop of stone. The two of them had luckily phased in close to one another and quickly found this place to hole up and scout. There was only one way up here and Lynn had her pistol trained on it while Blake sent scouting drones out over the ruins. It was vital that they understood the lay of the land before sending up the flare.

There were cadets on the ground nearby. She could hear them moving about in the other fragmented buildings. Briefly, there were voices. Lynn nodded her head down and to the left, and Blake nodded back that he understood.

The recon drones started pinging locations with quick, red lasers, indicating that they identified other cadets. Most of the pings were happening around the same area to the southwest of their position.

Blake said quietly, "They are grouping up southwest of here. Looks like a palace."

"What about to the north of us?"

"There are a couple of cadets in the building over there," he indicated, pointing toward his ten o'clock.

"I didn't see a ping, how do you know?"

"Saw the blokes."

Lynn looked out the window toward the building Blake had indicated. She didn't see any movement, but she trusted him. She turned her attention to the palace in the distance; the lasers from the scouting drones had disappeared, but she knew most of the cadets would be around there. Also, based on the terrain around them, that would be the landmark around which they would converge. Their plan could work; they would have a good start on those fools if they moved away from the palace.

"All right, I'll get the flare," Lynn said.

"No. We have to get those ones down there first."

She knew he was right, they were far too close, but a pit formed in her stomach when she heard him say it. If either of them died, it was over. Grantitan was under siege and there was no more time to mess around with this test. They had to pass.

"Look," he continued, urging her to peek out the window. "I count three of them."

"I see one." A woman passed by a blown-out section of wall briefly and disappeared into the ruins again.

"See the stairs beyond the building?"

Peering out over the roof, Lynn saw a staircase enclosed by stone walls on either side ascending to the next level of the city. She nodded to Blake.

He instructed her softly, "We fly through that building, kill the wankers, and go out and up. Hole up again in the house on the left, at the top of the stairs."

Again, she nodded in agreement. He waved her over to him and she slid over to the opening in the wall.

"On three."

The two of them stood up and Blake counted down with his fingers. Three, two, one—Blake tossed a decoy grenade onto the ground to the left of them, and with one quick dash, Blake vaulted out of the opening and across the alleyway, landing on the adjacent rooftop on his toes and rolling through to his knees. Lynn followed a second behind him. Both drew their silenced pistols and listened for footsteps.

"Contact!" someone said from inside the house as the decoy grenade made loud gunfire noises in the street. They heard footsteps heading for the staircase and Blake moved into position to ambush them as they came up. Signaling to a nearby hole in the roof, Blake wanted Lynn to drop in and flank them. At least, she hoped that was what he wanted, because she was going for it.

"Cloak," Blake commanded, making himself invisible. Lynn mirrored him.

She peered into the hole and there was already a male cadet poking around below. Lynn jumped into the hole, knife drawn, and buried the brutal steel into the back of his neck. Gunshots rained around her in response and Lynn scurried behind a wall. Shots ricocheted every which way.

During a brief pause in the barrage, there was a gurgling sound as Blake came down the stairs and slit someone's throat.

"What the—?" The woman's voice was nearby.

Lynn could tell she was right around the corner, so she drew her pistol, swung around the wall, and buried two shots in the woman's back. Blake picked up their power cells as he crossed over to Lynn.

"Quickly," he urged. Cloaks still active, the two of them hurried to the stairs as planned and got up onto the second level of the city, entering the house on the left. Heading upstairs, they deactivated their cloaks and set up the same defense as before, with Lynn trained on the stairs and Blake beside the window.

Lynn took a moment to carefully prepare the flare while Blake made sure the coast was clear. Once she launched it into the air, the two of them donned their cloaks once more and scurried through the city and to another building near the edge, where they set up a perimeter once more to scan to woods that bordered the city.

"Anyone follow?" Lynn asked.

"I can't see any—" Blake began.

A canister came flying in the window and bounced off the wall, rolling right up in front of them, and cracked open, dispensing poisonous gas into the room.

"Bullocks!" Blake exclaimed, "Jump!"

He was already out the window. There was no time to think about how high up it was. All she could do was do her best to land right and pray she could get to safety after.

Only neither of those happened.

She cried as she landed off-center and her ankle twisted inward, sending her face first into the dirt. When she looked up, she was surrounded and Blake was on his knees, flanked by two men with guns trained on his skull.

Including the two on Blake, there were five of them. One of the guys grabbed Lynn's neck and forced her to her feet, taunting her, "Well, look what we have here. I was hoping I'd find this one."

"She's cute, right?" another one said, to the amusement of the group.

"Cowards," Blake sneered.

Hitting him in the back of the head with his pistol, one of them shouted, "Shut up!"

Lynn was instantly enraged. No way she went down like this.

"Too bad she has a terrible personality," Lynn replied. Mercilessly, she deployed a blade from beneath her left wrist and quickly jabbed the one holding her in the trachea. Blood sprayed on her as he struggled to grab his neck and stop the bleeding. Too late for him.

"Oh, hell no!" one exclaimed as they all panicked and turned their guns on her. Lynn pivoted to her right, activating her ARM and spraying one of them with lethal poison. Blake reacted perfectly, disarming one of the men. Unfortunately, in the meantime, one of the attackers got a shot off in Lynn's knee and she fell onto her back in agonizing pain. Blood trickled into the dirt and the man loomed over her. Reflexively, she went for her pistol, but he shot her in the hand and laughed at her again while she writhed in searing pain and screamed. "You got some fight in you, Corithian humping slut."

"Cowards! I'm gonna kill you!"

He laughed and said, "That seems unlikely."

Now there were two of them standing over her, and the third had wrestled Blake into submission with his knee on Blake's shoulder blades, pressing him into the dirt.

"You are gonna watch this first, then we will take care of you," the man told Blake.

The other guy seemed provoked by something. Looking past where Lynn lay, he yelled, "Hey! Over here, we got one of them!"

Great, Lynn thought, more of these gutless pansies. How embarrassing. To think that she even thought they had a chance of surviving this was absurd. She could conclude that just by staring at the stubs of what used to be her ring and pinky fingers.

"You want to do the honors? We get to kill the Corithian, though."

It sounded like three pairs of boots approached her head, then Lynn heard a familiar voice reply, "Wow, great job. Don't mind if I do."

Her body was shaking and things around her were a bit of a blur, but she could still see Sam standing over her, the barrel of her pistol directed at Lynn's skull. Praise be to whatever God was out there, she smirked. These guys had no idea they were about to get popped.

Three rapid shots escaped into the air and their attackers dropped dead. Sam's pistol retracted and her powerful arms scooped Lynn up off the ground while Siefer helped Blake to his feet. Lynn cried in pain as Sam hustled into a destroyed tavern, bouncing her up and down in her arms.

Sam deposited her onto the dusty bar top and Lynn heard Kiah say, "You are okay."

Lynn screamed in agony as she felt healing drones searing her bleeding flesh with cauterizing lasers. Kiah appeared beside her and held her hand. "It'll be over in a minute."

"There's more of 'em coming over there," Blake said. Sam got up from beside Lynn and went over to Blake and Siefer, who were keeping watch beside a blown-out section of wall.

Beside herself, Lynn managed to sit up and ask, "What took you so long? For Christ's sake!"

Sam turned around and hushed her, indicating that enemies were nearby. Kiah retracted her drones for the moment and everyone went silent.

There was an odd sound outside. Whoever it was, they were making a ruckus. Sam must have caught sight of it, because her expression molded into pure and absolute dread. "Oh, just kill me now," she said.

11

As it happened, Alex had phased into the test within spitting distance of Jett. Unfortunately, the immediate commotion around them indicated that they were not alone. A shallow, man-made trench was carved out between where Jett and Alex crouched behind ruined buildings, too exposed for them to cross over right now. Upon initial scouting, Alex saw at least three cadets in the vicinity, two of which took roost on a rooftop maybe ten to twelve meters ahead of them. Jett seemed to see them too.

Producing a decoy grenade, Jett indicated his intention to Alex and signaled for him to wait. He tossed the decoy as far as he could to the west, setting off fake gunfire noises and alerting the cadets on the high ground. They turned their scopes and Jett shuffled across the trench and crouched next to Alex. Real gunfire suddenly broke out near the decoy and it looked like the cadets on the rooftop were engaging someone to the west.

"Too easy," Alex joked as they watched the fight.

"Come," Jett instructed, signaling for Alex to follow. "Let us capitalize."

Alex followed him into the trench, which split off to the east a few meters behind where they were camped, and they quickly crept around the periphery of the conflict until they came out at an old, crumbling blacksmith shop. The forge was surrounded almost completely on all four sides, with only one wall compromised by a wide, diagonal crack in the stone.

"Can you close that?" Jett asked.

"No problem."

Alex used the golem to pull together stones from outside and pile them compactly in front of the opening, leaving only a few inches of exposure near the top. Meanwhile, Jett rigged the door to the smithy with explosives.

"Okay, this is sufficient," Jett decided. Alex followed Jett up to the second level of the shop, which seemed like it would have once been the blacksmith's home, and took a position beside one of the windows. Jett set up by a window on the opposite end of the room.

"We gonna wait here for the flare?" Alex assumed.

"It seems wise. There is a large palace due west," Jett answered, pointing away from the window where he was. "Should the battle converge there, Lynn will be wise enough to travel away from it. That means the flare will probably appear from your direction."

Alex peered out the window carefully, scanning the terrain. Between them and the tree line was maybe a quarter mile of ruined city, the ancient buildings resting upon three different levels that were separated by stairs.

"You think she will go toward the forest?" Alex asked.

"Yes. That would be strategic, as it is far from the epicenter of this simulation and we can more easily evade detection."

"I'll keep my eyes out."

A few minutes passed with relative calm. Distant sounds of cadets fighting could be heard, but nothing stirred within Alex's field of view. Until a loud crashing sound, like that of iron pots hitting the ground, echoed down the street outside of Alex's window, followed by a blaster charging and a series of small explosions. Alex could see someone escaping out a window a couple structures over from him and, as she tumbled onto the ground, a laser blast took a chunk out of the windowsill where she had been. That's when he noticed: the woman was Reanyn.

"Jett! Come here, Reanyn is down there."

Jett shushed him as he slid over to the window.

"She's in trouble," Alex pointed out. "If she dies, we can't win."

"How many are in pursuit?"

"I don't know, but we have to go."

At that moment, Alex caught sight of the guy chasing her. Without thinking, Alex called forth a narrow pillar of stone and slid down onto the parallel street. He rushed through a nearby alleyway and interjected himself between Reanyn and the man pursuing her, preparing for battle.

The man yelled something obscene as Alex burst out from the alley. He fired at Alex and missed widely. Before he could shoot again, Alex trembled the ground beneath him and the man lost his footing. Following up with a quick and precise conjuring, Alex impaled the man with a rock spike.

Reanyn emerged from a building ahead of him, having seen the massacre. "Wow, you got him. Thank you."

"No worries," Alex replied. "We are a team, after all."

"Alex!" Jett exclaimed, exiting the alley from which Alex had just come. "The flare!"

Alex looked up to see the ruby red glow of Lynn's signal ascending high into the sky, not far at all from where they were.

"Come on!" Alex said, taking off toward the flare.

12

"Holy hell ..." Kiah said ominously.

"Siefer!" Sam summoned him. "Do you see that?"

Siefer crept over to the destroyed wall and peered out. Meanwhile, Lynn was biting the hilt of her knife, trying to resist screaming in agony as Kiah's drones cauterized her fingers and removed the bullet from her knee.

"Grothians," Sam lamented.

"Damn," Siefer said. "How are we supposed to beat three templars?"

"I say we don't," Blake said. "Wait the wankers out and let everyone else deal with 'em."

"Great, except that we released the flare. The others are going to go to those woods beyond them. No way we get by those templars undetected," Sam reminded him.

"I'm sayin' just give it a minute. Someone else will engage, then we can go."

Lynn yelped in pain, biting with all her might on the knife as the drone's appendages plunged into her knee and tore out the bullet.

Kiah rushed back over to her and stroked her forehead, trying to comfort her. "Almost done, hang in there. Try to stay quiet."

"I hate you," Lynn grumbled. She squeezed her eyes shut and felt tears escaping the corner of her eyes as the drones closed the wound.

"Whoa, whoa, look," Siefer said suddenly, summoning the others to a window on the western face of the tavern.

Blake approached the window. "I bloody knew it!"

"Are they fighting?" Kiah wondered.

"Yeah," Siefer confirmed. "There is a group of cadets over there drawing their attention."

"We gotta go, now," Sam urged, readying her weapons. "Come on, Lynn, on your feet."

Kiah recalled her drones and joined Sam at the destroyed wall as everyone prepared to rush. Painfully, Lynn slid off the bar top and onto her ravaged knee. It wasn't pretty, but she could get through it. Not like it was her real knee anyway, she laughed, trying to block out the pain. She'd wake up after this good as new and wouldn't even remember this pain. Just push through.

"Remember," Sam said. "If we get into it with 'em, use your mantras so they can't read your mind."

"Roger," Kiah said.

"You all ready for this?" Siefer asked.

"Tip top," Lynn joked.

"Okay, let's do this," Sam commanded. "You see that building over there? Looks like a school? Go along that stone wall and over that hill. We can wait inside the tree line up there for the others."

"Cloaking devices if you have 'em," Blake added as they all hustled out of the tavern toward the school.

"No, save your cells," Sam disagreed.

They got over to the school and had made it about halfway down the perimeter wall when an erratic ball of blue energy cut in front of them and devastated a large section of the wall. All of them jumped over the wall and into the schoolyard for cover. Peering over the edge of the wall, Lynn saw two tall and lanky Grothian templars in the middle of the street, surrounded by an arcane aura of blue light. Their suits were metallic and fibrous, conforming to their bodies, and one, who seemed to be a male, had a helmet that was sleek and intimidating. The other, a female, had no helmet; she wore a silver circlet around the crest of her head, resting perfectly against the light aqua-colored skin of her forehead and tucked behind her pointy, elongated ears. Her eyes were like big globes of blackness.

Sam turned to Lynn and handed her an assault rifle. "Here," she said. "I'll engage, and you cover me." As Lynn took the rifle, she couldn't help but look concerned.

"Okay," Lynn agreed, not seeing a better option. "I've got you." Sam must have seen the pause in her expression, because she tightened her metal fist and beat it against her armored chest, holding out two fingers in a peace sign and winking at her. What a crazy woman.

"Here we go," Sam said. "Don't let 'em think."

Courageously, or perhaps foolishly, Sam signaled for them to wait, and she exposed herself to the templars.

They trained on her and Sam taunted them. "Come get me you bastards!"

The one with the helmet seemed to vanish, dashing too quickly to see, and he appeared a second later behind Sam with a long, serrated blade drawn, and lusting for blood.

Sam whipped around and mercilessly smashed the Grothian's helmet with her metal arm, eliciting a pair of sparks on contact, and sent the templar sliding across the dirt.

"Now!" She called to Lynn and the others.

Everyone unloaded their weapons on the templars as Sam thrust jumped and escaped to a rooftop across the street.

The templar who had been knocked down vanished almost instantly, leaving nothing but dirt to catch their bullets. Meanwhile, the female with the circlet just stood where she had first appeared, gazing at them with those deathly eyes. She erected some kind of barrier, remaining stoic as gunfire ricocheted off of her invisible wall.

"Damn it!" Blake exclaimed, stopping to reload.

Perplexed, Kiah stated the obvious. "We have to try something else."

"Enough of this." Siefer got up from his crouched position and slung his rifle over his back. Going right out onto the street, he faced the female templar. Siefer began to conjure a ball of orange energy in his palm and, with a cocky smile, he held it out toward the templar and said, "Let's see you block this."

Sam came down from the rooftop at the same time and flanked the templar. Lynn watched anxiously as the two of them prepared their weapons to blow the templar away.

Sam's blast came first and the templar easily dashed away before the ground cratered beneath it. A split second later, Siefer's ball of energy erupted, deepening the crater.

As the templar vanished, Lynn could sense it all around her. A female voice entered her head. *Death awaits you.* Utterly terrifying. It sounded far away, crackled, like a quiet ghost in a static holo-TV. If she was using telepathy, she was probably trying to read Lynn's thoughts. Over and over, Lynn repeated in her head "bravo, right, center," as her eyes darted wildly around, searching for the rogue templar.

"Siefer!" Sam warned from across the street.

Even though Siefer was a good fifteen feet from her, Lynn could see the expression of dread take shape on his face, as if every hair on his body was standing and stiff and his heart was crippled with paralyzing fear.

It appeared in an instant, those black, empty eyes piercing Siefer's soul as he stared straight into them. He tried to raise his arm to defend himself, but it stopped in midair and his whole body seemed to be frozen. At that moment, Lynn felt a strange pressure in the air, an evil, paralyzing aura of indescribable influence. There was a stomach curdling crack as Siefer's forearm was mercilessly snapped telekinetically, the bone emerging at a forty-five-degree angle. The skin around the break began to peel back and tendons popped and twisted as the templar made Siefer's arm into a carnival of gore. Boy did he scream. Lynn thought she was going to be sick.

"Don't just sit there!" Kiah said, aiming at the templar.

"You'll hit Siefer!" Blake warned.

Sam thrust jumped and landed next to Siefer, rounded up a charged, metal fist and delivered a massive punch to the templar's barrier, stopping her from channeling and knocking her backward. The templar dashed away quickly before Lynn and the others could fire on her. Now that the templar had released his body, Siefer collapsed onto his side and cried in agony. Sam powered up her arm cannon and stood over Siefer, protecting him from further attack. As both templars emerged once more, she lifted it and launched another blast at the male templar. Blake tossed his bladed boomerang while Lynn and Kiah opened fire on the female.

"Get out of the street!" Kiah exclaimed.

"I know!" Sam shot back.

"Now! We can't do this forever!"

Sam held out her hand and Siefer grabbed it with his one good hand, letting Sam pull him to his feet, then she scooped him up in her arms and thrust jumped away from the fight. They landed behind Lynn, in front of an old, rusty swing set and Sam deposited him carefully onto a small patch of yellowish-green grass.

"Don't you die!" Sam instructed Siefer before jumping back into the fight.

Blake's boomerang zipped past the male templar, who dodged it gracefully, and when it reached the female, she held up her hand and stopped it in midair. A blue aura traveled from the templar's hand to the boomerang and she took control of the killing machine, sending it soaring at Kiah. It was so unexpected and so fast that Kiah barely moved it time and the whirling steel deathtrap devastated her, slicing her left arm entirely off and taking a chunk of flesh out of her shoulder and abdomen.

"Kiah!" Lynn screamed as Kiah's blood splattered everywhere, soaking Lynn and Blake.

"Bloody hell!" Blake exclaimed, trying fruitlessly to recall his weapon.

Kiah cried in agony, "My drones, in the pouch ... my drones!"

Blood was spilling everywhere and the templars were preparing another attack. No way they could fight these two off and help Kiah. She was going to die, Lynn realized, and they were going to lose.

Just as Lynn thought all hope was lost, she witnessed the best possible thing that could have happened at that moment.

Alex, Jett, and Reanyn descended the hillside behind the school and unleashed their weapons on the templars. Drone lasers, streaks of lighting, and spikes of rock had the templars on the run. A moment later, Karson and Leon emerged from the tree line and added to the barrage. The only thing missing from this glorious moment were the goddamn chariots and white horses.

When they reached the bottom of the hill, Leon was closest and Lynn called to him, "Leon, we need you!"

Leon stopped beside Kiah and gasped. "My God, woman, hang in there, okay?"

Frantically, Kiah said, "Hurry up, my drones, I'm bleeding out!"

"Here's the two of hers," Blake said, handing Leon the little metal spheres from Kiah's pouch. Leon took them from Blake and combined them with three of his own, morphing them into drones, and started the process of cauterizing Kiah's wounds.

Meanwhile, Lynn jumped over the schoolyard wall and joined Jett as he engaged the female templar. Together with Sam and Karson, they broke the templar's concentration, forcing her to drop Blake's weapon, and got her on the defensive. Lynn and Jett blocked her energy attacks with pulse shields and Sam and Karson counterattacked her with perfect timing. Somewhere behind them, Lynn heard Alex and the others clashing with the male templar. They kept the pressure on and after two more rounds like this, the female templar finally fell to her knees, her power waning. Sam stood before her, a sadistic grin on her face, and broke the templar's neck with a quick and brutal snap.

Upon the defeat of his comrade, the male templar seemed to panic and tried to escape, dashing away from Alex's rock spikes and rushing down the road.

"Don't let it get away!" Alex shouted.

Indeed, there was no way Lynn was going to allow that. With complete and total focus, Lynn held two explosive ninja stars between the fingers of her one fully equipped hand and she tracked the escaping templar with narrowed eyes. When he was at perfect range, Lynn flicked the deadly stars at him, missing barely with one and landing the other in his back, just below the shoulder.

The templar stumbled out of his rapid dash, catching himself on his knees and reaching around to touch the vicious wound on his back. Before he could get to the steel, the star exploded, blowing his arm clean off and leaving him a struggling mess of half-consciousness. Lynn approached him slowly, tolling the bell for him with every step. The others gathered around as Lynn drew her serrated knife and did the honors, burying the final stab straight through the bastard's heart.

"Yeah, you eat all of that! How's that feel?" Lynn taunted the templar's corpse.

"Nice work everyone!" Alex cheered.

"Yeah, totally awesome!" said Reanyn.

Jett, ever the pragmatist, interrupted the celebration. "Lest we forget, there were three of them. Let us regroup and move to the tree line."

"Jett's right," Sam agreed. "Let's go get the wounded."

The seven of them returned to the schoolyard, where Siefer was back on his feet and observing as Leon finished up on Kiah. She looked an absolute mess, and Lynn didn't blame her. Not long ago, she had been lying under those drones getting stabbed and burned. Come to think of it, now that the threat had passed, Lynn was starting to notice the throbbing pain in her leg again.

"How is she doing?" Jett asked. "Can we move her? We must move to an area less exposed than here."

"I am fine," Kiah said stubbornly.

"No, you are blown in half," Sam corrected. "I'll carry you." She looked at Siefer and winked. "You are on your own, big guy."

"No problem," he cocked. "Just a flesh wound, eh?"

Just as Sam scooped Kiah into her arms and the group was about to move, something started to happen. It felt like the air was dissipating, like everything around them was becoming lighter. Lynn would have thought maybe she was just feeling woozy from her injuries, but everyone in the group seemed to be aware of it. They had all stopped and started looking around suspiciously.

Finally, Blake voiced his concern. "You guys feel that?"

"Yeah," Reanyn confirmed. "It feels ... weird, what is happening?"

"I feel like I'm falling asleep," Alex said.

No, Lynn realized. It was actually quite the opposite. They were waking up! That meant ...

"I think we did it," Lynn said.

"Did what, lass?" Leon asked.

Picking up on her hypothesis, Jett answered for her. "We passed the Prism Gauntlet."

In a manner that was wonderfully familiar to Lynn, the world began to fade and she felt like she was drifting away, waking slowly from a dream. It seemed the algorithm was finally pleased. Soon, the cadets would wake up in their pods, surrounded by their envious peers as they earned the right to say forever that they were the first ones in their class to become Prism soldiers.

BLACK SKY

1

Beneath the bright, nearly full September moon, a carnal celebration ensued inside the grand ballroom of Raynor Academy. It had taken only about ten days after Lynn's group became the first to conquer the Prism Gauntlet for the remaining cadets to follow suit and have their worthiness evaluated. A total of fifty-four cadets evening in formal tuxedos and long dresses arrived for the to be honored for their achievement of becoming Prism soldiers. It was a rich event, and all had to be on their best behavior. Prism elites and influential donors would be present, they were told.

This wasn't Lynn's glass of wine, but Zach informed her that it would be both rude and unwise not to rub shoulders at this most prestigious event. She didn't even own a formal dress, but that excuse didn't work for Zach either. Apparently, he had worked too hard grooming her for this moment to let her embarrass him. He made her go with Rachel to pick something out, a pain she hoped never to suffer again, and they settled on a long, strapless black dress, black heels, and corsage with black lace around a deep blue rose. Later, she had her hair and makeup done and picked out a pair of simple silver earrings to wear. Rachel proceeded to insult her taste and to insist she wear opal to complete her outfit, a suggestion which Lynn resented but ultimately succumbed to. How much fluff would she be asked to accept, anyway?

Lynn had to admit, though, she did look amazing.

She entered the ballroom, lit opulently by golden chandeliers, music and merriment surrounding her, the banisters bearing the insignia of Prism draped neatly over the balconies above, and found herself amazed. All of this was for them. They had really done it.

"Whoa! Look at this!" Alex marveled as he entered the ball. Reanyn was with him, holding his arm, and Lynn supposed she wasn't surprised.

"Oh, wow!" Reanyn said, her eyes wide. "We did it, Alex!"

"Hell yeah we did! Lynn, do you see this?"

"Pretty pretentious, huh?" Lynn said. "I guess that's how you know we are really in."

They made their way to the center of the ballroom, where everyone was gathered in front of a raised platform beneath red velvet curtains and Prism banisters. In the center of the stage was a simple podium, flanked on either side by the flags of Gran Karisu and the Sarian Empire. Along the periphery of the stage, the officers of Raynor Academy stood at attention in full Prism formal attire. Their various capes, insignias, and tassels made for a colorful array of achievement and added to the wondrous prestige of the event.

"This reminds me of graduating college," Reanyn said.

"I wouldn't know," Alex joked.

Lynn spotted the Corithians in the crowd and Jett seemed to notice her at the same time. He shot her the most handsome smile and she smiled back, blushing a little. For a moment, they looked at each other like that. Man, he looked good.

"Here comes the headmaster," Alex said. The music suddenly died out as he approached, and everyone went silent.

"Ahem. If I may," the headmaster spoke into the microphone as he took his place at the podium. "Good evening ladies and gentlemen, and welcome to this most illustrious evening. I am Headmaster Lucian Everett, and I am proud to be your host. With us tonight are fifty-four elite soldiers who have broken the standard of excellence and raised the bar for another generation of Prism cadets. With them, there are a great many individuals in this room who have contributed in various ways to their success. Tonight, we honor their achievements, and we honor your contributions."

Applause followed the headmaster's address, and he continued with the sort of typical commencement rhetoric. Lynn wasn't really listening. Although she had never graduated college, she had been to enough of these events with Dean when she was younger to know the key components of them. This speech was not for her, but for the people with the pocketbooks.

Headmaster Everett had to make sure the people who bankrolled him knew what kind of great product they were paying for.

While she listened to the headmaster's monotonous dribble, Lynn's mind began drifting toward the topic of her true interest: what was to come next. Now that they were Prism soldiers, they could go back to Grantitan and help liberate them from the Grothians. Finally, Lynn would not just sit idly by and watch the world burn.

This had been exactly what she had told Zach the day before, when he was coercing her to get into this dress. He started babbling on about "destiny" and the same crap he always did, asserting that she and Alex would go to Taland next for more advanced, individual training. Lynn was furious; how much "training" did they need? They had just beaten two Grothian templars in the Gauntlet; so as far as Lynn was concerned, they had trained enough, and that's what she told him. Lynn was done playing Zach's games. No more training, no more simulations, no more puzzles. It was time for her to act and do the things she set out to do.

Something like ten minutes later, Headmaster Everett was wrapping up. "And so I bid you, eat, drink, dance, and enjoy this most joyous of evenings. Prism associates, get to know the soldiers of Sari's future that you have helped produce, and to you new Prism soldiers, meet your benefactors and future employers. Thank you all for coming and I hope you enjoy the evening."

Another round of applause concluded his speech as he exited the stage. The officers were at ease and leaving the stage as well, indicating that everyone may break away from the group. People started talking and the music played once more as the event came alive.

"Come on, Alex, let's dance!" Reanyn said, pulling on his arm.

"Yikes," Alex said, pretending to be uncomfortable, "I guess that's my cue. See ya later, sis."

"Good luck," Lynn joked, smirking at him as Reanyn dragged him away. She was happy for him. Reanyn's personality was quite fitting for a relentless optimist like Alex and Lynn knew they would be great together.

As for Lynn, she was perfectly happy to make her way to the edge of the room and keep to herself. She had never been one for schmoozing or dancing. Champagne wasn't bad, though, and Prism had spared no expense on the white bubbly of the evening.

She was leaning on the wall, sipping her fizzy alcohol, when Zach and some other guy approached her.

"And this is my other student, Lynn Palmer. Lynn, this is Sal Brigande," Zach introduced her against her will.

"A pleasure," Sal said, extending his hand.

She shook his hand and returned the gesture with intentional exaggeration. "The pleasure is mine."

"She is a bit rough around the edges, but very, very talented," Zach assured him. "This is the one who figured out the crash test."

"You're one to talk," Lynn commented.

Sal laughed. "Yes. Zach is well known for having a certain candor. I expect so much of his prodigies. Well done, by the way. The crash test has filtered out many would-be legends. I understand you were part of the first team to beat the Gauntlet as well?"

"That's right," Lynn pat herself on the back. "Actually, my idea led us to victory."

"I like your confidence. Perhaps we will have another conversation in the near future."

"Captain Brigande is my mentor," Zach said. "You would do well to listen to him, should your paths happen to cross."

"Gotcha," Lynn said. "Well, Captain Brigande, until we meet again."

"Likewise, Ms. Palmer," Sal replied.

"Enjoy yourself," Zach insisted. "You've earned it."

With that, he and Sal were off to the next adventure and she was back to sipping champagne. It felt good to hear him say that—"You've earned it"—even though she was still irritated with him. Lynn supposed that expression was as close to "I'm proud of you" as anyone could get from Zach, which was a sentiment she didn't realize she wanted until just then.

Jett approached her, looking handsome as hell in his black tuxedo and white shirt and bow tie, and held out his hand.

"May I dance with you?" he asked.

She sipped her champagne and answered nonchalantly, "I don't dance."

"Well, you can't just stand over here by yourself."

"Who says?"

"This is our evening. You ought to enjoy the fruit of your efforts."

Lynn grimaced. "Doesn't it bother you that we are drinking and dancing and celebrating while Grantitan is under siege?"

As always, Jett provided a perfect rebuttal. "All the captains are drunk anyway. We couldn't leave if we wanted to. Tomorrow will come sooner than we think. Come on, dance with me."

"Like I said," Lynn replied after a pause, "I don't dance."

"Well, I think it is only fair."

"What is fair?"

"We passed the test."

"Yeah, so?"

"So, you can dance with me. I can't distract you now, right?"

Rolling her eyes, she gave in. "Okay, *one* dance."

He smiled and held out his hand once more, and this time she accepted it and followed him onto the dance floor. They were in the center of the action; the music was picking up and the people around them were alive with the enjoyment of the evening. He did have this charm about him that Lynn couldn't help but be enamored with. Though she wanted nothing more than to leave this place, Jett did have a point. It was only a few hours. No point in being miserable the whole time.

"Have you done this before?" Jett asked.

"What, you don't think I'm cultured enough?" she joked.

"You said you don't dance."

"But I didn't say I *can't* dance."

To punctuate her statement, Lynn grabbed Jett's hand and placed his other hand on her back. Her other hand came to rest on his shoulder, and she stepped into him with her right foot. Her left foot followed gracefully, and Jett took her cues, quickly slipping into a waltz.

"You are quite versed, I must admit," he complimented her as they wove between other dancers on the floor.

"I had to learn all this crap when I was a girl. My father wanted me to be 'well mannered' and whatnot."

Jett laughed. "Yes, as you might imagine, the life of a baron's son was fraught with similar expectations."

"Oh yeah?" she asked, noticing the tempo of the music picking up. "You know this one?" Releasing herself from his hold, she broke into a quickstep, slower at first, so he could follow, then faster, until they were dancing around the center of the crowd with rapid and precise movements. People were noticing them and moving back, giving them space for their spectacle.

She held out her hand to Jett and leaned back her head as he pulled her in to him and spun her around. When she finished the rotation, she felt herself trip slightly and start to fall, but Jett saved her from humiliation by dipping her and making it look like part of the dance. Thank God, she thought, how embarrassing.

"It's the heels." She laughed as he pulled her back up. She unbuckled the heels and kicked them into the crowd. One woman had to dodge out of the way as she kicked the shoe past her head. Lynn and Jett laughed out loud as she angrily denounced Lynn's manners. Thankfully, people stopped watching them after that and went back to their business.

"No excuses now, right?" Jett teased, leading her into another dance.

Lynn narrowed her eyes and pretended to make an offended face as she got in step with him. It was so much easier on bare feet. Losing herself in the moment, Lynn danced skillfully with him for several more minutes, until eventually the music slowed dramatically, and she fell carelessly into him.

They danced slowly and she laid her face on his chest. Nothing had felt this right in a long time, she realized. All the anger and the anxiousness she felt was fading into the romance of this moment. Everything was perfect. Maybe it wouldn't be so bad to let him in.

"You are really quite good," he said.

"Didn't think I could keep up with a prince, did you?"

"Not many people can. However, you are not most people. You could do anything you decided to do."

"Nice line," she joked, smiling up at him. "Bet that works on all the village girls at home."

"It works on the castle girls too."

Surprised by his cleverness and his secret levity, she just laughed. What a man he was; so handsome, heroic, genuine, and yet soft and relatable. That was it, she couldn't help herself. Slowly, she closed her eyes and kissed him softly.

"You want to go outside?" she asked, gazing into his dark blue royal eyes. "It's getting stuffy in here."

"After you."

Jett followed her through the crowd toward the exit. On their way out, Lynn saw Alex standing against the wall, drinking champagne and laughing with Reanyn and some rich donors. He shot her a wink as he saw her pulling Jett out the main entrance.

"Ooooh, it's chilly out here!" Lynn commented as her bare feet touched the stone stairs.

"Yes, it is nearly autumn, isn't it?"

"Wow, look at the moon!"

She ran down the stairs and over to the huge monument of Harold Raynor, the founder of Epilogue City for whom the academy was named, and stood on its big square base. From here, she looked up over the top of the ballroom toward the bright yellow, nearly full moon. Jett ran over to the monument to catch up to her.

"I've never seen a moon this bright!" Lynn marveled, pointing at the glowing sphere. "Seriously, look at that!"

"We have moons like that before the harvest season on Corinth. It is said to be the turning point, the changing of the seasons."

"Wow ... I want to see it someday. What's it like there, where you grew up?"

"What do you mean? The planet, or the castle?"

"Both."

"You'll see it someday, now that you are a Prism soldier."

"Come on," she scoffed, coming down from the monument. "You gonna be like that?"

"The wonder of new worlds is part of it, is it not? I wouldn't want to spoil it."

"I suppose. At least tell me this: are there huge monsters where you live, like the ones here on Gran Karisu? I should know that before I go there."

"Not at all." He laughed. "Most of our wildlife is harmless."

"Most?"

"Well, like all worlds, we have our dangers."

"But nothing you can't handle, right?" Lynn smiled and stole another kiss, letting her hands rest on his chest and her body slip into his comforting embrace.

Jett stroked her cheek and touched the back of her neck as he kissed her again. She lifted herself onto her toes and trapped his neck between her arms as the passion between them intensified. His hands explored the contours of her body and she felt her stomach flutter as he reached her hips and pulled her into him. Clearly asserting her desire, she let him lift her as she touched the sides of his face with each hand and kissed him passionately. It had been a long time since Lynn had been in the context to think about sex, but in this moment, all those feelings were rushing back into her. Screw it, she thought. Whatever happened after this, wherever they were deployed and whatever challenges they faced, it didn't matter. Lynn knew exactly what she wanted tonight.

She slid out of his hands and grabbed his wrist, smiling flirtatiously. Softly, she said, “Come on,” and led him away.

2

"So, I assume that by now you have heard all the details about Grantitan?" Zach asked as he poured three generous portions of scotch into solid crystal tumblers. Lucas had arrived earlier that evening, and as much as he had wanted to jump into everything then, Zach knew his appearance at the ball was an obligation best not shirked. So, when he had glad-handed a sufficient number of palms, Zach slipped out of the black-tie affair and back to his office, where Rachel and Lucas were sitting in front of his desk. Each took a drink from Zach as he returned to the desk and plopped down in his usual seat.

"Yeah," Rachel said. "Though you probably know more than we do."

"The details are still unclear, but I think we both know the implications."

"Grantitan's been hot for a while anyway," Lucas reminded him. "Even when we were there, it was ready to blow up."

"Yeah. The Grothian betrayal was inevitable. I have always said that. Unfortunately, the timing could not be worse."

"Is there ever a *good* time for war?" Rachel questioned.

Finally trying his scotch, Lucas nearly spit it out and said, "My God, man, what is this garbage?"

Chuckling, Zach replied, "That is culture, my dear friend." Tipping his glass, Zach took a swig and turned his attention to Rachel, "Anyway, right now is a particularly inconvenient time. Yes, the wheel of fate is indeed a curious cog."

"You always do this," Rachel said, annoyed. "Just get to the point." Lucas laughed at Rachel's accurate characterization of Zach. Anyone who knew him would say that he could be obtuse and long-winded. Zach even laughed at himself a little as he sipped his scotch, remembering the first night he had seen Lynn at the Haxenburg. She had been drunk off her ass and said the same thing. Oh well, he was who he was.

"Well," Zach began, standing up from the chair and wandering over to the window, "I asked the two of you here because I need a favor. Lucas, you already have an idea of it, I venture. With everything that is going on, things are likely to heat up soon, and I don't know how that will impact my agenda. If I am called away ..."

He paused, swishing his drink and letting the single large ice cube clank on the sides of the glass.

"Rachel, there is something about Alex that I am going to tell you, and you must swear to me that this thing I tell you will stay between the three of us."

Lucas looked with disbelief as Zach prepared to reveal their secret. Admittedly, Zach was nervous about this, but he knew he had to have contingencies, and if there was anyone around here that deserved any modicum of his trust, it was Rachel.

"When I met Alex and his sister, they should have been crushed by the side of the Calivian airblading stadium. Do you recall, when that space debris crashed there over a year ago?"

"Yeah, the same morning I texted you about it," Rachel remembered, her expression marked by curiosity.

Zach wandered over to the decanter to top himself off as he continued. "Well, the reason they survived is nothing short of what the average person would consider a miracle. But those like us, we know better."

"Just tell me the point!"

He turned to face her as he delivered the purpose of his tale. "Alex caught a giant slab of concrete with his bare hands. That's how they survived."

Wide eyed, Rachel repeated his words. "He caught it? With his bare hands?"

"Yup," Lucas confirmed.

"But ... that's impossible, unless—"

"Yup," said Lucas once more.

Making his way back to the window, Zach elaborated. “That’s what I have been doing for the last year. Lucas and I, we trained him, unlocked his power. Rachel, we watched Alex break a mountain with the palm of his hand.”

“My God,” Rachel said, “So the Alderian myths are true after all?”

“I always thought they were just stories,” Lucas admitted. “But I saw it with my own eyes.”

“Wow ... what about the sister? Lynn, right? She doesn’t seem special, from what I have seen, anyway.”

“Lynn is an ordinary human,” Zach explained. “They are not blood related. However, we trained her because I feared that Alex wouldn’t come without her. In the process, we found her to be a formidable Prism cadet as well.”

“Don’t underestimate her,” Lucas agreed. “She put Zach on his ass after two months, and she was a civilian. No military background before this.”

“No experience at all? That does surprise me.”

“Yes, it surprised me as well,” Zach confessed.

“Zach would end up in something like this, wouldn’t he?” Lucas joked.

“Always full of surprises,” Rachel said.

“I am trusting you,” Zach reminded Rachel. “No one can know about all this, for obvious reasons. People would try to exploit Alex.”

“Oh, I agree. What are you planning, though? At some point, you have to expose him, right? Otherwise, what are we doing here?”

“Someday. I’m just not sure when that is. There is so much we don’t know.”

“Maybe this is why the Grothians attacked Alder twenty-two years ago.”

Lucas agreed. “Yeah, good point. I bet they knew about the Alderian’s power.”

“And that’s why they are still occupying it,” Rachel supposed. “Anyway, what was the favor you were talking about, Zach?”

Zach walked back to the window, searching for the best way to phrase his request. It was an odd one, this quest, for it had no finite result nor specific timeline. Instead, all he could say was that there was this elusive objective, some unseen paradigm, and it was somewhere in the galaxy, though exactly where was a good damn question. The other three pantheons: the phoenix, the hydra, and the gryphon ... they must exist. How did the power come to be? Could Alex learn them all, or was he born with only one? These questions had to be answered, but they also couldn't risk the wrong people answering them. He was about to formulate all of this into a response, then he happened to glance out the window.

"Never mind," he said instead.

Confused and irritated, Rachel asked, "What do you mean, never mind?"

They must have seen the look on Zach's face, because both Rachel and Lucas got up and joined him in front of the window. They were all silent as they processed what they saw. Zach knew there was only one thing to do.

"Find the headmaster ... and get your rykai suits."

3

"Where did you come from?" Lynn wondered, staring down at their feet intertwined in the misty slits of moonlight poking through the curtains. Her arm was around him and her other hand was busy circling two fingers around his chest. Hardened from training and peppered with small scars and a burn mark on his left breast, Jett's skin was imperfect with purpose. Not the skin she would expect of a man who grew up in a palace. Such an anomaly, this man. But then, wasn't Lynn an anomaly herself?

"Where do any of us come from? It's about where we end up, right?"

She thought about that before answering, "I suppose it is really about the journey."

"Yes, that is true." His hand touched her chin and tilted her head up to his. Looking at her with those soft and beautiful eyes, he said, "May I say, it is my pleasure to have shared this journey with you."

"Me too."

He leaned in and kissed her, and she returned his graces, letting her passion escape errantly as she nuzzled into him and their naked bodies pressed together. She could have stayed like this forever. Jett was so noble, so strong, and so passionate, not like anyone she had ever met. Lynn trusted him completely. Dare she imagine, perhaps she even loved him. She had never felt this way with someone before.

Over and over she kissed him, rolling herself on top of him and letting the sheet slide carelessly off her back. She felt his hands caress her bare skin and felt the hot breath between them as she hovered over him.

"What are you waiting for?" she whispered, enticing him and licking his bottom lip seductively.

Jett accepted her temptation and they ravaged each other's bodies once more until both of them were satisfied and laying in their own sweat.

Breathing heavily, Lynn said, "Wow. That was amazing."

A moment later, Jett turned onto his side to look at her and said, "I feel so natural with you. I don't know how to describe it."

"I think I know what you mean." It was an elusive sentiment, but Lynn felt it too, like she could let her guard down, be a real person for once and let her worries just drift away.

"You are so beautiful. I could be with you like this forever."

She bit her lip and laughed. "Until I ask you to make breakfast, right?"

"I'll make you whatever you desire," he smiled back.

"Damn right you will."

For a moment, she tried to picture what it would be like to have a prince make her breakfast in bed. She imagined a gratuitous spread of meats, cheeses, and Corithian fruits. She pictured Jett wearing an apron and giggled. Lynn tried to imagine him in the kitchen, but she just kept picturing places from Grantitan. She wanted so badly to see Corinth and all the other places in the galaxy that she had never seen before. Being with Jett had awakened a sense of wonder inside of her that, at one time, Lynn might have thought was dead forever.

"What do you think will happen next? Now that we are Prism soldiers?" Lynn couldn't help but ask. She knew she shouldn't bring her mind back to these contemplations, but she couldn't help it.

"There is no way to know for sure. We will fulfill our destinies, however they may manifest."

That wasn't really an answer. She knew she was bound for Grantitan, to fight the Grothians. What she actually wanted to know was what would happen to them, whether she had taken this chance in vain or if her heart could thrive after all, but the words wouldn't form. Whether it was pride or cynicism or maybe both, Lynn couldn't bring herself to ask him the real question: did he want to be with her.

As if reading her mind, Jett touched her cheek and said, "Whatever destiny my future holds, I hope that it includes you."

Lynn fell into him and they were about to kiss again when they were startled by the sudden sounding of the campus PA system, which was loud and sounded very urgent.

"What the hell?" Lynn exclaimed as she jumped a mile.

"The PA," Jett said. "At this hour, it must be an emergency."

"What did it say?"

Jett put up a finger to indicate he wanted to listen, and the message began to play again.

"Attention all personnel, cadets, and faculty," the PA blared. "A Grothian fleet has entered the airspace around Epilogue City. All soldiers and cadets are to follow protocol Delta. This is not a drill or a test. I repeat, this is not a drill or a test. All soldiers and cadets, follow protocol Delta."

"Oh my God!" Lynn gasped. It was really happening! This couldn't just be another elaborate test, could it?

Jett jumped up and started to dress. Urgently, he explained, "Protocol Delta is the contingency for hostile invasion. We have to get our rykai suits and find Zach immediately."

Actually, she knew what protocol Delta was. All of them had been made to read the same manuals in their first week at the academy, but there was a more pressing concern in her mind: where was Alex? She didn't want to be separated from him if the Grothians were really attacking.

Scrambling out of bed and clothing herself haphazardly, Lynn decided not to voice her concern. At least, not yet. The first priority was going to be getting weapons, then she would find her brother.

"Are you ready? Let us go to the armory, quickly," Jett insisted.

"Yes, right behind you."

The PA message was blaring on repeat as they came out of the room and into the courtyard, where they could see more clearly the threat looming before them. Up above the courtyard, the massive Grothian destroyer hovered, draining the once peaceful night sky of all hope and beauty. Nothing but death remained.

"Come on! We have to get back before they descend!" Lynn said before sprinting off across the campus.

Jett was right behind her and she was sure he had said something back, but her brain scrambled the words. She was focused only on one thing:

getting her rykai suit. This was it, the reckoning that Zach had always said was coming.

They reached the armory in record time and went straight to the armament pods. Several of the campus staff were already suiting up and preparing for battle. Cadets were trickling in and the faculty were directing them to battle stations.

"Lynn," Jett got her attention before he stepped onto the platform. "Do you see Instructor Brine? We need to report to him once we have our suits."

"Right," Lynn agreed halfheartedly, already involved in selecting her armaments. If there was time for that, sure, that was the protocol. However, those ships were closing in fast.

A moment later, Lynn locked in her selections and the machine roared as it constructed Lynn's rykai suit straight onto her body, piece by piece.

Sure enough, Lynn heard explosions outside. So, it had begun.

As they came out of the pods, an officer stopped them and said, "Cadets, the headmaster has activated emergency protocols, who is your commanding officer?"

Jett responded, "sir, Instructor Brine, sir!"

"Instructor Brine's unit is assigned to the airfield bunker; you are to report there at once."

"We are on our way, sir!"

Lynn wasn't on her way. Instead, she disregarded the officer and went for another exit.

"Cadet Palmer!" he called. "You are ordered to report to the airfield at once!"

"Lynn!" Jett beckoned. It was no use; Lynn wasn't going to wait in some bunker while the Grothians murdered her brother. She had been helpless once, as a little girl inside a storage chest, watching the slaughter of her parents. Then she had been helpless for years as the planet of Grantitan crumbled around her in the aftermath of these Grothian bastards. Not today. Never again.

She left the armory and immediately saw the carnage across the campus. A crumbling, half-obliterated structure struggled to stand where the ballroom had been, and smoke billowed from ominous fires that spread from within the great cavity made by the Grothian pulse cannon. Above her, the black sky became a tapestry of death as dark blue orbs of light dropped enemy soldiers to the ground and the ships fired bright green and red lasers at defensive structures on the ground.

Lynn ran across the campus grounds, stopping for a moment to avoid a laser beam from above, which tore a hole in the ground ahead of her.

"Lynn, wait!" Jett called, finally catching up to her.

"I am going to the ballroom."

"I know. I will go with you."

Another explosion happened nearby, reinvigorating Lynn's sense of urgency. All she could think about was making sure Alex was safe.

"We have to hurry!" Lynn said, taking off again.

She only made it a few steps when a laser blast from one of the ships decimated a column to her left and sent huge chunks of stone flying dangerously around the area. With heroic effort, Jett activated his pulse shield and pushed in front of Lynn, repelling the collateral damage.

"Are you okay?" Jett asked.

"Fine." Lynn had equipped one of those too; she would have to remember to use it.

As she was about to move again, Lynn suddenly felt tense and the air became much denser, like all the air was being sucked out of it. A thin blue slice of energy appeared before them, expanding outward and crackling with intense energy. From within the energy, a Grothian templar materialized.

"Rush it!" Jett ordered as he drew his rifle and opened fire. Instantly, the templar teleported away. Lynn spun around and put her back against Jett's and they both prepared to deploy shields. Her heart had never beat so fast and her eyes were dashing so quickly that everything was a blur. Where was it?

Surrender, Lynn heard from nowhere.

"There!" Jett pointed as it appeared to their right.

It struck with a pulse of blue energy in the shape of a ring, fired precisely from a small cannon attached to its right arm. Just in time, Lynn deployed her pulse shield and absorbed the blow, but the impact was unfathomable. The tiny ring had been only about the size of a car steering wheel but possessed so much power that when it hit Lynn's shield the impact knocked her ten feet away and onto her back.

Give up and die quickly, the templar demanded, ready to fire again.

Getting to her feet, Lynn brushed herself off and stared violently at the templar. Her fingers rested on her weapons. Surrender wasn't part of the plan; not today, not ever. These bastards were responsible for everything. She was done bowing to them.

"Never," Lynn said.

Very well.

4

It was approximately ten minutes till ten p.m. when the headmaster first declared over the intercom that Epilogue City was under attack. About half the cadets had left the ball before then, but Reanyn had wanted to stay, so of course Alex obliged. When the headmaster came on, the officers present in the ballroom told everyone not to panic and to make their way to the exits in an orderly fashion. They were then to go to the armory, where they would get their rykai suits and be told where to report.

Just minutes after the first announcement, a horrific explosion rocked the ballroom as the Grothian destroyer tore through the building with a pulse cannon.

Alex and Reanyn were far enough from the epicenter to evade death, but the impact sent a shockwave through the area that launched them through the air. When he landed, Alex felt dizzy and disoriented. His head was an echo chamber for the faraway sounding screams of the people around him.

He heard Reanyn calling to him. Snapping back into it, Alex sat up and looked around. Half of the ballroom had been hollowed out by the blast and fire was everywhere. People were rushing around the ruins, searching for colleagues. Officers were barking orders, trying to organize the chaos.

"Alex! Over here! I need help!"

He caught sight of Reanyn's body and was horrified to see her torso wedged between a pile of rubble and a crumbled column that had fallen down amidst the destruction. Blood drizzled down the side of her dirt-covered face.

Alex ran to her and grabbed her hand. "I am going to get you out, okay?"

"I can't move Alex, I'm stuck, you have to get me out!"

"I know. Stay still, okay?"

He dug around Reanyn's torso, removing loose rocks where he could. He tried to lift the pillar, to no avail. It was a miracle, the way it landed—

there was another small cube of debris that held the pillar up just enough that it hadn't crushed her. There was no way he was moving it, though. Unless ...

"Hurry, Alex!"

Reanyn started to panic as they heard more explosions and gunfire outside. Approaching a shattered window nearby, Alex peered outside. Dozens of Grothian dropships were flying low toward the campus as the destroyer above pelted the ground with cannon fire. It was absolute madness.

"Don't leave me!" Reanyn pleaded. He would never. He just had to make certain the coast was clear.

Alex took one last glance around the area, and when he was certain no one was near, he closed his eyes and placed his hands on the pillar of stone. If he could catch a slab of the stadium, he could lift this up.

"What are you—" Reanyn started.

"Hold on," Alex interrupted. "I'm getting you out of here."

Alex calmed his mind and focused all his energy on the pillar in front of him, and he felt a tingling sensation in his hands. The sensation traveled through his body as Alex exhaled and got a firm grip on the bottom of the pillar.

Bending his knees and taking a huge breath, Alex exerted incredible effort on the pillar. Amazingly, he felt the massive column inch upwards ever slightly. He was doing it! Adjusting his position, Alex went at it again, grunting barbarically as he lifted. His breath was fast and hard, and he could feel his arms beginning to shake, but the pillar had moved another inch.

"I can move!" Reanyn declared, trying to wriggle her way out from beneath the deathtrap. She had made it out a few inches before getting caught at the hip.

"Hurry!" Alex groaned, desperately trying to hold on.

"I'm still stuck!"

He could see her struggling and knew he was going to have to raise it one more time. Gathering all his energy, he once more lifted the pillar with inexplicable power. Once he had brought it up, Reanyn was able to slide out from beneath it to safety. Finally, Alex dropped the pillar with a huge crash and a cloud of dust. His arms were throbbing, but there was no time to worry about himself. He rushed to Reanyn and knelt beside her.

"Are you okay?" he asked.

"You saved my life, how did you—"

"I'll explain later. Can you get up? We have to go."

As the initial shock of her ordeal wore off, Reanyn looked down at her legs and realized they had been badly damaged. Alex noticed as well; at least one was broken.

"My leg!" she cried.

"No worries, I'll get you out of here."

Ignoring the pulsing pain in his arms, Alex scooped her up carefully, tossing her arm over his shoulder and lifting her onto one foot. She winced in pain and stumbled into him as he tried to guide her out of the building.

"I'm sorry."

"It's okay. We have to move; I'm gonna pick you up, okay?"

She cried out as he lifted her beneath the knees, but she was okay once Alex got going, and the two of them swiftly exited the burning ballroom. Outside, a cloud of darkness enveloped the campus.

A young, female officer was helping lagging cadets and directing traffic. She yelled, "Hurry up and get to the armory!" Alex hurried down the stairs and approached the officer.

"Her leg is broken," he explained.

"Cameron! Elliot!" she called to her subordinates, before turning back to Alex. "We'll take her. You proceed to the armory."

He didn't have a chance to respond before the woman was already rushing to help another person coming out of the ballroom and two men were taking Reanyn out of his arms and placing her onto a stretcher.

"Alex, be careful," Reanyn pleaded as they were carting her away.

"I will," he promised.

Chaos encroached upon him as Grothian dropships released soldiers and the fighting began. There was gunfire everywhere, both from the soldiers on the ground and the ships in the air. Ground defense systems were activated and made deafening sounds as they attacked the enemies in the sky.

Alex was making his way to his destination when a series of explosions rocked the ground between him and the armory. A pair of Grothian fighters had cruised by and released a salvo toward a nearby anti-air cannon. The crafty ships dipped and dodged around the cannon as it counterattacked with quick laser bursts. In the middle of all this, two hovering vehicles had cut across the stone path in front of Alex with such speed that he was staggered by the wind gusts that followed them. As quickly as these vehicles passed, Alex saw them complete a one hundred eighty degree turn and come back toward him. The hovering vehicles looked like militarized Jeeps with armored cages on top.

His heart racing, Alex sprinted away from them, toward the armory. He may have to fight, he lamented, knowing full well he couldn't outrun those vehicles. Without a rykai suit, he would have to use his power.

One of the hover-vehicles pulled up just ahead of him. From it Zach yelled, "Alex! Get in!" Lucas was in the passenger seat in Zach's vehicle, and a second later Rachel pulled up beside Zach in her own vehicle.

Wasting no time, Alex jumped into the back of Zach's war machine and held onto the cage.

"Thank you," he said. "I can't believe this is happening!"

"Believe it," Zach replied, before punching the gas again.

"Where is your sister?" Lucas yelled over the chaos.

"She left the ball earlier; I have no idea! I was going to find her—"

Zach interrupted, "No time! If she listens to the PA, she'll go to the airfield."

"Why are they doing this?" Alex asked.

"Because they can," Zach answered simply.

The Grothian fighters came in for another sweep and Zach jerked the vehicle hard to the left as cannon fire rained down in front of them. In the process, he nearly rammed Rachel and she had to slam on her breaks, causing her to fall behind.

"Damn it!" Zach exclaimed. "We have to get our birds up there!"

Lucas pointed up ahead, "That's a templar!"

Curiously, Alex pulled himself up above the cage and looked. Since they had veered off, they were curving around the central garden square, near the armory, trying to turn around. Sure enough, in the middle of the garden, among broken columns and crumbled stone, a tall, elven looking templar was embroiled in combat. One of the two soldiers that the templar was engaging was Jett, and the other was his sister.

"Lynn!" he cried, too far away for her to hear. Dropping back into the vehicle, Alex beckoned for Zach to stop. "My sister is over there! We have to help her!"

For a second, Zach seemed to ignore him.

"Stop the vehicle!" Alex repeated. "I am helping my sister!"

Alex tried to assert himself closer to the front seat and Zach slammed on the brakes, thrusting Alex back against the back of Lucas' seat. Zach turned the vehicle and stopped skillfully in front of the square.

"You are a pain in my ass," he said. "Stay here."

"No way!" Alex objected.

"You don't have a rykai suit," Zach insisted. "Lucas, get them to the airfield."

"You got it, boss," Lucas complied, taking over the driver's seat as Zach exited the vehicle. Alex watched as Zach approached the square and prepared himself for combat. From a holster at his hip, Zach withdrew a small metal hilt, which he quickly transformed into a full-length, electrified bo staff. He held out his other arm toward the templar and released a charged blast of bluish-orange energy from a small cannon that appeared on his forearm. What seemed like a disproportionately large explosion followed, and the templar vanished.

5

From Lynn's right, she heard someone shout her name. A huge explosion followed and the spot where the templar had been standing went up in fire and shrapnel. Stunned, Lynn spun around and saw Zach in full rykai gear, wielding an electrified bo staff and a pulse cannon on his arm. With an urgency she had never heard in all the time she had known him, he shouted, "Run!"

"Hurry, get in!" Lucas called to Lynn and Jett as he pulled the armored hover-Jeep up beside them. Jett stepped inside the vehicle and held his hand out to Lynn.

"Come on!" he beckoned, pulling her up into the vehicle.

"Sis, thank God you are okay!" Alex exclaimed.

"Alex! I was so worried!"

Lynn felt tears of joy forming in her eyes as she embraced her brother. At least that was one less thing she had to worry about.

"Hold onto your pants!" Lucas said, kicking the vehicle into gear and spinning the Jeep around violently.

"What about Zach?" Lynn asked, turning around to see him locked into a furious battle with the templar.

"The big man can handle himself," Lucas assured her. "We didn't spend the last year and a half training you two so we could toss you to the wolves."

He punched the gas and they were off, flying through a crescendo of chaos in the middle of the campus. All around them, Lynn could see Grothian soldiers deploying out of dropships and engaging the Prism forces, who were holding their ground at fortified locations around the campus. Enemy fighters still dominated the sky, though at least now they were being contested by Prism aircraft. They could fend them off, Lynn told herself, this was not the end.

Upon arriving at the airfield, they were immediately entangled in the conflict. Lucas plowed through the middle of a dozen Grothian soldiers and zipped through two barricades outside the main hangar of the airfield, where he brought the vehicle to an abrupt halt. Behind them was a tall bunker housing a massive ground-to-air defense turret. The blasting of its guns was so intense the ground felt like it was shaking.

"About time you showed up!" Terif called as they piled out of the vehicle. "Where is Zach?"

"He is on his way," Lucas said.

"What about reinforcements?"

"Any time now. Planetary elements were activated as soon as we detected the Grothians."

An explosion at the barricades cut their conversation short. Alex and Lynn huddled behind Lucas' Jeep as bits of concrete and tarmac hailed from the sky. People were crisscrossing and guns were firing everywhere. She peered around the Jeep and saw Sam crouched behind one of several barricades between them and the killing fields, giving the Grothian soldiers hell along with a dozen others. Blake and Leon were behind another barricade with a few others.

"Get on that ship!" Terif ordered the platoon, as another dropship managed to evade the turret and drop a fresh lot of Grothian soldiers.

Rushing around the Jeep, Jett yelled, "Come on!"

"I don't have a suit!" Alex reminded him.

"We have to hold them back!" Jett insisted, tossing Alex his rifle.

"It's too late!" Sam said. "They are going to overrun us. If they get up here the shield battery is toast."

"What do we do, then?" Lynn asked.

Terif said the thing Lynn already knew, and she was so ready to do: "We fight."

6

Sparks erupted in crackling bursts from Zach's staff as he parried the dual energy blades striking him in rapid succession. The templar was fast and vicious, but Zach had trained his whole life for this. His focus was absolute and his strikes were precise, calculated, and autonomous. In his mind, the only thing that existed was his mantra. After one particularly intense bout, Zach saw an opening and knocked the templar back. He lifted his arm and deployed the cannon on his arm again, only this time he didn't intend to fire it. The templar would just dodge it. Instead, as the cannon deployed, he simultaneously pointed his staff to the right and fired a bolt of electric energy from the tip of his staff, perfectly striking the templar and launching him onto his back.

"You can't read my mind," Zach taunted his opponent. "Call off your troops or you will die."

The templar got to his feet and fired a ring-shaped burst of energy at Zach, who easily deployed an energy shield from his staff to deflect the attack. Seconds later, the templar was upon him again and Zach was defending against the barrage of energy blades. This time Zach separated his staff in two and evened the odds. The two dual-wielding soldiers raged across the square, flinging sparks everywhere. They fought in a circle around a stone fountain, leaving burn marks on the edge of the stone as their weapons slashed around furiously.

Finally, Zach began to tire, and the templar slashed Zach's shoulder and bicep. It was a flesh wound, but enough to disarm Zach and give the templar an opening for the kill. As the templar's other blade came around for his neck, Zach had the awareness to deploy his arm cannon and use it to stop the blade just in time. He fell to the ground, his cannon sparking and smoking from the blow, and grabbed the other half of his staff in time to make a shield to save himself from the next blow.

His next intuition was to fire electricity again, but the templar saw it coming and knocked his staff from his hand. Zach was terrified; he was losing it and the templar could probably read his mind now.

That's correct, the templar confirmed his suspicions. *No one can hide from me. In fact, it is you who is going to die.*

The templar held out his hand and Zach was lifted effortlessly off the ground, forced to hang helplessly in the air while the templar grinned sadistically. Telekinesis? Zach thought Grothian templars could only master one form of psychic ability. He had no idea that multiple disciplines could be learned, or that such a feat was even possible.

The templar hurled him through the air into one of the many columns still intact around the square. Pain surged through his body as his spine smashed against the stone and he fell to the ground. A small trickle of blood escaped Zach's mouth and he spit it on the ground.

A shadow loomed over him as the templar approached.

"Your people have persisted in ignorance and insubordination for too long," the templar explained. "It is because of this that we must restore order to the galaxy."

Of course, Zach already knew this. He had suspected all along that attacking Gran Karisu was just the Grothians' way of flexing, of showing them what they could do if they wanted to. They wanted Grantitan and all the other outer planets to understand that resistance was futile. When everyone saw how far-reaching and powerful the Grothians were, they would submit to their governments being usurped. There had never been peace, not truly. Though he supposed it didn't matter now, since he was about to die.

The templar charged his weapon and pointed it at Zach, preparing to unleash the ring of blue energy that would mean the end of him. At this range, his shield would break and he would be crushed, and there was no way he could dodge. The grin beneath the templar's steel-covered eyes suggested that he too was aware of the cards he held.

Refusing to accept his fate, Zach quickly, and without thinking, lifted his staff to fire a bolt of electricity. What happened next was wild.

The templar was stricken by a powerful blast of electrical energy and sent hurtling backward while the ring of energy it had been conjuring to eradicate Zach went soaring up into the air and inadvertently destroyed a passing Grothian fighter. Zach was relieved but also confused, for the bolt had never left his staff.

7

The one-hundred-meter stretch of field in front of the turret was a maddening cudgel upon Lynn's senses. With the Grothian forces inside the dome of the turret's shield, the airfield would be overrun in short order. At all costs, they had to protect the shield battery, lest they become exposed to the attacks of the Grothian destroyer as well.

"Stay together!" Jett commanded. "Just like the Gauntlet!"

Terif shouted to Alex and a half-dozen others at the barricades, "Cover us!" He led the charge, getting into Lucas' Jeep and driving it recklessly through the middle of the barricades and into the advancing line of Grothian soldiers.

As the enemy's line scattered, the Prism soldiers made their stand. Lynn tossed exploding shuriken and picked off two of them, while Sam thrust jumped into the fray and snapped one's neck on her way down. Blake's bladed boomerang took out a group of them and Jett's attack drone killed and disabled others. Leon tended to the wounded while Alex and the others at the barricade picked off soldiers at their flanks.

The first wave had gone well, but two more ships were deploying nearby.

"Quickly!" Jett urged Lynn, rushing the dropship. Lynn followed him and the two of them deployed their shields and fought with their backs to one another. Half of the Grothians were shot as they left the dropship, and the other half were dispatched by Lynn's poison and Jett's energy sword.

"Lynn!" Sam shouted from behind her. She spun around and her heart dropped. Charging her full force was a brutal, four-armed hulk of an ogre, even bigger than the one she had faced in the test. What was it doing here?

Just in time, she activated her shield and blocked a walloping backhand from the creature, knocking her several feet away and bouncing her twice off the battle-scarred ground before she came to a rest on her back. Her shield flickered and retracted.

She looked up in time to see Sam and Jett engage the beast. Sam thrust over its massive reach and put a shotgun blast of wild energy into the creature's spine. Jett directed his drone to fire lasers at its head, but the beast's familiar and impossibly hard carapace was not to be broken. Though it screamed in fury and pain, the beast lost no momentum and plowed right through Jett, launching him somewhere into the distance. Sam fired again and the beast turned on her. Wisely, she retreated, leaving the beast rampaging around the battlefield uncontested.

Lynn got to her feet and felt for her shuriken; they had worked before. That's when she noticed ... there were two more of the beasts. The Grothians were unleashing these natural siege weapons against them! Even if she could kill one, there was no way she could kill three. This was a death trap, being out here.

"Retreat! Fall back!" Terif was yelling as he stood up in his Jeep. Lynn's eyes darted around, looking for the best path back to the turret. There wasn't a good one, and there was no time; two of the ogres had spotted her.

She sprinted desperately toward Terif's Jeep. Luckily, he had spotted her and was backing up toward her. When she reached the Jeep, one of the ogres was nearly on top of her; there was no way Terif was getting away in time.

"Get down!" Terif yelled. Down? Why not in?

She heard the familiar whizzing sound and knew instantly why. Lynn dove to the ground beside the Jeep and Blake's weapon soared over her and collided with the beast. It sounded like a blender grinding up ice cubes as the twirling steel sliced into the carapace of the creature.

"Hurry up and get in!" Terif commanded. No arguments there. Lynn hopped in and Terif gunned it for the barricades.

"Are they controlling those things?" Lynn wanted to know.

"Just our luck, huh?"

The Jeep pulled through the barricades and they jumped out quickly. Chaos had descended upon the airfield when one of the ogres got behind the barricades. People were running and screaming and trying to survive.

Another dropship came down and two dozen Grothian soldiers advanced on the mostly unprotected barricades.

"We've been breached!" Leon exclaimed. "We have to retreat!"

"We can't hold this position!" Alex agreed.

As if to confirm their plight, a deafening explosion occurred nearby: the shield battery. Now there was nothing between them and the pulse cannons from the Grothian destroyer.

"Next will be the turret!" Terif shouted. "Everyone fall back to the docking bays. There is another battery there!" Jett, Sam, and Blake came over the barricades with Siefer and a few others, and Terif reiterated his orders.

"Jett, are you okay?" Lynn rushed over to him.

"I'm fine, and you?"

"Fine. Come on, we have to get away from here."

Most of the Prism forces were way ahead of them, but before they could move away from the barricades, a volley of laser blasts from the destroyer overhead laid siege to the nearby turret, rocking the ground around them.

"Oh God! Watch out!" Alex cried. It was too late. One of the Grothian soldiers who had breached the turret shield was aiming a rocket launcher straight at the barricade in front of them.

"Get back!" Jett demanded, activating his pulse shield and jumping in front of them just as the rocket fired. What was he thinking? He couldn't survive that!

"Jett, no!" Lynn pleaded. Without thinking, she deployed her shield as well and stood beside him. Everything happened within milliseconds, and then, with what Lynn could only assume was utter instinct, Alex held out his hands and called forth a wall of stone in front of them. All Lynn could process after that was the ear-shattering, mind boggling explosion. The wall imploded and huge chunks of stone bounced off Lynn and Jett's shields. The sheer wave of energy following the blast sent the Prism soldiers flying off in random directions. The last thing she remembered was being airborne, having no idea where she was or whether she was actually alive, then she felt a hard impact as she smashed into the ground and everything went black.

8

Her vision was blurry, her ears were ringing, and her brain felt completely scrambled. Lynn could feel her life flickering like a light bulb about to burn out. The scarred airfield around her filled with Grothians as her allies were defeated, one by one. Chaos transformed into somber surrender in the wake of the unfathomable power of the enemy. Jett must have been flung somewhere to her left, but she couldn't see him. Alex lay near her, wounded and unconscious. All signs suggested that the bell would soon toll for them.

"Alex ..." she nearly whispered, stretching her arm toward him weakly. Tears formed in her eyes and she kept calling to him as he lay still.

"Alex!" she cried, crawling over to him "Alex, Get up!"

Staring at his limp, tattered body, Lynn shook him over and over. She screamed at him, first in sadness and then in anger. It couldn't be ... not this way, not after everything they had been through. It just couldn't end like this!

She laid herself across Alex's chest, closed her eyes, and tried to block out the sounds of death. A faint tempo seemed to beat in her eardrum, was it Alex's heart? It was! He was alive, thank God! Erratically, her mind raced around. What about Jett, was he alive? And Zach? Where was everyone else?

Suddenly the sound of stomping boots and Grothians shouting grew dangerously near. Lynn fearfully opened her eyes, and instantly something flashed, blinding her momentarily. Something shimmering and bold. She wiped her eyes, but her tears were dry. What? It was still shimmery.

When her eyes adjusted, the light softened and she could see it. The shard was light blue and about two inches long, and it flickered with a bright iridescence. The most unusual thing about the shard was that it was embedded in Alex's forearm. Just above his elbow, on the inside of the arm, a chunk of flesh had endured terrible carnage, scooping out a cavity just deep and wide enough to reveal the bone upon which the shard was resting. The way it was sitting, partially secured inside Alex's muscle tissue, it had to have been there before. No way it landed there; Lynn could just tell. What the hell was she seeing?

Carefully, Lynn reached in with two fingers and removed the shard from Alex's arm. Holding it in the palm of her hand, Lynn was mesmerized by the radiant light pulsing from this tiny, crystal-like object. Suddenly, she had chills. Small vibrations emanated from the shard and it felt as though they flowed through her whole body.

She heard the Grothians and remembered that she was doomed. All around her, enemy soldiers poured into the airfield, yelling, dashing, and shooting at the Prism soldiers who lagged behind the retreat. Lynn slipped the glowing shard into the pocket on her right hip and watched intensely as the conflict played out before her.

The Prism soldiers fought valiantly, but they were no match for the overwhelming number of Grothians and it was too late for retreat or surrender.

Suddenly, an ominous presence overtook the air, making the area around her seem ten pounds heavier. For some reason, the Grothians stopped fighting and stood stoically in a semi-circle before the remaining Prism soldiers. Confounded by the situation, the Prism soldiers stopped as well, and for a moment, the dust settled. Something emerged from behind the Grothian ranks. It was so fast that it looked like just a blur of movement. The unknown entity came upon the Prism soldiers, killing them one by one in a frenzy of blood and severed limbs. Panic and wild gunfire did nothing to stop it. Everyone was killed in a matter of seconds.

When only one Prism soldier remained, the mysterious assailant finally appeared before her. He was a tall, thin, and brooding figure, made remarkable by the presence of several thick, snaky cables protruding from the small of his back. They seemed alive as they poked about, rising and coiling like the hair of Medusa.

He slashed the woman's arms with maniacal, metal claws, disarming her. With impossible speed, two of the man's snake-like cables lunged at the helpless soldier, opening up at the ends and stabbing both of the woman's legs with stiletto-like fangs. The soldier screamed and fell to her knees while the assailant snickered and grabbed her by the neck.

"Such fragility."

"Please, oh God! I surrender! I have a family!" She screamed desperately.

"Yes, beg me for your pathetic life. For you see ... I *am* God."

Before the woman could plead again, the assailant wrapped both hands around her neck and squeezed violently until no life remained. As the woman fell dead at his feet, the unknown assassin seemed to bask in his work.

He turned and faced Lynn.

Her heart nearly stopped.

When he had appeared, there were aspects of him that she had known instantly, but she didn't want to believe it. His figure, his voice, and his nine tail-like cables were darkly intimate to her. And now she knew for certain; for when the enigmatic man turned to her, she saw that on his face was the mask of a white fox.

9

"On your feet, soldier!" Zach heard Rachel's voice calling to him.

There wasn't much time; the templar was already up and firing another energy blast. Zach grabbed his two staff pieces and fused them together to make it whole again. He charged forward, called forth his energy shield, and thrust his staff toward the incoming blue ring. The two energy sources connected at an angle and Zach's staff split the ring in two, allowing both ends of the deadly blast to pass by him and explode on the ground far behind him.

He shot two bolts of electricity toward the templar, who dodged expertly and fired back. Zach had him on the run now and he was back in control of his thoughts.

"Attack to the right, now!" Rachel shouted, coming to Zach's side.

Zach attacked to the left and connected with the templar's torso.

"Now, finish him!" she demanded.

They both fired huge bolts of electricity from their weapons in rapid succession toward the damaged templar. Five, six, maybe seven bolts later, the ground was charred, smoke was rising from the craters of their attacks, and the templar was gone.

"Did we get it?" Zach wondered.

"I wouldn't be so sure."

"Not bad for a Sarian," Zach heard from somewhere behind them. Rapidly spinning around, he and Rachel lifted their weapons, but the templar wasn't there.

"It's in our heads," Rachel said. Zach felt that she was probably right, but kept scanning the area, just in case.

"Stay on your guard and use your mantras. This one is both telekinetic and telepathic."

"Whoa, Zach, Look! What the hell is that?" Rachel exclaimed suddenly, seeming to disregard Zach's warning. Something flashed before them and Zach looked up to see a huge plume of fire escape into the sky above the airfield. It was hard to explain, but it was unlike the shape or the nature of any manner of explosion he had ever seen. No, instead, this fire seemed alive, sentient.

"That's not normal," Rachel said.

"No, it isn't." The fire split off into furious arcs, descending inward like shooting stars until there was another flash and a wave of energy that whipped across the campus as if a bomb had just gone off. There was a wild screech, a valorous cry that could no doubt be heard across all the western spire. Zach's eyes bulged with curiosity and fear. "Neither is that."

It wasn't normal, but if Zach had three guesses about it right now, he would only need one.

"Come on!" Zach shouted. "We have to get over there!"

The two of them rushed into Rachel's Jeep and Zach slammed on the gas, hauling it over to the airfield.

10

"Who are you?" Lynn demanded as she stood before the Fox. Grothian soldiers surrounded her and raised their weapons as she confronted him. With one wave of his bloody claw, the Fox bid them stand down.

Ominously, he replied, "You know who I am. You have always known."

"No! You are no god! You are a murderer and a coward!"

"Really? Where, then, are *your* gods? Nowhere, because they exist only to laugh at you while the universe burns."

Words spilled out of her mouth automatically as years of bottled up rage overflowed from her brain. "Who is the one burning it? This is all because of you, isn't it?" As she let the rage pour out, her whole body seemed to intensify, to tighten and solidify with each wave of adrenaline that swept over her.

This was it. This was perhaps the moment that it had all been for.

The Fox just snickered and said, "I have no need to answer your questions. Now, you are boring me."

Guns pointed at her again and Lynn said, "You had no reason to kill my parents either!"

For a moment, the Fox stopped the Grothians, intrigued.

"That's right, you bastard! In the hotel, in Calivia! I know it was you!" She condemned him, "Now, I am going to make you pay for what you did. Take off that goddamned mask and show me who you really are!"

Lynn prepared herself to fight and the Fox sneered. "You ask me if this is because of me? Everything that is happening is because of the arrogance of mortals. You cannot kill me. You do understand this?"

Actually, Lynn understood nothing. The Fox, what even was he? The Grothians, the chaos, the randomness and the irony of everything she had been through ... how was she supposed to reconcile it? None of it mattered anyway. No way she was getting out of here, surrounded by these bastards. She had to kill the Fox, or else it would all be for nothing.

"We'll see," she said as she quickly drew her pistol and fired two shots.

The Fox flashed away, which Lynn expected. When he appeared beside her, claws slashing, she was ready and she adeptly deployed her pulse shield and bashed the Fox right in the face, deterring his attack. She followed up quickly by snapping her wrist and releasing poison toward the Fox, but he was too quick and dashed away before the lethal spray could disable him. From apparently nowhere, he slashed her shoulder with his claws, and she screamed in pain before he vanished again. All the Grothians around her laughed as they watched her struggle.

How the hell was he so fast? Lynn held up her blaster, searching for the Fox as the blur of his body vanished into thin air. Was he cloaked?

The Fox appeared before her and grabbed her wrist, pushing the gun upward as Lynn fired a shot into the sky. With her free hand, Lynn deployed a blade from atop her wrist and tried to impale the Fox, but one of his tails reflexively lunged out and coiled around her wrist before she reached his gut. Another tail emerged from behind him, revealing its pointed tip, and went for her thigh.

She yelled, "Overclock!" and the pulse-shield bracer on her left arm expelled a great wave of energy, bubbling outward from her body and knocking the Fox and his nine tails away from her. Thank God Jett had shown her this attack. She could only do that once or twice more, maybe, so she had better make the power cells count.

As the Fox recovered, she threw her shuriken at him, but his tails easily reacted to these, deflecting them toward the hangar to his left. Explosions destroyed parts of the wall, and a fire escape which was once attached to the building came crashing down onto the tarmac. Behind her, Grothian soldiers jeered at her with disgust.

Again, the Fox laughed and lunged at her. Lynn deployed her pulse shield on her right arm and her blade on her left and fought furiously as the Fox slashed at her and his tails struck from all directions. Lynn's adrenaline-infused rage and lust for revenge seemed to stifle her fear. There was nothing before her but absolute focus and a necessity to win, to kill the Fox. She had to do this for her parents, for all the people of Grantitan and

Gran Karisu and everywhere else in Sari where people suffered; and for herself, for the Fox was the epitome of evil and the conduit of death.

She and the Fox danced around the airfield and the Fox laughed as she parried and countered him. In one powerful maneuver, Lynn managed to cut the head off one of the tails and bash the Fox with her shield. While he was staggering, Lynn cut another of the tails. The other tails seemed craven at the sight of this, so Lynn lowered her shield, unsheathed her knife, and went in for the kill.

Unfortunately, the Fox was not so easily defeated.

She tried first to slice his neck open with her bladed arm, but the Fox ducked and avoided the attack. Lynn staggered forward and tried to swing back around with the knife, but the Fox pushed into her and got a hold on her wrist before she could. He powered into her chest, pushing her back into the wall of the hangar.

"Overclock!" she shouted again. Only, nothing happened. Her heart sank as she realized she had used too many power cells by keeping her shield active for so long.

The Fox grinned as he restrained her wrists against the wall. "Too bad."

Seven tails snaked around him, seeking revenge for the two Lynn had decapitated. Over and over, the tails stabbed her; small, shallow penetrations of about an inch or two, and never in vital places. Her arms, her legs, and her torso endured inexplicable pain as the tails exacted violent revenge on her. Meanwhile, the Grothians cheered and laughed at her pain.

Dozens of holes opened up in her flesh and Lynn screamed in agony, begging the Fox for mercy. "Stop! Oh God, stop! Just kill me you bastard!" Her hands started shaking and her body felt weak. Shock was setting in and Lynn could feel her mind going blank as she could do nothing except watch herself die.

Momentarily, the tails retreated, and the Fox crept close to her, until his face was inches from hers, and he whispered, "You look just like your mother did, Addilynn. So righteous, so pure, and unfortunately, so frail and weak."

Her heart skipped a beat and suddenly she was reinvigorated. He knew who she was? How could he? She was barely five years old, and she had been hiding; did he know she was there all along?

"No! How do you—" He was reading her mind, she decided. After all, he had to be a templar, right? There was no other explanation.

"I am God. I decide, Addilynn, and you have forced my hand, just like your father did. Now, I must bid you farewell. Another wasted, disappointing mortal."

As the Fox's tails reared up and prepared for the kill, something awakened inside of Lynn. It felt warm at first, then burning hot, like her body was tempered steel. And just as the sword is forged from a rod of iron, so too was her body transformed, weaponized by the hot embers of hatred and the hammer of revenge.

Lynn's body burned with intense heat and she blew the Fox across the square with a sudden release of incredible energy, an energy so powerful it put all the Grothian spectators on their backs as well. What was happening? She was aware of the transcendent state she was entering as she watched her arms glow and a tail of flame ignite at her shoulder and coil around her arm all the way to her palm. Fire emerged from her upper back and blew in the wind like a cloak. The fire in her palm swirled around into great balls of scorching-hot madness. All of this happened within seconds as the Fox tumbled across the ground and into the partially destroyed barricade near the airfield turret.

Something impossible was happening. Only, it wasn't impossible. Alex had caught the slab and broken a mountain in half. Zach had shown her a city in space and a planet full of rippers and ogres. Grothian templars had descended upon them and attacked them with telepathy. The Fox himself ought to be impossible. Indeed, nothing was impossible. In that moment, Lynn was naked and fearless, for she had become the decider.

Grothian soldiers, panicked and caught off guard, rose to their feet and reached for their guns, but Lynn's body was working with autonomous instinct. Fireballs escaped her palm with incredible speed, killing on contact all who would oppose her. After a dozen of them fell, the remaining Grothians fled in fear, leaving the Fox alone in her line of sight.

"This can't be!" the Fox stammered. His suit was destroyed and his mask charred from Lynn's blast. The Fox was just another mortal. No dashing away this time.

Lynn wouldn't provide him with closure. Instead of answering him, she held her arms out to her sides and focused all her energy on the palms of her hands and her intentions toward the Fox. The fireballs in her hands grew in size and moved toward her chest, converging in front of her to form a huge, unstable ball of furious fire.

I am justice, Lynn thought silently and without rage.

The ball of fire burst forward toward the Fox, and as it traveled, it transformed into the shape of a great phoenix. Like a guided missile, the phoenix struck the Fox with deadly precision, obliterating him instantly and leaving only the charred remains of the barricade in its wake.

Ash and embers rained down around Lynn as she stood and stared at the place where the Fox once was. A heavy haze fell over the airfield. Lynn closed her eyes, and the flames on her back expanded into wings of fire and the incredible screech of the phoenix sounded across the western spire.

Tears of pure wonder and relief moistened Lynn's face as she fell to her knees and the wings of fire dissipated into smoke. She looked up at the sky and she could see blue as the Grothian ships began retreating. Everything was going to be okay.

Her body cooled and she began to feel lightheaded and sick. Pain shot through every inch of her body as the strength of the phoenix left her. Looking down at her body, she noticed her rykai suit was destroyed and she was almost naked and covered in burns, especially her arms and hands, which were badly charred. She started to shake and her consciousness was waning.

Oh well, she thought. *If I die, at least I killed him*. One last time, she looked up and saw the sun appear from behind the massive hull of the Grothian destroyer before she let her eyes close and her body fall face first onto the scorched ground.

FROM THE MIDST

1

The chaos of the night melted into a bitter, amber-colored dawn as the sun rose over the besieged city. Alex was in pain, but he would live. Other than the gaping hole and broken bones in his forearm that were covered with thick bandages and a molded cast, Reanyn had been able to heal him. His sister had not been so lucky.

From the moment he came to, Alex stayed by her side in the tattered academy medical facility. The burns were serious, the medics told him, and she would have to remain in a coma for a day or two until the healing serum they injected her with could ease most of the pain. In addition to the burns, she had been stabbed everywhere and her thigh and her back had been slashed to shreds. They said there was a slight chance she would not make it the two days, the carnage was so severe. But Alex wouldn't believe that. Lynn was the strongest person he had ever known and there was no way she would give up now, not after everything they had been through.

In the background, Alex had the galactic news playing nonstop on his phone. No one seemed to know why the Grothians attacked or why they didn't finish the job, but clearly, the Sarians had done something right. Soon after the Grothians retreated from Gran Karisu, Sarian armadas, supported by Prism no doubt, arrived on Grantitan and drove the templars' forces off the planet. For once, it looked as though there was hope of releasing outer Sari from the grip of the Grothians.

"They are moving some of the patients to the *Leviathan*," Jett said as he walked into the room and sat beside Alex at Lynn's bedside. "They can provide better care in the ship's medical bay."

"That's a good idea," Alex said.

"Would you like to get some air? You have been here all night. I will stay with her."

Alex stared at the wall for a moment, a mixture of fatigue and anxiety swirling around his brain and slowing his thought process, and finally replied, "Sure, that would be nice. I'll be right back."

He got up from his chair and went to the hall, stopping at the doorway for a moment and looking back at his sister. It was so unreal to see her lying there, unconscious, with all those bandages wrapped around her body and a tube in her mouth. *Come on sis*, he prayed, closing his eyes and listening to the gentle beeping of the monitors around her.

The hallways were a mess: gurneys everywhere, equipment scattered, and medical staff rushing about and talking quickly. Some of the lights were blown out and parts of a couple rooms were destroyed, with debris spilled out into the hall.

When Alex finally got outside, he lit up a smoke and walked across the grass toward the edge of the spire. Smoke still rose from a section of the northern spire even now, nearly nineteen hours after the Grothians had retreated. The skyways were eerily empty, and the only sounds were those of emergency and military vehicles traveling between epicenters and doing damage control. In the aftermath of the previous night, Epilogue City faced a stark reality indeed.

Alex heard footsteps approaching him as he exhaled into the wind.

"Long night," Zach said, joining Alex with a lit cigar. "Glad you both made it."

"Me too. So, you think Lynn is going to be okay?"

"Yeah, I do. She is one stubborn woman. Worse than my ex-wife."

Alex laughed. "Yeah, she is tough as hell."

Zach took a big puff of his cigar, polluting the air with thick, acrid smoke, and added "She is also the phoenix."

In his surprise, Alex swallowed suddenly and nearly choked on his own spit.

"What do you mean?" Alex demanded in a fit of coughing.

"Approximately what it sounds like," Zach answered, not satisfying Alex at all. "You have manifested the power of the golem, and your sister has manifested the power of the phoenix."

"What? Since when? How do you know this? What happened?"

After Zach took a moment to collect his words, he went on to explain his insanity.

When Zach and Rachel had arrived at the airfield, the Grothians were already retreating, and what was left of the Sarian forces had pulled back to the airfield's southern turret. Few were alive on the decimated strip of land near the northern turret. Methodically, they searched among the bodies for survivors. When Zach came upon Lynn, she barely had a pulse and her arms looked like the remnants of a forest fire. The rest of her body had lesser burns, which was perhaps lucky, for the burns had also cauterized her many flesh wounds and probably saved her from bleeding out. In ordinary circumstances, this would be sort of a miracle, but Zach knew better. This was just like the day at the stadium. The only questions were *how* and *why*.

They found Alex shortly after and called in a medical unit to take him, Lynn, and the few other survivors away as soon as possible. In the meantime, Zach examined the battlefield and put the clues together. All the defeated Grothian soldiers were scorched to oblivion in nearly the same way. Where a barricade used to be there was a blackened crater, from which a trail of charred tarmac led all the way back to where Lynn lay motionless, a circle of soot around her. Ashes were all over the area. This was not the kind of scene caused by any weaponry that Zach knew of. Even fire-based rykai suits wouldn't produce this much by-product.

Then he saw something shimmering.

Resting between Lynn's thigh and her melted rykai suit was a diamond-like shard. Zach dislodged it and held it between two fingers, observing its perfect texture and flawless appearance. In that instant, he felt something powerful coursing through his body. Zach could sense the rage and the retribution of the phoenix with every fiber of his being. It was as if he had become possessed, enchanted by some unseen, unimaginably powerful spirit. This was it; he just knew it. The shard was how the Alderians had invoked the planet. Though he had no idea how this would work, Zach was certain of his hypothesis.

Alex was beside himself with amazement.

When Zach was through telling all of this, he took another long puff of his cigar and stared into the distance, letting Alex take it all in before he produced the incredible conduit of power and held it out in front of him.

"Unbelievable," Alex said, mesmerized by the glimmering sliver of crystal, "But, wait ... did my sister have that all along? How come her power didn't manifest when you trained us, like mine did?"

"I don't know," Zach admitted. "We will have to ask her when she wakes up. In the meantime, I bet there is a shard inside of you somewhere."

"Really? Oh yeah, I guess that makes sense."

"Come on, let's go find it."

Flicking his cigar off the edge of the spire, Zach turned to go, and Alex hurried after him. It was time to unravel this Alderian myth once and for all.

2

"Hold on," Alex asked, power walking up beside Zach. "Where are we going? I want to be there when my sister wakes up."

"Me too. I want to know all about her shard, but this won't take long."

"Well, we don't want to bombard her when she wakes up, she needs a chance to decompress after everything."

"No time for that," Zach insisted. "The bigwigs are going to debrief us soon, now that order is nearly restored. We have to get our story straight before that."

"What story? What are you talking about?"

In his usual fashion, Zach only gave him a half answer. "Whichever story doesn't involve shards that grant you and your sister superpowers."

Alex followed Zach back into the medical facility and down the busy hallway as he objected, "So, you want me to lie?" Not that Alex was surprised.

Zach cut to the right suddenly and flung open the door to a partially destroyed room. Once inside, Zach prompted Alex to lie on the still-intact exam table and pulled a high-tech-looking scanner out of one of the drawers.

"What is that?" Alex asked, sitting on the edge of the table.

"It's going to show me if any more of these are under your flesh," Zach replied, first scanning the shards, then making his way over to Alex. As he began slowly looking over Alex's body, starting from the top of his head, Zach answered Alex's previous question. "As for the debrief, you wouldn't be lying. As far as we know, this is all theoretical."

"But it really isn't, is it?"

"Maybe not, but anyway, our coming here was conditioned upon a lie, so it would be pointless to diverge from that now. Similarly, the same dangers I expressed on Grantitan with regard to revealing your power are even greater now."

"How so?"

Zach started bending down to scan Alex's dangling knees while he answered. "Before, you were some unknown, superhuman prodigy. Now, there are two of you and there are likely conduits, meaning there is potential that others may steal and invoke the shards."

Alex understood well enough, he supposed. They didn't know enough about the shards to know how they actually worked, but if they assumed the shards somehow granted powers, like the ones depicted in the Alderian myths, they wouldn't want the wrong people getting them. It was hard to imagine what it would be like if the Grothian templars got the shards. Sari would be doomed.

There was one problem with all that, however: Alex had shown Reanyn his power. On top of that, he had no idea how many people at the bunker saw him raise that wall and would put together what really happened. Actually, if he really thought about it, it seemed unlikely that anyone besides Reanyn would be able to say with any degree of certainty that Alex had powers. There had been so much chaos at the airfield that it would be easy to deny. So, maybe all he had to do was talk to Reanyn. At least, he hoped so.

"So, what do we say?" Alex asked.

"Sit still," Zach demanded, ascending Alex's body with the scanner. "We tell them what happened. You were out cold before anything happened, so how would you know? I arrived after everything—"

"Okay, I got it. I won't say anything. Are we going to keep this a secret forever, though?"

"If we have to." Scratching his chin and looking awfully intense, Zach asked, "Why is there no shard?"

"Is the device busted?"

"No chance. You don't have a shard in you ..."

At the same time, Zach and Alex shifted their eyes to the bandages on Alex's arm. If there had been a shard, it could have been there. After all, when Alex had woken up, the nurse explained to him that the hole had been deep and wide, exposing almost two inches of bone on his forearm.

Before either of them could articulate it, Alex got a text from Jett.

"My sister is awake," Alex read aloud. "I'm going to see her."

Alex slid off the table and right into Zach's intense grip. Squeezing Alex's elbow, Zach said sternly, "Remember what I said, when you go into debrief."

"Right. I understand."

3

Something marvelous, unprecedented, and symbolic swept into Lynn's mind as the Grothian ships departed the atmosphere of Gran Karisu. Her body was failing, and her eyes slowly closed, allowing her to drift away into some unknown purgatory. Here, a sense of euphoria she had never felt before seemed to erase all angst, negativity, and pain. For a time, she felt totally untethered, as if her body and her soul were at once unshackled and unbeaten. Gentle rays of sunlight kissed her face and drew her tormented self out of the dungeon and into a world unseen, smiling and full of hope. Across a golden plain, she saw two great skyscrapers, the blinding light of the sun reflecting off their smooth chrome exteriors. Great shadows stretched across a river and into the field where she stood, her hand shielding her eyes from the brightness and her hair and her sundress undulating gently in the wind. The long, ambitious shadows shrank as she came closer, becoming smaller and smaller. Lynn walked through the river with no regard for its roaring current, pursuing the shadows all the way to the base of the buildings, until they disappeared completely inside the massive structures. Only her shadow remained.

That's right; tremble before me, she thought, making a fist that sparked with fire. *You and your kin have no country here, for I am the decider now.*

For how long she lingered in this wild state, Lynn had no idea, but eventually what she assumed to be reality broke through and she saw Jett before her.

"Lynn, you're awake!" He leaned down beside her. "We were all worried. I am so glad you are okay." The nurse removed the tube in her mouth and Lynn choked and coughed profusely. She sure didn't feel "okay."

"Where am I?" Lynn asked deliriously.

She heard Zach's voice next as he and Alex burst into the room. "Still at the academy, unfortunately."

"Sis! You are okay!" Alex exclaimed, rushing over to her.

Lynn examined her bandaged arms and the crummy hospital bed in which she lay, and cracked a smile. Looking at Zach, she joked, "What, no handcuffs?"

Zach laughed heartily.

"You would say that," Alex said.

"Well, come on, really." She laughed. "Also, how about a drink? My throat is so dry. How long was I out?"

"About twelve hours," Jett responded, grabbing a cup of water from her bedside and helping her to sip from the straw.

Lynn sipped the water and complained, "I guess I have to ask for the good stuff, huh?"

"What would you like?" Jett asked. "I will get it for you."

"Something forty proof or higher."

Alex objected, "You shouldn't drink right now."

Turning toward him, Lynn winced in pain and said, "It's a joke, dummy."

"Are you in pain?"

"Obviously."

"I shall ask the nurse about pain medication," Jett offered, getting up and leaving the room.

"Sorry sis," Alex said. "I'm just glad you are okay." He touched her hand, or rather the bandage-covered appendage that used to be her hand, and looked at her empathetically. She really was lucky to have such great people in her life.

Zach approached the bedside, where Jett had been, and said, "Alex, if you would, give us a moment?" Alex seemed hesitant for a second and Zach followed up, "Don't worry. No stress."

"All right," Alex agreed. "See you soon, okay?"

Alex gave her a smile and touched her forehead. Once Alex had left them, Zach sat in the chair beside the bed and folded his hands together as he often did when he was about to explain something pretentiously.

"What do you want?" Lynn asked.

"How long did you have this?"

Zach reached into his pocket and pulled out the crystal shard Lynn had found, flashing it before her for a few seconds before sliding it back into its hiding place.

"I found it during the battle."

"Found it where?"

"It was inside Alex's arm."

A look of fascination swept over Zach's face as he exclaimed, "I knew it! Lynn, that shard gave Alex his power. The fact that you possessed it during the battle is what gave you the power of the phoenix as well."

"Wait, how did you—"

"I saw the soot, the ash, the burn marks ... no weapon could have done that. Lynn, we have discovered the secret of the Alderians! It is this shard!"

Bewildered, she asked, "But, how—"

"I don't know, but is it really less believable than a race of people who can spiritually invoke the powers of the planet? We have to test it."

"How do you want to do that? I'm still half dead, remember?"

"I'll test it myself. If I can invoke the shard, we will know it is definitive. The most important thing, however, is that we can't mention this when they debrief us."

Zach continued droning on and Lynn was about to object, but instead her energy was drawn to something else. She realized, sort of half-coherently, that Zach was suggesting the mythical powers she and Alex had obtained came from the use of the shard, and some random corner of her brain decided to conflate this with the Fox. His speed, his inhuman ability, and his apparent omniscience ... were they results of a shard as well? What were the chances that only one of these existed in the universe? She would bet her life there were others. She pictured Alex's ravaged body, and even more so her own body, and realized the shard had remained in perfect condition in both cases. If she had killed the Fox, then ...

"We have to go back to the airfield," Lynn said urgently.

"What? Did you hear what I said?"

"Yes, lie at the debrief and blah, blah, blah," Lynn recited, unhooking herself from her IV and various wires and tubes. "But none of that matters if we don't go back now."

"You need to keep that stuff on—"

"There is another shard."

Taken aback, Zach asked, "What do you mean, you saw one?"

"Just take me there. Don't you trust me by now?"

Zach thought about it for a moment, then he gave in and helped her escape.

4

It had actually been quite easy to slip out of the medical building; the perks of traveling with a Prism officer, Lynn supposed. All it took was for Zach to insist that he was moving her to the *Leviathan* on orders from Lucian Everett and no one second-guessed them. Absently, she thought she ought to text Alex and Jett and let them know she was with Zach, but she had no idea where her phone was right now, and the sense of urgency to get to the airfield was overwhelming.

When they got outside, Zach helped her into his Jeep and they headed over to the airfield.

Lynn gazed at the incredible destruction around them. "This place is ruined."

"Yes. I'm afraid it will be a while before we can train any cadets here."

"Why did they retreat?" she wondered. Seeing everything now and remembering the battle, Lynn couldn't understand it. The Grothians were winning, and by what seemed like a significant margin.

"There was only one destroyer. They caught us off guard, which is why we lost, but they never intended to conquer us."

"What do you mean?"

"They knew reinforcements would come, that's why they retreated when they did. All they wanted was to demonstrate their ability to attack inner Sari."

"Those bastards."

"Whether their attack was to their benefit remains to be seen."

"How so? It looks pretty successful to me."

"The Grothians retreated from Grantitan this morning."

"What?"

"Prism armadas arrived to support the freedom fighters and they overpowered the Grothians. The other outer planets will soon follow, I expect, now that they know what is possible."

"I can't believe it ..."

Shock and joy overtook her at the thought of the Grothians fleeing her home. Maybe, at last, they could be free. People could start to have hope again, rebuild the lives they always dreamed of. Her friends and family ... they were going to be okay. Everything was going to be okay.

They pulled up to the airfield and got out of the Jeep. People were working diligently on repairing the turret nearby, but the barricade and the surrounding bits of charred tarmac remained untouched. Lynn hurried over to the barricade where the Fox had been just before she had vanquished him. Bending down beside the crater, she closed her eyes and images of the Fox rushed into her mind. She remembered details sporadically, like being surrounded by Grothians, feeling a surge of rage-infused adrenaline when he had said her name, and the fire conjuring around her as the Fox was helpless before her. She wished she had been close enough to him at the end to have seen his expression. Now, she opened her eyes and saw only a pile of ash where he had been.

"What was it like?" Zach inquired, standing behind her. When she didn't answer for a few seconds, Zach added, "The phoenix. What did it feel like?"

"I barely remember," Lynn admitted. "I felt this feeling of, I guess, transcendence. It was like I had been possessed by something godlike. I couldn't feel pain or emotions. I was just totally calm, I think, and then I just knew what to do."

"I felt something similar when I removed the shard from your body."

As Zach answered, Lynn stared at the ash inside the crater. She knew there would be a shard in there, and she knew what it would mean if there were.

Zach continued, "It is extraordinary. You killed a dozen of them, at least. Granted, at some cost to yourself, it would seem. When Alex first caught the slab it almost killed him, but after I trained him, he could break a mountain without a scratch on him. I assume I can do the same with you and tame the phoenix."

Lynn was listening, but as she did, she decided to sift through the ash. Sure enough, at the bottom of the pile of ash and soot was a shimmering crystal shard.

"Just like I thought," Lynn said.

"What?" Zach asked, bending down beside her. He saw the shard and his face lit up with amazement.

"Another shard?" he marveled, picking up the shard and comparing it to the one he had found on Lynn's hip.

"It belonged to him ..." She trailed off. It only made sense. As soon as Zach suggested that she and Alex had obtained supernatural powers from the shard, she just knew the Fox had been carrying one too. There was no other explanation for him.

"Who? Was it a templar?"

"The Fox."

"You defeated the Fox? The nine-tailed templar?"

"Sounds like him."

Zach was stunned. "He is one of the most feared of the Grothian warlords we know of. Prism has only seen him a handful of times. Lynn, do you realize what this means?"

It meant her quest was over, she had done what she set out to do. Her parents were avenged and the galaxy was a safer place now with that murderer and psychopath dead.

"It means we can win," Zach continued. "We made peace all these years because we feared the templars. We have been under their thumb, constantly waiting for the other shoe to drop. We gave up so much, but now ... now we know."

Suddenly Lynn was aware of her pain again. Her meds must be wearing off. It probably didn't help that she was out here shoveling soot around.

"Are you okay?" Zach asked as he seemed to notice her discomfort.

"It hurts."

"Yeah, we ought to get you back. Come on."

She allowed Zach to help her up and they got back into the Jeep.

As they drove back, Zach continued his victorious rant. "I can't believe this. Lynn, you and your brother have changed everything." Lynn just closed her eyes and leaned against the side of the Jeep.

A moment later, Zach said, "I'm glad you understood the urgency of your suspicion about the Fox. If someone else had found the shard, it would have been bad. Once we get you healed up, we must go to Taland. There, we can finish your individual training. Also, I know a guy, a real science whiz, who we can trust enough to reveal the shards to him. Maybe he can help us figure out more about the history of the Alderians and what we should do next. And of course, we have to get you using the phoenix more and figure out how to mitigate those burns. There is so much to do, Lynn!"

"No." Lynn said, exhausted. "I meant what I said the night before the ball. I just want to go home." The thought of everything that Zach was saying was just overwhelming. Sure, that stuff could be important, but she had done her part. She killed the Fox, and now, all she wanted was to see her parents.

"You can, after we finish your training."

"That will take years. Then there will be another quest. I'm tired. I played along with all this because I wanted to be stronger and be able to make a better life for Grantitan. I feel I can do that now. I just want to see my family," Lynn said.

After a brief silence, Zach replied, "Okay. I'll get you on the next ship. I'll have to arrange for you to see Hailey for your burns. That is, if you want to look normal again. Prism has skin grafts that will make it look like you were never burned."

That was too easy.

"That's it?" she asked, "No destiny or whatever? I thought all this was fated?"

"Maybe this is part of it."

"What, you think maybe I'll change my mind if you give me an inch?"

"No." He laughed. "Knowing you, you'll take a mile. I mean, maybe you are right. Maybe this was your quest. You defeated the Fox, Lynn, that's incredible. We have the shards now. I guess we have some time while I figure out what the hell all of this means."

Lynn smiled and closed her eyes again, letting herself relax for the rest of the short ride back to the medical facility. She was glad Zach understood. Honestly, Lynn couldn't be certain what came next. No one could. Perhaps she would decide to carry on someday, but there were things she wanted to do first. She would bear no guilt either, for she had done plenty, and it was time for her to rest.

5

It took only two days for them to get it together and put Lynn on a ship to Grantitan, which was surprising, considering everything that was going on. She had half-expected Zach to tell her that it would be weeks before Prism could spare the resources to take her home. As it turned out, there was a need for more personnel on parts of Grantitan to deal with the lingering loyalists who refused to accept the liberation. They were not a threat, not with all the Grothian fleets gone, but they were enough of a nuisance to require intervention. Zach helped put together a crew and a company of about one hundred soldiers to go to Grantitan immediately. Lynn would be transported with them and brought to the Hedron Center in Calivia for treatment.

Alex and Reanyn volunteered for the assignment immediately. Technically, Zach told them, they should complete advanced training in Taland, but this was a simple planetary assignment, and given that it would be a minute before Prism training operations would resume, an exception could be easily made.

The ship was boarding when Lynn arrived at the airfield in the early morning with Alex and Reanyn. A feeling of uncertainty haunted her as she gazed around at the ruined campus, still in awe of the scope of it all.

"This is it," Alex reminded them. "You ready?"

"All set! I barely had anything when I came," Reanyn said.

"Yeah, I guess, just ..." Lynn replied, unsure as she looked around the airfield. Jett was supposed to meet her. He had told her the day before that he was going to be staying on Gran Karisu for a while, doing whatever he could to help Prism reorganize in the aftermath of the attack. Lynn couldn't blame him for that. Even though she wished he would come with her, there was no good reason for him to abandon his duties for however long it would take her to recover.

"What? You forget something?" Alex asked.

Reanyn shoved him playfully. "She is looking for Jett."

"Oh." Alex sounded embarrassed. "Makes sense."

"Yo!" someone called from behind them. Siefer, Sam, Kiah, and Karson all approached them excitedly.

"Hey!" Reanyn greeted them. "Glad you came."

Kiah replied, "We just wanted to say goodbye and good luck."

"Thanks, you too," Alex said, shaking Kiah's hand. Everyone seconded the gesture with a nod and a smile.

"I'd shake your hand, but, you know," Lynn joked, holding up her bandaged stumps while everyone laughed at her.

"You were incredible," Sam commended Lynn.

"Yeah," Karson agreed. "All of you were."

"I'll miss you," Reanyn said, trying not to cry.

"We'll see each other again," Sam assured her.

Siefer agreed. "We are all Prism now. Those Grothians better keep on runnin', if they know what's good for them."

"Damn right," Alex said.

Sam pointed her metal index finger at Lynn and said, "Next time I see you, my Grothian kill count is gonna be higher, I promise."

"I'll hold you to it." Lynn laughed. "And you have to kill a warlord, or it doesn't count."

"All right, well, we gotta get going," Alex said.

"Okay, well, take care," Karson said. "Be safe."

Kiah seconded, "Stay in touch."

"We will," Reanyn promised, her face now saturated with sappy tears. Giving Kiah a big hug, she added, "You will always be my sister."

Siefer hugged her next and said, "We are all family now." Everyone said goodbye one last time before the three of them proceeded toward the ship.

Sam put her hand on Lynn's shoulder as she began to walk away. "Until next time," she said with a wink.

Lynn repeated, "Until next time."

Then, they were gone. Just before the three of them reached the ramp of the starship *Heimdall*, Lynn saw Jett, Blake, and Leon coming across the tarmac. Jett saw her and put his hand up as he hurried over to her.

"We'll save you a seat," Alex said before he and Reanyn went up the ramp.

"Thank you, I'll catch up in a minute," Lynn replied. As Jett came up to her, Lynn sassed, "About time. For a second, I thought you forgot about me."

"I would never," Jett assured her. "I was called on to make last-minute preparations. A team is going over to the northern spire this morning. I am so sorry."

"It's fine, I'm kidding."

He moved in close to her and gently held her bandaged wrists in his hands, his deeply passionate eyes conflicted by a juxtaposition of hope and sadness.

"You must be happy to be going home," he said.

"Sort of."

"It is a little bittersweet, I must admit."

"You could still come with me.

"I want to, but ..."

"We have other things to do, I know. I'd do them too, if I could," Lynn said.

She knew what he had really wanted to say because she wanted to say it too. In all the randomness of this quest, all the things she thought she knew that turned out to be so subject to change, there was only one thing at the end of it all that she could still say with certainty. There was also no way of knowing if that certainty was mutual or if it even mattered, unless she uncovered it now.

"I love you," Lynn said softly, pressing herself against him and slowly kissing him.

When she released him, she lingered inches from his mouth, awaiting his reply.

"I love you, too," he pledged, returning her kiss.

They kissed twice more before Lynn asked him, "Will I see you again?" It was sort of a stupid question, she knew, because the answer was the same as it was with all the others. It wasn't up to them. They were part of Prism now and they would go wherever people needed them. That was, if Lynn ever came back at all.

"I promise that you will."

He stroked her cheek and she knew he was sincere. In the background, Lynn could hear some officer yelling to her to get on the ship. It was time to go.

"I should go before they throw a tantrum," she said.

"Indeed, you must."

"I love you," Lynn repeated. "Wherever we are, it will be true."

"And I love you. Until our duty brings us together again, I shall dream about you every night."

"Me too."

One last time, they kissed each other and finally said goodbye. Lynn felt a lump in her throat as they parted ways and she boarded the ship. Before she knew it, she was strapped into her seat beside Alex and Reanyn and they were taking off. Everything was different now, she thought, as she felt the ship roaring into space. Reality was setting in a bit; no doubt her life would never be the same, but at least now, it felt like parts of it mattered.

Lynn couldn't wait to be home.

6

Lynn's arrival on Grantitan was peaceful and unceremonious. She came into the Calivian spaceport on one of the *Heimdall*'s dropships with a few other Prism personnel who had business in the city. Since she had lost her phone and not bothered to replace it before leaving Gran Karisu, no one even knew she was coming home. On top of that, she was arriving alone, as Alex and Reanyn had already gotten off the ship on the other side of the planet. Saying goodbye had been hard, but Lynn knew she would see them again soon.

When she limped her way down the ramp and into the spaceport, the only person there waiting for her was the infamous Hailey, Zach's perpetual on-call nurse.

"Right on time," Hailey remarked with a smile, hurrying over to Lynn and offering to take her bags.

Lynn allowed her to take them and replied, "Thanks a lot."

"You're welcome. Come on, my car's this way. We have to hurry; I'm due back at work soon."

Lynn hustled out of the hangar behind her and got into Hailey's little white car and buckled herself in while Hailey put her stuff in the trunk.

Hailey got into the driver's seat and Lynn said, "You would think Zach would give you a driver, at least."

"You know how he is. He keeps a tight circle. There aren't many people you can trust these days."

"I suppose. I hope he pays you well, anyway." He probably had an affair with her too, Lynn thought, only half-humorously.

"I've never regretted Zach's trust," Hailey answered vaguely.

They drove the rest of the way in relative silence. What were they supposed to talk about anyway? Lynn had known this woman all of five minutes. Instead, Lynn just peered out the open window, letting her hair blow in the breeze and watching all the familiar landmarks go by. Nothing looked different. Though, what did she expect? It wasn't like things would change overnight. Liberation was not acquired in a day. What had happened was a huge step, but they had more work to do, for certain.

When they got to the Hedron Center, Hailey escorted Lynn up to the fifth floor and brought her to the same wing where she and Alex had been the day the stadium blew up.

"What, is this the super-secret Prism wing? Pretty obvious," Lynn observed.

"Yes," she answered curtly, leading Lynn into one of the rooms, "Here is your room. I'll be back in a bit to get your treatment started."

"Wait, how long do I have to wait here?"

"Just a few minutes now, but once I start the treatment, it will take about a week."

"I have to sit here for a week?"

"Unless you don't want your pretty skin back, but you are young, so I wouldn't recommend that. Be back soon."

Without giving Lynn a chance to reply, Hailey was gone.

Lynn sat on the edge of the hospital bed and stared at the wall. Well, what now? Alex was gone for six weeks and apparently, she was going to sit in bed for a week. Boredom was inevitable. She was already bored and she had only been here for thirty seconds.

Something unexpected interrupted her lamenting.

"Addy? Oh my God, it is really you!" Beatrice exclaimed as she burst into the room. How did she know Lynn was here?

"Beatrice? How did you—"

Dean appeared in the doorway and answered her. "Hailey called us."

Beatrice rushed over and gave her a careful hug, noticing her bandages, and immediately started crying. "We missed you so much, Addy."

"I missed you too," Lynn replied, placing her bandaged hands awkwardly on Beatrice's back.

"What happened to you?" Beatrice demanded as she released Lynn and looked her up and down.

"Just a little scuff," Lynn said, downplaying it.

Dean jumped in. "It looks a wee bit more than a scuff." Beatrice's eyes were still scanning Lynn, clearly processing too much at once.

Lynn tried to shift attention away from her injuries. "How come you didn't answer when I called?"

Confused, Beatrice asked, "When did you call?"

"Right after the attack. I was worried about you, but no one answered my calls."

"Now you know what it is like to be us," Dean said, finding the perfect opportunity for a jab.

"Dean, stop it!" Beatrice scolded him. "Honey, the Grothians cut off communications. As soon as they took over, they stopped our phones, our networks, everything."

"That makes sense," Lynn said, doing her best to bite her tongue with Dean.

"We tried calling you after the Grothians left, but your phone was off," Beatrice said.

"It got destroyed, I think," Lynn guessed. "I was in the battle, on Gran Karisu. Did you hear about it?"

"Oh my God, Addy, you were in that battle? That's how you ended up like this? This is why we got so worried when you said you were leaving with Mr. Brine."

Lynn rolled her eyes and said, "I killed a templar, that's how I ended up like this. Look what those templars did here, how many people they killed or subjugated. Someone has to do it."

Intrigued, Dean repeated, "You killed a templar?"

"I killed the Fox."

"Who is the Fox?" Beatrice wondered. Dean didn't seem to know either.

"It doesn't matter. He was a feared Grothian warlord, a Prism most-wanted target. He attacked Gran Karisu and I killed him," Lynn explained.

"So, you passed the tests then?" Dean asked. "You are a Prism soldier now?"

"Yes."

"Well, hopefully you won't have to fight any more of them," Beatrice said. "They are saying the Grothians are willing to renew peace talks."

"They will never give us peace. Not for real."

There was an awkward silence, then Dean shifted the conversation. "We are proud of you, you know."

Lynn was too surprised to respond.

Dean continued, "I know I said you couldn't do it, but the truth is, I am a stubborn old man. I like things my way. That, and I thought you were being a little bull-headed back then."

Lynn laughed, holding back tears. "I was bull-headed. Still am."

"But you made it. You are a Prism soldier and because of you, people will have hope again. You should be truly proud of that." Now she was unable to hold back the tears.

"Thank you," Lynn choked out. "I love you. I am sorry about the things I said before I left."

"It's okay," Beatrice said, giving her another hug. "We are sorry for not telling you about your past and not believing in you."

"I don't care about that anymore," Lynn admitted. "I know you were trying to protect me. The past is the past."

"Oh, Addy, I love you. I'm so glad you are okay."

"I love you too."

Hailey walked back into the room with a tray full of all kinds of madness, interrupting the emotional reunion. "Okay, Mr. and Mrs. Palmer, I need you to wait downstairs. I am going to start the treatment now." Part of her was relieved. Making up with her foster parents was nice and all, but Lynn could only take so much of this.

"Okay," Beatrice agreed reluctantly. "We will see you soon, Addy."

"Get yourself well, you hear?" Dean added, "We love you."

"Love you. I'll come see you when I'm out," Lynn said.

Rolling up a cart to the bedside, Hailey started preparing for whatever crazy procedure she was about to subject Lynn to, taking a needle and syringe out of sterile wrappers and equipping it with some clear fluid.

"That was heartwarming," Hailey said with no emotion at all, still totally focusing on her work. "Lay back for me, please."

Lynn did as she was told and Hailey stuck her with the needle, startling her with the rudeness of it.

"You are going to be asleep for a bit while I do this first part. When you wake up, it'll be just a few days of rest and monitoring and you will be good to go. Sound good?" Hailey summarized.

"I guess it has to be, huh?" Lynn sassed, in reference to the needle that had already been injected into her.

Hailey just chuckled and said, "You'll be out in two minutes. Be right back."

She rushed out of the room and left Lynn drowsy and lost in half-lucid thoughts. A lump was still working its way out of her throat, but it wasn't sadness or anxiety. She kept thinking about Beatrice and Dean and how good they were. There were so many people who were good: Alex, Jett, Zach, and all the others. At some point, she had lost herself, and she realized that now. There were reasons to be cynical, sure, but there were also so many reasons to have hope.

There was another thing that kept floating around in her head as she was passing out: the Fox. Lynn had so many unanswered questions about him. How had he known her? Was he really the man who killed her parents, or was it someone else imitating the Fox? Was it truly the shard that was responsible for all of him? As she contemplated these questions, she realized that she may never know the answers. In fact, the answers were irrelevant. The past was the past, right? The Fox was dead, and that was the important thing. Even if the templar she had killed on Gran Karisu wasn't the same fox who had murdered her parents, she had dealt a mortal blow to the symbology of the Fox, the mysterious and hallowed concept that had spawned legions of violent crusaders all across the Sarian Empire. If another of the Fox's soldiers tried to rise up, she'd do it again, too. Lynn supposed that, for now, all she could do was focus on the present and the people who loved her, and that was exactly what she decided she was going to do.

7

By the time all the bureaucrats were finally done with him, Zach could have written a damn memoir about it all. Even by Prism standards this debrief had been excessive. He supposed, given the chaotic state of things, it made some sense, but still, he had better things to be doing. So he was in and out of that stupid building over the course of the week, breaking for only a couple hours a day, long enough to fill his stomach and see his prodigies blasted into space. Finally, on the fifth day, long after he had first considered unholstering his revolver and once again trying to blow his brains out, they finally released him from the academy. Not a second too soon.

He reached into his peacoat the second he was clear of those people and lit up one of his best cigars. Staring at his phone, he scrolled down his contact list, stopping at his daughter, Jaymi. His encounter with the templar had been brief, but it had reminded him how quickly it could all be over. For the past few days, he couldn't stop thinking about her.

After battling his nerves for a moment, Zach dialed her number. It rang three times and went to voicemail. Whether that was because she still didn't want to talk to him was hard to say, but he was done running from his stupidity. It was time to make amends. If nothing else, he had to try.

"Hey Jaymi," he spoke nervously into her voicemail box. "It's Dad. I don't know how much you heard about Gran Karisu, but I am okay. I got into it pretty hard this past year and ... well ... I'm sorry about the way I treated you and your mother. If you don't want to forgive me, I understand, but just know that I am sorry. Something kinda big is happening ... you might have heard ... so, I don't know how long I'll be traveling around. Anyway, I love you. If you—"

The answering machine cut out before he could continue. Zach was never good at that stuff and almost immediately wished he hadn't sent that message. It was so corny, and while he did mean what he said, he knew he couldn't make up for anything or be there for her any more than he ever was. His destiny was, is, and always would be in outer space. Regardless, at the very least, she deserved to know he was sorry.

"That it?" Lucas asked him as he approached from across the lawn.

Zach swiftly put his phone away and answered, "I imagine so, until the next idiot comes along."

"What took them so long? They only asked me, like, two questions."

The two of them started walking across the campus while Zach explained, "They wanted to know about the templar. How it fought, how it spoke to me, what kind of powers it had."

"That took five days?"

"After the second day, there was a lot of political meandering. Not all of it was debrief. You know, talk about the Grothian motivation and our next steps."

"You probably can't say, huh?"

"It wouldn't interest you. Plus, it's not what we are going to be doing."

"What do you mean? I am supposed to be retired." Lucas laughed. "You remember, you called me here for a favor?"

They had nearly reached the main faculty building, where Zach's office was, when Sal Brigande approached them.

"Commander Brine!" Sal called.

"Sir!" Zach saluted, followed immediately by Lucas.

After a brief and seemingly skeptical inspection of them, Sal addressed Lucas. "Corporal, will you excuse us for a moment?"

"Yes, sir," Lucas complied, making himself disappear.

Sal returned his attention to Zach and laughed. "At ease already, for heaven's sake! How long have we known each other?"

"Sorry, sir."

Putting a hand on Zach's shoulder, Sal said, "Well done, my boy! I don't know if your exploits are a better reflection on you or on the guy who trained you. Call me impressed."

"Thanks. You did teach me how to smoke a good cigar," Zach joked. Whipping out his case, he flipped it open and offered one to Sal, who accepted. Zach lit him up and the smoke was abundant between them as they spoke.

"You know, I was listening to the details about the battle. That templar having two powers was really unexpected, and you held your own, too. I was also intrigued by the fact that your pupil killed a dozen Grothians on her own, fresh out of the Gauntlet. She's not even done advanced training, has she?"

Sal already knew the answer, of course.

"She and Alex, they are quite the prodigal students," Zach boasted. "As for the templar, if you think about it, they've been waiting twenty years to attack us again. It makes sense that they were getting better all that time."

"True," Sal agreed, puffing for a moment before continuing. "Those Grothian bastards. They are wishing they didn't attack us right now; you know that?"

"Maybe. Or maybe they are gearing up for something bigger."

"No. They responded to our request for negotiation this morning. They are running scared. It's almost like we had something they never expected."

Zach's eyes grew large with surprise. "They are negotiating?"

"They are coming to the table, at least. Anyway," Sal said, and paused for a moment. "There was something else I wanted to ask you."

Zach had a feeling he knew what that something was, though he couldn't imagine how Sal had caught him in a lie. He had been so careful in his iteration of the battle and of the Fox's demise. What had he screwed up?

"If the Grothians don't negotiate, hell, even if they do, we are going to need more captains that have what it takes to stand against them. How would you feel about taking my place at the helm of the *Leviathan*?"

Certain he had heard incorrectly, Zach asked, "You want me to command your ship? What about you?"

"I am going to have too many ships to be encumbered by the captain's chair, I'm afraid."

"You made admiral? That's amazing, congratulations!"

"Congratulations to you, as well, Captain Zachary Brine."

Sal held out his hand and slowly opened his fist, revealing the insignia of the Prism starship captain, a small pin depicting a starship flying in front of a golden prism, suspended inside a ring of shiny metal. This was a dream come true. As Zach held it in his hand, he was speechless. Everything he had so carefully contemplated those fateful days following his witnessing of Alex catching the slab, it had all ended up as he imagined. Granted, Zach had never foreseen all the details of how this epic endeavor played out, but he had always known, from the very start, that he was pursuing a greatness beyond the capacity of himself as an individual. This was true of Alex and Lynn as well, and perhaps now it was true of some of the other cadets. This promotion, this expansion of his autonomy and ability to explore the vastness of the universe, was a confirmation of the destiny he had tacitly accepted since the moment he stood up in that diner in Calivia. Looking back at what he had been doing then, right before the explosion at the stadium, Zach felt so foolish. Why would he have ever considered killing himself? He tried to imagine if he had. Everything would have changed. None of this would have happened, and the secret to beating the Grothians would have never been found. Even putting all that aside, he couldn't do something like that for Jaymi's sake. She needed a father; even one who was hardly ever there was better than none at all.

"Thank you, sir," Zach finally said. "I am honored to accept this promotion."

Sal shook his hand and said, "You have earned it. You showed incredible bravery and valor against the Grothian forces, and your commitment to this academy and the production of dozens of the greatest soldiers in the galaxy have proven you worthy of leading your own starship."

"Your words mean more to me than anyone's."

"I just wanted to tell you personally before you are announced publicly. I am proud of your achievement and to be able to say that I trained you." Sal smirked a little at the last remark.

"Happy to improve your resume." Zach laughed it off.

"Oh, there is just one thing about the *Leviathan*. I am taking a lot of my people with me to positions that are open on the command ship. You will need to replace about fifty percent of your personnel, but you will have plenty of time to vet candidates before you deploy. I am going to have the ship for at least another month anyway."

With a slick and joyful smile, Zach replied, "That is fine. I already have a pretty good idea of who to pick."

"Very good. Well, Captain, we shall meet again soon. Congratulations again."

"It is my honor, sir."

Zach felt mesmerized with glee as Sal walked away. Everything he had worked for had paid off. Now, he was in charge of the future. With a huge grin on his face, Zach foresaw a great adventure around the bend. There were so many things to do! Excited, he pulled out his phone to text Rachel and noticed he had missed a call while he had been talking to Sal. There was one new voicemail in his box and a text from his daughter that read "I'm glad you are okay. I love you too." In the voicemail, Jaymi said "Hey Dad, I got your message. I love you too, and well ... I still think it's wrong, what you did, but, I don't know ... I still hope you come home someday. Love you, bye.". That moment, Zach promised himself that he would make the time to see her, no matter what. He couldn't be happier.

Returning from whatever hole he had been hiding in, Lucas asked, "What was that all about? Is he mad?"

Zach just chuckled, putting away his phone and puffing on his cigar. "No. Oh, and, you know that favor I was going to ask you about?"

"Yeah?"

"Well, forget it. I need a different favor now."

"Anything you need."

"I need you to not retire, because we have a crew to assemble."

8

Six weeks turned into nine while Lynn waited monotonously for Alex's return to Calivia. When she was finally discharged from the Hedron Center, Rami, Jocelyn, and a bunch of people she knew from university threw her a massive coming-home bash. Red's bar gave her a hero's welcome as she and her friends walked in. Apparently, Lynn's exploits on Gran Karisu had made it around the town and she had become an overnight legend. No one from this god-forsaken city had ever done something like that, and the drinks were flowing freely all night.

The peace talks with the Grothians had gone well, for now. Lynn wasn't important enough to know the particulars, but one of the few times she had spoken to Zach since coming home, he had told her the Grothians were negotiating and another attack was unlikely. She didn't trust them for a second, but at least they had gone nine weeks without a peep. Lynn must have scared them something good, beating their best man. She'd never stop grinning over that one.

Alex finally came home. She met him and Reanyn at the spaceport and drove them back into town and straight to Red's bar. Swinging open the old, rickety doors, Lynn announced, "Hey, Red! We got another homecoming here!"

"Lynn—" Alex started to object. Everyone turned and cheered at the sight of Alex.

"Oh, come on," Lynn urged. "Like we ever needed an excuse to get drunk? I think you earned it."

"You got me there," he laughed. He turned to Reanyn and said, "Wanna come meet my friends?"

"I'd love to!" she replied.

"Yo! Big man!" Rami waved them over. Jocelyn and Trey were already sitting with him at their favorite booth.

Alex and Reanyn went right to the table to say hello while Lynn went to the bar. By the time she got there, Red already had their drinks waiting.

"Thanks, baldy." She laughed, dropping thirty on the bar top.

"Anytime, Addilynn," he said with a smirk.

"I'm a war hero now, remember? You have to respect me."

"I bet you got lucky. Kill a hundred more of 'em and I'll be impressed."

"Piss off, baldy. Go grow some hair." Both of them laughed and Lynn took the drinks over to the table.

When she got there, everyone was goofing off and she heard Trey asking Reanyn, "So, you basically met this guy in a video game?"

"I guess," she answered shyly. "A pretty awful video game."

"But wait, how do we know that wasn't reality and what we are doing right now is the video game?" Rami pointed out.

"Don't do that to me," Jocelyn said. "Now I'm gonna be thinking about that all day."

Lynn weighed in on the discussion as she passed drinks around. "You know how I know this is reality? No one would program Trey that damn ugly."

"Hey, now," Trey said as everyone laughed at his expense. "I know you missed me, but settle down a minute, would you?"

Lynn pounded her whiskey and signaled for another, her way of "settling down," and plopped herself in the booth next to Alex.

"So, how long are you going to be home?" Rami asked Alex.

After a swig of rum and coke, Alex answered, "Not sure. Honestly, I haven't even gone home yet. We came straight from the spaceport."

"Are you both going back together?" Jocelyn wondered. "To Gran Karisu?"

Already quite drunk, Trey interrupted, "Yo, what's it like on Gran Karisu anyway? There's like, big monsters and stuff, right?"

"I already told you about it," Lynn reminded him, not hiding her annoyance. "And we don't know when, or even if, they want us back. The Grothians are supposedly gone now." Even with peace on the horizon, it did seem odd to Lynn how little communication she was getting from Prism. There had been some debate over how much time Lynn ought to take to recover, and since she had been cleared for duty over two weeks ago, all they had said was she would "receive orders soon." She texted Zach about it once, but he was dodgy. Honestly, she could have followed up more aggressively, but she still wasn't sure what the future held, and right now she was kind of happy to be in a holding pattern.

"Oh, come on, you don't believe that," Rami said. Lynn's next whiskey arrived, and she wasted no time tipping it back.

"I believe everyone wants peace," Reanyn disagreed with a rather corny tone. "Even the Grothians can't really desire war."

"I agree," said Alex.

"Well, either way, you two should go back," Jocelyn asserted, surprising Lynn.

Lynn slapped down her glass and asked, "Why is that?"

"Because what you did was amazing. You inspired people. You guys are heroes."

"Aww, shucks." Alex laughed.

"Seriously, though, you guys could kill *all* the monsters," Trey remarked.

Jocelyn had a point. Ever since she had been home, Lynn had seen things changing. It was slow, but sure; people had more hope now, more motivation. When she walked down the street, people recognized her, smiled at her, and saluted her. There were still crummy, dark parts of Calivia, sure, there always would be. But what seemed different now was that the good parts were starting to shine through.

Alex's phone lit up and he glanced down at it.

"What?" Lynn asked.

"Let's go smoke," he dodged, getting up from the booth. "Be right back, fools." Reanyn smiled oddly at him before going back to her drink.

"Hey," objected Lynn. "Wait, who texted you? Is everything okay?"

"Oh yeah."

As they passed through the doors onto the early evening street, Lynn began to get frustrated. "Well then why are you acting weird?"

Then she saw him.

Standing there, across the street from them in his cheesy Corithian slacks and frilly button-up shirt was Jett Shorin. His hair was a ruffled mess and his cufflinks were unbuttoned, just the way she liked him.

Alex smiled and said, "I forgot to mention, someone is here to see you."

Barely looking for oncoming traffic, Lynn sprinted across the road and into his arms. A taxi honked at her as it had to slow to avoid her, but Lynn couldn't care less. She had no words to describe that moment, seeing him there, melting into his arms, feeling his lips so intimately on hers again after expecting not to see him for so much longer.

"I told you I would see you again," Jett said, giving her that handsome smile.

"I didn't expect you so soon.".

"I can leave, if you want."

"No, I love it."

She kissed him again and nuzzled into his collarbone, his hands pressing against her back and drawing her close. She felt him stroke her hair and she ran her fingers down his chest.

"Since I am here, will you show me around your city?" he asked.

"It's a date."

She looked back across the street at Alex, who was minding his own business and smoking his cigarette.

"Alex!" he shouted to him.

Immediately, he turned his attention to her and replied, "I'll go home with Rami, you have fun!"

"Are you sure?"

"Positive!" He put out his cigarette and went back inside. Her brother was so great, setting everything up like this.

"Well then, shall we?" Jett asked.

"My car is this way," replied Lynn, taking his hand and leading him across the street.

Lynn was ecstatic. The evening was clear and beautiful, and she got to spend it with Jett. She couldn't think of a more perfect way to exist.

9

A perfect night flew by all too fast. They spent hours roaming around the city, doing nothing but enjoying each other's company. The last place Lynn ever thought could be romantic was Calivia, but anywhere was perfect with Jett. At one point, they wandered by the airblading stadium and Lynn showed Jett where it had all begun. Everything was fixed now. You couldn't even tell something had happened there. Finally, after they had gone to one of Lynn's favorite restaurants and gotten their fill of beer and fried foods, she invited Jett on a ride through the beautiful Calivian countryside to her parents' home, where she had been staying the past few weeks. The fading sunlight had barely become darkness when they arrived, alone, and became enveloped in the secluded intimacy of the night. If she had a choice about it, Lynn would have made this night last forever.

Of course, it wasn't her choice.

The next morning, Lynn's eyes opened to the unwanted presence of the sun creeping through the curtains of her old country bedroom. A pollution of dust and hair floated inside the angled rays of light as they crept across the carpet and onto the foot of the bed. She felt Jett stirring beneath her.

"Good morning," he said, touching her cheek softly.

"Good morning yourself." She smiled up at him.

He reached for his phone. "What time is it?"

"Not yet," Lynn protested, grabbing his wrist. "You said you would make me breakfast, remember?"

With a playful smile, he replied, "How could I forget?"

"So," she teased, "You better get to it." Lynn giggled quietly as she released his wrist and slid off the bed, grabbing her clothes and beginning to dress.

"Oh my," Jett said urgently. "It is later than I thought."

"You have to go back already?" It made sense, Lynn supposed, since it was over an hour back to the city.

"Soon, but I want you to come with me."

Suspicious, Lynn asked, "Wait, where are we going? Last time I checked you aren't from here."

"I saw a lovely breakfast café on my way in yesterday," he answered.

"Yeah right. What are you up to?"

"Just come with me," he insisted as he dressed himself.

She squinted her eyes at him. "Fine."

Once they were dressed, they went downstairs and into the kitchen, where Lynn opened the fridge and grabbed an iced coffee. Jett waited for her by the front door while she gulped the first third of it. After a long, refreshed exhale, Lynn followed Jett outside and got into his car.

As they began to drive away from the property, Lynn asked, "So, where were we going again?"

"Somewhere else." He laughed.

"God. Now you are officially as annoying as Zach."

"I am not sure if that is an insult or a compliment."

"Take it how you want, but I assure you, it was meant as an insult."

Jett laughed it off and kept driving through the countryside. Before long, they were on the highway and coming in fast to the central hub of Calivia. Lynn could see the college campus where she used to study on her right, and to the left the lowly district where she and Alex used to live. Somewhere beyond that were the mines where Alex worked, and a few miles north of here would be the tarp city, where all of this had taken hold of her. A powerful nostalgia came over her as they sped through all the familiar places. At last Jett took an exit and came to a stop beside a quaint little café. Lynn had been there once, maybe.

"You weren't kidding?" Lynn was surprised.

"I told you I would get you whatever you wanted."

The two of them went inside and the smell of coffee and bacon overtook her senses, instantly making her stomach growl.

"Good morning," a server greeted them. "Have a seat anywhere."

Making their way over to a small table, they sat across from each other. Jett remarked, "This place has a certain comfort about it."

"Yeah," Lynn agreed. "Do you have coffee shops on Corinth?"

"Of course, but as with many other aspects of this city, it is different."

The server brought them coffee and asked if they were ready to order.

"May I sample the crepes?" Jett asked.

"Crepes?" Lynn made fun of him. "I'll have the breakfast sandwich, extra bacon,"

"Sure, I'll be right back with that," the server replied, making a swift exit.

"What?" Jett wondered.

"Crepes are not a real breakfast," she teased.

"I didn't know I was in the presence of a breakfast connoisseur."

Jett smiled and sipped his coffee, and Lynn said, "It's a dessert, and not even a good one. Where is the meat?"

Soon their food came out. Lynn was ravenous, stuffing her face while she watched Jett carefully cut his crepes with a fork and butter knife and take calculated bites. She was torn between making fun of his manners and improving her own.

"You are missing quite a morsel of 'dessert,' you know," Jett said.

"And you are going to be hungry again in a half-hour. Hope your flight is a short one." Taking another bite, Lynn thought for a moment and said, "You never told me where they are sending you."

"That's because I don't know," Jett replied.

"Big surprise. I have been talking to Prism COs for the past week and no one is giving me any definitive orders. I am not even sure what I want to do, but you would think a supposedly 'elite' group like Prism could get their act together, huh?"

Jett laughed. "Yes, they can be quite mysterious."

"It's not even that. I mean, you know you have to leave today, right? And yet, you don't even know where you are going? That's crazy."

"I agree, but I believe all will be well in the end."

"I guess."

A few minutes later, they had finished eating, left a nice tip on the table, and gotten back into Lynn's car. Jett checked his phone again, probably worried about the time.

"Time to go?" Lynn asked unwillingly. She wasn't ready to say goodbye yet.

"Duty calls."

They got back in the car and took off toward the Calivian spaceport. Hard as it was, Jett's vigilance was one of the things she loved about him. As long as there were people to help, Jett would never give up. Perhaps that was how Lynn felt as well, in her own way. Maybe she had always known it to be her purpose, only it had been clouded by the anger and bitterness of her youth. Though she supposed she would never truly forget the tribulations of her past, one thing Lynn could be sure of was that it was different now. There were some things that did matter.

Lynn took the exit leading into the Calivian spaceport and pulled into the lot marked *Hangar Seven*, where Jett was supposed to go. She swallowed the lump in her throat as she put the car in park. This could be the last time she would see him for a long time—maybe ever, if the worst happened. She scolded herself; since when did she become such a sap?

"Will you come with me?"

Confused, Lynn replied, "What, to the gate? We can say goodbye here, right? I can't go inside, can I?"

"They will make an exception for Prism soldiers, I presume."

"Okay, I guess." Turning off the car, she got out and followed Jett over to the gate. Honestly, she didn't really want to prolong this. Goodbyes were already hard enough.

"Hello," Jett greeted the gatekeeper.

"Hello. May I see your clearance?" he requested, holding out his hand. Jett handed him a folder and the man flipped it open, perusing it for a few seconds before he closed it up and said, "Okay, you two are good to go," and handed the folder back to Jett.

"Thank you," Jett said, saluting the man before they passed by.

"What does he mean *we* are all set?" Lynn asked. "He didn't ask me for my clearance. What is going on?"

Jett delayed answering her as they power walked across the busy starship hangar.

"Did you hear me?" Lynn demanded.

"Hey, Lynn, you made it!" Someone yelled to her from up ahead. When they got a few steps closer, she realized it was Siefer. Beside him were Leon, Kiah, and Karson. Alex and Sam emerged from the huge starship behind them, laughing and joking with Lucas, who appeared a few seconds later.

Lynn was confused and slightly annoyed. "What is my brother doing here? Jett, what aren't you telling me?"

Alex came down the ramp of the ship and caught sight of her. His face lit up and he called to her and waved her over. "Lynn! Check this out!"

They joined the group right in front of the starship and Lynn noticed something familiar about it. This was the same starship they had boarded before the Prism test, the *Leviathan*. Why was Sal Brigande here, and what was everyone else doing with him? Lynn started putting it together.

"Isn't this awesome! I've never seen the outside of the ship this close!" Alex was like a kid in a toy store. Reanyn and Blake appeared from another group of Prism soldiers and joined them.

"Lynn, I'm glad you came!" Reanyn said excitedly.

"Good to see you again," Sam added. "Sooner than I expected."

Lynn turned to Jett and said, "I was on those orders too, wasn't I?"

"I thought Captain Brine would explain it better than I," Jett answered, scratching his head with an air of uncertainty.

Rolling her eyes, Lynn sighed, "Of course he would."

Sam took a couple steps up the ramp and called out, "Yo, captain! Your mistress is here! Oh, I mean, the other mistress!"

"Sorry I didn't tell you," Alex apologized. "Zach insisted, and you know how he is."

"Yes, I second that notion," Jett said.

"Whatever," Lynn dismissed. "Do you at least know where we are going?"

"We are going wherever the wheel of fate takes us," Zach declared boldly, strutting his way down the ramp in his impressive captain's attire.

Lynn walked right up to him, staring fiercely at him and his cocky grin, and asked, "So, you are just assuming I am going to go along with this?"

"You have so far," he pointed out. "Lest we forget, you were the one who begged me to take you to Gran Karisu in the first place."

"Only to prove you wrong."

"And prove you did. Why stop now?"

"Looks like you have plenty of people already. How incompetent are you anyway?"

He laughed that deep belly laugh of his and reached out and grabbed her wrist. She jerked back a bit, but he insisted, pulling her wrist out toward him. Turning her hand so the palm faced up, he deposited into it a small, silver locket with "LP" engraved on the top in italics. Attached to the locket was a silver chain, on which a small key was also threaded. He gave the locket a gentle flick, clicking it open slightly in her hand, revealing the radiant shard inside.

"I don't have any phoenixes yet," he said quietly. "That key goes to your personal cabin. Inside the cabin, I left you a new rykai suit. I think you'll find it accommodates the new you quite well."

She closed the locket immediately and gazed at its surface for a moment. Taking a deep breath, she replied, "You are relentless. No wonder you got divorced."

He just laughed again and addressed the group around the ramp. "All right you slack-offs, we are already behind schedule. Everyone get inside and prepare for takeoff!"

"Yes, captain!" They answered. Everyone started filing past Lynn and up into the ship while she still stood there, mesmerized by the power resting in her hand.

"I'll see you inside, sis," Alex said with an emphatic thumbs-up as he went by.

The last of the crew boarded the ship and only Zach and Lynn remained.

"I thought you were bringing these to Taland?" she asked, once she felt it was safe to discuss it further.

"I did." He smirked. "Tested the shards up, down, left, right, and sideways. I'll say this: nothing I could drum up was as cool as what you did."

"You mean, the shard worked for you?"

"Yeah, and my guess is they manifest differently in everyone. I already talked to your brother and gave him his shard back. We will have to implant that one in you like we did with his, once we get you settled onboard."

"There you go again, assuming I am going to get on your stupid ship. What if I just take this and leave? Did you think about that?"

"You could, I guess. At any rate, we are set for takeoff any minute." Zach stood there for a moment while Lynn just stared at the locket in her hand, deep in thought. Finally, Zach turned to go up the ramp. He stopped a few steps later, turned his head, and said, "Last chance."

The truth was, Lynn had no intention of saying no. If there was one thing she had learned from all this, it was that the galaxy may be a dark place, but it could get a whole lot brighter when there were people out there who were willing to stand up and fight. As much as she fantasized about staying in Calivia with her family and friends and stealing Jett away from Prism so they could go on some romantic journey to Corinth together, she understood that she had a greater calling. She had the power to stop the madness, to help the downtrodden, to make sure no one was ever shattered as she had been all those years ago. There was no doubt there were more like the Fox out there, and indeed, she would find them, and they would tremble before the fist of the phoenix.

"Let's get the hell off this stupid planet already," Lynn finally said, following Zach up the ramp.

As the ramp began closing behind them, Zach turned back to her, held out his hand, and said proudly, "Welcome to the crew of the *Leviathan*."

About the Author

Patrick Carpenter grew up in Sanford, Maine, where he spent the better part of his life. He has traveled to many places, but New England has a special place in his heart. It was here that he went to college at the University of Southern Maine and obtained his bachlelor's degree in Leadership and Organizational Theory. Before that, he received a Culinary Arts degree from York County Community College. Though he spent years in restaurants and banking, writing has always been his true passion, and creating this book was the most passionate work he has ever performed. Besides writing, Patrick enjoys hiking, fitness, gaming, cooking, and spending weekends with his family.

Thank you for reading. For more *Dark Ocean* content and other works by Patrick Carpenter, visit the website at epicartspc.com

Be sure to subscribe to get the latest updates on Patrick's work.

Also, you can follow Patrick on Twitter @PatrickRcarpen3

Made in the USA
Middletown, DE
06 July 2021

43618690R00222